Heartstone

Heartstone

Elle Katharine White

HARPER Voyager
An Imprint of HarperCollins Publishers

This is a work of fiction. Names, characters, places, and incidents are products of the author's imagination or are used fictitiously and are not to be construed as real. Any resemblance to actual events, locales, organizations, or persons, living or dead, is entirely coincidental.

Harper Voyager and [logo] are trademarks of HCP LLC.

HEARTSTONE. Copyright © 2016 by Laura Katharine White. All rights reserved. Printed in the United States of America. No part of this book may be used or reproduced in any manner whatsoever without written permission except in the case of brief quotations embodied in critical articles and reviews. For information, address HarperCollins Publishers, 195 Broadway, New York, NY 10007.

HarperCollins books may be purchased for educational, business, or sales promotional use. For information, please email the Special Markets Department at SPsales@harpercollins.com.

FIRST EDITION

Designed by Paula Russell Szafranski

Dragon art © VSForever/Shutterstock, Inc.

Library of Congress Cataloging-in-Publication Data has been applied for.

ISBN 978–0–06–245194–1

16 17 18 19 20   LSC   10 9 8 7 6 5 4 3 2 1

For Kelsey,
who has a Shieldmaiden's heart

NORTHERN
WASTES

the
OLD WILDS   Castle
                             Selwyn ·

                        LAKE
                        MEERA
RIVER
RUSHLESS   RUSHLESS
                WOOD
                WIDDERMERE
                MARSHES

        HARBOROUGH
        HATCH   Selkie's
                                 Keep ·

                · Hatch Ford   UPPER
                          RIVER   DEAN
                          HATCH
                                         Hallows
        DRAGONSMOOR   EASTWICH   LOWER
   · House Pendragon ARLE   DEAN
TYNE   · Lambsley
     · Ramshead
        MIDDLEMOOR
                   HART'S RUN   Cloven Cairn
                      North Fields   the FENS
 · Upper Westhull   · Merybourne Manor
              Little Dembley
 · Westhull   · Trollhedge   LESSER
        WESTWICH   EASTWICH
                                       RIVER
                                       MERYLE
 · Lower Westhull

                   Edan Rose ·   Edonarle ·
WAIN   Hunter's   RIVER
              Forge   WASH
   · Wain-on-the-Water
              LESSER
              WESTWICH   Wash ·

                                   Clawmouth ·

Heartstone

CHAPTER 1

AN INCONVENIENCE OF HOBGOBLINS

I'd never seen an angry hobgoblin before.

If this one wasn't my friend, it might've been funny. Tobble was red in the face before I noticed him in the grass by the garden wall, and since hobgoblins have green skin, that in itself was quite a feat.

"Tobble, what's wrong?" I asked in Low Gnomic, or what could've passed as Gnomic if I hadn't butchered it with my Arlean accent. The earthy words used by hobgoblins and other garden creatures sounded heavy and awkward on my human tongue, and Tobble had often despaired of my pronunciation. Today, however, he was too distraught to notice.

"Lord Merybourne has hired Riders, Aliza. Five of them! Do you know what that means?" he said. His head, which was round and homely as a potato, came halfway up my shin, and he clutched handfuls of his mossy hair as I knelt next to him. "We're doomed! Doomed, I say!"

I set my basket on the ground. "Slow down. Who's doomed?"

"Everyone! Gnomes, hobgoblins, half-goblins, all of us garden-folk."

"Why are you all doomed?"

Tobble clambered up onto my lap, leaving muddy footprints on the front of my dress. Eyes the color of wilted dandelions stared into mine. "There will be wyverns flying around the place!"

"Well, yes. The Riders ride the wyverns. Isn't that the point?"

"Aliza, wyverns *eat* hobgoblins!"

"Come on, Tobble. Nobody's going to get eaten. When's the last time you heard of a hired wyvern snacking on the locals?"

"I guess . . . never."

"Exactly. These Riders signed a contract. They're not about to let their mounts gobble up the garden-folk while there's work to be done. Besides, it's bad manners. Wyverns are civilized creatures."

"But what if one of them gets hungry? What if he can't help it?"

I squeezed his hand between my thumb and forefinger. "Tell you what. Just in case, gods forbid, Lord Merybourne happened to hire the rudest Riders in Arle, I'll ask him to set aside a few extra head of cattle for their wyverns."

Tobble grinned, showing a row of flat, brown teeth. Just as he opened his mouth to speak, a shadow fell over the garden. Wings beat the air behind us. *Large* wings.

My heart broke into a gallop as Tobble disappeared into the underbrush. Instinct told me to follow him, to run, to hide, but terror dug nails deep into my legs, rooting me to the ground. *Is this what Rina felt? Is this why she didn't run when the gryphons came for her?* The wingbeats grew louder and I picked up my basket. Not much defense against a gryphon's talons, but I wasn't about to go without a fight.

I turned to face the thing that blocked the sun.

Relief washed over me, warm and sweet, and I almost laughed. In the field beyond the garden wall, a dragon was descending.

The dragon's wings stretched the length of the field, and talons the size of plowshares scoured the earth where it landed. Pewter scales shone with a bluish-gold luster where the sun hit its sides, and I longed for a canvas and some paints to capture the sight, my fear forgotten.

A broad-shouldered figure leapt from the dragon's back.

"You there!"

The Rider's voice tore me away from the strokes of my mental paintbrush. I reddened as he approached and tried to wipe some of the mud from my dress, succeeding only in smudging it farther down the front. The contrast between us grew clearer—and more painful—with each step. Tooled in gold across the Rider's breastplate was the rampant figure of a dragon, the symbol of House Daired, and on the hilt of the sword slung over his shoulder I caught the bloodred glimmer of a lamia's heartstone. As my younger sister Mari once told me, the serpentine, scythe-wielding monsters called lamias were one of the *Tekari*, sworn foes of humankind. A lamia's heartstone would be a worthy pommel gem for a Daired's blade.

My gaze trailed from his heartstone to his face, and a new chill ran through me, though this one wasn't so much fear as a healthy dose of embarrassment.

Blast. He *would* be handsome.

Of course, he could've looked like the wrong side of a troll and his appearance would've still made me blush. By rights this Daired shouldn't have been here at all. Merybourne Manor sat at the heart of a poor county, the smallest in the island kingdom of Arle. Lord Merybourne ruled over farmers, craftspeople, and the occasional merchant, but no one rich or distinguished, and it'd taken us months to scrounge enough to meet the bond-price for a band of Riders.

My father, the Manor clerk and an old friend of Lord Merybourne, had spent weeks running the sums to see how we could afford it. Five Riders, five mounts, and food and lodging for a fortnight, in return for which they'd hunt down and slay the gryphon horde that plagued us. At twenty silver dragonbacks per Rider, the commission cost the Manor a total of one hundred dragonbacks.

Or, by my more practical calculation, the entire income of Merybourne Manor in a year.

Still, it had to be done. Lord Merybourne had sent the letters to the capital, Edonarle, and prayed some of the Riders would answer. And they had. It was only when my father received their signed contracts that we realized one of the Riders was a Daired.

Lord Merybourne had just about choked on his soup when Papa handed him the contracts, Master Daired's on top. Other Riders could win over the bear-like beoryns, and some of the older blood-lines could bond with smaller winged wyverns, but the Daireds alone, descended from legendary warrior Edan the Fireborn, were dragonmasters. Naturally, that entitled them to charge just about any bond-price they liked. Which, as we'd heard, was upward of fifteen gold dragonbacks per day.

Yet this Daired had signed Lord Merybourne's contract, accepting twenty silver dragonbacks for a whole fortnight's work. Knowing that, I expected I wasn't the only one who'd look on him with suspicion. Admiration and gratitude, of course, but suspicion too. No Daired in their right mind would stoop to visit Hart's Run on so slight a temptation as twenty dragonbacks . . . but here he was, striding toward me along the overgrown garden path, that strik-ing, battle-scarred face set in a look that confirmed my fears: Mery-bourne Manor was the last place in Arle he wanted to be.

And here I was, the first of the Manor-folk to greet Master Daired, sweaty, dirt-stained, hair all amuss, and staring like a half-witted schoolgirl. *Perfect.*

I dropped into the curtsy I used for strangers of uncertain rank, unsavory solicitors, and the man at the market who sells cut-rate mutton. As I straightened, I touched the four fingers of my right hand to my forehead in greeting. "Morning, sir."

With a flick of his wrist he returned the gesture. Dark eyes under brows sharp as knives raked across my face and dress, and, apparently not finding anything there to his liking, he fixed his gaze somewhere just over my head. "What's the quickest way to Lord Merybourne?"

"If you follow the path, it'll take you to the front of the Manor House. There'll be someone at the door to show you in."

Daired pushed past me, muttering something that might've been *thank you*, though it just as easily might've been a rude word in the dragon-tongue, Eth.

He didn't get far.

Unheard by either of us, Tobble and a dozen other hobgoblins had crept from the undergrowth as we spoke, crowding onto the path to watch our exchange. Their mossy green skin blended into the flagstones so well, Daired didn't see them at first. I did.

"Watch out!" I cried.

Tobble shrieked as Daired's iron-shod boot came down on his toes. Daired yelled in surprise and aimed a kick at Tobble's midsection, and Tobble's shriek turned into a keening wail as he sailed toward the hedgerow. I threw myself into the shrubbery after him. Leaves and branches tore at my side and I landed hard, Tobble cradled in the crook of my arm.

"Aliza! Are y-you all right?"

By sheer good luck we'd missed the thorniest part of the shrub. I spat out a leaf and set Tobble on the ground, relieved to find him unhurt. Despite their small stature, hobgoblins were hardy creatures. "I'm fine. Are—oh no. What are they doing now?"

We emerged from the hawthorn onto a battlefield. Shouting all manner of Gnomic curses, the rest of the hobgoblins had declared war on Daired, scooping up handfuls of mud and flinging them at his head, or, if they couldn't lay hands on enough mud, simply flinging themselves. Most only reached his knees. He battled off the inconvenience with kicks and, for those hobgoblins who managed to leap higher than his waist, with his fists as well, matching their curses with a few of his own, both in Arlean and Eth.

"We should probably help him," I said.

Tobble crossed his arms. "You do what you want. I'm going to watch."

Hobgoblins. Dodging the nearest projectile, I stepped over Tobble's screaming cousin and placed myself between Daired and his attackers. "*Gpheth!*" I cried. "*Stop!*"

The hobgoblins froze, mud dripping from their fingers. Daired froze too, his hand near the buckle that would release his scabbard from its harness on his back.

"Tobble's fine," I told the hobgoblins in Gnomic. "This man is Lord Merybourne's guest. Please, let him through. And no more mud!"

One by one, the hobgoblins dropped their missiles and slunk back into the garden, chirping their disappointment. I snuck a peek at Daired. Covered in mud and blisteringly angry, the man was a sight to make gargoyles tremble. He wiped the remains of one lucky shot from the corner of his mouth and spat on the ground. "What did you tell them?"

"I asked them to leave you alone," I said. "Really though, you didn't have to kick him. Hobgoblins are harmless."

"Tell that to my armor." Bending his head in the barest of bows, he turned on his heel and stormed down the path toward the Manor.

"Well, I never!" Tobble said. "What an awful man."

With a sigh I stooped to collect my fallen basket. The herbs I'd set out to gather lay trampled in the mud. "Tobble, I think I'll see about those extra cattle now."

INSIDE, THE KITCHENS WERE ALL ABUZZ WITH NEWS OF the Riders' arrival. I set my refilled basket on the sideboard and scanned the room for Cook. He stood by the fireplace, sweating and muttering as he supervised the seasoning of the stag rotating on a spit.

"Bloody Riders can't hunt their own meat now, can they? Make us cough up enough for a banquet when we've already—Aliza! Oh, thank the Fourfold God. Where's my rosemary?"

"I left it by the pantry."

"What good's it going to do my venison over there?" he bellowed. "Jenny! Jenny, get the rosemary! And where's my carving knife?"

Several maids looked up, eyeing first the knife in Cook's hand, then each other.

"Well, don't just stand there. Find it! And who's keeping an eye on the bread? Blast it all, people, this banquet is happening tonight, not next week!" He remembered me with a frown. "Miss Aliza, what are you doing here? The kitchen's no place for Manor-folk."

"You asked me to go collect some . . . never mind. Listen, I wanted to ask—"

"No, no, none of that! Unless you're here to tell me those Riders have brought their own feast, I can't have you in here."

"All right, all right. I'm going. And, Cook, the knife's in your hand."

A chorus of giggles erupted from the kitchen maids as Cook flushed and held up the errant utensil.

Unfortunately, he had a point. It'd taken a year's taxes and two loans from neighboring estates to cover the Riders' bond-price, and with the welcome banquet Lord Merybourne ordered on top of all that, it pushed us nearly to the breaking point. But I'd promised Tobble I'd look into the extra cattle, and the least I could do was ask. I'd have to talk to my father.

Long before I reached Papa's door, I heard Mama's voice echoing all the way down the spiral staircase, shrill and angry enough to frighten away even Lord Merybourne, should he have been unwise enough to wander this way. My younger sister Mari once speculated that Mama had some banshee blood on her side of the family. I trusted her judgment. Mama's half-brother, my uncle Gregory, had inherited a talent for gardening from his great-grandmother's dalliance with a wood-wight, so it wouldn't surprise me if one of Mama's ancestors had passed a little something down as well, though that relationship would take a good deal more explaining. Banshees, like lamias and so many other creatures of the Oldkind, counted themselves among the *Tekari*, and hated all humans.

My parents' conversation grew clearer as I climbed the last few steps.

"Surely you see what an opportunity this is!" Mama said.

"Yes, I do." Papa's voice was stern. "It's a chance to get rid of these accursed gryphons once and for all. Of all people, I'd think you'd appreciate that most."

"Of course, of course, but I'm talking about our daughters."

"Oh? Were they planning to slay some of the beasts themselves?"

"Robart!"

"If these Riders are apprenticing, I'll give my hearty consent to whichever girl wishes to take up the blade. You and I will both sleep easier if they know how to defend themselves."

"I'd sleep easier knowing they're looked after *now*, not ten years from now when they've finished their training."

"I was joking, my dear."

"Well, I'm not! And anyway, a husband lasts longer than an apprenticeship."

"Only if he's unlucky."

Imagining Mama's response to that, I took pity on Papa and knocked.

"Enter!" he called.

Mama paced in front of Papa's desk. "Aliza! What are you doing up here?"

"I had a question for Papa about Manor expenses."

Usually bored at the first hint of business, I expected her to make a quick exit. Instead, she stood and stared at me, toe tapping. "Well? Out with it."

"Papa, after the banquet tonight, how many head of cattle will His Lordship have left?"

He donned his spectacles and consulted the ledger at his elbow. "Cook agreed to make do with only one side of beef tonight, so that leaves two dozen dairy cows, six bulls, and ten steers. Why do you want to know?"

Forty animals. That was less than half the herd Lord Merybourne had owned before the gryphons descended. With winter coming and a hundred mouths to feed on the Manor, we couldn't spare many more. "It's nothing."

"And good thing too. Your father's in one of his moods," Mama said, glaring at Papa. "If you won't take an interest in your daughters' futures, Robart, then gods help me, I'll do it myself."

"I've no doubt you'll do a splendid job, Moira."

"I mean it! Where are these Riders now?"

"Lord Merybourne is welcoming them in the Great Hall."

"Excellent. Come along, Aliza."

"If you ladies are headed that way, perhaps you'd do me a favor?" Papa offered me a sheet of paper. "Take this to one of the Riders down there, name of Brysney. His Lordship wanted it signed as soon as possible."

Mama snatched the sheet from my hand. "Signed? What more would a Rider have to sign? He couldn't . . ." Her face brightened as she read it over. "Oh! Oh my goodness!"

"What, Mama? Papa? What is it?"

Mama circled the desk to keep the paper out of my grasp. "Robart, is he serious?"

"Quite. Master Brysney wrote to Lord Merybourne shortly after their contracts were sealed, asking if he knew of a suitable house in the neighborhood," he said. "His Lordship offered the North Fields lodge and, well, we now have a Rider paying rent."

"That's wonderful!" I said.

Mama waved a hand. "Yes, yes, wonderful. But how many *other* people know about this, Robart?"

"Besides us? His Lordship, Lady Merybourne, and Warren Carlyle," Papa said, naming Lord Merybourne's steward and the father of my closest friend, Gwyndolyn Carlyle. "Lord Merybourne will tell the rest of the Manor at banquet tonight."

"Well then, that doesn't give me very much time."

"Time? For what?"

"We have a long game to plan, and I'll not waste a moment," Mama said, eyes sparkling in a way that didn't bode well for me or any of my sisters. "I have to put the pieces in motion. Angelina needs a dress!" she cried, and before Papa could stop her, she was out the door.

"Aliza, my dear, for whatever happens tonight, please accept my sincerest apologies," he said as the door swung shut.

"Oh, don't worry. Anjey can hold Mama off." I could see now why Lord Merybourne wanted to throw the Riders a banquet.

With one of them renting the North Fields lodge, we'd be able to repay our debt to the nearby estates in months, not years. "Is it just the one Rider?"

"Just Master Brysney and his sister, Lady Charis. The others will stay with them while they're hunting the gryphons."

"*Brysney.* Why do I know that name?"

"The last contract they undertook was in Harborough Hatch."

"I . . . oh." *Of course.*

We'd all heard what the Brysneys had done in Harborough Hatch. Between rockslides, mudslides, and floods, news coming out of that county had always been bad, but nothing compared to the day the Lesser Lindworm broke ground outside of the city of Hatch Ford. Spawned from earth and the legends of nightmares, the venomous, worm-like *Tekari* terrorized the countryside for weeks, until twin Riders from the north, a brother and sister, flew in on the first winds of winter and succeeded where dozens of Riders before them had failed. Bards all around Arle sang about the battle, and though there were a dozen versions of how they'd done it, a few facts stayed the same: Master Brysney and Lady Charis slew the Worm, and paid the price for it. Lady Charis's wyvern died after the battle, poisoned by the Worm's incurable sting.

The bards didn't talk much about that part.

"I hope the gryphons won't be so difficult," I said.

"With five Riders and a dragon in the fight, I doubt it'll even come close to difficult," Papa said, shutting the ledger with a thud. Dust floated up from the faded pages. He fought back a sneeze. "If you're—*ah*—heading downstairs, would you take this to Master Carlyle? With my apologies. Next time I won't keep it so long."

"Do you want me to bring the lease too?"

"No, I'll take it down. I just wanted to see your mother's reaction," he said with a smile, which dimmed the more he thought about it. "And, er, on that note, keep an eye on your sister for me, will you? I've never seen Moira so determined. All joking aside, I wouldn't want her doing anything foolish to attract Master Brysney's attention."

"She wouldn't stoop *that* low, would she?"

"Who knows? All we can do is remind her that this Brysney, rich and single as he may be, is most definitely not here looking for a wife."

CHAPTER 2

LAVENDER AND LOST THINGS

Master Carlyle's study wasn't far from my family's apartments, tucked in the northwest corner of the Manor House behind the portraitless portrait gallery we used to store broken furniture, threadbare tapestries, and one really hideous suit of armor. The door to his study was locked, but torchlight flickered at the crack at the floor. I knocked. "Master Carlyle?"

The only answer was a thump and a crash.

"Master Carlyle? Is everything all right?"

"For gods' sakes, I'm coming!" He wrenched open the door. "Aliza? What do you want?"

"My father wanted me to bring your ledger back. He said he'll—"

He snatched the book from my hands. "Yes, yes. Off with you now. Goodbye."

The door slammed shut.

"... not keep it so long next time. You're welcome. Have a lovely afternoon," I said to the faded wooden panels. Warren Carlyle had never been a cheerful man, but he'd always been cordial to me, if only for Gwyn's sake. *Strange.* I picked my way past the unseeing eyes of the stuffed knight and headed for my family's apartments.

Mama greeted me at the door, face flushed, hair frizzy, and arms full of ruffled silk. "What took you so long? We're all in such a state!"

"What's wrong?"

"That whey-brain of a housemaid went off with the servants to set up the banquet at Hall-under-Hill before she finished the ironing. I've managed to press Angelina's things but I haven't time to fix her hair *and* finish the rest of our gowns."

"Why not ask Leyda to iron her own things?" No doubt it'd come as a novel idea to my sixteen-year-old sister, the care of her own belongings. "Want me to find her?"

"No, no, I will. You help Anjey."

"What about Mari? Is she coming?"

Mama sniffed. "Not likely."

I sighed. My seventeen-year-old sister, Mari, was sweet, shy, and cleverer than the rest of us combined, but she had an unfortunate habit of choosing the company of books to that of people. Following one memorable banquet—at which she discovered it was impossible to read over her dance partner's shoulder and maintain his good opinion—Mari had washed her hands of public gatherings in general, and after overcoming her initial disappointment in discovering she had a bluestocking for a daughter, Mama let her do as she pleased.

On this particular occasion, however, Mari's introversion served Mama's purposes well. As long as Anjey was willing to woo a Rider, I was confident Mama would leap at any excuse to keep at least one daughter safely indoors. In fact, if she didn't expect to get a son-in-law out of the excursion, she probably wouldn't have wanted any of us to go to Hall-under-Hill.

"Mari will be disappointed she didn't get to see Master Daired's dragon up close," I said. My sister was an expert on all creatures of the Oldkind, whether friendly, deadly, or indifferent to humans.

Her handwritten bestiary was her most prized possession. "He'd have been the jewel of her collection."

"It's a she, actually. The Daired dragon. Or so the maids are saying," Mama said. "Why not make a sketch for Mari, my dear? I know she'd appreciate that, and—that *is* mud on your dress, isn't it? Well, you're just going to have to make do with a cold bath. We've not a moment to waste!"

"Mama, the banquet doesn't start until sundown."

"Yes, and I'll not have my daughters stepping out of this house looking anything less than perfect. Perfection alone can capture a Rider's heart," she said, as solemnly as if quoting the *Book of Honored Proverbs*. "I *will* see one of you married to a Rider by Saint Ellia's Day, you mark my words. Now hurry!" She rushed out, still clutching the ironing to her chest.

"Is she gone?" My older sister's voice came muffled from behind the door to our room.

"Aye."

"Thank heavens. Come in."

I pushed open the door and stumbled over a hassock. "What were you trying to do, barricade yourself in here?"

"If it'd keep her from coming back." Anjey kicked the hassock out of the way. "She wanted to know how I felt about bonnets with bells. You know, so the Riders can pick me out of a crowd."

I looked around our room. The scent of lavender lingered around the dresses scattered over the bed and hanging over the wardrobe doors. I wondered how long Mama had been waiting to bring these reminders of her theater troupe days out of storage. One look was enough to tell me that the necklines on most were a few scissor snips away from making Anjey blush.

"It'd be memorable."

"I'm sure it would. What on *earth* is this?" Anjey asked, picking up one of the gowns between her thumb and forefinger. It was made of lace, a few panels of threadbare silk, and the unfulfilled dreams of what must've been a very lonely dressmaker. It fell with a soft slither onto the coverlet. "Do you think she'd mind if I wore an old potato sack instead?"

"Oh, shush."

"I'm seriously considering it."

"Tell you what. If you want to wear a potato sack, I won't stop you, but that means I'm going in *that*." I pointed to the lace-and-silk negligee. "It's the only way I'll get a look from these Riders."

She laughed, but it was true. Both as an artist and as her sister, I'd challenge anyone who didn't think Angelina Bentaine the most beautiful woman in Hart's Run. While the two of us shared the same brown eyes and Mama's copper complexion, Anjey had the finer features. I was squarer and more angular, lithe but not as delicate. Her hair fell down her back in glossy black ringlets, thick, wild, and the envy of all the women—and some of the men—in Hart's Run. Mine was lighter, flatter, and much less likely to inspire a ballad. Braided up with ribbons or the occasional flower, it suited me just fine, particularly as it didn't turn traitor at every change of the weather.

"Burlap or no burlap," Anjey said, "if we don't start getting ready now, Mama's going to have a stroke anyway."

I pulled my hair out of its pinnings. A few hawthorn twigs fell from its tangles. "True. And I need a bath."

"Yes, what *did* happen to you?"

"I'll give you three guesses."

"Jenny and Joe picked you for target practice?"

"Ha! They wouldn't dare. Not after last time."

"Battle with a troll?"

Might depend on whom you ask. "No."

"Did Tobble convince you to help him dig his fat uncle out of the potato patch again?"

"Closer. I met Master Daired in the garden," I said, and told her about the events of the afternoon as I drew my bath from the barrel the servants had filled that morning. As Mama predicted, I had to make do with tepid water.

"How extraordinary!" Anjey said. "I wouldn't have expected that of a Rider. Aren't they supposed to be, I don't know, more *gallant?*"

I pulled the bathing screen across the corner of the room. "They kill things for a living. It's not exactly an occupation for the tender-hearted."

"Let's at least hope the other Riders don't go around kicking hobgoblins."

I leaned back in the tub, combing out the rest of the hawthorn twigs. *Aye, let's hope.*

THE WATER WAS JUST STARTING TO TURN COLD WHEN A muffled shriek sounded from the next room. I sat bolt upright. "What was that?"

Something thudded against the wall, and my heart leapt into my throat. I threw on a robe and shoved back the bathing screen. Old, irrational fears rose up inside me as Anjey and I rushed next door. On the threshold of our little sister's room I froze.

Leyda lay sprawled on the bed, her eyes closed, feet dangling off the edge at an awkward angle. She didn't seem to be breathing.

For the second time in my life, the world ground to a halt.

Images from three months ago bled into edges of my vision, mixing present and past as I stared, not at Leyda, but at our youngest sister, Katarina, her body broken across the pasture wall, throat torn open by a gryphon's talons, unseeing eyes fixed on the Manor House, at once so close and so far away. She'd slipped away from her chores to pick flowers in the south pasture, and I hadn't noticed until it was too late.

Papa said my scream had roused the whole Manor.

Lord Merybourne sent his first letter to Edonarle the next day, pleading for Riders to come and free us from the horde's tyranny. The Riders took two months to answer, and in that time I tried everything I could to get rid of the sight of Rina's blood on my hands. Now, seeing Leyda lying there, it all rushed back: the red stains, the empty eyes, the horror, the loss.

I clutched at the doorjamb as Anjey brushed past me. "Leyda, is everything all right?" she asked. "We heard—goodness, Aliza! Are *you* all right?"

Leyda sat up.

My world righted itself. "I just thought . . . Leyda, you looked hurt," I said.

"What?" Leyda said. "Of course not. I'm fine."

Anjey touched my shoulder. She'd seen Rina's body too; she understood. "Well, you *were* just lying there," she said to Leyda in a fair imitation of our mother at her severest, "and you did scream."

"Because I have nothing to wear!" Leyda sighed and flung herself back onto the bed. "These Riders are the most important people to visit Hart's Run in *forever*, and I don't have any blasted trousers!"

I smiled. Of all of us, Leyda refused to be bowed by grief. "*Rina wouldn't want us to mope about like this*," she'd said after the funeral. "*She would've wanted us to live, and that's what I mean to do.*" So far, she'd kept her promise. She certainly intended to make the most of this evening. Tunics, belts, and gowns lay scattered across the furniture, along with slippers, mismatched gloves, several undarned stockings, and a few sashes nicked from Anjey's wardrobe. Nothing in the room looked as if it had been pressed in days.

"Don't be silly," I said. "Why would you want to wear trousers to a banquet?"

"Because they're *Riders*, Aliza. Riders don't wear dresses."

"Lucky you're not a Rider then," Anjey said.

"Aye, lucky me," she muttered.

Anjey pulled out a maroon gown from the place it'd been wedged between the bed and the nightstand. "Is this mine?"

"Don't be mad, please!" Leyda leapt to her feet. "I tried on everything else I have and it all looks so *dull*. I'll do your ironing for a week if you let me wear it, I swear!"

"Make it two weeks and you can have it. I was going to wear burlap anyway." She winked in my direction and tossed Leyda the dress. "Come on then. Let's see how it looks."

A FEW HOURS LATER WE EMERGED, FORTUNATELY FOR Mama's health without a stitch of burlap between us. After going through half a dozen gowns and most of Anjey's patience, Leyda at last returned to the maroon gown. Anjey wore midnight blue, and at her suggestion, I stuck with my favorite green dress.

Mama threw up her hands as we filed into the parlor. "It's about time! Another few minutes and we might've been late. I *will* see Master Brysney dance with one of you before the first course."

Papa rose from his chair by the fire. He'd added the simple heartstone pin Mama had given him on their wedding day to his customary black suit, but besides that he hadn't changed at all. "My dear, the first course will scarcely be out of the ovens by the time we get there. We have plenty of time."

"All the better. Now hurry, girls."

I read in Papa's smile what he dared not add aloud. *These Riders are here to slay gryphons, not dance country jigs. We'd best not get our hopes up.*

Outside the Manor House, we joined a stream of other families making their way to the banqueting grounds at Hall-under-Hill. Papa greeted the blacksmith and his wife as we passed their cottage. "Evening, Farris. Madam Farris."

"Evening, Sir Robart. A fitting evening for such a celebration, eh?" Farris said, and pointed upward. Clouds were gathering in the west, making it look as if some elemental dragon had ignited the sky, sending pillars of fire searing across the horizon. Adding to its beauty was the absence, at long last, of any gryphons. The presence of two wyverns, a beoryn, and a dragon were understandable deterrents.

"I'll say," Papa said as Mama sought Madam Farris's side. With two infant sons and no daughters, the Farris family posed no threat to my mother's matchmaking schemes, and she and Madam Farris soon fell to talking.

The bowl-shaped valley of Hall-under-Hill wasn't far from the Manor House. As we topped the last rise, I imagined the effect the sight might have on a stranger to the Manor. We were humble folk, yes, but we weren't *entirely* uninteresting. Hall-under-Hill was the wonder of the county. According to our bard, the former Lady Merybourne had surprised Old Merybourne so much when she'd agreed to marry him that he'd spent half his fortune creating a fitting venue for their wedding. From the hills of Hart's Run, Old Merybourne's goblin stonesmiths had hollowed out a floor large enough to fit several immense banqueting trestles, a bonfire the size of the millpond, and all the families of Merybourne Manor.

By the light of the bonfire I counted five Manor families mingling by the banquet tables. Lord and Lady Merybourne were there as well, and at their side were the guests of honor, each wearing the telltale leather breeches and iron-shod boots I realized must be synonymous with the title Rider. Four great beasts stood behind them. The fire reflected the glossy coat of Master Ruthven's beoryn, the liquid, intelligent eyes of two winged wyverns, and above them all, looking down from the height of a large cottage, was the Daired dragon herself. A shiver of wonder ran down my spine. It didn't matter that the creatures were *Shani*, the friends of humankind. In their own beautiful, civilized way, they were all still terrifying.

"That'd be them Riders, then?" Master Farris said to my father.

"So it would seem."

The blacksmith grunted. "They'd better be quick about this slaying business. I'd like to go outside every once in a while without worrying for my life."

Papa pressed his lips together, Mama turned pale, and Anjey studied the ground. Leyda trembled as she took my arm.

"Hush, John!" his wife said in alarm, seeing the effect of her husband's poor choice of words. "Oh, look at that. Madam Moore wants to see us. Have a pleasant evening, Sir Robart, Madam Bentaine!" She whisked her husband away toward the food and a quiet scolding.

"I think we're being summoned," Papa said, seizing the chance to change the subject. He nodded to Lord Merybourne, who was in fact waving us over.

"Sir Robart!" Lord Merybourne boomed, grasping Papa's hand and clapping him once on the shoulder. His Lordship never seemed able to say anything without booming. A big, barrel-chested man with a thick beard, his conversation was often accompanied by expansive gestures that one had to take care to avoid. After more than forty years of friendship with Lord Merybourne, my father had swifter reflexes than most men his age. He took a step back to escape a second bone-shaking clap on the shoulder. "Just the man I was looking for."

"Good of you to invite us," Papa said. "My family's been anxious to thank these Riders in person." He touched his forehead and bowed to the Rider next to Lord Merybourne. "Master Brysney. Once again, it's an honor."

"Likewise, Sir Robart," said the Rider. He was a fine-looking man, slim but muscular, with reddish-gold hair and the lilting brogue of Northern Arleans. Besides his distinctive outfit, the cut of his hair also betrayed his rank. Shorn on the sides but longer in the middle, it tapered into a leather-bound braid down his back in the traditional style of Arle's warrior elite.

"*Such* a pleasure to meet you, Master Brysney!" Mama said, pushing Papa aside and dropping into her deepest curtsy. "Moira Bentaine, delighted to make your acquaintance. We've heard so much about you. Why, just this morning my eldest—Angelina dear, come here for a moment, will you?—Angelina was saying how lucky we are to host Riders as distinguished as yourself and your sister." She clapped her hands. "What a wonderful reputation you have. My brother in Edonarle will hardly believe it when I tell him that the same two who slew the Lesser Lindworm of Harborough Hatch stayed at our Manor!"

At the words *Harborough Hatch*, the woman standing by Brysney's side looked at us, a stricken expression on her face.

Brysney's brow darkened. "We're honored to be of service, ma'am."

He turned away, but Mama plunged on, begging him to tell how they'd managed to kill the Worm. His look might have spelled doom for my mother's ambitions if Anjey hadn't intervened.

"Never mind that, Mama. Angelina Bentaine," Anjey said, stepping forward. "Pleased to meet you, Master Brysney."

Brysney's eyes widened.

Anjey held his gaze and smiled.

"I . . . pleased to meet you as well," he said.

"Anjey is my eldest," Papa said, doing his part to help us out of the mortifying hole his wife had dug. "This is Aliza, my second eldest, and this is my second youngest, Leyda."

Leyda dipped into a curtsy that would've been less wobbly if she'd not kept sneaking glances at the wyvern behind Brysney.

"Would you introduce your companions, Master Brysney?" Papa asked.

Tearing his eyes from Anjey's, Brysney turned to the other Riders, Mama's blunder with Harborough Hatch apparently forgotten. "Yes, of course. Sir Robart, Bentaine family, this is my sister, Charis Brysney."

Brysney's twin sister had a face that warranted second glances, though the second was bound to be surreptitious and, though admiring, a little frightened as well. She had a harsh, proud beauty, with red-gold hair, gray eyes, and a freckling of scars across her left cheek. She returned my father's greeting with a stiff nod.

Brysney continued. "This is our friend Nerissa Ruthven, and Nerissa's brother-in-arms, Bluescale Broadback."

Lady Nerissa was a short woman with a long face and three silver braids woven into her Rider's plait, though she didn't look much older than forty. A scaly head thrust over her shoulder, glittering cerulean in the firelight. Her wyvern surveyed us for a few seconds before withdrawing into the shadows with a snort.

"And this is my brother-in-arms, Silverwing Scytheclaw," Brysney said. A second wyvern raised a silver-scaled wing and spoke a few words in Vernish. "Silver's honored to be here, and we both look forward to spending more time in the country. He says he's never ridden such clean winds."

"So good of you to come," Papa said, and Brysney moved on.

"This is Nerissa's husband, Edel Ruthven, and his beoryn, Burrumburrem."

Ruthven was an enormous man, even larger than Lord Mery-bourne. Black-skinned and bald save for the Rider's plait down the center of his scalp, he bore three deep talon scars along his jawline. By the size and shape, I guessed they'd been a gift from a valkyrie. His chest was bare beneath his leather breastplate and the muscles in his arms were roughly the circumference of my head. One massive hand rested on Burrumburrem's shoulder. Like his Rider, the bear-like creature watched us with narrowed eyes. Ruthven gave only the barest of bows when Brysney introduced him.

"Master Ruthven," Papa said. "I trust you're all settled comfortably?"

Ruthven grunted something that might've been Beorspeak for all I could tell.

"Quite comfortably, thank you," Brysney translated. "Now last of all . . ." He looked around. "Ruthven, where's Daired?"

CHAPTER 3

HALL-UNDER-HILL

Daired was nowhere to be seen, though his dragon hadn't moved from her place behind Burrumburrem. Brysney addressed her with a few words in Eth. Her response shook the ground and rumbled in the chests of everyone in the vicinity, but by Brysney's expression, even she didn't know where Daired was.

"I'm sorry about that, Sir Robart," Brysney said. "He was just here."

Before Papa could tell him not to worry about it, Lord Merybourne announced the arrival of Cook and the kitchen staff, bearing a feast fit, if not for a king, then at least for the lord of a backwater country manor.

Papa bowed to the Riders as the rest of the crowd drifted toward the tables. "I'm sure we'll see him sometime tonight. Good evening, sirs. Ladies."

"Enjoy the banquet!" Mama called over her shoulder as Papa guided her toward the food.

Brysney stopped us before we could follow them. "Miss Angelina, may I have a word?"

Surprise flickered over her face, erased an instant later by the kind of smile Anjey reserved for people she liked, or at least wouldn't mind liking in the future. Dancing around the edges of that smile was a hint of coyness too, and I knew my sister well enough to read the subtext. Planned or not, Anjey meant to make the most of her new acquaintance.

"You may," she said.

Then again, she *had* always been partial to northern accents.

I pulled Leyda away to give them some privacy. "What do you think he's saying?" Leyda asked as we searched for a spot at the banqueting tables.

"Saying? Probably thanking her for changing the subject when Harborough Hatch came up. Thinking? *'Praise Odei, that might be the most beautiful woman I've ever seen.'*"

"You've got to admit, she has taste," Leyda said. She craned her neck to keep the Riders in view. "Did you see his armor? I think that was real silver. And those pendants Lady Charis wore in her hair; were those rubies? She looked so wonderfully *fierce*." She slipped into an open seat next to four-year-old Rya Carlyle, who was busy attempting to eat an entire turkey wing in one bite. "What I'd give to wear my hair like that. Do you think it takes long, all the braiding?"

"Longer than you could sit still for," I said, and gave the sleek black plait she wore down her back a playful tug. She stuck out her tongue.

"Rya, sweetheart, use your knife," Gwyn Carlyle said as I sat next to her. "Should we leave some room for Anjey?"

"I don't think she'd notice if we did." I gestured over my shoulder to the place where Brysney and Anjey sat, their heads bent close together in conversation.

"Well, well!" Gwyn said. "Just wait until your mother sees. Do you think she'll aim for a spring wedding?"

Coming from anyone else, I might've been embarrassed to know

Mama's ambition was so obvious, but Gwyn knew my mother almost as well as her own. In any case, she was right. After Rina's death, Mama had made it her avowed object to get her daughters out of Hart's Run. That gave us several options, but as we were all too old to apprentice ourselves to the crafting guilds and none of us had any interest in studying abroad in Edonarle, marriage seemed the surest way to get us under a safer roof. Unfortunately for Mama, until now young, single, well-armed men without ties to the Manor had been rather thin on the ground.

"I'd guess early winter. This afternoon Mama swore one of us would be married by Saint Ellia's Day."

"That's a pity. Anjey would've wanted lilies." Gwyn raised her glass. "Here's to the happy couple-to-be."

"Aye, I'll drink to that," Leyda said, stealing my wine and taking a sip. She giggled at my expression. "Come on, Aliza. A *Rider* in the family? What's not to celebrate?"

"What are we celebrating?" Rya piped up, air whistling through the gap in her teeth. She'd conceded defeat to the turkey and was now struggling to keep up with the conversation.

"Nothing yet," Gwyn said. "Give it a few months. Anjey needs time to work her magic."

Leyda frowned. "Months? She'd better be quicker than that. He's only here for a fortnight."

"No, he's not. You hadn't heard? Brysney's renting the North Fields lodge. He and his sister are in Hart's Run for the foreseeable future." Gwyn leaned forward. "They say he's running away from something tragic in his past."

"Really?"

"I thought it was his sister's wyvern who died at Harborough Hatch," I said.

"Well, yes, but that's not why they're here. I heard something awful happened to Brysney while they were in Edonarle. He took a contract in the country to escape it."

"I *knew* it," Leyda said under her breath, and snuck another glance at the table where Brysney and Anjey sat. "What happened? Did he have a falling-out with the king? Did his wyvern accidentally kill someone? Oh! Did *he* kill someone? A human, I mean? Or a *Shani?*"

Gwyn grinned. "Haven't a clue. We'll have to make something up."

For the next half hour we wove stories about Master Brysney's departure from Edonarle. The twang of a fiddle at last interrupted Leyda's tale of an ancient blood feud between Brysney and a family of beoryn Riders, and we looked up to see Barrett the cartwright tuning his instrument across the Hall. Davy, the carpenter's son, sat next to him with his goatskin drum. A stream of people had already started for the open space in front of the bonfire.

"Aye, Leyda, I'm sure there are all sorts of bounties on his head, which is why he's at a party in Hart's Run and not fleeing to Els or Nordenheath under cover of darkness," I said, facing the dancers. "Now, what do you say we show these Riders—"

My voice died in my throat.

A little girl twirled into the circle of firelight, her dark hair reflecting the glint of the flames as she spun on her father's arm, exactly as Rina had done every year at the Midsummer bonfire. She even wore Rina's favorite shade of purple.

"Everything all right?" Gwyn asked.

I blinked. Rina was gone. Nothing I could do now would change that. *But we're still here*, I thought. Nearby, Leyda rushed to join the circle, laughing, joyous, and every inch alive. The ache inside my chest dulled. It would never go away entirely, but seeing Leyda happy helped ease the pain. Rina always hated when people cried.

"Sorry, yes. Everything's fine."

"Evening, Gwyn, Aliza!"

We turned to see the apple-cheeked face of Henry Brandon, Lord Merybourne's bard, beaming down at us. At his side, Joe, the cooper, gave Gwyn a nervous wave.

"Oh, ask her already, Joe," Henry said. "It's not that hard. See?" He offered me his hand. "Care to dance, Aliza, or are you going to sit tonight out?"

"You wish."

To Gwyn's delight, Joe followed suit as the musicians broke into an old Hart's Run harvest jig. The four of us swung into the circle of dancers, singing, clapping, and stamping in time to the music until we were winded. As the last few notes dissolved into applause, Henry and I stepped out of the circle, desperate for a drink. We took our glasses to the crumbling perimeter wall and settled to watch the lines reform.

"Davy's in rare form tonight," I said. "I've never heard a Mad Robin played that fast."

"He is good, isn't he?" Henry stared into the bonfire, swirling his wine with a thoughtful look. "I've been thinking about offering him an apprenticeship."

"With *you?*"

"Good gods, you make it sound like I've condemned him to fifteen years in the oakstone quarries. I'm not a bad teacher."

I decided not to bring up his attempt to train the Manor hunting dogs to howl on key when he was fourteen. He'd taken away a crescent-shaped scar on his forearm and a healthy respect for all four-legged creatures with teeth. "I only meant . . . well, isn't it a bit early?" Henry wasn't much older than me, and he'd only been a full bard for a few years since the death of his old master.

"Wasn't my choice. Lord Merybourne wants me to have an apprentice. Davy's father says the boy can't tell oak from ash, and like you said, he's got a gift for music. Playing it, at least. I've yet to see what he can do with a sonnet." He tipped back the last of his wine. "Then again, if I wanted a storyteller, maybe I should've asked your sister." He looked around the Hall. "By the way, where is Mari tonight?"

"Home. You know she doesn't really enjoy this sort of thing."

"Socializing?"

"And dressing up."

"How does your mother feel about that?"

I gave him a look.

"Ah well. Poor, sweet Mari. I suppose it's for the best; it'd be hard to outshine the lovely Angelina from behind a book." He shot a wistful glance toward the bonfire, where my sister danced with Brysney. "*For ne'er the like to her shall see, though you shall seek eternally,*'" he murmured, quoting a line from "The Lay of Saint Ellia of the Shattered Bow." "You know, I think I might've actually had a chance with Anjey if I hadn't written her those verses when we were fifteen."

It was a small miracle I didn't spill my wine, doubled over as I was with laughter. "Oh, Henry, you should've seen her face when she wrote that rejection note," I said when I could speak. "She was *mortified!*"

"You wouldn't laugh if you knew the whole story."

"Oh, really? Try me."

"I was practicing sonnets, and Anjey was the only one on the Manor who fit the line '*wanton raven curls.*' I simply couldn't let that gem go to waste."

I smacked his shoulder. "Henry! Anjey really did get upset about that."

"And I wrote her a very nice apology letter. It's not my fault my master forgot to deliver it. Besides," Henry said, springing to his feet to avoid a second smack, "I wasn't about to ruin the drama. Unrequited love! It was the perfect tragedy."

I chased him around the arch and back out again into the firelight, but before I could catch him, Lord Merybourne gave a cry for "a song from Henry," and Henry stopped in his tracks. I narrowly missed crashing into him.

With a grin he shoved his empty wine glass into my hands. "Take care of that, will you? My skill is in demand tonight."

"This is not over!"

"I'd be disappointed if it was, my dear," he called over his shoulder.

A hush fell over the Hall as Henry took his place in front of the bonfire. Barrett struck a chord on his fiddle, filling the valley with the first notes of "The Lay of Saint Ellia of the Shattered Bow." I handed our glasses to a maid and sat on a fallen stone to listen. The tale of the ancient princess and slayer of the great sea-serpent was one of my favorites, and all teasing aside, Henry was the best singer in Hart's Run.

"Have a care, my friend."

In the stillness before Henry began, a voice spoke out of the darkness behind me. It was a deep voice, hardly above a whisper, but something about it unsettled me. A moment passed before I realized why: I didn't recognize it.

Curiosity tugged me away from the bonfire to eavesdrop on the conversation.

"You walk a perilous line," the strange man said. Beneath the man's impeccable Arlean I caught the trace of a foreign accent.

To my surprise, Master Carlyle answered. "You're one to talk," he said. "How'd you get into Hart's Run? Didn't someone notice?"

The stranger laughed—a low, dangerous sound. "You might say I've developed a talent for getting into and out of places without being seen."

"What do you want?"

"Your word, Master Carlyle, nothing more. I believe you are a man of honor, but my master has expressed . . . doubts. I'm here to provide some surety. We need to know you're both willing and able to keep your promise."

The stranger's voice had a hint of a hiss to it. I slipped into the shadows on the opposite side of the pillar, Henry and "The Lay of Saint Ellia of the Shattered Bow" forgotten.

"Yes, yes. He'll get what he's owed, and with interest," Carlyle said. "But no one hears of this. Do you understand? Your master never mentions my name, and neither do you. I won't be seen doing business with your *kind*."

"Let me advise caution, friend Carlyle." The stranger's voice fell. *"My master does not take orders."*

There was a shuffling sound. I dove behind the curtain of ivy covering the nearest arch. Through the leaves I saw Carlyle return to the banquet tables, his silhouette stocky and bowlegged against the bonfire. For a minute I crouched in silence, hardly daring to breathe as I waited for the stranger to step out into the firelight.

No one came.

Another minute passed, and fear once again gave way to nosiness. My hiding spot commanded a perfect view of the entire Hall. Whoever it was shouldn't have been able to slip past without me seeing him.

An icy breeze ruffled the ivy.

"You should mind your own business, little girl."

I whirled around, but the darkness behind me was empty. The stranger had disappeared, leaving me with a pounding heart and shaking hands, alone in the hedgerow.

Something rustled at my feet. "Aliza? Are you all right?"

Well, alone with a hobgoblin.

"Tobble!" I knelt next to him. "Did you see someone just now?"

"Huh? What, here?"

"Behind you. There was a man. A strange man." I felt the ground where he had stood, where he *must've* stood, searching for the indentation of a boot, a shoe, a foot, anything. Only unbroken grass stems met my touch. "He was right here, I swear!"

"I'm sorry, Aliza, I didn't see anything."

I peered into the darkness beyond the arch. If the man had hoped to stifle my curiosity by scaring me, it hadn't worked. "Never mind. What are you doing here, Tobble? You *do* know there are wyverns just over there, don't you?"

Tobble grumbled a few words in Gnomic.

"Sorry?"

"Er, about that," he said. "Chief Hobblehilt heard about our little skirmish in the garden this morning. He wanted to make sure that we, um, apologized to the dragonrider."

"And you volunteered?"

"*Ugh.* Cousin Nobble volunteered me."

"Oh dear. Anything I can do to help?"

"Yes! Can you translate for me?"

"You speak perfectly good Arlean."

"Well, yes, but *he* doesn't need to know that. And those wyverns are much less likely to eat me if you're there." He scrambled up my bent knee and swung onto my shoulder. "Please?"

"Fine. But you'll owe me, all right?"

"Aliza, you are my favorite human being on earth."

DAIRED WAS NOT MINGLING IN THE CROWDS NEAR THE tables, nor was he among the dancers. We snagged Anjey as she passed by the bonfire and asked her if she'd seen him or, failing that, if Brysney had. "Cedric just went to look for him," Anjey said, pointing to where the *Shani* creatures lounged between—or in the case of the two wyverns, on top of—the stone archways. "I think they're over there."

"She's looking happy," Tobble said as we made our way across the Hall.

"She's made a friend."

"Lovely. Er, Aliza? Would you mind steering a bit more to the right?" he whispered in my ear. "I think that blue wyvern just licked its lips."

I rolled my eyes but did as he said, not because I feared Bluescale might swoop down and snatch him from my shoulder, but because neither Brysney nor Daired were near them. "Look, if you're really so worried about it, can't Hobblehilt just send a note?"

"There! They're back there, behind that arch. See?"

I looked. Beyond the ruined wall, the two Riders stood close together. Even from a distance they appeared to be deep in conversation.

"Don't be silly! I'm not going to walk up and interrupt them."

Tobble smiled. "Of course not. We'll wait on the other side until they're finished. But nice and close, so we can hear."

A reflexive *no* rose to my lips, but cursed curiosity dug its claws into me once more, and my no was stillborn. I sighed. "You're a bad influence, Tobble Turn-of-the-Leaves. You know that, right?"

"Yes, yes. Now *shh*. I want to listen."

The musicians resumed a rollicking jig, which gave us plenty of cover to sneak closer. Keeping my head low, I sat on an overturned paver around the corner from the Riders. Tobble leapt down onto the grass and pressed his ear to a crack in the stone.

He needn't have bothered. Neither Brysney nor Daired made any effort to lower their voices. "Great gods, Alastair, you're impossible," Brysney said. "Are you even *capable* of enjoying yourself?"

"Not really, no. Certainly not here."

"You're being absurd. The country is a lovely place." Brysney breathed deeply. "Edonarle doesn't have fresh air like this."

"That's cow dung you're smelling."

"Yes, scoff all you like, you damp toadstool. I like it here. Given enough time, I might even love it. Charis was right; it's exactly what I needed. Might be a nice change for you too if you'd let it."

"I'm glad you like it, Cedric. Truly, I am," Daired said, sounding weary, "but I only came to this godsforsaken smudge-on-the-map because Charis asked me to, and because you needed a few familiar faces. We're here to do a job, not . . ." He seemed to be searching for the right words. "*Fraternize* with the locals."

"Doesn't mean we can't enjoy the scenery."

"Trees and mud and vermin-infested gardens. Not much to enjoy."

"I wasn't talking about the gardens."

"You can't seriously like these people, Cedric."

"Why not?"

"There's not a soul out there who'd have the first idea how to gut a gryphon, even if we laid it out dead in front of them and put the knife in their hand. The best of them would be worthless in battle."

"Not that I don't appreciate a good gutting," Brysney said, "but there are other skills in the world worth cultivating."

"Name one."

"Dancing."

Daired groaned. "Thell have mercy and kill me now."

"The great Alastair Daired, frightened by a country jig? If only the Broodmother of Cloven Cairn could see you now! She'd have given the wings off her back to find out your true weakness before you cut off her head."

"Give me a coven of lamias any day over a *jig*." Daired spoke the word like a curse. "In any case, you looked enough of a buffoon out there for both of us. I won't add to your embarrassment."

"Believe me, even if you did make a fool of yourself, I'd be the last one to notice. I've had more pleasant things on my mind."

There was a pause. "Are you talking about that girl? The one you were dancing with?"

"I wondered if she'd caught your eye," Brysney said with new enthusiasm. "I've met my share of pretty women, Alastair, but I've never known real beauty until tonight. Oh, don't make that face. If you saw her, you know it's true."

"I'm color-blind, not actually blind. Yes, she's pretty. It doesn't mean anything. You've courted enough brainless women to know that by now."

"Anjey is nothing like them," Brysney said, his voice growing warm. "*Any* of them. Hard as it may be for you to believe, I have learned from my mistakes."

"Prove it."

"Anjey's more than a beautiful face; she's clever and witty and kinder than any of the others. She came to Charis's defense the instant Harborough Hatch was brought up."

"Came to her defense?" Daired sneered. "What, did she drop her bonnet? Or swoon to create a distraction?"

The smile that had risen to my lips faded.

"She changed the subject."

"That doesn't count," Daired said. "Half of Arle knows that Harborough Hatch is a painful memory for you and Charis. This girl's no cleverer than the last because she—what?"

Brysney's laughter drowned out Daired's protests. "I get it now! You're still in a foul mood from this afternoon. Admit it! That's why you won't enjoy any of this."

"I was pelted with mud by a band of feral hobgoblins on my way to the last place in Arle I wanted to be," Daired growled. "Have you ever tried scrubbing mud out of chain mail? Of course I'm in a foul mood, and *why are you still laughing?*"

"Hobgoblin Girl—the one you told me about—I just realized who she is!"

"Don't tell me."

"'Dark hair, high cheekbones, wears flowers in her braid'? I'm no poet, but that sounds a lot like Anjey's sister."

Daired murmured something I couldn't make out.

"Aliza's her name, in case you wanted to know."

"I didn't," Daired said, "but let me guess. You're going to tell me that charm and wit run in this extraordinary family."

"Mhm. Beauty too. Don't tell me you didn't notice."

"The girl wasn't . . . plain," he said after a prickly silence.

"So?"

"So what?"

"So why not go find her? If you won't dance, at least strike up a conversation. What's the harm? You've already been, ah, introduced."

"And that was more than enough for me. Pretty or plain, I've got better things to do than socialize with a country wench who spends her time in the company of garden pests."

Tobble leapt for the crack in the wall, his little fists balled at his side, sputtering Gnomic curses. Just in time I caught his arm and pulled him back.

"These 'better things' you speak of," Brysney said, "would they consist of skulking around in the shadows like a warty gremlin? Because if that's the case, my friend, then there really is no hope for you."

"So you keep telling me."

"Alastair, please." Brysney's voice grew serious. "If you won't go out there for me or for these people, do it for Charis. She's having a hard time without Redtail. She won't admit it, but I can feel her pain. She *misses* him."

Daired was silent for a moment. "All right," he said, "but I swear, if you try and make me dance, tomorrow morning your armor will be hanging from the highest branch of the tallest tree in Hart's Run, and I'll give Silverwing six head of cattle not to bring it back for you."

"You know what?" Brysney said. "That wouldn't even begin to dampen my spirits."

CHAPTER 4

SHE-WHOSE-WINGS-BRING-THE-TEMPEST

The sound of footsteps sent Tobble leaping back onto my lap. "Can you believe what that Rider said? He can forget about an apology from me!"

"No, he can't," I said, pretending to relace my boot as Brysney and Daired strode out into the firelight. It took effort to disguise the twinge of bitterness his words had inspired, but even in my own head I wouldn't give him the satisfaction of making me angry. The man introduced himself to hobgoblins by kicking them across the garden. I shouldn't have expected much by way of manners. "You roped me into this, and I'm going to make sure you see it through."

"Aliza!"

"Not for him, silly, for you. Hobblehilt's going to have your head if you back out now." It was true. According to Tobble, the last hobgoblin who'd broken his promise to the chief spent half a day bobbing in the River Meryle, getting his toes nibbled on by trout. "Besides, imagine Daired's expression when he's forced to talk to us in front of the other Riders."

Tobble considered that for half a second before leaping onto my shoulder.

There were fewer Riders standing at the edge of the Hall than when I'd last seen them. After delivering Daired to the public's eye, Brysney had slipped away again, no doubt to find Anjey and claim another dance. Master Ruthven and his wife had also made themselves scarce, which left Daired, Charis, and the *Shani* to watch the merrymaking from the fringes.

A few eyebrows rose as I approached Daired, and not all of them human.

"You sure about this?" Tobble whispered.

No going back now. The bravado I'd felt in the shadows didn't last long under the fiery gaze of the dragon and her Rider, now fully illuminated by the blaze of the bonfire. Daired had cleaned up since I'd seen him in the garden. He'd removed every last trace of mud, a feat which, after seeing up close how many layers of linen, leather, and chain mail formed a Rider's armor, I had to admit was quite impressive. Two steel dragons curled around the heartstone set in the pommel of his sword, the bloodred gem clasped in their silver claws. It caught the firelight, throwing glints like sparks across his black hair. Like Brysney, he wore his hair close-cropped on both sides and longer in the middle, the ends braided in an intricate plait that fell past his shoulders. A single gold hoop pierced his right ear. Surprise mixed with the semipermanent look of disdain on his face as he recognized us.

I curtsied. "Master Daired."

"Friends of yours?" Charis asked Daired. As she spoke, the silver cord that bound her braid swung over her shoulder and two small adornments came clinking into the light, dark as wine and smooth as glass. *Wyvern scales.* She wore her tokens of mourning close to her heart.

"We met earlier, but I'm afraid we weren't properly introduced," I said to Daired. "I'm Aliza Bentaine."

"How can I help you, Miss Bentaine?" Daired said, avoiding my eye.

I fancied I could follow the train of his thoughts, and wished I could tell him exactly what I was thinking as well. *Why, yes, I did just hear everything you said about me. Luckily for you, I have good manners and won't mention it, but that doesn't mean you're not a cad.* "I'm actually here for my friend," I said as Tobble balanced on my shoulder, hands on his hips. "You might remember him."

"Yes?"

"Go ahead, Tobble," I said.

Tobble pulled himself up to his full height, which brought him level with Daired's nose. "I come on behalf of Chief Hobblehilt Sun-on-the-Riverbank, of the Hobgoblins of Merybourne Manor," Tobble began in Gnomic, "who, for reasons I can't fathom, thought we should be the bigger people and come apologize, even though you *clearly* started it."

Tobble! My mind raced. "Tobble says . . . he's here on behalf of his people, the Hobgoblins of Merybourne Manor, and he'd . . . like to apologize for this afternoon."

Tobble continued in Gnomic, brightening with every word. "You're a brutal, mean-spirited bully, and I think you got exactly what you deserve. My belly still hurts from where you kicked me. You know, I had to miss dinner tonight because of you." He folded his arms. "We were having my favorite fungi."

"He says it was an unfortunate misunderstanding, and hopes that you'll be gracious enough to overlook any damage they might have done to your . . . er . . . armor."

"I wish they'd used rocks instead."

"Please accept his apology," I said, and smiled and prayed like anything that none of the Riders spoke Low Gnomic.

Daired looked away. "Apology accepted."

"There. Happy?" I asked Tobble in Gnomic.

Tobble made a face at Daired. "You're a pompous, self-absorbed snotpig. I hope you get hiccups for a month."

"Thank you for understanding, Master Daired." Behind him his dragon shifted into the firelight, her eyes gleaming as she watched our conversation, and I remembered the sketch I wanted to make for Mari. "Would you mind if I drew your dragon?"

Daired frowned. "The hobgoblin draws?"

"No, sorry, that was me."

Again his dark gaze raked my face as if searching for something. I couldn't tell what it was or if he'd found it, the artist in me momentarily distracted by his eyes. They were beautiful, a rich brown with long lashes. It'd been hard to tell when we'd first met, as most of the time they'd been covered in mud. *No, not beautiful.* I checked myself. *Beautiful* wasn't a word suited to someone who kicked hobgoblins.

They were nicely symmetrical, that was all.

"You don't have anything to draw with," he said.

I pulled a folded piece of parchment and a linen-wrapped stick of charcoal from my pocket and held them up. Next to him, Charis said something in a creature tongue—Eth, I guessed, though it might have been Vernish. Regardless of the language, I recognized the tone. My drawing tools somehow warranted her mockery. My face grew warm, but for Mari's sake I held my ground. Daired answered her with a few words in the same language.

"Sir?" I asked, but before he could reply, I was fairly bowled over by a grinning Leyda.

"Aliza!" she cried, clinging to my elbow. The scent of wine followed her, and I stifled a groan as I stuffed my drawing utensils back in my pocket. She gave both Daired and Charis a frank once-over, her gaze lingering on their weapons. *"Introduce me,"* she said in my ear in a voice that wasn't even close to a whisper.

"Lady Charis, you've already met my sister Leyda," I said, emphasizing the *already met* part in the hopes that Leyda would come to her senses.

She didn't. "Lady Charis, they say you can throw a dagger from fifty paces and hit a hobgoblin's big toe. Is that true?"

Tobble yelped and sat down hard on my shoulder, tucking his feet under him.

"I've never tried it," Charis said.

Leyda turned to Daired. "You must've killed hundreds of *Tekari*, Master Daired; all the songs say so. Which were the fiercest? My sister Mari thinks lamias are the worst, but I think it'd have to be gryphons. Do you ever make them plead for mercy before you kill them?" Her eyes grew round, mesmerized by the golden dragon crest on Daired's breastplate. "Have you ever lost a battle?"

"Leyda, don't be silly," I said, pulling her back before she could reach out, touch the emblem, and send her sister to an early grave from the embarrassment. "Of course he hasn't. Now, if you'll excuse—"

"Why would you say that?" Daired asked.

I blinked. "Well, you're still alive."

"You don't have to die to lose a battle, Miss Bentaine."

"I didn't think *Tekari* accepted surrender."

"They don't. When Riders fight, it's not only our lives at stake," he said. "There's more to us than your folktales might suggest."

I opened my mouth, then shut it just as quickly. The words of some of Henry's bawdier limericks about Arle's warrior class came to mind, and I hoped what Daired said was true, almost as much as I hoped he left Hart's Run without hearing those particular folktales. "I'm sure there is. Leyda, we should—"

"Do you really have to have noble blood to become a Rider?" Leyda asked Charis. "Or can anyone take up the sword?"

Charis undid the clasp on the leather strap that held her scabbard in place on her back. It swung into position at her hip, and she drew it, holding it out for Leyda to admire. "Of course anyone can take up the sword, child," she said, with a condescending smile. "But fortunately for Arle, the *Shani* have higher standards."

Leyda's face fell.

"Which is why the Free Regiments exist," Daired said. "Rangers don't ride *Shani*."

"And speaking of *Shani*, Leyda, we'd better be getting Tobble back home," I said.

"What? No!" Tobble said in Gnomic. "I want to stay for the party."

"Play along," I growled in the same language. Muttering his disappointment, he swung down from my shoulder and clambered over to Leyda. She cradled him against her chest with her free hand, making no effort to resist as I turned them both toward the bonfire. "Tobble says it was a pleasure to have met you both," I said to Daired and Charis. "Have a lovely evening."

"Miss Bentaine, you're forgetting something," Daired said.

"I am?"

"My dragon would like a word with you."

Both Leyda and Tobble looked up at me, their expressions caught somewhere between amazement and alarm. "Go," I said, nudging my sister in the direction of the tables. "Help Tobble find some dinner."

Daired's dragon arched a sinuous neck over his shoulder as Leyda and Tobble scurried off. Even several strides away I felt waves of heat radiating from her. She lowered her head and watched me with unblinking eyes the color of fire opals before speaking another few words in Eth. "She says you forgot about your sketch," Daired translated.

I fumbled for my parchment and charcoal. "You're right. Thank you . . . Drakaina," I said, taking a gamble and using the address Mari had once informed me as the only way a *nakla*, or non-Rider, dared speak to a dragon. Drake *for males,* Drakaina *for females, and gods help me if I'm wrong.*

The dragon let out a deep, chest-rumbling laugh.

"Have I said something wrong?"

"My name, Miss Bentaine, is *Ahla-Na-al Kanah-sha'an-Akarra,*" the dragon said. "She-Whose-Wings-Bring-the-Tempest in Arlean, and I'm nowhere close to being the Drakaina. I am, however, thoroughly flattered that you would confuse us." She raised one wing and folded it back so that the claw on her wing joint touched the ground. "You can call me Akarra."

"Pleasure to meet you, Akarra."

"Likewise. Now, where will you sketch this masterpiece of yours?"

Beyond her left wing, the bonfire cast enough light to draw by. "Just over there. It won't be much of a masterpiece, I'm afraid. My sister Mari couldn't make it tonight, but she would've loved to see you."

"How thoughtful." She settled onto the ground and folded her wings. "Would you like to include Alastair?"

Daired and I raised our heads at the same time, and looked at Akarra with expressions that both said *please no.* "That's not necessary," I said.

He bowed and backed away to join Charis, who was having a quiet word with her brother's wyvern.

"Oh, just as well. He'd never be able to stand still," Akarra said, and struck a regal pose. "Lucky for you, I don't fidget."

True to her word, Akarra remained motionless while I drew, surveying the banquet with a noble air that was both a delight and a challenge to capture. Several minutes later Daired wandered back, remarking on something in Eth. She replied without moving, which seemed to irk him. He spared me one last look before disappearing into the shadows beyond the wall.

I finished the sketch with little time to spare. As I stowed my charcoal, His Lordship's booming voice announced one final song from Henry Brandon, and I knew what would follow. As soon as Henry finished, Papa would collect his family and badger us home before Mama had a chance to propose to Brysney in proxy.

"All done?" Akarra asked when I hopped down from the wall. "May I see?"

I held the parchment as close to her as I dared, hoping that a stray spark or even the heat of her words wouldn't send my work crumbling to ashes.

"Mhm. It's been a long time since I was small enough to see myself in a looking-glass, but I'm sure that's what I would see if I could. Well done, Aliza." Looking over my shoulder she said, "Ah, Cedric. Who's your friend?"

The last words were addressed to Brysney and my sister as they approached, hand in hand, breathless from dancing. Anjey's eyes grew larger the closer they came, and she stared first at Akarra, then at me, clearly shocked to see me on first-name terms with a dragon.

"Akarra, this is Angelina Bentaine," Brysney said. "It looks like you and Aliza are already acquainted."

"Aliza has been sketching my portrait, Cedric. I'm sure even that vain wyvern of yours has never had finer."

"Really?" said Brysney. "In that case, I may have to commission your talent on behalf of my Silverwing someday."

"I'd be happy to, sir."

"Excellent!"

Anjey nudged him.

"Right. Miss Aliza, my fellow Riders and I would like to start hunting the gryphon horde as soon as possible, but none of us have the faintest idea where to start." He glanced at Anjey, whose hand he still held. "I've already asked your sister, but I was hoping I could persuade you to assist us too."

Anjey's astonishment on meeting Akarra was nothing compared to mine. *What on earth could we do to assist a band of Riders?* On that point, at least, Daired and I had no cause for argument. Anjey and I would be useless on the battlefield. "I'd be glad to help, Master Brysney, but I'm not sure what we could do."

"Tomorrow we're going to start a sweep of the woods between here and the North Fields lodge," he said. "You ladies know the area, and Miss Anjey tells me you're both fine horsewomen. You could be our guides."

My anxiety eased. Giving my sister an excuse to enjoy Brysney's company would've been reason enough, but truth be told, I was eager to spend time outdoors. It'd been too long since we Manorfolk had been able to go for a stroll in the woods without fearing for our lives.

As long as we don't go through the south pasture. No matter how much time passed, I didn't think I could ever face that field again. For all I knew, Rina's blood still stained the stones of the pasture wall. I'd take the Riders anywhere in Hart's Run they wanted to go—except there.

"Count me in, Master Brysney."

TO ANJEY'S DISAPPOINTMENT, PAPA CUT OUR TIME AT the banquet short soon afterward. The instant Henry finished his song, Papa appeared out of nowhere and made the polite but firm suggestion that we return to the Manor House. A sullen Leyda and Mama, whose wine-glazed eyes brightened when she saw her oldest daughter with Brysney, were already in tow. I introduced my family to Akarra before Mama could say something we'd regret later.

"An honor, Bentaines," Akarra said, extending one wing in what seemed to be a dragonish curtsy.

Papa apologized for taking us away. "We've got to get back to our other daughter," he said as Brysney drew Anjey aside for a few last private words.

"Ah yes. Do give Miss Mari my best."

"Thank you, we will. Goodnight, ma'am," Papa said. "Girls? Come along."

When we returned to our quarters at the Manor House, I found Mari lying on the drawing room floor, asleep before the dying fire. Various books and journals lay spread around her, her precious bestiary serving in place of a pillow. "We missed you tonight," I whispered, pressing a kiss to the top of her head. "A dragon was asking about you."

Mari shifted off her bestiary and mumbled something before drifting back to sleep. I lifted the corner of the book, slipped my drawing of Akarra in between the pages, and crept out.

CHAPTER 5

THE PROS AND CONS OF WEARING TROUSERS

Morning came too fast, announced by both the rising sun and someone shaking my shoulder. Stupid with sleep, I pushed the shaker away and rolled over. "Go 'way."

The pillow disappeared from beneath my head.

"Hey!"

"Get up!"

Bleary-eyed, I sat up and blinked until Anjey came into focus. One hand held my pillow; the other was on her hip. Dressed in a loose-fitting shirt and the only pair of trousers she owned, she'd already washed and done up her hair in a long braid.

"What're you up to?"

"The Riders, Aliza! We agreed to help show them around North Fields today, remember?"

"Course I remember," I mumbled, stealing the pillow from Anjey's side of the bed, "but 'stoo early. Later."

"Cedric wanted to get an early start. His wyvern thought there would be rain today and they want to make the most of the weather while it's clear." Again the pillow disappeared. "So get *up!*"

"All right, all right! You win," I said, and disentangled myself from my blankets with a sour look, "but you get to explain to Papa where we're going."

"I will. Now get dressed!"

Anjey shouldn't have agreed so quickly.

We found our family at the breakfast table. Leyda hunched in a chair between Mama and Papa, her head in her hands. Mari sat across from her sister, a prim smile on her lips as she buttered her toast.

"And where exactly are you two going dressed like that?" Mama asked as soon as she noticed our trousers.

"The Riders are surveying North Fields this morning. Master Brysney invited us to join them," Anjey said.

Mari set down her toast. Papa looked up from his eggs. Even Leyda raised her head.

"Oh! Oh, goodness!" Mama cried. "He asked for *both* of you?"

"But *why?*" Papa asked.

"As guides. The Riders want Aliza and me to show them around the area."

"Didn't I tell you, Robart?" Mama said. "When do you meet him, my loves?"

"As soon as possible," Anjey said.

"What? What are you waiting for? Go, go!" she cried, shooing us with her hands, but Papa pushed back his chair and blocked our way.

"Absolutely not! Angelina, Aliza, stay where you are. I will not have my daughters gallivanting off around North Fields in the company of strangers and dangerous beasts."

"Papa, we'll be perfectly safe," Anjey said.

"No. You're not going."

Mama sprang to her feet. "Robart, think what you're saying! They need our girls' help. Would you deny them that?"

"Moira, it's *dangerous*. I'm not going to lose another daughter to those creatures."

For a moment we were all silent, trying hard to avoid looking at the empty chair where Rina used to sit. Mama collected herself first. "You know as well as I do that there could be no safer place in all of Hart's Run than with those Riders," she said in a softer voice. "Why, it'd be more dangerous for Mari and Leyda to visit the milliner in Trollhedge than it would for your girls to go with Master Brysney."

"My love—"

"No, Robart, it's settled. They will go, and they will go with your blessing."

He sank into his chair with a sigh. "Fine. Anjey, Aliza, you may go on one condition. Be *careful*, my dears. Promise me you'll be careful out there."

"We will," Anjey said. "Of course we will, Papa."

Mama smiled in triumph as she sat, shook out her napkin, and began to work on her toast as if nothing had happened.

"Good." Papa waved us away and returned to his breakfast. "Now, do as your mother says. Off with you."

THE SUN HAD JUST BRUSHED THE WEATHERVANE ON THE roof when we emerged from the stables, leading two of His Lordship's horses and an irritated stableboy. As residents of the Manor House, we had permission to use what horses we wanted, provided they weren't needed elsewhere on more important business. The stableboy knew this, but he had a hard time believing that Anjey and I had been summoned on an errand for the Riders, and after our second attempt at explaining things failed to make any impression, we gave up and saddled the horses ourselves.

The lad followed as we led them from the stable, teasing us the entire way to the front courtyard. There he fell silent. Five Riders stood waiting for us, their formidable mounts ranged beside them.

"Don't worry," Anjey told the stableboy, "we'll have the horses back by nightfall."

"We'll even brush them for you," I said.

"Aye, Miss Anjey. Thanks, Miss Aliza. Er . . . enjoy your ride," the boy said, then turned bright red and hurried away.

"Good morning, ladies!" Brysney cried from Silverwing's back. "Where do we start?"

I swung up onto my horse, a solid and dependable bay gelding. It'd been a long time since I'd ridden, and it felt good to be in the saddle again. "The river path might be easiest for those not flying," I said. We were the majority. Though a massive creature built for strength and speed, Ruthven's beoryn had no wings, and Charis rode a beautiful gray mare.

"The river it is. Miss Anjey—"

"Are we going or not, Brysney?" Ruthven said.

A grumbling thundercloud might have sounded less irritable. Burrumburrem shifted from paw to paw at his side, the fur along his spine rising in a reflection of his Rider's mood. Seeing a full-grown beoryn in daylight for the first time, I no longer wondered why the original Arlean settlers mistook their kind for bears. As tall as a draft horse and thick with muscle, Burrumburrem couldn't have weighed less than ten men, and the fangs that peeked out from either side of his snout were as long as my hand. His pelt, however, was gorgeous, a deep amber-brown with glints of gold. I quelled the desire to stroke it and see if it was as soft as it looked. Mari had drummed *Shani* etiquette into us quite well over the years, and I believed her when she said we were, as she put it, under *no* circumstances to *ever* touch a Rider's sworn companion creature. At best it would be disrespectful. At worst . . .

Mari hadn't elaborated on the *worst* bit. She hadn't needed to. I kept my horse away from the beoryn, and the gelding, for his part, was happy to maintain his distance from those glistening fangs.

"Ruthven's right," Charis said. "Take the wing already, brother. We need to keep ahead of the weather."

Brysney's wyvern spread his wings with a snort. We set off.

We took the path that wound alongside the River Meryle, and thus through all of Merybourne Manor. Silverwing flew as close to our horses as he could, dipping and banking so that Brysney could snatch the occasional word with Anjey. Early-rising villagers greeted our little party as we headed north, and Brysney's attention to my sister didn't go unmarked. Davy and a band of his friends visiting from Little Dembley even had the gall to whistle at them both as we passed their yard. Brysney, fortunately, didn't seem to notice. Daired, Charis, and Ruthven ignored the townsfolk altogether, but Nerissa was a little more pleasant, returning the fourfold greeting to anyone who touched their forehead or shouted a good morning.

We soon crossed the old stone bridge that marked the border of the inner Manorlands. Beyond its arches, the River Meryle deepened, gathering speed and strength from the tributaries that trickled in from the hills. Past the bridge, the land too grew wilder, and Charis, Anjey, and I soon had to pick our way through a tangle of vetch, flowering phlox, and sticky ferns. Ruthven's mount waded in the river, while his wife and Brysney hovered overhead on the backs of their wyverns. Akarra brought up the rear. She also walked in the river, Daired sitting high and proud on her back. I caught him looking at me more than once, his frown a mixture of curiosity and suspicion. No doubt he thought I'd snuck Tobble or one of my other hobgoblin friends along for the ride.

After a half hour navigating the river path, our group broke through the fringe of thinning trees. I blinked in the sunlight. Acre upon acre of wildflowers sloped into a wide valley before the woods claimed the land again, filling the hills on the horizon with tossing green. In the far corner of the fields we could just make out a sprawling stone house. A smudge of smoke rose from the chimney, thin and gray against the trees. Based on what Papa had told us, Lord Merybourne had already ordered most of Brysney's and Charis's belongings into the lodge, and from what it looked like, several of the servants had stayed on to prepare for their arrival.

"Welcome to North Fields," I said.

Burrumburrem shook himself and Ruthven grunted. Charis and Nerissa thanked us for leading them there, and Daired said nothing at all.

Silverwing touched down next to Anjey. "It's absolutely perfect," Brysney said.

"Perfectly *impractical*," Nerissa said. "Cedric, if it comes to a fight here on the fields, we'll never be able to keep the high ground."

Charis stood up in her stirrups and scanned the valley. "I don't see any other open ground. Alastair?"

"No," Daired said. "It's not ideal."

Akarra spread her wings and gave them an experimental flutter, sending leaves and twigs scuttling out from under her. "Not bad for a quick ascent. We could always chase them into the valley from the woods. Silverwing and Bluescale can flush them out, and Burrumburrem, Charis, and I will take care of them once they're here."

"My thoughts exactly," Brysney said. "Miss Anjey, have you noticed the gryphons congregating in any particular place?"

"They've always come from the forest." She pointed northeast, where the hills were rocky and the trees grew dense. "Over that way. We call it the Witherwood."

Ruthven spoke for the second time that morning. "Those rocks would make good cover. Burrumburrem and I will scout the area," he said, and without waiting for a response, his beoryn broke into a lope that took him and his Rider out of sight in a matter of minutes.

Nerissa sighed. "I'll go keep an eye on them."

"We'll ride toward the lodge," Brysney said as Nerissa's wyvern leapt into the air. "Meet us there when you're finished."

Her answer, if she gave one, was lost in the sound of Bluescale's wingbeats.

"Shall we?" Brysney said to Anjey. "I'd like to see—"

"Sssssss!"

Even Daired jumped as Akarra hissed. "What's wrong?" he asked.

She faced the forest and cocked her head. A sliver of fang showed beneath her curled upper lip. "*Shh. I'm not sure.*"

A gust of wind spiraled through the underbrush and my horse shifted beneath me. In the woods, something rustled.

"Akarra?" Brysney whispered. "What is it?"

Her only answer was to spring roaring into the air, for at that moment a gryphon came hurtling out of the shadows of the trees with a soul-curdling shriek.

My horse gave a screaming whinny and leapt sideways, nearly unseating me. Wings unfurled, the gryphon's leonine hindquarters rippled as muscles stretched to their breaking point. In a flurry of blood-matted feathers and scales it sprang for the neck of Anjey's horse, talons raking flesh as it struggled to push itself into the air. Her mare reared, lashing out with her hooves, but the gryphon ignored the horse in its panic to get airborne. I caught a glimpse of the gryphon's yellow eyes, wide and mad with fear, before Akarra lunged forward and ended its life with a single snap of her jaws.

No Rider could have kept their seat better than Anjey. The mare stumbled and dropped to her knees, blood pouring from her neck, and Anjey threw herself from the saddle before the mare could crush her. Relieved to see her clear of the horse, my panicked mind didn't register the new danger for several seconds.

She didn't rise from where she fell.

"Anjey? *Anjey!*" Before I knew what I was doing, I was at her side. "Are you all right? Angelina, answer me!"

With a grunt she rolled over, her face white and racked with pain. Blood stained her cheek. "No trouble, eh?" she said.

The horse's neck was not the only thing the gryphon's talons had raked. Anjey's sleeve was torn open and four lacerations ran lengthwise across her forearm. They were bleeding heavily, soaking the front of her shirt.

"Papa isn't going to be happy when he sees this," she said.

Brysney appeared at her other side. His face went white as hers. "Anjey, no . . . !"

"Brysney, can you bind this?" I asked.

"I—yes. Yes, of course." He pulled a knife from a sheath strapped to his calf, but he had no loose shirt to cut for bandages, only polished leather plates. He swore.

"Give it to me."

Brysney gave me the dagger and I cut away the hem from my own shirt, willing my hands not to shake as I handed him the strip of cloth. As he wrapped Anjey's arm I squatted beside the dead gryphon, at once transfixed and appalled by the sight. Its wings were twisted and broken, its talons still dripped blood, and its mouth hung open in a scream that would never again be heard.

Mama's words came to mind as Daired climbed down from Akarra's back and nudged the carcass with the tip of his sword. We should have been safe with the Riders. Gryphons weren't the most intelligent of the *Tekari*, but they weren't stupid. Even if this particular gryphon had been one of the duller ones, it should have fled from Akarra, not flown straight into her jaws.

Unless, of course, it'd been fleeing from something else.

Only then did I notice my horse had bolted.

Akarra growled. "Riders, on your guard!" she cried. "There are more!"

I leapt to my feet. We could hear the cracking branches and frenzied gryphon shrieks for ourselves. They were coming, not from the northeast as we'd expected, but from the west. Charis drew her sword and wheeled her horse around to meet the creatures. "Cedric, get those two away from here!"

"Miss Aliza, can you help your sister to that ridge?" Brysney pointed to a hill about a bowshot from the forest's edge.

"Aye."

"Good. Here, take this." He pressed his knife into my free hand. "Just in case. Silver and I will be right behind you."

I eased a hand under Anjey's shoulder. "Can you stand?" She tried to sit up, clutching her arm. Blood was already soaking through the bandage. "One . . . two . . . three."

Anjey straightened, swayed once, and steadied herself against me. Slowly we started for the hill. "What about the others?" she asked.

"They'll be fine. This is what they do. Just keep walking."

She obeyed, but each step drained a little more color from her face. When we reached the crest of the hill it was all I could do to keep her from crumpling to the ground. I eased her down on a grassy patch and crouched beside her, Brysney's knife drawn.

"How's the pain?" I asked once she'd caught her breath.

"It doesn't feel as bad as it looks."

"It looks terrible."

"You're quite the comforter," she said, attempting a grim smile. "I didn't say it doesn't hurt. Once the shock passes it'll hurt plenty."

"We'll have you safe inside with clean bandages and plenty of wine before that happens."

"Please do. Especially that wine bit," she said. "Aliza, what was that gryphon *doing*, attacking us like that?"

I looked toward the eaves of the forest, where the Riders stood in a line, weapons drawn. "If I didn't know any better, I'd say it looked scared. Like it was being hunted."

"By what?"

The clamor from the woods grew louder. "I have no idea."

CHAPTER 6

THE LOWER WESTHULL RANGERS

No sooner had I finished speaking than half a dozen gryphons broke through the undergrowth. Like the first, they ran in a fearful frenzy, heedless of everything in their path.

Everything, perhaps, except a full-grown dragon.

Their shrieks of alarm echoed over the fields as they tried to check their flight away from Akarra's dragonfire, Silverwing's talons, and the Riders' swords. Some of the luckier ones were close enough to the woods to retreat that way. The rest either took to the sky or made the vain but valiant attempt to fight.

Possessed of the strengths of both an eagle and a lion, gryphons could be formidable creatures, but they were deadlier and more coordinated in large numbers. Scattered by surprise, the few gryphons that attempted to stand their ground were soon decapitated, eviscerated, immolated, or run through. At least one beast found itself dispatched by all four means. Akarra and Daired chased the gryphons that flew. None of them reached the ground alive.

And still we hadn't seen what had driven them to us. Anjey squeezed my hand weakly as Brysney, Daired, and Charis made their way toward the ridge. "We'll have quite the story for the stable-boy, won't we?"

"We certainly will."

"He'll—oh, blast everything," she said. "Aliza, the *horse*."

I'd forgotten about her borrowed mare. It lay dead at the edge of the forest, surrounded by gryphon carcasses.

Anjey bit her bloodless lip. "Do you think Lord Merybourne will be angry?"

"You couldn't have prevented it."

"It's not me I'm worried he'll blame."

I followed her gaze to the place Silverwing had landed. Brysney sprang from his back and ran to Anjey's side. "We need to get you inside." He slid one hand beneath her shoulders and the other beneath her bent knees, lifting her as if she weighed as much as a dried leaf. With Silverwing hovering beside them, Brysney started for the lodge, my sister in his arms.

Akarra touched down next to me, and Daired leapt to the ground with his sword drawn. Charis joined him. "Any ideas what we're dealing with, Miss Aliza?" she asked. "You haven't hidden away any direwolves or valkyries in this part of the county, have you?"

"None that I know of."

"Pity."

Before I could reply, a band of armed men and women on horseback charged out from the eaves of the forest. It was a small band, but well disciplined. The slain gryphons gave them only a moment's pause. As soon as they caught sight of our party, they whipped their horses into a gallop and headed straight for us.

"Oh, *Thell*." Charis lowered her sword. "Did your Lord Merybourne happen to enlist a regiment of Rangers and forget to tell us about it?" she asked me.

"Of course not," I said. "Lord Merybourne has no—"

"Yes?"

No money to pay another band of wandering mercenaries, I'd wanted to say. "No need for Rangers," I said instead as the regiment gained the bottom of the hill.

Daired sheathed his sword as the leader of the company halted in front of us. Each of the Rangers wore the dark red cloak of the Free Regiments over leather hauberks or mail shirts, and by the tattered state of their uniforms, I guessed they'd been on the road for a long time. Most also wore light helms on their heads. The leader removed hers to reveal a woman's face, sweat-streaked and hard-featured, with a jutting chin and small, sharp eyes. She gave Daired a smart salute. "Good morning, sir!"

He did not return the salute. "What's your business here?"

"We had a report of gryphons in the area, sir. My name is Forstall, captain of the Lower Westhull Rangers. Our regiment left Hallowsdean a fortnight ago looking for work. The rumors brought us here." She eyed Akarra. "We had no idea there were already Riders engaged. Apologies if we intruded."

"You don't owe your apology to us, Captain Forstall," Charis said, nodding toward my sister. Anjey and Brysney had nearly reached the lodge. "Only to that lady there."

Forstall shaded her eyes. "What happened?"

"A startled gryphon is more dangerous than you might think. The lady took a talon to her forearm. Next time you may consider looking ahead before you go driving out a horde like that."

"Begging your pardon," Forstall said. "We took reasonable precautions. Our scout reported no habitations out this way, barring that lodge over there, and we thought it was empty. We didn't think there would be anyone in harm's way."

"In that case, you might want to use a different scout."

"I'll keep that in mind," the captain said coolly. "Before we leave, would one of you point us to the nearest town? If we're not needed for the gryphon hunt, my men and I would like to find some other employment in the area."

Charis looked at me. "Miss Bentaine would be better able to answer that."

"Ma'am?" Forstall asked.

"Do you have a map, Captain Forstall?" I asked. It wouldn't be difficult to direct them back to the Manor without one, but the last thing His Lordship needed to deal with was an unexpected regiment of Rangers. Sending them to Trollhedge or Little Dembley would be much easier for everyone.

"Of course. Wydrick?" Forstall called to her men.

One of the Rangers urged his horse forward. "Captain?"

"The map, Wydrick, if you please," Forstall said, and as she spoke, heat rippled through the air, followed by the thinnest of hisses. I glanced over my shoulder to see what was the matter.

Every single hair on the back of my neck stood on end.

It was as if Forstall had called for a basilisk instead of a man. Both Akarra and Daired seemed petrified by the sight of Ranger Wydrick. Akarra's mouth hung open, her breath boiling the air around her. Daired looked as though a ghast had sucked the life out of him.

Wydrick held out a rolled sheet of parchment. "The map, Captain."

Akarra reeled as if she'd been stung. Twice Daired's hand reached for his sword, but each time something seemed to defeat him and he fell back, his face fixed in an expression of mingled shock and fury.

Captain Forstall gave dragon and Rider a curious look before noticing the map. "Not to me, Wydrick. To the lady there."

Wydrick dismounted and strode over to me. His face was pale

beneath his white-plumed helmet, and beads of sweat dotted his cheeks, but besides that he betrayed no great agitation as Akarra hissed again. He saluted. "Ma'am."

The hand Daired had raised to his sword fell to his side for a third time, empty and trembling. Snarling something in Eth, he leapt on Akarra's back and she sprang into the air. Within minutes they were no more than a dark dot in the sky above us.

"What was that all about, Wydrick?" Forstall asked.

"Can't say, Captain." Wydrick removed his helmet with a lop-sided grin. Piercing green eyes met mine. His fair hair was tousled and sweaty from their ride, and his formidable jawline sported several days' worth of stubble. "I don't think your dragonrider likes me very much."

I returned the smile, but his attitude puzzled me. I didn't see how anyone could stand a few paces away from fiery death and joke about it minutes afterward. If it were only Daired who'd reacted so strangely, I might understand brushing it off; his bad temper seemed perennial. But Akarra? *There must be quite a story there.*

I looked at the map he offered. It showed all of southern Arle, ranging from Hallowsdean on the east coast, to the peaks of wild Dragonsmoor in the northwest, to Edonarle, the king's city on the southernmost shores of the island. The hills of Hart's Run lay north of Edonarle, crammed like a cartographer's asterisk between the more important counties of central Arle.

"Where would you say we are, Miss . . . ?"

"Bentaine, Master Wydrick." I pointed to a patch of parchment above the line that marked the northern border of Hart's Run. "This is North Fields, where we are now." I tapped an inky splotch a quarter of an inch below it. "The town of Trollhedge is just about here. They should have accommodations for a regiment of Rangers."

"Thank you, Miss Bentaine." He rolled up the parchment and replaced it in the folds of his cloak. "I hope we can stay. It's a beautiful area."

"Indeed it is, Wydrick," Forstall said. "Now, if it's not too much trouble, the rest of us would like to find lodging before this weather turns sour."

"Yes, ma'am." He touched his fingers to his forehead, once to Charis and once to me before he remounted his horse. He smiled too, but only to me.

"Farewell, Lady Rider, Miss Bentaine," Captain Forstall said. "Give our best wishes to the injured lady for her speedy recovery."

Charis inclined her head just enough to avoid being uncivil, though not enough to avoid being unfriendly. I curtsied goodbye.

With a shout, Forstall wheeled her company around and led them back down the hill. A minute later Master Wydrick's white plume disappeared in the shadow of the trees.

Yes, there's definitely a story there.

SAVE FOR THE INVITATION TO RIDE BEHIND HER AND MY acceptance, neither Charis nor I broke the silence as we made our way to the lodge. Both Silverwing and Captain Forstall's predictions of ill weather had come true; by early afternoon the clouds were piling up thick and fast, and the breeze that had first announced the oncoming gryphon had strengthened to a gale. Rain rode the wind, stinging our faces as Charis handed the mare's reins to a waiting groom.

Since the gryphons had descended on Hart's Run, few Manorfolk had dared to risk a visit to the lodge, but Papa had taken us to North Fields several times when we were younger and I remembered it well. From ground to gables it was just shy of the height of the Great Hall, with a roof of slate tiles and heavy timbered windows. Nothing grand, but the inside was comfortable, and most of the time it offered some charming views of the fields.

Currently, the predominant view was mud.

I picked my way through the puddle-strewn courtyard, leaping from cobble to cobble and cursing the squelchy feeling seeping up through cracks in my boots. *Oh, blast—*

A long hiss sounded from around the side of the lodge. I paused in the middle of a puddle, debated for a second, and headed for the side yard. *It's not as if I could get much wetter.* I rounded the corner of the lodge.

There I stopped. Akarra lay on the ground, her forelegs tucked beneath her and her head level with the paving stones. Mist rose in clouds from her scaly hide. Daired knelt next to her, one hand on her neck, staring out into the fields with a vacant, troubled look in his eyes. He was soaked to the skin.

"Master Daired, are you all right?"

He didn't respond. Folding my arms against the chill, I wondered whether or not to call again or follow Charis indoors, but before I could do either, Daired turned and looked at me. Or rather, he looked in my direction. His gaze ran through me like a spear, but I didn't think he saw me at all. He didn't look like the scornful Daired from the banquet, or even the silent Daired from this morning. Those dark eyes looked haunted.

After a moment he turned away.

I hurried inside, shaken and not quite knowing why.

The other Riders sat in the main parlor before a roaring fire, Ruthven and his wife included. The lodge steward appeared at the same moment I did. "Ah, Miss Aliza! I didn't realize you were also joining Master Brysney's party," he said, gray whiskers trembling beneath a capacious nose. I gathered he was already calculating without pleasure the extra preparations my presence would require.

"Sorry to be a bother, Henshaw. This was all rather unexpected."

"I've a room made up for your sister. Shall I do the same for you?"

"No need. I'll stay with Anjey."

"Very good, Miss Aliza." He bowed and backed out of the room.

"We may be here for a while yet," Nerissa said, peering out the window. "I don't fancy flying in this weather."

Ruthven grunted in agreement and Charis heaved a sigh.

"Miss Aliza, come sit by the fire and dry off," Brysney said.

Wringing water from my hair, I joined Anjey by the hearth, pleased to see some color returning to her cheeks. Brysney had found some clean rags and rebandaged her arm, and it looked as though the bleeding had slowed. I worked up my courage to lift the corner of the cloth.

And hastily covered it again.

"Nasty wounds, Miss Anjey," Charis said, looking over her brother's shoulder. "They'll need to be stitched soon."

I swallowed hard. Anjey looked at me, then at Brysney, but before I could take responsibility, he reached for her good hand. "I'll do it."

"We'll have to clean them first," I said. That at least I knew a little about. My uncle Gregory had taught me wood-wightish herblore during my summer visits to Edonarle, and in the years since I'd done what I could to develop my skills as an herbmaster. "I'll see what Henshaw has in the storeroom."

I found Henshaw in the kitchens. He pointed out his store of herbs and unlocked the wine cupboard, muttering various prayers under his breath. To my disappointment, he didn't have anything stronger than dried passiflora and a basket of leaves from the vine we at the Manor called hush. Ground and mixed with honey, it made a paste that could numb pain, but not to the degree Anjey would need. I left the kitchens with the hush, a bottle of honey, and a jug of Henshaw's strongest wine.

In the parlor, I found Brysney laying out clean cloths on a table close to the fire. Half a dozen lamps burned around it, filling the room with a steady yellow light. Betsy, the North Fields maid, was already busy boiling rags in a pot over the fire. She, Anjey, and Brysney were the only ones in the room; whether out of weariness or indifference, Charis and the Ruthvens had elected not to stay and watch.

I poured some wine for Anjey. "Sorry, dearest. This was all he had."

"I'll take whatever I can get."

It took real effort of will to concentrate on preparing the honey-and-hush salve, rather than on Brysney as he selected the longest of the needles Betsy brought to him, or on my sister as what little color she had drained out of her face. The hush made a messy paste. I washed my hands at the ewer basin, scrubbing them clean in the hottest water I could bear.

"Ready?" I asked Anjey when we finished.

"Wait." She poured another cup of wine and handed me the jug. "Ready."

Bracing myself, I pulled away the bandages. Four lacerations ran crosswise down her forearm. They were shallower than I'd first thought, but that was little comfort; I could still see the yellowish white of exposed fat beneath the broken skin, and muscle beneath that. My insides churned. *Breathe. Do what needs to be done.* "I am so sorry," I said, and poured the wine over the wounds.

She bit back a yelp.

Beads of sweat stood out on both our foreheads by the time

I'd finished cleaning her injuries. I exchanged places with Brysney, feeling quite certain I wouldn't be able to stomach any sort of food for at least a week.

To his credit, neither the blood nor the gaping flesh seemed to give him pause. He smiled at Anjey. "You've nothing to worry about. I promise I've done this many times," he said, and threading a freshly boiled needle with clean thread, began stitching.

Anjey's fortitude impressed me. Her pain showed, not in her face, but in her grip as she squeezed my hand under the table. It didn't take long for me to lose feeling in that hand.

"You're very brave, you know," Brysney told Anjey as he readied a new needle. "I've seen young Riders cursing and moaning over injuries half as bad as this."

Leaping at the distraction, I pressed Brysney for more details of his life as a Rider, or anything else to take Anjey's mind off the stitching. And, frankly, mine as well.

"Ah, Miss Aliza, beware! You've given me the one thing Riders crave above all else."

"What's that?"

"Permission to make ourselves sound more heroic than we actually were."

"By all means, tell us," I said. "Exaggerations included."

For the next hour we listened to his tales: of dances with wild wulvers and the great chase of the ghostly White Stag, of merfolk choirs on the shores of Lake Meera and battles with the savage centaurs that guarded the Widdermere Marshes, and of selkie sightings off the coast of Hallowsdean. Brysney turned out to be an excellent storyteller, and Anjey's grip loosened as he swept us up in the rush and excitement of his adventures.

One tale, however, he didn't share. Brysney never once mentioned the slaying of the Lesser Lindworm of Harborough Hatch.

"THERE." MINUTES AFTER HE FINISHED TELLING US ABOUT his first encounter with a gale of mischievous nixies, Brysney sat back in his chair. "That should do it."

Anjey and I both exhaled at the same time. Cautiously she moved her fingers.

"Better?" he asked.

"Better," she said. "Thank you, Cedric."

Cleaning up the remains of our operation gave me enough cover to hide my smile. No matter that the two had been strangers three days ago, Brysney and Anjey were now firmly in first-name territory. After one party had seen the inside of the other's arm, I supposed some social boundaries were bound to blur.

Night had fallen during our surgery. Rain pounded against the windows, the darkness outside riven every few minutes with lightning. I wrapped Anjey's arm with more clean cloths soaked in the honey-and-hush mixture, and Brysney and I helped her up the stairs to the room Henshaw had prepared. We bid Brysney goodnight on the threshold.

Anjey's brave veneer crumpled the moment I shut the door. She collapsed onto the bed.

"How's the pain?" I asked.

"I wouldn't say no to more wine."

"Give me a minute." I slipped back downstairs and fetched the wine jug, a cup of hot water, and a handful of mint leaves. "Here."

She sipped the wine as I prepared a cup of mint tea, which she drank obediently. The honey and hush, together with the wine, seemed to ease the worst of the pain, and after half an hour or so under my ministrations, she fell asleep. I stayed awake for a little longer, watching and worrying. When at last I knew I could do nothing else to make her comfortable, I curled up at her side and fell asleep.

My dreams that night were confused, full of fangs and horse screams and the yellow stare of a gryphon, chased by Daired astride a maddened Akarra. And above it all watched a fair-haired stranger with pale green eyes, his laughter even louder than the dragon's roar.

CHAPTER 7

THE WITHERWOOD

In the morning Anjey was worse.

My heart sank when I inspected her arm. The skin around the stitches was tight, red, and warm to the touch. A fast-moving infection had set in, and my salve hadn't been enough to stop it. I folded back the bandages, shuddering to think what horrible things those claws had torn before they raked my sister's arm. *Dead things, foul things, dozens of things that could kill her from the inside in a matter of days . . .*

I felt her forehead and my heart sank even lower.

She woke at my touch. "Something wrong?"

I tried to smile. Worrying her would only make it worse. "Besides the fact that you took a talon to the arm yesterday, I'd say everything's just fine."

"It's hot in here."

What else can I do? What else does she need? I laid a cool cloth on her brow, racking my memories of Uncle Gregory's lessons for something that would help. *What's strong enough to fight—? Oh.* I wondered if the Fourfold God enjoyed the cruelty of the coincidence. *Of course.*

Anjey watched without stirring as I pulled on my torn shirt, muddy leggings, and boots still damp from yesterday's soaking. "Where are you going?"

"I need to see if one of the Riders will fly back to the Manor and let Mama and Papa know we're alive. They must be worried sick." I didn't tell her where else I planned to go.

"I can't decide whether Mama will be pleased or horrified when she finds out. To know that Cedric and I are in the same house for the indeterminate future, or to know that I'm here without the proper wardrobe?"

"She won't know what to do with herself. Are you hungry?"

Anjey grimaced.

"Not at all? Something to drink?"

She licked her cracked lips. "Aye, please."

"I'll send a maid up. And I'll be back soon," I lied.

Brysney was awake and pacing when I came downstairs. Behind him, Silverwing lay sprawled on the hearth, his tail wrapped around the leg of a chair pulled close to the fire. He raised his head when I entered the parlor. Brysney stopped pacing. "How is she?"

"Not good. It's infected."

"Badly?"

"Yes. She needs stronger medicine than what we have here."

"What does she need?" Brysney asked in a voice that told me he would've walked to the highest peak of Dragonsmoor if I said there was an herb growing there that would save my sister.

I sank on to the arm of the nearest chair, rubbing my temples. "The only thing I can think of is ashwine root."

"I've never heard of that before."

"It's a local plant. Potent against infection, but not very common."

"Where do we find it?"

"Before the horde descended, we could always find some around the Witherwood."

If I'd had any lingering reservations about Brysney, his reaction dispelled them like the sun on mist. He tightened the straps of his scabbard against his chest and smiled. "In that case, we'd best get ready. We've got a busy day ahead of us."

"No, Cedric, there's no *we*." The chair in front of the fire moved, and a glowering Daired rose to face us. He crossed the room in several long strides. "You're not a Rider, Miss Bentaine. There's no way we're letting you go into this Witherwood."

I bit my tongue. His gallantry did him credit, but in the moment it was maddening. "Ashwine root is hard to find. If you want to gather enough and be out of there before dark, you'll need me with you."

"Describe it to us."

"I can't." I thought of Anjey lying upstairs, waiting for my return. She'd be waiting a long time if the Riders denied me. I wouldn't return without something to help her, and if I had to, I'd go to the Witherwood by myself. Ashwine looked like at least three other creeping greens, two of which were poisonous. Smell alone could identify it beyond all doubt, but the scent of ashwine was too subtle to describe with any precision, and it faded not long after it was picked. "I mean, I can, but not well enough to stake my sister's life on it."

"She's right, Alastair," Brysney said. "Miss Aliza, I'm going to wake the others. Nerissa and Ruthven can take word back to your parents that you're alive. The rest of us will head for the Witherwood," he said, and hurried out.

Daired turned back to me. "Charging into a gryphon nest is no little thing, Miss Bentaine, especially for a *nakla*. It'll be dangerous."

"I know."

"Do you?" He came closer. "Do you have the slightest idea what it takes to face a horde of gryphons?"

"A knack for squeezing into small spaces. Master Daired, you're not going to change my mind. I'm coming with you."

"It's not your responsibility to take on these creatures. It's ours."

"And it's mine to help my sister."

"You're sure the infection is serious?"

"I know the start of blood-fever when I see it."

The long, thin scar along his right temple drew tight as he furrowed his brows. "I can't make you stay, can I?"

"No."

"Fine. If you must then you must, but before I let you walk out that door, you're going to have to promise me something."

Before you let me? Oh, Master Daired, I'd like to see you try and stop me. "What's that?"

"Don't die today."

"Thank you, sir. Now that you mention it, I'll make a point not to."

"Good," he said, and pushed past me without another word.

Brysney had gathered the rest of the Riders in the front hall of the lodge. All but Charis took the news of Anjey's ailment without comment, and she said nothing beyond the fact that none of this would've happened if Lord Merybourne kept something stronger than wine in the lodge. The part of me that didn't prickle at her haughty tone wondered if she was right. My gaze wandered from the smattering of scars that covered her left cheek, to the line over Daired's temple, to the claw marks that marred Ruthven's face. The gods of the Riders were Mikla and Thell, Protector and Unmaker, and death was their trade. Each of them must've treated worse injuries than a talon gash in their careers, and did so with no herbmaster on hand to fix them up with a healing poultice. They did what they could with what they had and lived through it, each battle bringing new scars to boast of to their fellow Riders.

That, or they died.

The thought was less comforting than I hoped.

As the Riders headed outdoors to prepare their mounts, I sent a maidservant up to Anjey's room with a tray of tea, a pitcher of water, and strict instructions not to tell my sister where we'd gone until we were out of sight of the lodge.

Outside, the rain had stopped. Mist shrouded North Fields, thick and ghostly. More mist hung about Akarra, whose entire body let off clouds of steam in the damp air. She stood with her head bent next to Daired's.

"I understand we're going to a place called the Witherwood, Miss Aliza," she said as I approached. "How far is it?"

"From here, an hour's hike in good weather. It's a steep climb."

"In that case," she said, settling on the ground and beckoning me forward with an outstretched wing, "we'll all ride."

My mouth fell open. Brysney raised an eyebrow, and beneath him Silverwing let out a hoot of surprise. Nerissa and her husband looked at Akarra's offered wing before urging their mounts away from the lodge, as if eager to distance themselves from the undignified scene.

His face red, a speechless Daired gaped once, twice—but when he found his voice, he put it to good use. "Akarra!"

What followed was a strenuous protest in Eth, no doubt filled with furious reminders that I was a *nakla* and thus had no place astride a Daired dragon, and with pointed entreaties to consider the shame she'd bring upon herself to bear said *nakla*, and, judging by the tone, with a curse or two for good measure.

"Alastair, I don't give a fewmet for what the Drakaina thinks, or anyone else for that matter," Akarra said when he'd run out of breath. "This is life and death. We'll only waste time if you make Aliza walk, Charis will do no better on that mare of hers, and Silverwing can't take the extra weight." Daired started to protest, but a thunderous glare from Akarra silenced him. "You won't win this battle, my *khela*, so don't bother arguing. If you feel so strongly about it, you're free to stay here. I'll take them myself. Come along, Aliza," she said. "Charis, you too."

If it weren't for the need that drove us into the Witherwood in the first place, I would've refused. The idea of riding a dragon went against every custom I'd ever heard of, spoken and unspoken, yet the thought of Anjey's suffering made me brave, and deep down, I couldn't deny the flicker of excitement at the prospect of *flying*.

I clambered atop Akarra's back, using her foreleg as a mounting block. Her hide was warm, almost hot to the touch, and I saw at once why Riders wore the clothes they did. *Shani* only suffered a saddle in battle, which meant that most of the time, leather breeches and iron-shod boots were all that stood between a Rider's legs and the skin-shredding scales of their mount. Still, for a moment I savored the feeling, uncomfortable though it was. *A nakla sitting astride a Daired dragon? What Mari would give to see this!*

Daired climbed up behind me. "Tuck your feet under her shoulder spikes and lean forward," he said, wrapping an arm around my waist. I stiffened. "No, Miss Bentaine, I'm not going to let go," he said, his voice gruff and much closer to my ear than I felt was necessary. "It's for your own safety."

I glanced over my shoulder. He stared straight ahead. Behind him, Charis sat with folded arms, smirking. *She* didn't need anyone to hold on to her.

"Everyone settled?" Akarra asked.

Daired replied testily in Eth.

"Excellent," Akarra said. "Aliza, if you'd be so kind to point us in the right direction?"

I told her how to get there, wondering aloud if the mists would make it hard to find.

"Oh, don't worry. If a horde has nested there, you can be sure we'll smell it long before we see it. Now, I'd recommend you brace yourself."

I obeyed, clutching the spikes in front of me as her muscles coiled beneath us. Tighter, and tighter—

She sprang into the air.

Then I understood what Daired meant.

Oh gods, please don't let go! In a panic I gripped his arm as my stomach made a nearly successful bid for freedom, that spark of excitement extinguished in a flood of terror. Akarra banked to the west, and I screwed my eyes shut, grateful I hadn't eaten breakfast.

The nauseating sensation steadied but didn't subside as Akarra's powerful wings carried us across North Fields. Daired didn't let go and didn't speak, save to ask once, brusquely, if I was all right. Sick, dizzy, and half giddy with vertigo, I gritted my teeth and nodded. The Riders could have the sky if they wanted it. *Give me earth and growing things*, I thought as I clung to his arm. *You can keep the wind.*

As Akarra predicted, the smell of rotting flesh first signaled we were getting close. Soon her wingbeats slowed, and I worked up the courage to open my eyes. The forest sloped up in front of us as we glided over the thinning trees and rocky outcrops.

"The Witherwood is beyond the ridge," I said, my voice shaky.

She descended into the nearest clearing, her claws sinking into the leaf litter that covered the forest floor. As soon as we touched the ground, I breathed the most sincere prayer of thanks I'd ever said to every facet of the Fourfold God who was listening.

Silverwing landed beside us. "This the place?" Brysney asked.

"Aye, this is the Witherwood," I said, trying to figure a way to the ground that didn't involve me falling in a heap. The odds weren't in my favor.

Seeing my hesitation, Daired offered me his arm, but as my legs had taken on the consistency of jelly, it turned into less of a dismount as a graceless crumple. He ended up catching me awkwardly by the elbows and setting me on the ground.

"Thank you," I said, too relieved to be on solid earth to worry about being embarrassed.

He dropped my arms and stepped away as if my touch stung.

"If we're to find this ashwine plant quickly we'd best split up," Brysney said. "If you could describe it to us, Miss Aliza, we'll call for you if we think we've found it."

"You're looking for a woody vine with narrow leaves and clusters of purple flowers. It grows in shade and on rock faces. Look around the boulders first."

Charis frowned at our surroundings, the straggling trees made even more sinister by the shape of the crags in the mist. "This is bad terrain for a fight."

"Let's hope it doesn't come to that," Daired said, releasing his scabbard from its harness on his back. "Start looking."

OVER THE NEXT HOUR I WORKED NEXT TO THE RIDERS, inspecting, reinspecting, and discarding a number of vines that looked like ashwine but were either common throttleberry, flowering blue murmurry, or the vine hush. Silverwing searched with us, but Akarra stayed crouched in the same place she landed, fearful of alerting the horde to our presence if she moved about too much. For a few minutes before we began our search, Brysney and Charis debated whether or not it'd be better to flush the gryphons out all at once and be done with it. Charis said it would be easier to choose our own battleground if we made the first move, but Brysney overruled her, claiming that a fight would delay our errand and risk needless injury to everyone involved.

He said everyone, but he meant me. I silently thanked him.

The sun was high behind the clouds and we were all feeling hot, sweaty, and discouraged when Brysney at last let out a stifled cheer. Charis and I abandoned our search and joined him in a little copse farther down the hill. Lichen-covered boulders stood like sentinels around three sides of the grove, and up the tallest climbed a slender brace of purple-flowered creepers.

"Is this it?" Brysney asked.

I knelt beside the vine and broke off a leaf. The smell of wood smoke and sour earth filled my nose as relief filled my heart. I tugged on the base of one of the ashwine plants. Its roots ran deep. "Yes, this is it. May I borrow your knife?" I asked. Brysney handed me his dagger and I scored the earth around the ashwine with the tip of the knife, working the vine this way and that until the whole root clump came free with a soggy squelch. "This should—"

A screech sounded from just beyond the edge of the hollow, followed by the sickening crunch of bone and the noise of steel meeting feathered flesh.

I leapt to my feet. Brysney and Charis drew their swords and started toward the sound, only to be driven back as Daired came hurtling down the slope, his sword bloody and his face grim. Silverwing followed, half flying, half running, his jaws red with the same blood.

"How many?" Charis asked.

"I don't know. One dropped on me from above," Daired said. "I heard others stirring beyond the ridge."

The last word hadn't crossed his lips before Akarra's roar filled the Witherwood, drowning out the clamor of the waking horde.

Daired didn't give me a chance to panic properly. He grabbed me by the shoulders and shoved me into a cleft between the boulders. "Remember your promise," he said through clenched teeth before joining Brysney and Charis in their headlong dash toward the ridge.

I pressed myself into the gap between the rocks, wishing the hammering of my heart didn't sound so loud in the stillness of the hollow. *A knack for squeezing into small spaces.* My words from earlier echoed in my head like a bad joke.

The battle cries and gryphon screams beyond the ridge hadn't been going on for long before a shadow swooped across my hiding place, followed by another, then two more. Gryphons were retreating into the forest, some flying, some leaping from tree to tree, their talons scrabbling for purchase on the bark, silhouettes black against the green-tinged mist. One injured beast misjudged the distance between trunks and fell, sending branches, feathers, and its own broken body spilling into the clearing ten strides from my hiding place.

Terror shot through my veins like ice water. If it charged I had no place to run, and screaming for help might bring other gryphons before the Riders returned. I held my breath, withdrew beyond the curve of the boulder, and waited. The fallen gryphon lay still for a minute, its breathing labored. Another minute and its breath grew ragged, mixing with the wet gurgling sound of its own blood. When the gurgling stopped I risked a second glance.

Its head snapped up.

In the space of a heartbeat, the gryphon rallied the last of its strength and scrabbled to its feet. Guided by *Tekari* instinct even on the brink of death, it rushed toward me, wings dragging on the ground, beak open, squealing with pain, and rage, and the unquenchable desire to kill.

With every ounce of strength I possessed, I brought Brysney's dagger down into that burning yellow eye.

The shriek that came from the gryphon's throat surprised me more than the bone-jarring contact, but that was nothing compared to the shock I felt as blood gushed out over my hand. I stumbled backward as the feathery body crumpled, the dagger buried in its eye socket.

My breath rattled in my ears. I stared at the creature twitching at my feet. Even deep in its death throes, its talons raked the ground, reaching for me to rend, to kill.

Rina's little body broken over the wall, her throat torn open, blood pouring out over the stones . . . her voice silenced, eyes blank . . .

Again I saw the scene in the south pasture. Again I felt my sister's head against my chest, cradled there in that minute after I found her, before I could admit she was gone, in that moment when I still thought she could be saved. Again I relived every instant of pain, every wave of horror and confusion and sorrow, each throb of my heart as it broke, and broke again, until I didn't think there were any more pieces left to break.

And suddenly the gryphon before me was the same gryphon that had killed my baby sister. For all I knew, it might be. It didn't matter; they were all the same, the *Tekari*. They all wanted us dead.

Someone screamed.

The next thing I knew, I was on top of the gryphon, Brysney's dagger in my hand. Blindly I stabbed, once, twice . . . five times, ten times . . . All the anger, all the pain I'd kept inside since Rina's death came out on the point of that knife, buried deep in the body of her killer.

The scream faded to sobs, and strong hands dragged me off the gryphon carcass.

"Let me go! It killed her!" The strangled voice that came from my throat didn't sound like mine. I tried to fight my captor, but the more I struggled the tighter he held me. "She was twelve! She was only *twelve*," I sobbed.

"Aliza! *Stop!*"

At Daired's voice, the nightmare dissolved. I came back to my senses to see that he had both arms around me, trying desperately to wrest the dagger out of my death-grip.

"You're safe! It's dead," he panted. "Drop the knife before you hurt yourself."

I looked down and saw blood. Horrified, I flung the dagger away.

Daired let go, and like identical lodestones we sprang apart. I tried to move away, but the gryphon's corpse sprawled behind me, its empty eye socket fixing me with its final, gruesome taunt. *See what you've done?* it said. *You, who pride yourself on healing things, of doing no harm? Do you see what you're capable of?*

Furiously I wiped my hands on the edge of my shirt, but the blood wouldn't come off.

Daired pulled a soft cloth from a pouch at his belt. "Here. Use this."

I took it and scrubbed my hands like a madwoman.

"You've never killed before."

"No." My insides felt like water, icy and boiling all at once. I rested my hands on my knees and took a shaky breath. "No, I haven't."

"It's a day you don't forget." He picked up the dagger and offered it to me. "Cherish it."

I recoiled from the dagger still dripping with blood, and from the man who seemed to take such satisfaction in it.

"Miss Aliza!" Brysney said, rushing down the slope before Daired could speak again. He stopped next to me, taking in the sight of the gryphon carcass at my feet. "Are you all right?"

I closed my eyes and took stock of myself. *I killed something, yes, but it would've killed me. I'm still alive, and—* My eyes snapped open and I searched the ground, praying we hadn't trampled the ashwine. Relief washed over me as I saw purple flowers poking out near the base of the nearest boulder. I stooped to collect the fallen vine. "I think so. Just shaken."

Charis topped the ridge behind her twin, the flat of her sword propped against her shoulder. "Has our little herbmaster managed to stay out of trouble?" Her eyes fell on the dead gryphon. "Oh."

Brysney grinned. "Exactly. Miss Aliza, I believe you've earned your first blade."

"I'm sorry?"

"It's the first test in our trials to become a Rider: the taking of a life. Our first kill earns us our first blade. *Nakla* or not, you should have something to mark the occasion, and I have plenty of knives to spare. Alastair, would you mind?"

Daired scoured the blood from Brysney's dagger with a handful of damp moss, wiping it clean with his cloth. Again he presented it to me, this time with a bow. "Aliza Bentaine, this belongs to you."

I took it from him the way I might take a live snake. "I, um . . . thank you."

"Yes, congratulations," Charis said. "I'm sure your family will be thrilled when they find out they're living under the same roof as a gryphon slayer, Miss Aliza. Now, can we get back to the lodge? There's nothing more to kill here."

Brysney nodded. "Let's get the others."

Assisted by Silverwing, Akarra had finished off the few remaining gryphons at the crest of the Witherwood, though many had escaped into the lower forest. I appreciated that she and Silverwing didn't bother asking about the blood covering my shirtfront. With help from Brysney I climbed atop Akarra's back—clumsily, since I held both ashwine vine and dagger. If the others took note, neither Charis nor Daired mentioned it. In fact, Daired said nothing at all as we flew over North Fields.

He did hold on to my waist just a little bit tighter than he had before.

CHAPTER 8

SPARRING

If I'd thought I escaped danger by leaving the Wither- wood, I was mistaken. Anjey looked angry enough to hit something when I returned to the sickroom. If it hadn't been for the weakness of the fever, she probably would have.

"How *dare* you, Aliza?" she said after I'd explained what'd happened. "How could you leave without telling me? You could've died!"

"I'm sorry. I promise I wouldn't have gone unless it was necessary, and I didn't tell you because I didn't want you to worry." As I spoke, I unwrapped the bandage on her arm. The redness had spread, and pus had begun oozing from between the stitches in places.

Anjey's face went a sickly green color, and her anger evaporated. She looked away as I washed her arm with warm water, coated the wounds with a paste of salt and ground ashwine root, and wrapped it again in clean bandages.

"Better?"

Slowly the tension went out of her shoulders and she relaxed against the pillows. "Yes. I'm sorry I yelled at you."

"Don't be. I'd've done the same. Now, drink this," I said, handing her a cup of mint-and-passiflora tea. "You need to rest."

She drank. After a minute she closed her eyes and her breathing steadied. "'Liza? Tell Cedric . . . thanks," she mumbled before sinking into sleep.

A maid met me in the hall outside our room, her arms full of what on closer inspection turned out to be some of my own gowns. "Begging your pardon, miss, but the lady Rider and her 'usband just come from the Manor with these," she said. "They say your mother sent them for you and Miss Anjey."

I thanked her and was about to take the gowns when I remembered the bloodstained state of my current outfit. "Better leave them in the room, Betsy. Right now I need a bath."

IF THERE WAS SUCH A THING AS MAGIC IN THE WORLD, I was convinced it existed in the simplest comforts: hot bathwater and clean clothes. Scrubbing away the filth of battle and two days' worth of worry for my sister worked wonders for my anxious mind, and by the time I stepped out of the tub I felt better than I had since leaving the Manor. My growling stomach, now fully recovered from our flight, reminded me of the breakfast I'd skipped, and I dressed quickly, wondering if Henshaw still made his famous browned biscuits.

Halfway down the stairs I remembered something and changed my course from the kitchens to the courtyard. My boots sat where Betsy had left them near the servants' door at the back of the lodge, still damp from yesterday's puddles. With the only alternative being the pair of slippers Mama had sent with our dresses, I headed outside barefoot.

The midafternoon sun had burned away the morning fog, but clouds dotted the sky and the wind blew from the north. I crossed the courtyard to the garden behind the lodge, or what would've passed as a garden if someone had ventured to maintain it. Since the gryphons' descent, the grounds around Merybourne Manor had returned to their wild roots. Weeds choked the footpath to the garden, and the walls surrounding it were made less of stone than masses of ivy and moss. They broke the wind and left the garden quiet, filled with the rich, damp scent of growing things.

I paused at the gate to pluck a few white-tipped moorflowers from where they grew nestled beneath a fern. There was no abbey at North Fields and no cantor to take my prayer of thanks, but in my experience the Fourfold God had never been a stickler for ceremony, and if I remembered right, the lodge had a perfectly suitable alternative.

My bare feet made no noise on the moss-covered cobbles as I picked my way toward the four-faced statue of the Fourfold God standing on a small dais in the center of the garden. Lichen lined the folds of their carved robes in living wrinkles of green and brown, and spiders' webs hung from eight stone hands, raised in blessing over the occupants of the derelict garden.

Both of us.

Daired knelt at the base of the statue, his back to me. His sword lay on his knees, and his head was bowed.

I drew back behind a clump of juniper. I couldn't tell what astonished me more: to find a stranger in this hidden place, or to stumble across a Rider in prayer. From what I'd seen, the worship of Mikla and Thell didn't take place in quiet gardens and solemn abbeys. Theirs was the sanctuary of the battlefield; theirs was a baptism of blood.

Curiosity rooted me to the spot when I should've left him to pray in peace. *What does a Daired pray for?* I pushed aside the juniper and stepped into the clearing, making as little noise as possible. He knelt at the corner of the dais between the depictions of Mikla and Thell. Mikla's veiled face looked to the west, and he bore a shield marked with his sigil and his name, written in both Arlean and Eth: *Mikla—Protector, Shield of the Faithful. An-Tyrekel.*

Thell alone of the Four wore no veil. Her blank eyes stared south, and her hands were open and empty. Two names were carved in the stone beneath her feet. *Thell—Unmaker. Ket.* Of the little Eth I knew, that word stood out, cold and heavy and unmistakable. *Death.*

Daired touched four fingers to his forehead, lips, and heart before standing. He sheathed his sword without turning around. "I'm surprised you found this place," he said. "I didn't think you prayed anymore."

Well, blast. No retreat now. "Master Daired. I was going to say the same thing."

He whirled around. If I'd been standing there stark naked with the severed heads of a lamia and a valkyrie in my hands, he couldn't have looked more shocked. "Miss Bentaine!"

"Am I intruding?"

"You're . . . no."

"Were you expecting someone?"

"I thought you were Charis," he said. "What are you doing here?"

The opportunity was too good to miss. "Looking for hobgoblins, of course. But now that I'm here, I might as well say thank you." I stepped around him and knelt between the Janna and Odei facets of the Fourfold God.

Janna faced east, her beech leaf sigil clasped in her stone hands. Tendrils of ivy curled at her feet. I brushed them aside to read the names: *Janna—Provider, She-Who-Sustains. Ahla-Na Lehal'i.* To her left, the final facet of the Fourfold God faced north, bearing the shard of lightning that sparked creation. *Odei—Creator, He-Who-Begins. Ah-Na-al Akhe'at.*

I laid the moorflowers in front of Janna and made the fourfold gesture. "For guiding us in the Witherwood, and for healing my sister."

"How is she?" Daired asked after the requisite moment of silence.

"She'll live, gods willing." I stood and swept away the dead leaves and bits of moss that stuck to my skirt. "Thank you, by the way."

"For what?"

"For taking me with you."

"If I recall, I didn't have much choice."

"True."

His gaze lingered on my bare feet. "Were you hurt back there?"

"I'm fine. How'd you find this place?" I asked, eager to avoid reliving the battle. "Even I wasn't sure it was still here."

"The manservant mentioned it. Miss Bentaine, you're not—?"

A shadow fell over the garden. We both looked up—Daired with one hand on his sword hilt, me with muscles tensed, ready to run—but it was only Akarra. Her wings sent the ivy rustling around us as she soared toward the lodge.

Daired bowed. "Good afternoon, Miss Bentaine. I'm glad your sister will live," he said, and hurried out of the garden, leaving me wondering what else, besides a Rider and a worthy acquaintance, he thought I wasn't.

ANJEY WAS AWAKE WHEN I RETURNED TO OUR ROOM AF-ter lunch, bearing a tray of Henshaw's browned biscuits and a bowl of stew. Her eyes were bright, but not with fever, and her appetite had returned with a vengeance. While she ate I inspected the ash-wine poultice. My heart leapt to see how much the swelling and redness had decreased.

"Uncle Gregory would be proud," Anjey said as I applied fresh ashwine and wrapped her arm again. "He couldn't have done it better."

"He would've scolded me for letting it get infected in the first place."

"Aliza, don't say that."

"I should've asked the Riders to go for ashwine yesterday."

"You did what you could. None of this is your fault."

"How about this? The faster you get better, the less I'll worry."

"Deal." She pushed off the blankets and swung her legs out of bed. "Grab me a gown, will you?"

"What are you doing?"

"Getting better."

"I meant you needed to rest!"

"I've been resting all morning. I need some fresh air."

"This has nothing to do with wanting to see Brysney, obviously."

"Don't be silly." She grinned and started for the ewer basin, arm clutched to her chest. "Of course it does. Now help me get dressed."

WE FOUND BRYSNEY DOWNSTAIRS BY THE FIRE. HIS FACE lit up when he saw Anjey at my side, her arm in a sling I'd fashioned from half a pillowcase. After assuring him that she already felt better and hinting that a bit of fresh air would be welcome, he ushered us both outside.

Behind the garden, a field sloped away from the back of the lodge. The other Riders had already turned it into an exercise ring, tamping down the long grass and smoothing the ground with their iron-shod boots. Ruthven and his wife crouched and stretched in some sort of complicated calisthenics at the far end of the ring, which the *Shani* watched with interest. Nearer to the lodge, Daired and Charis sat on the garden wall cleaning their weapons.

When he saw us, Daired leapt down.

"Ah! Miss Anjey. Good to see you on your feet," Charis said, sighting along the length of her sword. "Won't lose the arm, then?"

"Doesn't look that way."

"Cedric, Charis, what do you say to a Sparring?" Daired asked before Charis could continue. "It's been a while. We could use the practice."

The twins had no objections, and at the prospect of a little entertainment, Anjey and I didn't either. Daired and Brysney drew their swords as Charis went to fetch the others. With one eye on my sister to make sure she was watching, Brysney practiced a few feints.

"You better be careful," I said in Anjey's ear. "The right smile at the right moment and he won't stand a chance."

"Shush."

"You know it's true," I said as Nerissa, Ruthven, and Bluescale joined the Sparring circle. Akarra, Silverwing, and Burrumburrem officiated from the perimeter as the fighters took their places, Brysney positioning himself so he could keep Anjey in view. "Don't smile!" I whispered.

"*Shush!*"

With a single high note, Silverwing trumpeted the start of the fight.

Each Rider rushed into the center of the ring, meeting in a melee of swords and wings. Charis engaged Daired at once, then turned from him to face Ruthven's attack before she'd gotten her first real thrust in, only to have him duck under her sword to swing at Brysney's unprotected back. Brysney sensed the blade and spun away, leaving Ruthven to battle Nerissa as Bluescale swooped in on Brysney from above. Brysney leapt over the wyvern's barbed tail to cross swords with Daired, whom Charis chased once more. Again and again they whirled around each other, finding and changing partners faster than a country jig.

Silverwing growled a low note and the game changed.

Ruthven turned his blade upon his wife, who equaled him blow for blow with a strength and ferocity belied by her stature. Daired battled Bluescale with his back to Brysney, who now fought Charis. I followed Daired's movements with an artist's appreciation; whatever faults he might possess, the man was worthy of his family name. The red stone embedded in the pommel of his sword shone like a drop of living dragonfire, bringing a spark of color to the otherwise bloodless battle.

Again Silverwing trumpeted, and without missing a step the combatants turned from their first partners to face another. Nerissa whirled to meet Brysney's blade as Ruthven swung his greatsword over her head to counter Bluescale's attack. Daired soon drew my attention again, however, for now Charis challenged him, and at once I saw there was a reason she'd helped cut down the Lesser Lindworm of Harborough Hatch. In a dizzying circle they spun around each other, swords flashing, matching parry for parry and thrust for thrust.

It was mesmerizing.

A growl from Burrumburrem and a hoot from Silverwing announced the end of one duel. I turned just in time to see Ruthven throw down his greatsword, the tip of Bluescale's barbed tail pressed under his ear. Grinding his teeth, Ruthven stalked off the lawn to watch the rest of the Sparring from the sidelines.

Distracted by her husband's defeat, Nerissa leaned too far into her thrust, and with a sidestep Brysney threw her off balance. Before she could regain her footing, he placed his blade against her throat. "Yield?"

Nerissa let her sword fall to the grass. "Yield."

He lowered his weapon and she joined her husband.

Brysney skirted Daired and Charis and sat next to Anjey. "What do you ladies say to our little game?"

"You're all very good," Anjey said. "Do you spar often?"

Brysney plunged with delight into a description of their battle habits. Anjey leaned closer to listen, and I lost track of what they were saying as the last combatants drew near enough for me to overhear their conversation. The fact that they could keep up a steady stream of banter while dueling hammer and tongs impressed me almost as much as their fighting ability.

"How does Julienna get on nowadays?" Charis asked, aiming a kick at Daired's knee. "It's been a long time since I've sparred with her."

Daired evaded her kick. "She's a better fighter than I was at her age."

"Has she"—Charis ducked beneath his sword—"killed yet?"

"Her first last summer," he said, leaping away as she drew a dagger with her free hand.

"Anything like mine? Twin trolls in the morning and a mad centaur in the afternoon?"

"Hardly." He glanced in my direction, and for an instant our eyes met. "She killed a gryphon, just like Miss Bentaine."

The point of Charis's sword dropped a few inches as she followed his gaze.

"She'd love to see you next time you're in Dragonsmoor," he said. "I promised—"

Charis sprang at him, bringing both blades in a singing arc toward his head. Daired rolled out of the way, the point of her dagger scoring a line along his gauntlet. It took an undignified scramble to escape her next blow. He staggered to his feet, and with a crash their swords met in midair. Beads of sweat stood out on Charis's forehead as she tried to pivot around their crossed blades, but Daired blocked her with his arm, earning another gash along his gauntlet.

Brysney and Anjey had stopped talking. They too watched the battle, spellbound.

Charis spun. Her dagger flashed in her hand as she dodged the sweep of Daired's sword and sprang up behind him, the edge of her knife pressed against the side of his neck. A tiny line of blood welled up below his ear. Her eyes blazed. "Yield?"

"Not . . . to . . . you."

And it was over. He moved so fast I couldn't tell how he did it; all I saw was a flash of steel and Charis sprawled flat on her back.

Daired laid his sword across her throat and wiped away the trickle of blood with the back of his hand. "Do *you* yield?"

"I . . . yes," she whispered.

"Well done, Alastair!" Brysney said. "And you too, Charis. Excellent fight."

Akarra and the other Riders echoed the sentiment, but none seemed to have any effect on Charis. Grudgingly she allowed Daired to help her to her feet. She leaned close and said something in his ear before stalking away.

Neither Anjey nor Brysney noticed. They'd moved on to talk of what Henshaw might be persuaded to make for dinner, and after taking leave of me, they headed for the lodge.

"Miss Bentaine?"

I turned back to the Sparring ring. Daired came toward me, his sword in one hand. With the other he drew a long knife from his belt. "Yes?" I said.

He flipped the knife, caught it just below the tang, and offered it to me. "Now you've seen how it's done. Would you like to learn?"

"I'm . . . what?"

"You'll want to be prepared for the next creature you must kill."

I looked over my shoulder, half expecting to see a gryphon diving for us, or a charging centaur, or, at the very least, an inconvenience of hobgoblins brandishing sticks and mudballs. Anything out of the ordinary to explain such an offer. After I'd assured myself that we were not in immediate danger of being gutted, trampled, or pelted with mud, I faced him again. "What creatures do you imagine I'm going to go around killing?"

"You live in Arle, Miss Bentaine. You never know when or where the next *Tekari* will strike."

"Of course, but . . ."

"You've already earned your first blade. I can teach you how to use it."

The edge of his knife caught the sun, gilding the steel with white light. *Hot blood pouring out over my hands as the red rage fell, and with it, the gryphon . . . hatred and fury dissolving into tears . . . the sick, empty feeling of having taken a life . . .*

"Thank you, Master Daired," I said, "but I'd rather not."

"You'll have to start from—what?"

"I don't want to know how to kill things."

He frowned. "You don't want to know how to protect yourself? After that gryphon—"

"Aye, I understand. It would've killed me if I hadn't stabbed it. And yes, I'm glad I'm not dead, but I don't ever want to have to make that choice again. I'm not like you, Master Daired." My gaze fell to my hands clasped in my lap. "I can't wash the blood off so easily."

He sheathed his sword. "No. I suppose not. Good afternoon, Miss Bentaine," he said, and without so much as a nod, turned on his heel and walked away.

I didn't see him for the rest of the day.

CHAPTER 9

LIEUTENANT PUNCH

The next morning Anjey and I joined the Riders for breakfast in the parlor. No sooner had we entered than Brysney beckoned for Anjey to take the empty seat next to him, and as she filled her plate he asked after her health, how she'd slept, and did she at all feel up to showing him the statue of the Fourfold God rumored to be hidden on the grounds after breakfast?

I heard their conversation without really listening. As a rule, mornings and I barely tolerated each other, and with my brain still fuzzy from sleep, I was happy to eat my breakfast in silence. Daired came in just before we started our second pot of tea, his hair damp and his boots spattered with mud, which he tried scraping off on the doorjamb before giving up, spearing a slice of cold pheasant from the sideboard, and sitting next to me. I smelled grass, wet leather, and a rich, smoky scent that reminded me of Akarra.

"Where have you been, Alastair?" Charis asked. "You missed our debate. Nerissa thinks Elsian steel performs better in battle, but I know I've heard you swear by that forge-wight Orordrin's work."

"Akarra and I've been scouting the nearby woods," he said. "And yes, I stand by that. Forgemaster Orordrin's are the only blades I'll carry."

Nerissa added another lump of sugar to her tea. "Elsian steel is lighter."

His mouth full of pheasant, Daired only shrugged.

"How's your arm, Miss Anjey?" Charis asked.

"Much better, thank you."

"I hope Cedric managed to stitch straight this time."

Brysney looked up. "I always stitch straight!"

"Didn't even give you a decent scar, I expect. Alastair should've offered to help. No one can stitch up wounds like he can." As if it were the most casual thing imaginable, Charis lifted up the corner of her tunic to show a fine white line running across her stomach. "Remember our battle with the troll troop of Selkie's Keep?" she asked Daired.

"That's not something you forget," he said, still intent on his breakfast.

She pulled her tunic down. "A troll took a swipe at me with his tusk. I took his head, but he left his mark. Alastair sewed it up, and now you'd hardly know anything happened."

"Don't praise him too quickly," Brysney said. He unbuckled the leather band he wore around his wrist and slid up the sleeve of his tunic to show a ragged scar slanting down the inside of his forearm. "You forgot this."

Anjey stared at it. "What happened?"

"This, Miss Anjey, is how the Daireds and the Brysneys first met. It was a long time ago. We were still Riders-in-training, without wyverns or dragons to our names. Our family was making a tour of Arle, and we decided to spend Saint Ellia's Day at a town on the outskirts of Dragonsmoor, near House Pendragon. The country around there is—"

"Wild as winter and just as unforgiving," Charis said.

"Well, yes, but that's what makes it breathtaking. When the sun rises you can see the dragon's eyries on the peaks, and at night the summit fires shine for miles—"

"Until a blizzard blows in from the moors and you freeze to death," she said.

"We'd just settled in at Lambsley when that almost happened. Charis and I wanted a glimpse of House Pendragon before the others, so we snuck out and headed for the hills as a storm blew in. And who do you think we found as we were climbing the crags near the house?"

Daired wiped his mouth and set his mug down hard on the table. "They found me."

Brysney grinned. "Doing what?"

"Battling a pack of direwolves."

The image of any Rider, even a Daired, standing alone against a whole pack of *Tekari* was enough to rouse me from my morning stupor. "By *yourself*?" I asked.

His dark look couldn't disguise the touch of color that came into his cheeks. "A Rider must trust their own fighting skills before they can rely on their mount's. It was just an exercise."

Brysney laughed. "Say what you like, Alastair. You're grateful Charis and I found you when we did. When our parents sent us on our solitary runs they only had us face a gryphon each, like all sensible Riders do. You don't take on a direwolf pack by yourself."

Daired shrugged and returned to his plate, cleaning up the last bits of pheasant with the air of a man who hoped the conversation would take another turn. Brysney, however, wasn't satisfied. He had my sister engrossed in the story, and I doubted he could deny Anjey anything when she looked at him like that.

"The pack was a half dozen strong. Alastair had his back to the cliff face, one blade against six beasts the size of mules, each with fangs longer than my finger. The snow was coming on hard too, and the wind was rising—that stinging, biting kind of wind that makes you think you'll never be warm again."

"Until you drive your sword through a direwolf's heart," Charis said. "Then the blood flows and you're fighting for every breath and each second is its own adventure, and you don't have time to worry about things like the cold."

"How poetic," Brysney said. "And that's all fine until somebody misses their stroke and a direwolf gets a mouthful of me."

She grimaced. "*You* were out of position."

"*You* misread my signal."

"I couldn't see through the snow!"

"Suffice to say," Daired spoke over them, "we fought, Cedric got bitten, I beheaded the alpha, and the rest of the pack scattered." He pushed his empty plate away. "I tried to return the favor by stitching up Cedric's arm. For some reason he didn't appreciate that."

"Because it got infected! Alastair's father had to call for the physician from Lambsley." Brysney flexed his arm, pulling the scar tight against his shifting muscles. "Left me with this."

"Don't pretend you don't like telling the story," Daired said. "You tell everyone you meet about that scar."

"That's not true." Brysney looked at Anjey. "I don't tell everyone."

"Edel, Nerissa, how long did it take him when he first met you?" Daired asked.

"I heard Cedric tell that story at a banquet at our first muster in Edonarle," Nerissa said. "We'd known him for an hour."

"Half an hour," Ruthven grunted.

A trilling whistle sounded outside before Brysney could defend himself. "Ah, good," Nerissa said. "Bluescale's back. Alastair, he says Akarra wants to see you."

Her announcement ended breakfast. Daired hurried out, followed soon by the others. Brysney and my sister invited me to join them as they went in search of the statue. I declined, certain they'd enjoy their time more without me. Anjey was in good hands, and I had other plans.

BY THE TIME I'D CHANGED INTO SUITABLE RIDING clothes, the sun had burned away the last shreds of morning mist. Clouds like spun cotton drifted low in an eggshell-blue sky. Deep in the forest, a cicada droned, and over the hills a few swallows dipped and swung, snatching insects off the tops of the grasses. I breathed in the smell of clean earth as I made my way to the stables. Contrary to what Daired might think, the country *did* have its charms.

A soft whinny greeted me as I approached the stable. The bay gelding hung his head over the stall door, nose wrinkling as he searched for the apple in my pocket. He'd bolted when the gryphons attacked but found his way back to the lodge later that night. I offered him the apple and slipped inside to brush him. As I worked, dust floated up in clouds, hanging in the slant of sunlight falling through the windows, and he leaned into me as I loosened the clumps of mud caked across his withers. Whichever groom had brought him in from the fields had done a shoddy job of cleaning him up, and it took me almost half an hour to make him presentable.

"There. That's better, isn't it?" I said, hefting the saddle over his shoulders.

His ears flicked forward as the stable door creaked open. Voices drifted through the dusty air. "He's utterly, *disgustingly* infatuated."

I froze, my hand on the saddle girth.

Charis continued as she and her companion walked down the aisle toward the gelding's stall. "This is exactly what we didn't want to happen. We took this contract to help him forget."

"To be fair to Cedric, it does seem he's forgotten," Daired said.

They stopped at the stall across from mine. With a joyous neigh, Charis's mare thrust her head into the aisle to greet her Rider. Charis patted her neck. "No, he hasn't, and he never will. He's my twin, Alastair. I can *feel* it. Every time he looks at that Bentaine girl, he sees—"

Daired caught sight of me and seized her shoulder. "Charis."

I nodded to them and continued saddling the gelding as if I hadn't heard a thing. Part of me wished I hadn't. The other part, the one that never regretted eavesdropping, seethed under their glares, desperate to know what Charis thought her brother saw when he looked at "that Bentaine girl." Tightening the last buckle, I led the gelding out of the stall, keeping him between us so they couldn't see how much self-control it took for me to keep a rein on my tongue.

Daired followed me outside. "Going somewhere?"

I swung into the saddle. "Just taking him for a run."

"Are you sure that's wise? The rest of the horde is still out there."

"I'm not going far," I said, and nudged the gelding with my heels.

The horse gave a little nicker, nuzzled Daired's offered palm, and stayed put. Daired stroked the gelding's nose. "I'm beginning to think you like chasing trouble, Miss Bentaine."

"Perhaps I do. Are you going to let me pass?"

"You're quite reckless for a *nakla*."

And you're insufferably condescending, I wanted to say, but Charis spared us both from such mutual honesty. She rode out of the stable bareback astride the gray mare.

"Mind if I join you, Miss Aliza?"

"Not at all. I was just—"

Like a bolt of silver-and-flame-colored lightning, Charis and the mare shot away. My horse leapt after them, and I let him run. The clack of hoofbeats on stone deepened to the thud of hooves on springy turf as we cleared the courtyard. I gave the gelding his head. The wind twisted my hair into hopeless knots and my eyes streamed, his mane stinging my face as I bent low over his neck. We crested hill after hill, tasting the rain-washed air, savoring the touch of the sun, and enjoying the kind of freedom I hadn't felt since the gryphons descended on Hart's Run.

Halfway around the fields I caught up to Charis. She looked at me over her shoulder, grinned, and kicked the gray into a gallop again. Trees whipped past me as I followed her along the border of the forest, branches smearing like streaks of green paint in my peripheral vision as the gelding tore after them. The lodge came into view as we circled the last bend. Beneath me his stride lengthened, hooves pounding the ground, eager to overtake the gray. The gap between us closed to a few yards, then only a few feet—

The gray surged forward, leaving the gelding in her mud-splattered wake. She crossed in front of the gate three full lengths ahead of us.

Sides heaving, the gelding slowed to a trot. I could almost feel his disappointment.

"Well run, dear heart," Charis said to her mare. She looked up to where Daired leaned against the gate and said in a louder voice, "Want to join us, Alastair? There was another horse in the stable."

"I'd rather watch."

She smiled. "Oh, come now. Afraid you might lose?"

"You're one of the best horsewomen I've ever met, Charis, and you know that mare would do anything for you," he said. "If there's any Rider in Arle who could beat the two of you bareback, it's not me."

"If you say." Charis gave me a sideways glance and inclined her head. There was no warmth in the gesture, but no hostility either, and she made no attempt to hide it. "Still, Miss Aliza ran a good race."

"Her form could use practice," Daired said.

I dismounted, resisting the urge to roll my eyes. *First it's too dangerous to go riding, then I need to practice?* "I'll keep that in mind."

Charis frowned to see me out of the saddle. "Won't you race again?"

I patted my gelding's sweat-soaked side. "I'm not sure he has another in him today."

"Fair enough. Alastair, I'm going to scout the far side of the fields. Tell Cedric where I've gone, will you?" He nodded and Charis kicked the mare into a canter, which took them beyond the crest of the hill in a minute.

Wings beat the air behind us. The gelding shifted uneasily, and I ducked as Akarra swooped low overhead, followed by Bluescale and Silverwing. Against the windswept sky they gamboled and frolicked, chasing each other and snapping at the occasional bird stupid enough to fly too close. Like steel striking flint, their grace was the spark of inspiration, and I hurried to unsaddle the gelding, already sketching their forms in my head.

I noticed Daired watching me when I emerged from the stables. He hadn't moved from his place at the gate, eyes fixed on me with an intensity that made me blush. I had no wish to impress him, but it still stung, the way he'd singled me out for such blatant criticism. *For gods' sakes, stop looking at me already!* I thought as I escaped into the coolness of the lodge. *You have a dragon, and she's dancing. Get your priorities sorted.*

BY THE TIME I'D FOUND A FEW SHEETS OF PARCHMENT and blackened enough sticks for charcoal, Akarra and the wyverns had flown away. I wandered into the garden to see if any other interesting subjects would present themselves.

As it turned out, one did. By name, rank, and all.

"Ma'am!"

I jumped as the ground beneath my foot shifted and the narrow, sloping head of a garden gnome popped up. "Goodness, you scared me!" I said in Gnomic.

"Apologies," the creature said, snapping a salute. Unlike their rounder, fatter hobgoblin cousins, gnomes were thin and angular, with tough, bristly skin and beards like wires. They served as guardians of the garden-folk, and in my experience, handled their jobs with deadly seriousness. "Lieutenant Punch, at your service!"

"Aliza Bentaine, Lieutenant. Pleased to meet you."

"The pleasure is mine, ma'am. I was hoping I'd find you here; word on the underground is that you and your sister came out this way. Chief Hobblehilt of the hobgoblin contingent has nothing but commendations for your service to the garden-folk. I understand you saved a hobgoblin citizen from dismemberment by a dragonrider the other day."

"Well, it wasn't exactly—"

"And guarded the hobgoblin envoy to those same Riders without thought for your own safety, which has led to a peace between the invading *wyverns*"—he shuddered over the word—"and the rest of us."

"Thank you, Lieutenant, but it didn't happen quite like that," I said, wondering what kind of rumors Tobble had been spreading.

"Nonsense! You're too modest, ma'am. I have these reports on excellent authority." Sweeping the tail of his mud-colored uniform behind him, Lieutenant Punch bowed. "I wished to convey my thanks in person. You, Aliza Bentaine, are an exceedingly admirable human being."

"Oh. Thank you."

The gnome straightened and scanned the area. "Now, forgive me, ma'am, but would you say we're quite alone here?"

I looked around. "Aye. Why?"

Punch sprang onto the garden wall and beckoned for me to come closer.

"Is something wrong?"

"Hush! Not so loud!" he whispered. "It's true I wanted to thank you, but that's not the only reason I'm here. Field Marshal Bunch needed someone to get close to these Riders, but he didn't want one of us in danger. He heard of your reputation and asked me to recruit you."

"*Recruit* me? Whatever for?"

"You're the only human the garden-folk trust right now." Punch shook his head. "These are dangerous times, Miss Bentaine. Dangerous times indeed. We hear things down in the Underburrow, things we don't like. The earth is unsettled, and so are we. We need your help to make sure these Riders don't turn their mounts on us when they're done with the gryphons."

"Lieutenant, I promise they're not going to start hunting the garden-folk after the gryphons are dead."

His face fell.

"But I'll keep my eyes open, and if I see anything suspicious, I'll let you know straightaway."

He brightened. "That's all we ask. Miss Bentaine, you have our thanks. I—say, were you drawing something?" he asked, noticing my parchment and charcoals. He stroked his whiskers. "You, ah, weren't in need of a subject, were you?"

"Interested?"

"Well, my orders are to report back to the Field Marshal as soon as we've finished, but seeing as you offered . . . I don't see how I could say no."

Eagerly he struck a pose, one hand on his flint knife, the other shielding his eyes from the sun as he gazed into the middle distance. For a minute his face contorted as he searched for an expression somewhere between courageous and majestic. At last he settled on something that made him look a bit like he needed to find a chamber pot.

"Will this be a portrait?" he asked as I marked out the first few features. "With paint and a frame and everything?"

"I'll see how it turns out."

"Do you think they'll hang it in the Underburrow someday?" he asked, nose wrinkling gleefully at the prospect. "Maybe after I'm killed in battle?"

As far as I knew, the Great Mud-Flinging of a few days ago had been the most action any garden creature had ever seen in defense of their territory. Punch and the rest of the gnomes probably cursed the fact that they'd missed it. "If you ever die in battle, Lieutenant, I trust Field Marshal Bunch and Chief Hobblehilt will make sure you're remembered properly."

"You couldn't add a few wyverns flying in the background? You know, for effect?" His carrot-colored eyes sparkled. "Or maybe one lying dead at my feet?"

A twig snapped behind me. Punch took one peek over my shoulder, shrieked, and dove into the bushes on the other side of the wall.

"Vermin really are everywhere, aren't they?" Daired said.

I rolled up the unfinished sketch with a sigh. "Is there something I can do for you, Master Daired?"

"No." He clasped his hands behind his back and studied the surrounding woods. "More something I can do for you. The other day in the Witherwood, you said something as you stabbed that gryphon. You said 'it killed her.'"

A cloud fell across the sun.

He spoke low and quick. "Your youngest sister, Katarina, died in a gryphon attack, didn't she? Master Henshaw said you were the one who found her body."

My voice abandoned me. Mouth dry, eyes burning, throat tight, I could only nod.

"I'm sorry. Seeing someone you love like that, it's a terrible thing. What you did in the Witherwood was justice. Blood for blood, blow for blow, death for death. It's Mikla's way."

"Why are you telling me this?"

"Because *nakla* or not, I stand by what I said before. With your bloodline you'll never be able to bond with a *Shani*, but Arle always needs defenders. Given training, I think you could be one of them." He sought my eye. "You couldn't save your sister, but someday you might be able to save another in her place. Let me teach you."

Blood thundered in my ears, pounding in time to the words that rang like hammer strokes against the walls of my heart. *Nakla or not . . . you couldn't save your sister.* It didn't matter that he was right. It didn't even matter that he'd offered to train me; I heard nothing beyond my little sister's name on his lips. With less consideration than it would've taken to comment on the weather, he'd laid open my heart's deepest wound and poured salt on it.

And looked damn smug about it too.

My tears dried. Grief, like water in a well-worn riverbed, had run its course. Only anger remained. "Thank you for your offer, Master Daired," I said, "but as you were so kind to point out, my sister is dead. Whether I do it well or not, killing things won't bring her back." I stood and curtsied. "Good afternoon."

LATER THAT NIGHT, I ASKED ANJEY IF SHE FELT WELL enough to travel.

"I don't think my arm would fall off if we had to leave tomorrow, but I wouldn't argue with anyone who said I should stay put for a few more days," she said.

"We need to leave."

Her smile dimmed. "What's wrong?"

"As long as we're here, the Riders won't go after the rest of the horde."

"And when you say Riders, you mean Cedric." She picked a stray thread off her bandaged arm. "You're right, of course."

"Don't worry, Anjey. If Brysney has any say in the matter, you'll see him again soon. In fact, with any luck, I bet he'll be giving you a heartstone before year's end."

"You think so?"

"Whatever other admirable qualities Brysney possesses, dearest, subtlety is not one of them. You'd have to be a fool not to see he's in love with you. Trust me. He'll be back to the Manor in no time."

"Well, in that case," she stood, "we'd better get Mama ready."

I laughed. "Mama? Good gods, she'll be fine. It's Brysney who needs to be warned."

EARLY THE NEXT MORNING WE SET OFF, RIDING DOUBLE on the gelding with our bag of clothes between us, Brysney and Silverwing flying alongside as our escorts. We passed Daired and Charis in the courtyard of the lodge. She bid us a stiff goodbye before returning to sharpening her sword. He touched four fingers to his forehead and said nothing, but I felt his eyes on us until we'd passed over the hill and out of sight.

MAMA GLANCED UP FROM HER CHAIR BY THE FIRE WHEN Anjey, Brysney, and I entered our family apartments. The darning egg in her hand slipped from her grasp and rolled across the floor.

Brysney picked it up. Smelling faintly of sweat and wyvern, dressed in his armor with a sword at his hip, he looked out of place in our parlor, and given his sheepish expression, he knew it. He presented the darning egg to Mama with a bow. "Madam Bentaine. I'm sorry we weren't able to send word earlier—"

Mama didn't let him finish. She leapt to her feet, shoved him aside, and threw her arms around Anjey and me. "Oh, my darlings, you're safe! You've no *idea* how worried we've been. Are you all right?" She held up Anjey's arm. "Does it hurt? Can you move your hand? That lady Rider didn't tell us much. She said that you'd been attacked—oh gods, we feared the worst. And then Lord Merybourne wouldn't let us go out there after you . . ."

"It's all right, Mama, really," Anjey said. "I'm fine. Aliza cleaned it and Cedric stitched it up. I'll be good as new in a few weeks."

"My clever girl." Mama brushed the hair out of my eyes and smiled before pulling us into another embrace. "You're both so *brave!*"

"Mama," Anjey whispered in her ear, "you're forgetting someone."

"Oh!"

And she whirled and threw her arms around Brysney, armor, scabbard, and all.

"*You!* Thank you, sir, thank you!" Mama said. "Thank you for keeping them safe."

"It was an, er, honor, ma'am. I, ah . . . I'm afraid I have to be going though."

That brought Mama back to her matchmaking senses. She stepped away with a look of reproach. "But, Master Brysney, you just arrived! You must stay for a cup of tea. Hilda?" she called into the next room. "Hilda, fetch some tea, will you?"

"Really, ma'am, that's not necessary. My wyvern is waiting outside."

Mama heaved a dramatic sigh, one that had years of practice and some professional experience behind it. "Oh, I suppose you're right. It was a pleasure to see you again, sir. You have our undying gratitude," she said, touching her forehead. "I hope we can repeat this visit another time. Perhaps with tea?"

His escape route now clear of motherly impediments, Brysney relaxed and returned the fourfold gesture. "I look forward to it. Miss Aliza, Miss Anjey, until next time."

As the door swung shut behind him, a yawn sounded from across the parlor. Leyda stumbled out of her room in her nightshift. "Morning, everyone. Mama, have you seen my—?" She blinked. "Anjey! Aliza! Did I miss something?"

It was good to be home.

LATER THAT AFTERNOON, AFTER PAPA FINISHED HIS LEC-ture to us about the dangers of not listening to his advice with a pat on the shoulder and a reminder to close the door as we left his study, I headed for the Carlyles' apartments. In the aftermath of our trip to North Fields, I'd almost forgotten Master Carlyle's mysterious friend at Hall-under-Hill. Now my curiosity came flooding back, and I wanted answers.

Gwyn greeted me at the door. "Aliza! I didn't know you were back. Come in, come in." She showed me into the parlor, where a fire roared in the grate. "I heard you had quite the adventure. Tell me everything."

I did, omitting only the part where I'd stabbed the gryphon. Someday I'd tell her, perhaps, but not today. Today I wanted to distance myself from death.

"And you *rode* the dragon?" she asked for the second time after I'd finished. "I thought that was forbidden for a *nakla.*"

"So did I, but Akarra insisted. I think there are exceptions when it's life or death."

"That's incredible."

"And terrifying. I don't ever want to do it again. My stomach isn't built for heights."

"That's too bad." She laid another log on the fire and wiped sooty hands on her apron. "Any developments with our happy couple?"

"Nothing *official*, but the two of them could hardly take their eyes off each other. If he doesn't find some excuse to visit soon, I'll be shocked."

"He'll—oh, bother. That might not be a good idea."

"Why not?"

"We're expecting a guest tomorrow." She lowered her voice. "I forgot you hadn't heard. It's the dreaded heir. Lord Merybourne says he'll be here for the fortnight."

That was news indeed. Everyone on the Manor knew that Lord Merybourne had named some distant cousin on his mother's side heir to his title, but we didn't often talk about it. Lord and Lady Merybourne still mourned the loss of their young son from many years ago, and as they were both long past childbearing ages, neither liked the reminder that their beloved Manor would pass to a stranger. Nor, frankly, did Gwyn and I, since it meant our fathers ran the risk of being replaced. "What's his name again?"

"Curdle-something-or-other? Father just always calls him *the dreaded heir*. He should be arriving tomorrow afternoon. And I'm sorry, Aliza, but His Lordship asked your father to help show him around when he arrives."

Papa disliked both small talk and strangers, and faced with both in the form of Master Curdle-something, I had the feeling he'd call on me to help ease his burden. "Thanks for the warning," I said.

"Speaking of fathers, do you remember seeing yours at the banquet at Hall-under-Hill?"

"Now that you mention it, not really, but I wasn't keeping an eye on him. Why?"

I told her about the conversation I'd overheard. "Does it mean anything to you?"

"No. It . . . no."

"What is it?"

"Nothing." She stood. "Just do me one favor, will you?"

"Of course. Anything."

"Don't tell anyone else."

CHAPTER 10

TROLL TROUBLE

Gwyn's warning echoed in my ears that evening and most of the next morning. As expected, Papa asked me to join him in welcoming the Merybourne heir. Noon found us standing at Lord and Lady Merybourne's side in front of the main doors to the Manor House, but my mind was elsewhere, contemplating voices without faces and threats in the dark.

With a creak, the coach-and-four came to a stop in front of the steps. The curtains flicked aside, then shut again to the sharp rapping of metal on glass. The coachman climbed down from his perch to open the door, muttering under his breath.

A silver-tipped cane preceded Master Curdle-something, questing out from the inside of the coach like a cat's paw. Boots followed it, their leather surface burnished within an inch of their lives, reflecting their master's face when he at last emerged: the thin, bespectacled face of a plain young man trying everything in his power to look distinguished. Blond curls flounced around his head, and he had knotted at his neck the most fantastic confection of mint-and-lavender-colored cravat I'd ever seen.

"Master Curdred! What an honor!" Lord Merybourne boomed.

Curdred paused in front of the coach to pull an impractically embroidered handkerchief from his waistcoat and brush few crumbs from his shirtfront. "The honor is mine," he said, and swept into the most elaborate bow I'd ever seen. "Wynce Curdred, your humble servant."

I bit my tongue to keep from laughing.

"OH, GWYN, IT WAS PERFECTLY *GHASTLY!*"

If anything, Leyda's account of our dinner with Curdred the night before fell short of the mark, and after breakfast, we'd seized on Gwyn's invitation to join her on an errand to Trollhedge. If she'd proposed a barefoot hike up the snow-covered Dragonsmoor Mountains, I would've taken her up on that too. Anything to get away from the toadying little magistrate.

"I hope you didn't say that to his face, Leyda," Gwyn said as the three of us started up the last hill outside of Trollhedge, walking with heads bent beneath a tent of sharpened poles. Flimsy defense from the gryphons, perhaps, but it at least offered the illusion of security.

"You know what? I wish I had!" Leyda said. "If that overstarched fop becomes lord at Merybourne Manor, then I'd much rather try my luck out in the wide world."

I shushed her because I was her older sister and I had to, even though I felt the same. If nothing else, dinner with Curdred had given us a taste of what life at the Manor might look like if he became Lord Merybourne. Under his ruthlessly fashionable guidance, we'd be forced to part with many things, including meat and comfortable clothes, and roving *Tekari* notwithstanding, I'd sooner join Leyda in exploring Arle than suffer through that.

"He couldn't have been that bad," Gwyn said. "Mother told me this morning she wished she'd gotten an invitation."

"Trust me, you were all happier staying put." Leyda shook out an imaginary napkin over her lap and spoke in an admirable imitation of Curdred's voice. "What *splendid* rutabagas, Lady Merybourne! The venison is . . . nice too, I'm sure. No, no, Sir Robart, I won't have a slice. Did I forget to say? I don't eat meat. You really shouldn't, you know. It's most unhealthy. Didn't I mention it, Miss Aliza? I've had the magnificent fortune to be named magistrate of Hunter's Forge. The youngest in the town's history too! You've heard of Hunter's Forge, of course."

I laughed as Leyda put a hand to her chest, immersed in the ridiculous character of Wynce Curdred. She gasped, fluttering her other hand in front of her face like a handkerchief.

"You haven't heard of it? Why, Hunter's Forge is home to the finest blacksmiths in Arle! You *must* know of Forgemaster Orordrin. His workmanship is sought all over the world. And not only that, but our hamlet also serves as the gateway to Edan Rose."

Leyda's look of horror was spot on; Curdred had looked at me with the same dismay when the name *Edan Rose* failed to trigger instant awe.

"But Miss Aliza, *surely* you know it? Edan Rose is the home of Lady Catriona, matriarch of the mighty House Daired!"

"He only told us eight times," I said. "You'd think he lived there himself, the way he described it. This Lady Catriona likes to have him around, gods know why."

"Perhaps for his fashion sense," Gwyn said, and we laughed again.

"Aliza, do you think the Rangers will still be in town?" Leyda bounded ahead of us to the crest of the hill where the tent of sticks petered out. Dust billowed beyond the ridge, sending a yellowish-brown cloud creeping toward us. "I'd love to see one of them up close."

"I don't—wait, how did you know about the Rangers?"

"Their captain stopped by the Manor the other day. Do you know—?"

"Leyda, look out!" Gwyn cried.

My sister shrieked as a dark shape loomed out of the dust cloud, followed by another, then a third. Within moments we were surrounded by a troop of trolls.

Don't run don't run don't run. I reached for Leyda's hand.

We all knew what we were supposed to do, but obeying the *walk, don't run* rule got a lot harder when there was an actual troll in your path, and not Henry Brandon playacting for the children in his fake trollskin. The real things were much more frightening, their shortsighted eyes rimmed in red, hides mottled with the dried blood of whatever animal they'd last killed. Horn-like tusks swept the ground in front of them as the troop sniffed the dirt, moving slowly but methodically up the hill, sometimes on four legs, sometimes on two. Seeing them like that made it easy to imagine them slow creatures, too bulky or dumb for speed, and I understood the temptation to run. Any decent athlete might think they had a shot at escape, but the moment they bolted, they'd learn firsthand the futility of a troll race. The trolls always won.

Luckily, they didn't much care for the taste of human. Trolls were neither *Tekari* nor *Shani*. They were the *Idar*, those Oldkind that were indifferent to humans, but that didn't make them any less dangerous. When rabbits and other small game were scarce on the ground, trolls had been known to take a bite out of the unwary traveler. We'd all seen those merchants and traders coming through Trollhedge with the telltale missing hand or peg leg.

Our only choice was to keep quiet, keep moving, and pray they weren't hungry.

I started forward.

"What are you doing?" Leyda whispered. "You're not supposed to move!"

"No, you're not supposed to *run*. Come on. We've got to get to the gate."

Gwyn took Leyda's free hand, and together we pressed through the crush of troll-flesh, doing our best to breathe through our mouths. The creatures smelled foul. A few gave us sidelong glances as we passed. One of the smaller ones paused to sniff me. Another bumped Leyda, who screamed and let go of my hand.

Something black whistled overhead.

The young troll in front of me reared up on its hind legs, a crossbow bolt sticking out of its throat. I threw myself out of the way, hitting the ground hard as the troll fell, its tusks gouging a furrow in the road where I'd been standing.

Its cry roused the rest of the troop. They bunched together in a knot, tusks scything to and fro as they searched for the source of the alarm. One stayed apart, coming toward the fallen troll with a high-pitched wail in its throat. The juvenile mewled and writhed, its thick-fingered hands too clumsy to pull the arrow from its neck. The older troll pawed at the arrow, still wailing. I scrambled to my feet.

"Get out of the way!"

A man in a Ranger's cloak leapt in front of me, crossbow in hand.

"*Wydrick?*"

"The same, ma'am, and very glad to see you again," he said without taking his eyes off the troop. "You and the other ladies might want to make for the village. I'll handle the beasts."

Gwyn grabbed my arm and pulled me away from the wounded troll, who was now snorting curses in a trollish dialect of Low Rhoc. "Why did he shoot it?" I hissed in her ear. "We were almost through!"

"Maybe he thought we were in danger," Leyda said. "Aliza, you didn't tell me you knew one of them!"

I know a fool, that's who I know, I was tempted to say, but the sight of Wydrick standing unmoved in front of a troop of angry trolls forced to swallow my words. Wise or not, I couldn't fault his courage. His judgment? That remained to be seen.

"Do we leave him?" Leyda asked.

"You heard what he said. We need to get to the village, and—Aliza! You're bleeding!"

I looked down. A gash ran down the back of my right hand where the troll's tusk had nicked me. "Oh. Ow," I said as the pain began to register.

"Come on. Madam Moore will have bandages and salve." Gwyn took me by the arm and hurried me through the gate. "Leyda!"

"Wait! He's coming too."

Wydrick ran down the slope, crossbow at the ready as the young troll rolled to its feet, the arrow broken off below the arrowhead. The rest of the troop grunted angrily but dared not pursue Wydrick so close to the borders of the town, and once the young troll rejoined their number, they lumbered off.

"Are you all right?" Leyda asked Wydrick.

"I'm fine, miss, but never mind me. How's the lady?"

"It's just a scratch," I said. "Really, I'm all right. Master Wydrick, why were you shooting at them?"

"I heard a scream, Miss Bentaine. I thought . . . well, I thought you might be in danger."

My anger ebbed. Not all of my anger—my hand still hurt like the blazes—but enough to accept his offer to escort us back to the regiment's quarters.

The Trollhedge guesthouse was a low building built of dark wood and crumbling brick. A number of Rangers sprawled on chairs around the inn's frowsty main parlor, some reading, some playing ninechess, some eating, and some snoring in front of the fire. Wydrick stowed his crossbow above the mantelpiece and swept aside the sword-belts and canteens piled on the nearest sofa. "I'm, ah, sorry we don't have a proper sitting room."

I told him not to mention it as Gwyn inspected my hand. Leyda stayed standing, staring at the red-cloaked men and women with unabashed interest. She caught the eye of a lunching Ranger, a young, mousy-haired man with the longest nose I'd ever seen, and smiled.

The man sprang to his feet, brushing crumbs off his hauberk. "Oi! Wydrick, a little warning? You din't say we were expecting guests!"

"Ned, we're expecting guests. Oh, look, they've arrived."

"Have you got any bandages, Master Wydrick?" Gwyn asked before the younger Ranger could reply.

Both men looked guilty, and, after a few minutes' rummaging, produced a length of linen and a bottle of oil of the Saint Marten flower. Gwyn helped me clean and wrap my hand. The gash turned out to be more of a graze, though by the profuseness of Wydrick's apologies, I would've guessed I needed my hand amputated at the wrist.

"I can't tell you how sorry I am. I swear, Miss Bentaine, if I'd known you weren't in danger—"

Ned snapped his fingers. "*Bentaine!* I *knew* I recognized you. You're the lady from the hill, aren't you? The one with the Riders?"

"Aye. Aliza Bentaine."

He bowed. "Edward Dennys of the Lower Westhull Rangers, but everyone calls me Ned. Pleased to make your acquaintance. Is your sister all right?"

"She'll be fine, thank you. Master Dennys, Master Wydrick, this is my friend Gwyn Carlyle and my younger sister—"

"Leyda Bentaine," Leyda said, squeezing beween the Rangers. "Pleasure. Do you get to kill many *Tekari?*"

"Leyda!" Gwyn and I said together.

Ned beamed and Wydrick touched his forehead, looking pleased. "We do what we can to protect those who need it, Miss Leyda," Wydrick said.

"Can I see your sword?"

"Sir, you don't—" I said, but before I could stop him, Wydrick drew his sword.

"Finest forge-wight work you'll ever see," he said, holding it out in front of him with a grin. "Never notches, never rusts, and never needs sharpening."

"Yes, and you don't ever let the rest of us forget it," Ned muttered.

"When you decide to fight with something better than that old firepoker of yours, then I'll let you boast all you want."

Leyda studied the blade with artless admiration. "Is that a dragon?" She pointed to the molding around the tang, the creature's steel hide worked with gold wire. "It's *gorgeous.*"

Gorgeous . . . and familiar. I'd seen that same emblem before, rearing rampant on a Rider's breastplate and curled around a bloodred pommel gem. I looked up at Wydrick in surprise. *What are you doing with a Daired sword?*

Leyda reached for the hilt. "Can I see how heavy it is?"

"Gwyn, didn't you need to order something from Madam Moore?" I asked, loudly and with a gentle nudge to the ribs.

"I—oh yes. Of course. We'd better go before she closes shop."

Wydrick sheathed his sword. His grin faded. "Sorry, miss. Perhaps another time."

"Thank you for the bandages, Master Wydrick, Master Dennys," I said, ushering Leyda toward the door by the elbow. "Have a good afternoon."

Dirt hung in the close-packed air of the streets outside, tingeing everything in shades of dun. Iron-gray clouds piled overhead, glimpsed through the nets draped across the road to discourage gryphon attacks. "Why did you do that, Aliza?" Leyda asked as we waited for a wagon laden with wine casks to rumble past. "Why do you *always* do that? They were answering my questions!"

"They were being polite. You were not."

"They didn't mind. Gwyn, tell her they didn't mind."

Gwyn smiled as we started across the road, dodging foot traffic and mule-drawn carts. "That Ned fellow wouldn't have minded if you'd asked him to calculate how much earth a loaming of gnomes displaces in a year. I think he liked the attention."

"Thank you," I said. "Leyda, you can't just—what are you doing?"

Leyda stopped in the middle of the street and crossed her arms. A young woman in the white tunic of an apothecary's apprentice almost upended her tray of unguents over Leyda's shoulder, swearing as she swerved to avoid her. "Make it up to me, Aliza," Leyda called over the noise of the crowd. "Just this once. Come with me to the lithosmiths."

"Leyda, get out of the road!"

"Not until you say you'll come with me."

Gwyn touched my arm. "Go with her. It's all right; I'll stop by Madam Moore's and find you when I'm done."

"Are you sure?"

"Yes, of course. I'll see you in a bit," she said, and followed the girl in the white tunic toward Smallbalm Street.

I threw up my hands. "Fine, Leyda! We'll go to the lithosmiths. Now get out of the street!"

She sidestepped the fishmonger's son pushing his wheelbarrow of ice chips and sawdust and hopped onto the curb with a grin. "Oh, don't look so cross. At least I *asked* you this time."

Aye. Small blessings. "Come on."

THE CRAFT OF ARLEAN LITHOSMITHS HAD LITTLE TO DO with gold, or silver, or any kind of precious metal. Their trade, first and foremost, was in heartstones.

The finest lithosmiths in Hart's Run did business out of Trollhedge, and their shops occupied the long, fortified building at the western end of the market. Nets woven from rope as thick as my wrists hung from poles above the rooftops, casting crosshatched shadows over the cobbles. A man and a woman stood guard at the door to the closest shop. The man had a dagger strapped to his hip; the woman held a small crossbow. They looked us over with narrowed eyes but let us pass.

It was cool and dark inside. The only light shone from the covered lamps hanging overhead, illuminating the glass-covered boxes scattered around the shop, and the heartstones glittering inside them. Leyda dashed forward with an exclamation of delight.

Our entrance conjured the proprietor from a back room. Thin metal files and chisels fine as quill pens stuck out from his massive white beard, like twigs in a walking bird's nest. He beamed at us. "Well now! What brings you ladies here this afternoon? Looking for something to give your true loves, eh?"

"Just browsing," I said, and his face fell.

Leyda pointed to a teardrop gem of deep plum. "What creature is that from, sir?"

"Fascinating gem, that one." The man pulled a file from his beard and tapped the box. "That was the last drop of lifeblood bled from a valkyrie's heart."

"And that?"

"The bluish-gray? A gryphon, miss."

"What about this one?" I nodded to the cloudy white stone hanging on a golden chain behind a case on the wall.

"Miss has rare taste, I see. That'd be the heartstone of a banshee. Very hard to come by. Very"—he slipped into the lamplight and frowned at my obvious lack of a purse—"*expensive.*"

"Are there other rare ones here?" Leyda asked.

The man offered to show her a fine cutting he'd made of a nixie's heartstone, but when she insisted on finding the rarest Trollhedge had to offer, he at last admitted, grudgingly and in an undertone, that one of the lithosmiths farther down the row had the sapphire heartstone of a siren on display.

With an "*I'llbeovertherefindyoulaterAliza,*" Leyda rushed outside in search of it.

"If you're not here to buy, girl, I don't want you hanging about," the proprietor growled as the door swung shut behind her. "Go trouble someone—"

"Miss Aliza?"

I turned. Wydrick's silhouette filled the doorway, his red cloak twisted in a lump over one shoulder. Dust and dead leaves swirled in around his feet. He was slightly out of breath.

"Anything the matter?" he asked the proprietor.

The man gave Wydrick's red cloak and sword-belt a long, calculating look. I saw scales in his eyes, weighing the trouble of making a complaint against the trouble of involving a Ranger in his business. The scales tipped in favor of the latter. "Nothing at all, sir." He returned the metal file to his beard and shuffled back to the room behind the curtain.

"Thank you, Master Wydrick," I said, "but what are you doing here?"

"Your friend at the apothecary said you'd come this way. Miss Aliza, I didn't steal it."

"Steal what?"

"My sword. You recognized the dragon; I know you did. I saw how you looked at me. I need you to know I didn't steal it."

"I never thought you did," I said, surprised.

"You—really?"

"No, of course not. Why would I?"

"But you're from Merybourne Manor, aren't you? I heard Alastair Daired was working for Lord Merybourne."

"He is."

He rubbed his forehead. "And he didn't say anything about me?"

"Not a word."

The shadow over his face lifted. "Oh. Ah, good."

From the back room, the sound of a metal file on stone grated against the silence. "If you don't mind me asking, Master Wydrick, why would you think he had?"

"It's a long story."

"I don't mind summaries."

"Well . . . I suppose I'll feel better once someone else here knows the truth." He leaned against the edge of the nearest table. "Alastair's father gave me the sword."

Whatever I'd expected, it wasn't that. I pretended to inspect the brown heartstone of a troll in the glass case beneath my fingertips as he continued.

"My mother was a Ranger and a friend of Lord Erran Daired. He took me in after she died, gods grant them both peace. Alastair and I grew up together at House Pendragon."

"Really?" The words spilled out before I could stop them. "What happened?"

"You mean why is he a Rider with a dragon to his name while

I'm a wandering mercenary with only a mangy nag for a mount? Alastair's damnable pride, that's what happened," he said with a sneer. "Lord Erran's last wish before he died was for me to have a dragon of my own. He made Alastair promise: when the time came, I would have a chance to compete in the Rider trials. Alastair broke that promise."

"He didn't let you compete?"

"Oh, Miss Bentaine, I *wish* that's all he'd done," he said. "The day before the trials, I found my horse dead in its stall. Its throat was cut, and on the door was a note: '*This is the only mount you deserve.*' It was in Alastair's writing." Sadness deepened the creases on his forehead as he stared out the shop's single window. "That horse belonged to my mother. It was the last thing of hers I had."

Even with my opinion of Daired already low, I'd not imagined him capable of that kind of cruelty. "Didn't you tell a magistrate?"

He laughed. It was the bitterest laugh I'd ever heard. "No magistrate in their right mind would entertain a case against Family Daired. Justice can't touch them, and neither could I, so I packed my things and left House Pendragon. After that—"

A bell jangled at the front of the shop and a young couple walked in. The proprietor emerged to greet them, casting a look of deep disapproval in our direction when he saw we'd not left.

Wydrick lowered his voice. "That's an even longer story, and I won't bore you with it. Suffice to say it brought me here." He bowed. "Thank you for not thinking the worst of me, Miss Aliza. I won't take up any more of your time."

With a swirl of his cloak, he ducked through the door and out of sight.

I turned his story over and over like a puzzle stone in my head as I went in search of Leyda. I found her and Gwyn admiring the siren's heartstone in a shop at the end of the row, this one guarded by two men, a dog, and a sign warning thieves that any attempts to rob the place would result in the removal of a hand or, as it said below in smaller, handwritten print, other critical bits of anatomy.

"Can you imagine what it took to find that?" Leyda said, tracing the heartstone's outline on the glass. "Do you think it was a Rider or a Ranger who cut it out?"

"I don't think Riders do that anymore," Gwyn said. "*Vesh* scavengers probably collected it after the battle. If they're quick enough, they—yes?"

A snub-nosed boy with sunburned cheeks stood at her elbow, plucking her sleeve. "Are you Gwyn-do-lyn Carlyle?"

She crouched to his level. "Aye, that's me. What can I do for you?"

He held out a folded sheet of paper. Ink stained one edge; the other looked as though it'd been cut, hurriedly and with a dull knife, from a larger sheet. "Fer yer farther."

Gwyn took it. "From who?"

"Master's friend, miss. Din't say his name."

"Thank you. I'll be sure to give it to my father."

"Afternoon, miss," he said, and scurried behind the row of heartstone cases. The curtain to the back room flicked open to admit him, and I caught a glimpse of an enormous figure draped in black before it fluttered shut.

"What was that all about?" Leyda asked. "Who—Gwyn?"

Gwyn's face had gone whiter than a banshee's heartstone. The hand that held the note trembled. She shoved it in her pocket before either of us could read it.

"Dearest, you're pale as a ghoul. What's wrong?"

"We need to go. Now."

CHAPTER 11

RIDDLES AND ROAST GRYPHON

Gwyn refused to talk about the note, save to say it concerned a business matter of her father's, and hearing the warning in her tone, I didn't press her. In a rare bout of maturity, Leyda didn't either, filling our journey instead with talk of Rangers and precious heartstones. We returned to the Manor without incident, seeing neither hide nor horn of the troll troop, and once inside, Leyda dashed off to share what she'd learned with Mari.

I followed Gwyn to her family's apartments. "Gwyn, talk to me, please. If something's wrong, I want to help."

"That means a lot, Aliza, but I can't talk about it. Not yet."

"Gwyn, you—"

"Do you trust me?"

"Of course."

"Then don't ask me again. As soon as I'm able, I'll tell you. I promise."

"All right."

"Thank you." She shut the door, leaving me alone in the hallway with too many questions and no idea where to find answers.

THAT NIGHT AS ANJEY AND I GOT READY FOR BED, I CONfided in her not only about Gwyn and the note but also about Wydrick. She listened with surprise as I described his history with the Daired family.

"How strange," she said. "Was that why Daired was so upset to see him at North Fields?"

"It must've been."

"Do you really think he killed Wydrick's horse? I mean, we both know Daired's proud and unpleasant, but that's downright cruel."

"You didn't see his face when Akarra suggested I ride."

"Was he that angry?"

"Angry doesn't cover it. When it comes to defending his family's dragons, I don't think there's anything he wouldn't do."

Anjey couldn't argue with that, and as the fire was already on its last log, we blew out our lamps and climbed into bed. Sleep drifted over me in minutes, warm and comforting as our goose-down coverlet, and I dreamed of far-off lands and dangerous men, of long vendettas and the color red, and of great beasts roaring, roaring . . .

I blinked, suddenly awake. That wasn't a dream. Deep in the woods, something *was* roaring. I sat up. Anjey snored softly beside me, untroubled by the sound. For a while I listened as the roars grew fainter, until I heard nothing but the chirping of summer's last crickets outside the window. When the roars didn't resume I lay down again, puzzled but too tired to think what it could've been. I'd work it out in the morning.

I didn't need to. Mama burst into our room just after dawn. "Wake up, girls, wake up!"

Anjey groaned and rolled over. "What's wrong, Mama?" I mumbled.

"It's the Riders! They killed the last of the gryphons last night. The horde is destroyed!"

"What?" I rubbed my eyes. "All of them?"

Mama thrust a sheet of paper in my hands. "See for yourself. Brysney came to deliver this an hour ago." At the name Brysney, Anjey opened her eyes and sat up. "Read quickly, both of you," Mama said. "Your father doesn't know I have it."

The fuzzy words grew clearer as my body caught up to my waking brain.

> To Lord and Lady Merybourne, the tenants of Merybourne
> Manor, and all residents of Hart's Run in the surrounding villages:
>
> It gives us great pleasure to inform you that last night the
> remainder of the gryphon horde was hunted down and killed in
> the woods along the eastern border of your estate. The terms of our
> contract have now been fulfilled.
>
> However, as new neighbors, we would like to take an
> opportunity to share your joy. Lord Merybourne, we propose a
> feast, in one week's time, to be held in your Great Hall for all who
> wish to celebrate the end of these creatures' reign. If you will supply
> the guests and the hall, we will supply everything else.
>
> Cordially,
> Cedric Brysney, Silverwing Scytheclaw
> Charis Brysney
> Nerissa Ruthven, Bluescale Broadback
> Edel Ruthven, Burrumburrem
> Lord Alastair Daired, Ahla-Na-al Kanah-sha'an-Akarra

The blank space by Charis's name stood out like a missing tooth, ugly and painful.

"Next week?" Anjey asked, reading it over my shoulder. "That's awfully generous. Can things be ready in time?"

Mama snatched the letter from my hands. "Depend on it, my

dear. And if it looks like they won't, I'll set up the Great Hall myself."

THE WEEK BEFORE THE BANQUET PASSED IN A FURY OF preparation. The Riders were as good as their word, paying for cooks from Trollhedge and Little Dembley and even two casks of Garhadi ale from the wine merchants in Edonarle. Akarra and Daired left the morning after Lord Merybourne received the letter, returning three days later with the casks clutched in her talons.

Woodcutters from the nearby villages came daily to the Manor, bearing carts of logs and brushwood for the fires. The weather had taken an unexpected turn, sending the chilly fingers of autumn creeping across the morning and evening hours. My sisters and I watched the carts stream into the courtyard from our drawing room window, huddled under shawls and extra-thick stockings. Manorfolk bustled beneath us, more than usual for the cold weather, but after spending so long cooped up inside, the chance to walk without fear under the open sky was too good to pass up.

The day of the banquet dawned cloudy and wet. Anjey remarked on the Riders' timing as I helped her dress. Her arm was healing well, but some things still gave her trouble, and even without injuries neither of us could manage a corset without assistance. Puffing and pulling, I cinched her laces tight as she braced herself against the bedpost.

"They chose the right day . . . to have . . . a party," she panted. "Nothing else worth . . . doing around here."

"There." I stepped back, my fingers striped red and white from the effort. "You're trussed."

She pulled on a plum-colored gown and I did up the buttons along the back. "Any word from Gwyn?" she asked. "I haven't seen her around lately."

"Me neither, but she asked me to trust her, and that's what I'm doing. What do you think of this one?" I held up my favorite green dress.

"You wore that to the last banquet. Wear the blue one."

In the hall outside we heard the beginnings of a high-pitched argument. Leyda wanted to wear trousers; Mama said if she did, she'd have to enjoy the party from our apartments.

"At least Mama won't have to worry about being late," I said.

The door to Leyda's room slammed shut.

Anjey arched an eyebrow. "Let's hope we all make it in one piece."

TRUE TO FORM, MAMA ROUNDED US UP AT QUARTER TO six and herded us out of our apartments, Papa, Mari, and a surly Leyda—who'd settled at last on the same dress she wore to Hall-under-Hill—included. Mari had surprised us all when she announced she'd be joining us, but Mama was delighted. She didn't even scold her for bringing her bestiary.

"What do you think you're going to do with *that?*" Leyda asked Mari as we headed for the Great Hall, scowling at the book under her arm. "You're not going to try to read and dance again, are you?"

Mari flushed. "If you must know, I'm working on my wyvern sketches." She stuck out her chin. "I want to make sure I get the proportions right."

There was the sound of a walking stick *click-clacking* down the corridor behind us.

Leyda looked over her shoulder, gasped, and hurried on ahead.

"My dear Bentaines!" Curdred called.

Papa paused long enough to give him an anemic smile. "Master Curdred. Good to see you again."

"What an exciting evening we have ahead of us!" Curdred said.

"I can't wait to meet this Daired of yours. Have I mentioned that his aunt, Lady Catriona, is an acquaintance of mine?"

The Manor House grew larger with every moment spent in Curdred's company, turning a few minutes' walk into a journey taking upward of an eternity. After hearing more than he could stand about Lady Catriona's many accomplishments, Papa interrupted long enough to ask Curdred how he liked Hart's Run.

"It's a *charming* county, Sir Robart, but it can't compare to the grandeurs of Edan Rose. You understand I—oh, I believe I'm wanted. Good evening!" he said, catching sight of Lord Merybourne across the corridor.

My family heaved a collective sigh as he strutted away, and we descended the final flight of stairs in peace.

I had to look twice at the man standing at the door to the Great Hall, greeting guests as they filed inside. Brysney wore a pale blue surcoat over a black tunic, his family crest on a silver pin at his shoulder. The way he brightened when he saw Anjey warmed my heart.

"Sir Robart! Madam Bentaine, I'm so pleased you could come," he said.

"Thank you for having us, Master Brysney," Papa said. "And bless you for ridding us of those beasts."

"It was an honor, and I'm glad you could make it. And all your daughters too!" Brysney said, bowing over Mari's hand. "A pleasure to meet you, Miss Mari."

Mari stammered out a hello, staring first at Brysney and then at Silverwing behind him.

"Now please, enjoy yourselves. There's food inside and plenty of wine. Sir, ma'am," he greeted the Martells behind us. "Good evening, and welcome."

Anjey tugged my sleeve as Mama and Papa headed into the Hall, her eyes fixed on Brysney. "I'll find you later, all right?"

"Don't distract him *too* much," I said in her ear. "He's still a host."

She squeezed my arm once before joining Brysney at the door. He didn't pay much attention to the guests who arrived afterward.

Inside, the Great Hall rang with laughter, chatter, and, among those perched by the casks of wine, a song or two. An enormous fire blazed on the hearth at the end of the hall. Trestle tables lined the walls, loaded with a hundred different dishes. My mouth watered as the smells wafted toward us. Roast deer and wild fowl, mince pies, dumplings, peppered greens, candied walnuts and sweet cream puddings, and—

I stopped at the platter in the center of the table, my appetite evaporating. There, spread-eagle on an oaken slab, was the cooked carcass of a gryphon.

"Have you never eaten your enemy, Miss Aliza?"

As if drawn to my disgust, Charis appeared at my side. Like her brother, she'd abandoned her armor for the occasion, wearing instead a navy surcoat with a hem that swept the ground. Her unbound hair hung around her shoulders in a curtain of saffron and copper.

"I didn't realize it was a common practice."

She laughed. "How else do you celebrate a victory?"

"Is gryphon meat edible?"

"It is when it's been roasted in dragonfire," she said. "Excuse me, Miss Aliza. I have to pay my respects to His Lordship. Have a pleasant evening."

"You too." *Enjoy your gryphon.*

I caught sight of Gwyn and crossed the Hall to greet her.

"Aliza! You look lovely," she said, taking my hand. If her father's business matters still troubled her, she gave no sign of it, though she didn't offer any explanation for her absence in the last week. I kept my promise and didn't ask.

"So do you! Is that a new dress?"

She pleated the gray skirt between her fingers. "This? No, it's an old one of Mother's. Aliza, come look at something." She pulled me aside and pointed at the food. "What on *earth* is that on the table?"

The centerpiece had already drawn considerable attention from most of the young boys in the room. They stood around it half awed, half disgusted, daring each other to take the first bite.

"Roast gryphon, apparently."

She shuddered. "*Ugh.* I'd call it barbarous, but if the Riders do it then it must be the height of fashion. Have you tried any?"

"Not a chance. I'd like the rest of my supper to stay down, thanks."

"Wise choice. Here." Gwyn plucked two glasses of wine from the tray of a passing maid and handed one to me as the musicians struck up their first notes. "May as well start with this. Good health!"

"Good—"

"Good health indeed! And *delightful* good luck as well!" Preceded by his ever-present cane, not a curl of his hair out of place, Wynce Curdred slipped into our conversation with the grace and tact of a senile centaur. "Such elegance and beauty all in one place. Why, I might almost believe I was back at Edan Rose. Who's your friend, Miss Aliza?"

"Master Curdred, this is Gwyndolyn Carlyle."

"Charmed," Gwyn said in the high voice that told me she was trying hard not to laugh.

"Likewise. Now, pardon the interruption, but I had to seize the opportunity; Miss Aliza, would you favor me with a dance?"

"What, now?"

"I never pass up a chance to dance! I've made it a rule for myself."

"But I hadn't—"

"Excellent!" He took my arm and tossed his cane to Gwyn.

"Master Curdred, really!"

He took my goblet and handed it to an increasingly astonished Gwyn. "I can't tell you how many times Lady Catriona has recommended it as beneficial exercise."

"Sir, no one else is dancing."

"All the better to start." He drew me toward the middle of the floor and waved a hand at the musicians. "A gavotte, if you please."

Barrett and Davy looked at each other blankly.

"*Mad Robin*," I mouthed, and Barrett struck up the appropriate note on his fiddle.

Gwyn wasted no time. Depositing Curdred's cane and the wine goblet in the arms of a nearby maid, she seized Henry Brandon and pulled him over to join us. I gave them both a look that said what I couldn't as Curdred hopped forward in time to music that only he seemed to hear, as it certainly wasn't the Mad Robin. *Thank you for saving me.*

Gwyn smiled and Henry winked.

A moment later Brysney led Anjey out to the position next to Gwyn and Henry, sending murmurs of delight rippling through the Hall. The stares of the other guests didn't seem to bother either of them, though I did see Anjey wince when Mama realized what was going on. Her delighted conjecture as to when the wedding would take place was loud enough for half the Hall to hear.

I fought the heat that crept into my cheeks as the dance progressed. Tall and gangly, Curdred was all knees and elbows, and each seemed to be in the wrong place at the wrong time. Unconcerned with trivial matters like keeping the beat or paying attention to his next steps, he nonetheless managed to maintain a steady stream of conversation throughout the dance.

"Do you know if the Riders plan to stay long in this area? Lady Catriona was surprised to hear that a manor the size of Merybourne was able to afford five Riders, and one of them her own nephew!

"I'm fortunate to have acquaintances in the highest circles of Edonarle society. There's Lady Catriona, of course, and this Daired, not to mention her other nephew. He's a Rider and captain in the king's army. And one can't forget the company I have the honor of hosting at Hunter's Forge. Our town has the finest smithies in the country, Miss Aliza, and you wouldn't believe the number of famous Riders who bear our workmanship. I understand Master Daired himself wields a fine example of Forgemaster Orordrin's smithcraft.

"Of course, when I inherit Merybourne Manor I intend to move here. I mustn't sound ungrateful, but the magistrate's lodge in Hunter's Forge is nothing compared with Merybourne Manor House. I'll not have my children raised in anything less!

"Well naturally, the future mistress of Merybourne Manor *must* come from humble roots. I've made it my mission in life to engage in all manner of philanthropic acts, and who better to start with than my wife?

"Miss Aliza, I must say that shade of blue suits you very well." Only as we neared the end of the dance did Curdred remember he was speaking to another person. As the steps slowed he gave my gown an appraising glance, lingering just long enough to make me uncomfortable. "Yes, very well indeed."

All his comments but the last received a vague, polite response. It didn't matter what I said; as soon as I spoke he'd change the subject as if he hadn't heard me. Curdred's final statement received a glare that might've cautioned him against speaking again if he'd seen it, but as his eyes were fixed on a point considerably lower than my face, he missed the warning.

Not a moment too soon, Barrett fiddled the last few notes of the Mad Robin. Never before had I been so relieved to curtsy a farewell. I hurried back into the crowd, leaving Curdred in the center of the dance floor, panting but looking pleased with himself. I'd not gone more than a dozen steps before, to my surprise, Gwyn turned to him and asked if he'd join her for the next dance.

Henry tapped me on the shoulder. "Fancy another, or did Master Gangles tire you out?"

"Only my patience. Come on. Let's make it easier for Gwyn."

He swung me back into the circle of dancers. "Have you tried the gryphon yet?"

"Not a chance! You?"

"I can celebrate the end of those creatures' tyranny without having to pick their meat out of my teeth." He nodded over my shoulder. "Aliza, is that Daired in the corner there?"

I looked where he indicated. A tall figure, skeletally thin, stood next to the casks of ale, wrapped in a cloak that hid most of his face. He poured a glass but didn't drink it, unseen eyes fixed on the dancers. On Henry and me, I realized after a moment. "No. Why?"

"You said he was tall and dark, and I can't say I recognize him. Daired's one of the only people here I haven't met."

"Now that you mention it, I don't recognize him either." Something about the thin figure turned my insides cold, but besides Henry, no one else seemed to notice him. "He's not Daired."

"No, he's not. Because that would be me."

Daired stood beside us. My foot came down hard on Henry's toe.

"Sir," Henry said, touching his forehead with a pained smile. "I don't believe we've met. Henry Brandon, Merybourne bard."

"So I gathered. Miss Bentaine, may I?"

"I, um . . ."

Fumbling over excuses, I looked to Henry for help, but he was already backing away, hands in the air. "*Your business*," he mouthed. I resisted the impulse to stick out my tongue at his retreating back, reminding myself to chide him later. Daired waited for my answer, as still and expressionless as a stone.

"You may."

He pulled me close as the musicians started a tune somewhere between a Mad Robin and a waltz. Though rough and calloused, his hand was warm and his grip tight. Again I smelled that smoky smell: rich, wild, and just a bit heady. He'd kept his leather armor beneath his surcoat, which shone burgundy when the light hit it. The golden dragon crest of House Pendragon reared rampant on Daired's left shoulder, right above his heart.

For several minutes we moved through the steps in silence, his critical gaze never straying from my face. Once or twice it seemed he wanted to speak, only to change his mind and shut his mouth. Baffled at first, and then a little annoyed, I at last said what I—and everyone else who gave us a second glance as we passed them—was thinking.

"I'm surprised, Master Daired. I didn't think you danced." *Something about "Thell kill me now" comes to mind*, I wanted to add, but thought better of it. Truth be told, he had no reason to be ashamed. For all his protests, Daired was an excellent dancer.

"Why would you think that?"

"You didn't dance at the last banquet."

"I didn't know anyone worth dancing with."

"In that case, I'm flattered you asked me."

"I'm a host," Daired said, and for the first time avoided my eyes. "It'd be rude not to show my face out here at least once. You were . . . convenient."

My eyebrow shot up. *Because heavens forbid Alastair Daired be rude to his guests.* I wondered if he'd asked me to dance to renew our last conversation and finish his lecture on the merits of the warrior life-style. If he did, I decided, then iron-shod or otherwise, I'd find some way to step on his toes before the dance ended.

"Are you enjoying the banquet?" he asked.

"Not at all."

"Oh?"

"There's not nearly enough trouble," I said.

The ghost of a smile played around his lips. "Perhaps next time we should bring in a live gryphon instead of a roasted one."

"You'd not have many friends left at Merybourne Manor if you did."

"Of all people here, Miss Bentaine, I'd think you'd be the least intimidated by a gryphon." We circled each other, palms touching. "You wouldn't run."

"Of course I would."

"Toward the gryphon."

"Toward the door, like every other sensible person in the room." I racked my mind for a new subject, preferably one that didn't revolve around bloodshed. "Now that your contract is fulfilled, do you and Akarra think you'll return to Dragonsmoor?"

"We haven't decided. If there's reason enough, we may stay."

"You don't think the gryphons will come back, do you?"

"That's not—never mind," he said. "Tell me, Miss Bentaine, how long has your family lived in Hart's Run?"

He talked like he fought: shifting, dodging the expected, no doubt doing his best to catch me off guard. *A second Sparring it is.* "My parents came from Edonarle when my sister Anjey was born. My father used to work for one of the accounting guilds."

"And they moved here?" What he didn't say, I understood. *Voluntarily?*

"My parents didn't want to raise children in the city, and Lord Merybourne needed a clerk. He and my father had known each other since before His Lordship inherited the Manor. They're old friends."

"Ah."

"I'd ask about your family too, Master Daired," I said when he offered nothing beyond that dismissive syllable, "but there's really no need."

"You know us that well?"

"I *did* pay attention in my history lessons."

"Myths and legends and watered-down folktales, Miss Bentaine. There's more to my family than your people might think."

"My people?"

"*Nakla.*" His voice dripped with contempt.

Now there's something the stories don't mention. I linked arms with Lady Merybourne and moved away from Daired. *Insufferable arrogance* didn't set the right tone for a heroic ballad. We met again in the center of the floor as the music quickened and the dancers broke off into two lines for a reel.

"What happened to your hand?" Daired asked.

I looked down. The graze on the back of my hand still stood out red and angry, though it'd stopped hurting a while ago. "I had a run in with a troll's tusk last week." A name floated to mind, borne on the crest of my less-than-better judgment, but I didn't care. I wanted to see his reaction. "That Ranger we met at North Fields came to my rescue, actually. Master Wydrick."

Daired stopped in the middle of the dance floor.

"You know him, don't you?" I asked.

"I . . . knew him."

"From what I hear, you didn't part on the best of terms."

Anjey and Brysney executed their turn around a motionless

Daired. "You heard right," he said at last, each word forced through clenched teeth.

"I'm sorry to hear it," I said. "Probably wasn't in Wydrick's best interests, making an enemy in House Pendragon."

"It's in no one's best interest to make us their enemy, Miss Bentaine, and that man was never fit to live under the Pendragon roof. Keep that in mind before you stoop to defending him." The music ended with a flourish and he bowed. "Good evening."

My mind whirled as he disappeared into the crowd, curiosity far from satisfied. Of one thing, however, I was certain. Even disregarding his cruelty to Wydrick, Alastair Daired was the rudest, most unpleasant man I'd ever met. His arrogance even made Curdred look affable by comparison; at least the magistrate bumbled by in preening ignorance. There was something much more calculating about Daired's conceit, more self-aware, and no matter how much I liked Akarra, I wouldn't be sad to see him leave Hart's Run.

A prickling started on the back of my neck as soon as I stepped off the dance floor, or rather, I became aware of a sensation that had been building for several minutes. Across the Hall, the hooded figure standing by the casks of ale lifted his goblet to me, and beneath the shadow of his hood, I saw the flash of a smile.

It was the grain of sand that broke the sphinx's back.

I'd faced enough riddles for one night. Willing or unwilling, this stranger might give me some answers, if not about Wydrick and Daired, then at least about what was troubling Gwyn, or what he'd demanded from her father that night at Hall-under-Hill. Question after question filled my head as I pushed my way toward the mysterious figure.

When I reached the table, he was gone.

CHAPTER 12

THE PINK BROOCH

The stranger failed to show himself for the remainder of the night, though not for lack of searching on my part. I even rounded up Henry and Mari to keep an eye out with me; Henry because he'd noticed him first, and Mari because it looked as if she had nothing better to do. Finding him involved little socializing and quite a lot of sitting in corners and watching people, a task at which Mari excelled. To our disappointment, the hooded man eluded our sight, and by the time Brysney called for a final song from Henry, we'd given up hope.

The evening, however, was far from a loss. Anjey was in a playful good humor the like of which I'd rarely seen before. Mama and Leyda only left the dance floor once to snatch a bite of supper, and Papa, after sampling the Garhadi ale, even allowed Mama to drag him into a jig. We all left long after midnight, exhausted but in good spirits.

I didn't see Daired again that night.

THE MANOR WOKE LATE THE NEXT MORNING. NO DOUBT many nursed wine-induced headaches, but I suspected most people stayed in bed simply to keep warm. While we'd been celebrating, autumn snuck in early. In the morning the grass was stiff with frost, and the new fire crackling in our grate did little to heat the room.

As I searched the wardrobe for my favorite shawl, a knock sounded at the door and our housemaid poked her head inside. "Begging your pardons. Miss Aliza, Sir Robart's asking for you in his study."

"Thank you, Hilda. Anjey, tell Mama to start breakfast without me, would you?" I said, and hurried out without my shawl. Papa didn't often call for me.

He answered at my first knock. "Come in, my dear, come in." He spoke in the high, cautiously polite tone of voice that told me he wasn't alone, and I pushed open the door with something close to nervousness fluttering in the pit of my stomach.

I was right. He wasn't alone. Daired stood and bowed. "Good morning, Miss Bentaine."

"Aliza. Shut the door and have a seat," Papa said. "Master Daired keeps the ledger for his band of Riders. Now that the horde is destroyed, he wants to settle accounts with His Lordship."

I frowned. Lord Merybourne had paid the Riders their bond-price when they arrived. *What more did they want from us?* "Is there something I can help you with, Master Daired?"

"I wanted you here because you witnessed the gryphon attack."

He spoke evenly, and I heard no anger in his voice. Whatever emotions he'd felt during our conversation about Wydrick he'd now subdued, but despite recovering his calm, I doubted he'd forgotten. I doubted a man like Daired ever forgot.

"The beast killed one of Lord Merybourne's mares. We should've been able to prevent the attack, so we're honor-bound to pay for the horse." Daired untied a leather purse from his belt and handed it to me. "Your father has agreed to abide by your judgment, Miss Bentaine. Do you say that's a fair price?"

With a cheery *clink*, fifteen gold dragonbacks tumbled out into my hand.

I looked up in alarm. Even Lord Merybourne's prize stallion wasn't worth more than ten dragonbacks. Daired watched me as I considered the small fortune in my palm. *If I said yes . . .* I traced the profile of Edan the Fireborn stamped into the gold. A few extra dragonbacks *would* help lessen the Manor's debt, and it wasn't as if Daired needed them. *It'd ease Papa's mind too. He wouldn't have to . . . no.*

I slipped the coins into the purse and handed it back to Daired. Tempting as it was, I wouldn't lie to my father. "You're too generous, sir. That horse wouldn't have sold for half that price, and the incident was an accident. No one can blame you."

Daired took the purse with an odd smile and set it on the desk before Papa. "Then let's say it's for the horse, as well as any outstanding expenses from the banquet. Sir Robart, pass on our regards to His Lordship for his hospitality."

"I will, of course, and thank you for everything you've done here. Best of luck on your journeys beyond Hart's Run, and do say farewell to the Ruthvens for me."

"You're leaving?" I asked without thinking, and Daired stopped in the doorway.

"Akarra and I have business elsewhere. So do Edel and Nerissa."

"And we consider ourselves fortunate for even so brief a visit," Papa said. "Aliza? Show Master Daired to the front hall, if you would."

I followed Daired out of the study and into the corridor. If he'd not tell me the object of his game, I'd at least make sure I understood the rules. "Master Daired, wait."

"Yes?"

"What's this about?"

"I'm sorry?"

"Fifteen dragonbacks is far too much for that horse, and you know it."

"Just for the horse? Yes. Not for everything else."

"The banquet wasn't worth fifteen gold dragonbacks either."

"I know."

"Then what is it for?"

Daired closed the distance between us. The sunlight streaming in from the windows cast shadows along his jaw, illuminating dark circles under his eyes. He looked like a man who'd gone a long time without sleep. "We should've been able to better protect your sister at North Fields. Consider it compensation on her behalf."

Ah. He'd been wise not to mention that in front of my father. Around Papa, Anjey and I had taken to pretending the gryphon attack had never happened, and Rider or not, Papa wouldn't have appreciated a reminder of how close he'd come to losing another daughter.

"How considerate."

"It's my duty. I wouldn't leave with a debt like that unpaid."

"No. I don't suppose you would," I said. "The front hall is this way."

I'd almost reached the door when a hand on my shoulder stopped me. "Miss Bentaine, how long is the Lower Westhull Regiment staying in Hart's Run?"

So Wydrick *was* still on his mind. "I don't know. There's usually work in the winter guarding the merchants' convoys to Edonarle, so I'd guess they'll stay through the spring."

Daired released me, his frown as fearsome as ever I'd seen. "I wouldn't count on it. Good morning, Ali—Miss Bentaine," he said, and wrenched open the door.

"Master Daired, what a surprise." The perfectly coiffed head and violet cravat of Master Curdred peeked over Daired's shoulder. "And Miss Aliza! Just the lady I wanted to see. If you don't mind, Master Daired, I'd like a private audience with Miss Aliza."

To tell which of us was more surprised would be impossible, but Daired recovered faster than I did. Without a word to Curdred, he bowed and hurried out the door.

"How can I help you, Master Curdred?"

"If you'd take a turn with me about the hall, I'll tell you," he said. "Perhaps you've been wondering why I decided to visit Merybourne Manor so suddenly."

"Not really, no."

He didn't seem to hear me. "It was over dinner nearly a month ago. Lady Catriona looked straight at me and said, 'Wynce, it's about time you get a wife.'"

I froze. *Oh gods, please be joking.*

"And I thought, where better to find a wife than at the Manor I am to inherit? It'll save a great deal of adjustment when we take possession, which is sure to suit all parties. Miss Aliza, are you well?"

"Forgive me, Master Curdred, I must've—"

"Take a deep breath, my dear. I haven't even gotten to the best part," he said with a chuckle, taking one of my hands. It took all the self-control I possessed not to jerk away. "Aliza Bentaine, you are one of the loveliest women I've ever met, and I'm confident that you'll bear lovely children. I'd consider myself the most fortunate man in the world if you'd take me as your husband." He stopped and faced me. "Marry me, Aliza."

"No."

He laughed. "I beg your pardon?"

"No, Master Curdred."

"I'm afraid you might've misunderstood. I was offering you my hand in *marriage*." A moment's fumbling in his pocket produced a silver brooch with a small pink stone in the center. A nixie's heartstone. "Not to mention, of course, this Manor."

"I understood you, sir, so please understand me. I will not marry you."

"But . . . why not?"

Where do I even begin? "Because we're ill-suited to each other, among other reasons."

"What other reasons?"

"I have no desire to marry you."

Curdred stepped closer. "But what of my desire, dear Aliza?"

"It's *Miss Bentaine*, sir, and I believe our private audience is over." Leaving him blinking in astonishment, I all but ran out of the hall.

FOR TWO DAYS I TOSSED CURDRED'S PROPOSAL OVER IN my mind and still came no closer to believing it. In twenty-three years my experience with love had been limited, but I'd always assumed men went about selecting a wife based on more than the potential beauty of their children. Or, for that matter, on an acquaintance that had lasted longer than one family dinner and a single disastrous dance.

When I shared the news with Gwyn, her reaction wasn't what I expected.

We sat in her family's parlor huddled close to the fire, hands wrapped around steaming cups of tea. The solitude was a treat; both Rya and Madam Carlyle were visiting Madam Moore, and Master Carlyle had holed himself up in his study. As I finished my story, Gwyn set her cup on the table.

"Curdred came to Merybourne Manor to find a wife?"

"At first I thought it was a joke. I *hoped* it would be a joke, but he meant every word."

"Interesting." She gazed into the fire, shadows flickering over her face. "Tell me something, Aliza," she said after a minute. "What would you do if you learned an unpleasant truth about your father?"

"What do you mean?"

"Say you discovered your father had done something awful, and to cover it up, he'd fallen in with bad company."

I forgot about Curdred. "Gwyn, what's going on? What did your father do?"

"I think . . . I think he's been embezzling from Lord Merybourne." Her shoulders slumped at my horrified expression. "No, I *know* he has."

"*What?* How?"

"I found his ledger. His real ledger, not the one Sir Robart's been using. My father's been skimming dragonbacks off the Manor accounts for years now."

I sat back in my chair, struggling to make sense of it. "But . . . *why?*"

"Oh, Aliza, I wish I knew. After so many years of service, maybe he thought Lord Merybourne owed him something." Gwyn studied the threadbare cushion beneath her, tracing the fraying seam with a finger. "Or perhaps my father is simply a greedy man."

"Why has no one noticed?"

"You know Lord Merybourne. He never checks his books, and even if he had, Father always had the false ledger."

"Is that why your father's been so upset lately? He knows you know?"

"He doesn't know I know. I wasn't supposed to find the ledger, but I was curious, and he'd been acting so strangely. And now . . . now I almost wish I didn't. Because that's just the start of it. Remember that note that boy gave me in Trollhedge?" I nodded. "It was a message from his creditors."

"Oh no."

"Father must've panicked when Lord Merybourne announced his plan to hire the Riders. From what I can work out, he borrowed enough from these people to replace what he'd stolen, so when His Lordship collected the dragonbacks for the Riders' bond-price—"

"No one would be the wiser."

"Exactly. Except now Father owes them. And, Aliza, he doesn't have the money."

I thought of the shadowy figure beneath the arch at Hall-under-Hill, and of the hooded man at the banquet. "Do you know who his creditors are?"

"No. Someone from Lithosmith's Row, I think, or maybe one of the *Vesh*. The note didn't have a name."

"Gwyn, I'm so sorry."

"Aye, me too."

"Tell me how I can help."

She didn't answer right away, watching the flames dancing in the grate. "I have an idea, but first I need his ledger. I need to know exactly how much he owes."

"You don't know where it is?"

"He moved it after I found it the first time. I can look in our family's apartments and his study, but I need your help to search the rest of the Manor." Footsteps sounded in the hall outside, and Gwyn grabbed my arm. "Please, whatever you do, don't tell anyone about this. Promise me, Aliza!"

"I promise," I said as little Rya bounded into the room.

"Look what Mama found!" she shrieked, leaping into her older sister's lap and holding up a sticky pinecone. She shook it in Gwyn's face. "It's full of seeds."

Gwyn laughed and picked the pine needles from Rya's hair. "That it is, sweetheart. Look at you, all a mess!"

"Thank you for the tea, Gwyn." I stood. "I'll keep an eye out for that book."

Over Rya's tangled black curls, Gwyn mouthed *thank you.*

"Goodbye, Aliza!" Rya said. "Come back soon!"

I showed myself out.

WHERE WOULD A MAN LIKE CARLYLE KEEP SUCH A DAN-*gerous secret?*

With Gwyn busy putting on a brave charade for her family, I had to search on my own, and for the next few hours I pondered that question without success. If he hadn't hidden it in his rooms or in his study, then where? Carlyle wasn't the kind of man to entrust his private ledger to someone else's keeping, even if they didn't know what it was. On a whim I searched the Manor library, thinking he might've been clever enough to hide one book among many, but after several hours' examination, I came away with nothing but a dusty dress and a knot in my neck.

Discouraged, I returned to my family's apartments for dinner. Mama couldn't wait to tell me that Anjey wouldn't be joining us, as Brysney had stopped by that afternoon and asked if she'd accompany him on a tour of Trollhedge. With a twinkle in her eyes, Mama declared she had no idea when they'd be back. Happiness for Anjey buoyed my spirits, but as the meal went on they soured again, too consumed with worry for Gwyn to pay much attention to the rest of the conversation.

At least until Leyda mentioned Curdred.

My head shot up, praying she hadn't somehow heard about his proposal. All things considered, I wasn't prepared to explain that to my family.

"The man is *insufferable.* I don't think he can go more than five minutes without looking in a mirror," Leyda said. "He actually pulled me aside today to tell me my frock didn't match my hair ribbons!"

Mari snorted into her napkin. Papa smiled. "Well, my love, you *are* wearing plaid, and that ribbon you had on this morning was striped," Mama said.

"I didn't say he was wrong. But you don't just go up and tell people things like that! Honestly, the man's got less sense than a stuffed peacock, and he's about as vain as a live one."

I set down my spoon. If Mama or Papa answered, I didn't hear. *Stuffed.* The word rang in my head, conjuring images of dim corridors draped with moth-eaten tapestries. *Could it be so simple?* Carlyle would need to keep the ledger close. If it wasn't in his study or his apartments, that left only one place he could hide it.

Excusing myself on the merits of a sudden headache, I slipped out before anyone could protest and headed for the northwest gallery.

A single torch burned at the end of the hall, lit by some superstitious servant who didn't like to cross the gallery in the dark. The half-light made it worse. Curtains hung over the windows, musty and patterned with cobwebs. Drafts seeped through the cracks of the bricked-over fireplace, sending waves of dust skittering like ghouls across the floor and the cloth-shrouded furniture. A slinking sense of dread followed me as I picked through the piles of domestic debris, stopping in front of my last, best hope.

The stuffed knight stared down at me.

Most of the plates of armor had rusted shut. The visor alone submitted to any sort of persuasion, albeit with a creaking and groaning loud enough to rouse the whole Manor. I stood on my tiptoes and peered inside the helmet, but the light was too low to make anything out. I reached inside and felt around. The soft body of a mouse moved beneath my hand, and with a squeak it scuttled away. Beneath it I felt only gnawed scraps of velvet. I sank back onto my heels under the crushing weight of disappointment. The ledger wasn't there.

"Looking for something?"

I spun around . . . and bit down on a scream.

The stranger from the banquet stood a few paces away. The tattered black cloth of his cloak enveloped a figure of inhuman thinness, and his—for whatever that cloak disguised, the voice was male—hooded head brushed the cobwebs hanging from the chandelier. In one gauntleted hand, he held a small leather-bound book. "For this, perhaps?"

Don't run; get answers. Fear can wait. "Who are you?"

"No one important."

"Tell me your name."

"*Tsk.* I thought you Arleans were supposed to be politer."

"You can't have cornered many of us in dark hallways, then," I said, hoping my voice sounded stronger than it felt. "What's your name?"

"What will you give me if I tell you?"

"I won't scream."

With a laugh like rasping metal, the creature bowed. "You drive an easy bargain, miss. I am but a humble minister in the service of the Silent King of Els, and by that token, I'm afraid I can give you no name."

"You're not . . . human, are you?"

"Thanks be to the Twins of the Desert, no. The Silent King chooses sturdier servants."

"If you're not human, are you *Shani?* Or *Tekari?*"

The minister snorted. "What makes a creature friend or foe to your race? Do *you* even know? My loyalty is to the Silent King; whether that makes me your friend or foe is up to you."

Tekari, then. The desert kingdom across the southern ocean had always been a mystery to us, and with good reason. Tales told around Arlean dinner tables spoke of vast wastelands inhabited by *Tekari* and *Idar* who hunted humans for sport and of great, ancient cities buried in the dunes, filled with people whose blood had long ago mixed with the Oldkind. Whatever the myths, the truth had never ventured past Elsian shores.

Until now. "How did you get inside the Manor?" I thought of his appearance in the Great Hall. "And why has no one noticed you?"

"Secrets and shadows are my business, young lady, and I take care to mind my business in strange places." As he spoke, the air around him grew inky, blurring the outlines of his robe. At a motion of his hand, the darkness dissipated. "I must say, I didn't account for you and the bard being able to pierce this disguise at the banquet, but that was my mistake. You artists are always seeing things that aren't there."

"What do you want from Master Carlyle?"

"Ah, now we get to it." He stepped closer, cloak billowing around him in a way that even the drafty hall could not explain. I took a step back. "The poor conniving steward finds he can't escape the hole he's dug for himself, so he sends this upstart chit in his place. To do . . . what exactly? *Talk* him out of his debt?"

"No." I stared at the Elsian minister where his eyes should've been, had they not been sunk in shadow. "I only want the ledger."

"Why? The steward already knows what's in it."

"I'm not here for Master Carlyle." I held out my hand. "Give it to me."

"You have courage, girl. I'll grant you that."

"I'm not going to say it again."

"Oh, I believe you." His gaze poured over me like the heat of a fever. "You're marginally clever, finding Carlyle's hiding place. I'd like to see what you'll do when you're desperate," he said, and the book burst into flames.

This time I did scream.

I stumbled back as an eerie blue light bathed the gallery, emanating from the fire the creature had conjured in the palm of his hand. The minister circled me, cradling the ball of flame until the last pages of the ledger crumbled to ash. Tongues of blue fire curled around his fingers like serpents, licking hungrily in my direction.

"Now, I told you once to mind your own business, but since you've ignored my advice, let me leave you with this—and if there's an ounce of sense buried beneath that foolish bravado of yours, perhaps this time you'll listen." He stopped pacing, and with a shake of his hand extinguished the flames. "Things are now in motion, old, deep things that you cannot stop, cannot defeat. All *Tekari* whisper it to one another: lamias and banshees and valkyries and direwolves and sirens, and even the great sea-serpent, slumbering in her fathomless depths."

"What do they whisper?"

"Do you truly want to know?"

I didn't. I did. I had to know. "Tell me."

"*It is coming.*"

With a screech and a rush of wind, the creature vanished.

I STAGGERED FROM THE GALLERY ON SHAKY LEGS, DESperate for a glimpse of sunlight, of clean sky, of *anything*. It took a few minutes for me to rally my nerves and climb the stairs back to the Carlyles', and once there, Gwyn had to pull the story from me bit by bit, through shivers and angry tears.

"Gwyn, I'm so sorry. I tried—I tried to stop him," I said when I'd finished.

"I know. You did everything you could."

"What do we do now?"

"There's only one thing to do; but, dearest, there's no more *we*. I won't ask you to put yourself in danger again. Not for me, and especially not for my father."

"I don't care—"

"No. I've made up my mind. One way or another I'll figure it out, but I have to do it on my own." She squeezed my hand. "Go home, Aliza. You've done more than enough for today."

I wanted to protest, to press my case, but she wouldn't hear another word about it. At last I did as she said and returned to my family's apartments. For hours that night I lay in bed and stared at the ceiling, exhausted but unwilling to sleep. I didn't want to dream of talking shadows and cryptic warnings and smiles without eyes.

I did anyway.

THREE DAYS PASSED WITHOUT WORD FROM GWYN OR sight of the Minister. More than anything I wanted to share what I'd learned with Anjey, but for Gwyn's sake I kept her father's secret. All I could do was wait, and hope, and warn Leyda and Mari to stay out of the shadows.

On the third day, the news broke. Late in the afternoon our maid announced a visitor. I rushed into the parlor to find Gwyn standing by the fire, wrapped in a shawl. She looked up as I entered, a sad smile on her face.

"I have good news, Aliza."

"What? What happened?"

"I bought us some time." She let the shawl fall to the crook of her arm, revealing a brooch of twisted silver wire and the small pink heartstone of a nixie.

I drew back as if a serpent lay coiled on her breast. "You're . . . *no.*"

"Aye. Curdred and I are engaged. He asked me this morning."

"Gwyn, you *can't.* Please! Think this through. There must be another way."

"Do you honestly think I'd have accepted him if there was another way?" She sank onto a sofa, her head in her hands. "Listen to me. I have thought about it. I've done nothing but think about it. There *is* no other way. You said the Elsian minister was looking for surety from my father. Well, now he has it. If Father fails to pay, I won't. I'll have the means."

I stared at her, too stunned to speak.

"The magistrate of Hunter's Forge is no pauper, you know," she said after an awkward silence.

"No amount of money is worth your life."

"And what about my sister? Is it worth Rya's life? Do you want to know what'll happen to her if my father doesn't pay?" Tears filled her eyes as she pulled a familiar scrap of paper from her pocket and tossed it to me. "See for yourself."

I smoothed out the note from Lithosmith Row.

> *My dear Carlyle,*
>
> *My master has graciously extended the date of your first payment. Should you miss it again, you will find yourself in a most unfortunate predicament. There are many dangerous creatures creeping through the wilds of Arle, sir, and it would be a shame for your youngest daughter to encounter one of them.*
>
> *Consider this a friendly warning.*

I handed it back to her. "I see."

"Then tell me I'm doing the right thing." Her voice fell and she closed her eyes, gripping the brooch so hard her knuckles turned white. "Please. Even if you don't agree, I need to hear someone say it out loud, or I don't know if I can bear it."

"Oh, Gwyn." She'd been brave, braver than anyone I'd ever known. I could be brave for her. "You *are* doing the right thing." I took her hand. "And I wish you both every happiness."

CHAPTER 13

A PRIMER IN FOLKLORE

Not long after the news of Gwyn and Curdred's engagement spread across the Manor, Gwyn came to me with another note. "Our maid brought this to me this morning," she said, her face grave. "You need to read it."

> *I know why you accepted that imbecile from Hunter's Forge. If you wish to take on your father's burden, then so be it. You are his surety. I look forward to renegotiating the terms of interest with you on my master's behalf, which I will deliver upon my return from Els. You will hear from me again before year's end.*

There were scorch marks along the edge. I gave it back to her. "Does Curdred know?"

"No. And I won't tell him unless I must, but if the Minister is returning to Els, this at least gives me some time to plan. We're safe." She threw the note into the dying fire. "For now."

SAFE, MAYBE, BUT NOT HAPPY. THE THOUGHT CROSSED my mind a month later on the eve of Saint Ellia's Day as I helped

Gwyn dress for her wedding. Beneath the blue silk and patterned mantle of an Arlean bride, she wore the strained look of a soldier preparing for battle. For her sake, I tried to stay positive. From what I'd seen, Curdred did seem genuinely besotted with Gwyn, and it made it a little easier to imagine a happy future for them when at least one party approached it with such enthusiasm.

A little, but not much.

I stood at Gwyn's side when the cantor gave them their vows. In lieu of actual friends, Lord Merybourne stood at Curdred's. Madam Carlyle smiled and clapped when the cantor tied the cord of four strands around their hands and pronounced them husband and wife. Master Carlyle watched his daughter in silence, his stare glassy and hollow. I thought I saw tears gathering in the corner of his eyes as Gwyn and Curdred walked out of the abbey together, but if there were, he didn't let them fall.

Lord Merybourne's carriage arrived after the ceremony to take them to their home in Hunter's Forge. I led the meager crowd in throwing copper half-trills in the air for luck, wishing them all the best in their new life together, and trying not to cry as the carriage disappeared around the curve of the road.

ANJEY DID HER BEST TO COMFORT ME IN GWYN'S ABSENCE, but within a week of the wedding we received more troubling news. Brysney delivered it one morning, calling on us in the front parlor with the most forlorn expression I'd ever seen.

"The king has called a muster in Edonarle," he said. "All Riders, I'm afraid. The Free Regiments too. He wants us to renew our vows of loyalty to the kingdom."

"How often does he call for these musters?" Anjey asked. I could tell she was working hard to disguise how much this news devastated her.

"Usually once every five years, but our last one was three years ago. I didn't expect another so soon," Brysney said. "Believe me, Anjey, if I had a choice I wouldn't leave Hart's Run for all the kings in the world."

She blushed and murmured something about his duty to Arle and how she respected him for it, but even that did nothing to settle Brysney's mind. He paced back and forth across our parlor, boots drumming an agitated rhythm against the floor.

"I hate to be giving up the North Fields lodge so soon after settling, but I have no idea when I'll return. The king keeps no schedule with these things. But the *minute* the muster is over," he said, holding out his hand to Anjey, "and I do mean the minute, we're flying back here and taking it up again."

Anjey took his hand. "What if Lord Merybourne's found another tenant?"

"I'll bully them out. Or Silver and I will camp in the fields. It doesn't matter. I *am* coming back for you." He pulled her close and pressed a kiss to her forehead. "I'll write to you every day."

"And I'll write back." She gave him a little push toward the door. "Go. Your sister's waiting for you."

"Every day! I mean it," he said as he backed out of the parlor, remembering at the last second that I was also in the room. With all the attention he could spare from Anjey, he bid me farewell, which meant he gave me a halfhearted nod without taking his eyes off my sister.

"I mean it too," Anjey said. "Goodbye, Cedric."

My heart broke with her as we sat on our window ledge and watched Brysney fly away on Silverwing, accompanied by Charis on her mare.

Brysney was the only one who looked back.

That same afternoon we received another visitor. I just about knocked over my inkwell as Hilda announced *Master Wydrick of the Lower Westhull Rangers*.

"Good afternoon to you, sir," Mama said, patting her hair into place and curtsying as he strode inside, his plumed helmet tucked under one arm, fur-lined cloak thrown back over his traveling pack. The dragon-hilt sword glittered at his hip. "So pleased to meet you, Master Wydrick."

He bowed. "The honor is mine, ma'am. I'm sad this is both the first and last time I've had the pleasure of visiting, but as your lovely Aliza was my first friend in Hart's Run, I thought it was only appropriate to say goodbye in person."

"How very kind of you!" Mama said, nudging me. "Don't you think, Aliza?"

There was a thud and a scrabbling sound from Leyda's room.

"Yes, very kind."

A door burst open and Leyda rushed out into the parlor, panting, eyes bright. "I thought I heard . . . oh! Master Wydrick, I didn't realize you were here."

He gave her a smart salute. "Miss Leyda."

"What a coincidence you should—" Her face fell as she noticed his pack. "Wait, you're not going, are you?"

"To Edonarle, yes."

"No! *Must* you?"

"It pains me more than you know, but yes, I'm afraid we must. The king takes these musters very seriously."

"Does the whole regiment really have to leave?" Leyda asked. "What if there are monsters to slay while you're away?"

Wydrick laughed. "He'll not keep us Rangers long. A month, or two at most. Riders get the worst end of these things; he might keep them until spring. In the meantime, the army will maintain patrols. Or perhaps you were looking to slay a monster or two yourself, Miss Leyda?"

The idea seemed to strike my sister with some novelty, and I spoke up before she could make an impulsive declaration to join the Free Regiments. "Thank you for coming, Master Wydrick," I said. "We wish you all safe travels."

"I hope I'll have the pleasure of seeing you again after the muster." He pressed four fingers to his forehead. "Until then, farewell."

WITH THE DEPARTURE OF THE RANGERS AND THEIR RED cloaks, the last of the color drained out of Merybourne Manor. I missed Gwyn more every day. We wrote as often as we could, and through her letters I learned all about Hunter's Forge and the great, the beneficent, the magnanimous Lady Catriona Daired. Gwyn introduced at least one new adjective for Lady Catriona per letter. She said Curdred had hundreds more. It cheered me to read a lively tone in her letters, though I wondered that she said almost nothing of her husband, save that he was an attentive magistrate to the people of Hunter's Forge. Their marriage, while by no means rapturous, seemed at least cordial. I took some small comfort in that.

Even better, in a letter sent two months after she'd left Hart's Run, Gwyn shared news of Els. She told me she'd received another note, delivered just as mysteriously as the first, which contained only the words *Martenmas, one year hence.* It gave her hope, she said, as she felt confident her father could repay his debt to the Silent King by then.

She didn't mention how much he owed.

While Gwyn's correspondence eased my mind, however, Anjey's lack of letters soon began to worry me. I teased her the night after Brysney left as she sat down to her desk to pen a letter, but she said love had done stranger things. Her confession startled me, for it was the first time she'd put words to what I knew she felt. She smiled at my surprise. "When it comes to love, Aliza, I've been reserved enough for a lifetime. Cedric is worth a little daring."

After that I no longer teased her.

The day after the Riders' departure she sent her first letter by carriage-post from Trollhedge, and I waited with an anticipation almost matching hers as the carriage returned six days later with fresh letters from Edonarle. None bore Anjey's name. Neither did the next week's post, nor the next. Papa and I tried to comfort her as each post carriage dropped its bundle of disappointment off at the Manor. We assured her that the Riders would be kept so busy with the king's business that Brysney wouldn't have time to reply, no matter how much he wanted to. A month after the Riders left, Anjey rallied, writing with renewed hope.

Still she heard nothing.

Midwinter Quarters and the Long Night passed, and then the New Year. A rare snow blew down from the north, drifting over the hills and valleys of Hart's Run in unforgiving heaps, white in the sun, blue in the shade, and bitterly cold. My sisters and I spent our time huddled close to the fire in our parlor, reading, sewing, drawing, or in Anjey's case, writing.

Nothing.

Mama managed to contain her distress at Brysney's silence in Anjey's presence, but she wasted no opportunity to curse the faithless Rider when Anjey was out of earshot. "And to see them together anyone could have *sworn* he was in love with her," she said. "To think! I'd planned for a wedding here by Saint Ellia's Day."

For once I agreed with Mama, yet for Anjey's sake I held out hope that something besides a change of heart had kept him from replying to her letters.

By spring that hope began to fade.

Winter left as abruptly as it had come, blown away on a warm southern wind. Manor-folk wandered outside as soon as the robins began singing in earnest, enjoying the sun and the gryphon-free skies. One day, while inspecting the Manor garden for the first hints of foliage, I stumbled across Mari crouched on the grass, one ear pressed to the ground. Her bestiary lay open on the blanket next to her.

"Mari? What on earth are you doing?"

"*Shh*. I'm listening."

"For what?"

She waved me away. I sat on the blanket and waited. At last she sat up and crossed something out in the margin of her book.

"Hear anything interesting?" I asked.

"No."

I looked over her shoulder and tried to read what she had scribbled out. "Did you expect to?"

"Have you spoken with Tobble lately?"

"Not since autumn, but the garden-folk have been hibernating. Why, have you?"

Mari shook her head. "Now that it's warmer, I thought we'd have seen them around, but nobody has. I talked with Master Rett and the other groundskeepers yesterday, and they haven't seen a single hobgoblin since the snows came." She thumped the ground with the heel of her hand. "I was looking for their Underburrow. I wanted to make sure they were all right."

"That's sweet of you, Mari, but you shouldn't worry. It was a hard winter, and they're probably too snug down there to bother coming out until midspring." I caught her pencil as it started to roll off the book. "I'm sure everything's—hold on a second. What is that?"

"Huh?" She looked down at the sketch I indicated. "Oh. It's my chapter on *Shani*. That's a forge-wight."

"What's it holding?"

"Fire."

My blood ran cold, then hot. *Shani*, the friends of humankind. Yet the drawing she'd made looked exactly like the robed and gauntleted Elsian minister, right down to his armored fist wreathed in flames, and *friendly* was the last word I'd use to describe him. "What did you copy this from?"

"I found it in Uncle Gregory's library last time we were in Edonarle. He's got loads of books about the Oldkind," she said, taking the bestiary from my hands and smoothing out the corner of the page I'd folded over. "Why?"

"Er . . . no reason." *None that I can make sense of.* "Mari, what do you know about Els?"

"No more than you. No more than anybody. They live in the desert, keep to themselves, and apparently their king doesn't talk much."

"Who do you think he is?"

"How on earth should I know?"

"You might have read something about it. You don't think they'd ever, I don't know, declare war on us?"

"They'd have an awful long way to come and pick a fight."

"Aye, you're right," I said, and tried to believe it. The Elsian minister's warning still haunted me, a sleeping dread that roused nameless fears in my heart. Nameless, and perhaps groundless, but that didn't stop me from worrying.

One week later, however, something happened that put our conversation and the fear it inspired quite out of my mind. Gwyn wrote to tell me that she was pregnant.

Over Leyda's giggles and Mari's speculations that she would

have a sickly, towheaded child, Papa agreed that I should do as Gwyn asked and accompany Madam Carlyle and Rya to visit her in Hunter's Forge.

Master Carlyle, I gathered, was not invited.

Several days later we set out in a hired coach, bearing our trunks and the best wishes of everyone from the Manor. Travel-sore and weary, we arrived in the village of Hunter's Forge just after sunset on the third day. The carriage came to a stop in front of an ivy-covered house at the edge of the village. Gwyn and her husband waited at the door, and only the sight of Gwyn's beaming face revived me enough to pay what amounted to a courteous greeting to Curdred. He bowed once before turning his attention to Madam Carlyle, intent on pretending I didn't exist.

After settling her mother and sister in their main guest room, Gwyn showed me to a tiny chamber under the eaves. "Oh, Aliza, you have no idea how glad I am to see you."

"Not as glad as I am to see you." My eyes flicked to her belly, where her pregnancy showed in the barest of curves beneath her dress. "How are you doing?"

"Well. Lady Catriona's physician is taking good care of us." She smiled. "As Wynce has said, living next to an obliging Daired *does* have its advantages."

"How are you doing with . . . other things?"

She sat on the edge of the bed. "I don't regret my decision, Aliza, if that's what you're asking. My family is safe. I have a home, a kind husband, and a child on the way. I'm content." She patted the mattress next to her. "How are things at the Manor? Tell me everything."

I sat, racking my brain for noteworthy news. "Honestly, there's nothing much to tell."

"The gryphons haven't tried to come back?"

"No, thank the gods. All right, let me see. Lord Merybourne paid off the loan from Lesser Eastwich last week, Henry officially took on Davy Martell as his apprentice, and Davy sang his first ballad at Spring Quarters. Henry was so proud. And—well, I've heard rumors that His Lordship might be looking for a new steward," I said. "Has your mother mentioned anything?" She nodded but didn't elaborate. "Your turn. Tell me more about Lady Catriona."

"You'll see for yourself soon enough," she said. "We're expected for dinner and a Sparring at Edan Rose tomorrow, so you'd better get some sleep."

I rose to unpack my trunk, but Gwyn surprised me with a fierce embrace.

"Thank you for coming."

"Oh, dearest," I said, returning her embrace. "You couldn't have kept me away."

CURDRED CARRIED ON PRETENDING I DIDN'T EXIST well into the next day, save for the hour before we were expected at Edan Rose. Sitting in the parlor with Madam Carlyle and Rya, I learned more of Gwyn's life in Hunter's Forge and what she thought of it, now untroubled by the threat of gryphons, banshees, valkyries, or any other sort of roving *Tekari*. No creature would dare attempt an attack within five leagues of Edan Rose, she told us.

"Are they afraid of Lady Catriona's ruthless hospitality?" I asked.

"Not Lady Catriona. Herreki."

"Who's Herreki?" Madam Carlyle asked, pulling Rya back from the hearth.

"Her dragon. *Ahla*-something-in-Eth-*Herreki*. She's the Drakaina of all Daired dragons."

"What's she like?" I asked.

"The Drakaina? I haven't met her yet. She usually has business with the Dragonsmoor eyries, but Wynce promised me she'll be here for dinner tonight."

A knock sounded at the door and Curdred poked his head in. "Darling, we really *should* begin getting ready," he told Gwyn, eyeing my plain frock in disapproval. His outfit, of course, would bear no competition. A waterfall of lemon silk cascaded from around his throat, the ends tucked beneath a waistcoat embroidered in ruby and amber thread. "We mustn't be late!"

Already frightened by her daughter's description of our soon-to-be host, Madam Carlyle swept Rya up and hurried to change. Less frightened but equally interested in meeting the Daired matriarch, I followed suit. At a quarter to six, the five of us bundled into the carriage Lady Catriona had sent for us, and at the stroke of six we pulled into the graveled drive of Edan Rose.

Instantly I repented of all the times I'd mocked Curdred for praising Lady Catriona's estate. If the house and grounds of Edan Rose couldn't inspire awe, nothing could. Two cottage-sized statues formed the gates to the main house: the left statue of Edan the Fireborn, the right of his dragon, Aur'eth the Flamespoken, sire of all Arlean dragons. Edan stood in salute, his sword raised to the sky as he and Aur'eth waited for the gods-sent phoenix that, according to the myth, would lead them to heaven. No one knew for certain what happened to the founder of Arle after he'd bound himself to the Flamespoken Sire and established Nan the Blind as the first queen in Edonarle. Whether he and Aur'eth actually did rise to take their place with the saints that day or whether they died like mortals none could say.

In any case, Edan Rose didn't seem to be the place to question the tale.

The house itself could've swallowed Merybourne Manor, Troll-hedge, and Little Dembley without thinking, and still have room for a dragon-sized Great Hall. Towers of reddish stone pricked the sky with their crenelated spires. Soft grass rolled underfoot, trim as a carpet, and one look at the steward who came out to meet us gave me a good idea what kept it that way. A scowl from her would scare even the most adventurous grass stem back into place. She introduced herself as Madam Kiery, told us Her Ladyship had a table prepared on the south lawn, and that if we'd be good enough to follow her, she'd be happy to show us to it.

Curdred didn't wait. He leapt ahead of Madam Kiery, effervescent in his eagerness to introduce Lady Catriona. Clutching Rya's hand, Madam Carlyle hurried after him. Gwyn and I came last at a slower pace.

"Nervous?" she asked.

"I'll let you know in a minute."

We rounded the corner of the house. Three figures reclined around a table set out on the lawn, their faces too distant to make out, but the silhouette of a dragon lounging behind the humans was unmistakable. I *knew* those pearly scales, that horned head, and that round, deep voice, now booming with dragonish laughter as we approached. *Akarra! But that means . . .*

Alastair Daired was here.

CHAPTER 14

AT THE GATES OF EDAN ROSE

"Well met, Miss Aliza!" Akarra said, her words resonating deep in my chest. "It's good to see you again."

From his place at the far end of the table, Daired stood and bowed, his expression fixed in a frown so fierce I wondered he didn't pull a muscle. "Miss Bentaine. Madam Curdred."

Across from Daired, a Rider with a crooked grin and an even crookeder nose leapt to his feet. "Alastair! You didn't mention you were friends of our guests."

"You *would* have known that if you'd been listening to a word I said just now." A woman with hair the color of old snow stepped forward from her seat at the head of the table. I tried not to stare. Red, shiny skin covered one side of her face, pulling her eyelid taut over her left eye. Rya gave a squeak of alarm, which her mother tried, frantically and without much success, to shush, but Lady Catriona didn't seem offended. She smiled at Rya. "Just an old scar, my dear. Nothing to be afraid of. Welcome to Edan Rose, Madam Carlyle, Miss Carlyle. And you too, Miss Aliza. I'm Lady Catriona Daired. Come, have a seat."

Over Curdred's expressions of rapture at the garden, the table settings, and even Lady Catriona's sword-and-gown ensemble, the young man with the crooked nose pulled out a chair next to him and motioned for me to sit. I took it gladly, as that was the farthest seat from Daired. "Thank you, sir. I'm afraid I didn't catch your name."

"Captain Edmund Daired. And that"—he gestured over his shoulder to where a wyvern with whitish scales sprawled on the lawn, snoring loudly—"is my dear friend and sister-in-arms, Whiteheart War-talon."

"Pleased to meet you both."

Whiteheart rolled over and muttered something in Vernish.

Captain Edmund laughed. "You must forgive her. It's a long flight from Upper Westhull, and we only just arrived this afternoon."

Before I could tell him that I didn't mind in the least, a low rumble shook the ground and a rush of wind swept the lighter items off the table. A shadow fell over the south lawn.

The Drakaina had arrived.

Herreki landed with the force of a small earthquake, claws the size of harvest scythes retracted so she didn't tear up the turf. With both wings extended over her head, Akarra bowed to the Drakaina and greeted her in Eth.

"Carlyle family, Miss Bentaine," Lady Catriona said, "allow me to introduce my companion-in-arms, *Ahla-Na-al She'gre-shal'an-Herreki*, She-Whose-Talons-Grasp-the-World, Drakaina to the House of Edan Daired."

I followed Gwyn's example and curtsied as Herreki strode over to the table. Larger than Akarra, her reddish-gold hide gouged with dozens of dreadful battle scars, I understood at once what Gwyn meant when she said that all creatures, *Tekari, Idar*, or otherwise, feared the Drakaina. Her hot yellow eyes licked over each of us in turn, yet she spoke civilly, welcoming us to Edan Rose in a voice that sent the wine dancing in our goblets, before growling to Akarra in Eth and springing once again into the air. With a dragonish sigh, Akarra flew after her.

"What's that all about?" Captain Edmund asked, shading his eyes to follow their flight into the gold-streaked sky.

"The Drakaina has a message from the eyries," Daired said.

"Don't mind them. Johns, bring the torches," Lady Catriona instructed the head servant. "Now, to dinner! We'll have to call Herreki and Akarra back here to warm our food if we don't get started."

A small army of serving maids in the golden dragon livery of House Daired descended on our table, laying out a feast to which even the Riders' banquet in Merybourne Manor couldn't compare. To my relief, there was no roast gryphon to be seen, though to be safe, I avoided the sizzling platter in front of Madam Carlyle, which looked suspiciously like braised valkyrie.

Lady Catriona at once turned her attention to Gwyn and the baby, leaving me free to learn more about Captain Edmund. He told me he was the second son of Lady Catriona's late brother Lord Rylan, who'd sent him into the army as punishment when his son chose to bond with a wyvern instead of a dragon.

Captain Edmund chuckled at my expression. "Surprising, isn't it? After all, what's a Daired without a dragon? But I've faced worse judgment for my decision, and so far I haven't regretted it. Whiteheart is a true friend, and I couldn't imagine a better comrade in battle."

"That's because you've never fought astride a dragon," his cousin said from across the table. With a sinuous *snick*, Daired drew a carving knife against a whetstone, ignoring Curdred's pointed remarks to no one in particular on how very *happy* he was to eat only vegetables.

"Did you hear that, Whiteheart?" Captain Edmund asked. "Are you going to defend our honor, or should I?"

"*Hrrrmph*. Remind me to disembowel him in the morning," came the muffled response from beneath her wing. Her Arlean had a Vernish lilt, with a hissing *s* and a slight trill on her *r*'s.

"I'm sure you're both brilliant warriors, Captain," I said. "Dragon or no dragon."

Captain Edmund shifted his chair closer to mine. "I'm glad you disagree with my cousin. In fact, while you're here, you must tell me what Alastair was like in Hart's Run."

I felt Daired's eyes on me, sharper than the knife in his hand. "He . . . did what he came to do," I said.

"Aha. In other words, he was dull as a spoon and ill-humored as the High Cantor," Captain Edmund said with a grin. "That sounds about right."

The carving knife sank into the haunch of beef. "I can hear you."

"I'm aware of that."

Instead of answering, Daired picked up his plate and, to the astonishment of everyone except Rya, who was busy hiding her asparagus beneath her napkin, and Curdred, who was in a state of great agitation because of the drop of wine he'd spilled on his sleeve, moved around the table and sat at the empty place on my left.

"Something wrong with the other chair?" I asked.

"Edmund's favorite pastime is finding new ways to annoy me."

Captain Edmund winked. "A childhood amusement I've never been able to give up."

"So I'll sit here," Daired said, stabbing the beef on his plate as if it'd done him some great personal wrong, "as long as it takes to defend myself."

"He worries I'm going to set about dispelling the mysterious air he cultivates among new acquaintances," the captain said. "Quite correctly, I'm afraid."

"Miss Bentaine isn't a new acquaintance."

"But I'm sure she has entirely too high an opinion of you anyway."

"Oh, you needn't worry, Captain," I said. "My opinion of your cousin is exactly where it needs to be."

"Good gods, Alastair, what's this? Your brooding charm and talent for dismembering *Tekari* has *not* left her in awe? You've failed your duties as a Rider, sir. I'm ashamed of you."

"I don't take contracts with the intent of impressing *nakla*," Daired said.

"No, we all know you take them in order to enjoy the delights of the countryside," the captain said. "From what I heard in Edonarle, Miss Aliza, Alastair was involved in at least two hobgoblin uprisings. Is that true?"

It might've been the torchlight, or the last rays of the setting sun, but I was reasonably sure Daired reddened. "The garden-folk will certainly remember him," I said.

"Fond memories?"

"Muddy ones."

Captain Edmund laughed. "Yes, Brysney mentioned that."

"He—you know Master Brysney?"

"Of course. The Brysneys are old friends of Alastair's. Cedric and his sister stayed at our city house during the muster." He leaned toward me. "Truth be told, I think Whiteheart fancied Brysney's wyvern."

From behind him came a murmured reply from Whiteheart that, though it was in Vernish, sounded rather like denial. I only half listened. Hearing the name *Brysney* shattered a dam inside me, and questions came flooding out. Confusion and curiosity gave them shape; two-thirds of a glass of excellent wine gave them a voice.

"Since you both saw so much of him during the winter, perhaps you could help me solve a mystery," I said when the captain finished teasing his wyvern. "My sister sent several letters to Brysney over the winter. Do either of you happen to know if he received them?"

The captain stroked his chin. "Letters? Well, if anyone would know it'd be Alastair. He spent half the muster in the Royal Post-house."

I turned to Daired. "Sir?"

"I don't know anything about your sister's letters."

"Do you know if he wrote to her?"

"I have no idea."

"*That's* hard to believe," his cousin said. "Brysney sent most of his post with you."

A furrow appeared between Daired's eyebrows, and refilling his wine glass suddenly took all his concentration. "He never sent anything with me."

"Then what were you doing at the posthouse so often?"

"I had business with my steward."

"Twice a day?"

"And my sister."

"Every day?"

"She needed advice."

"Are you going to finish carving the beef, Alastair, or should I come over and do it for you?" Lady Catriona's voice rang out over Curdred's tale of a harrowing escape from an unsavory cravatier in Hallowsdean. "And what's this about Julienna?"

Daired stood and took up the carving knife again. "Nothing, Aunt."

"Does that girl still insist on using two swords? I've told her so many times how impractical that is on the battlefield," Lady Catriona said, half to Daired and half to Gwyn, who sat next to her. "All style, no substance. She'll never sign a contract if she doesn't practice more with her longsword." She pointed a fork at Daired. "Make sure you pass that along."

"I always do."

"Yes, well, make sure it sticks this time. Now, Madam Curdred, tell me more about this craving you've had for pickled beets. My physician finds it fascinating."

I turned my attention to Daired to save Gwyn the embarrassment of answering Lady Catriona's question for the whole table. My curiosity was far from satisfied, and the way he avoided my gaze sent doubt creeping into my heart. "Are you sure Brysney didn't get Anjey's letters, Master Daired? Any of them?"

"As I said, Miss Bentaine, I had other things to do in Edonarle than keep track of Cedric's correspondence. I have no idea what letters he did or didn't get."

He didn't meet my eye as he said it.

No. A new thought flitted through my head like a gale of nixies, dark and just as troublesome. *He couldn't have interfered. He wouldn't. Unless . . . no.* Daired might be an arrogant cad, but whatever else he was, he was loyal to his fellow Riders. He'd never do something to hurt his friend, no matter how much he might disapprove of a Rider's relationship with a *nakla.*

And yet . . .

My internal debate raged through the remaining courses. Again and again I revisited the scene in our parlor. Brysney had promised to write to Anjey every day, and I'd sooner believe the sun rose in the west and dragons breathed ice than he would've broken that promise. Which meant that something—or someone—had prevented their letters from reaching each other.

And I had the horrible feeling that that someone was sitting next to me.

"Miss Aliza, is something wrong? You haven't touched your dessert," the captain said.

"It's . . . nothing. Just full."

"Right you are. Enough of food and talk. Time for entertainment! What do you think, Alastair?" he said in a louder voice, interrupting Curdred's monologue to Madam Carlyle on the merits of double-knotted cravats and Lady Catriona's advice to Gwyn on the best methods of breast-feeding. At the captain's suggestion both Gwyn and her mother looked up in relief. "Shall we settle once and for all which of us is the better fighter?"

"Of course! I nearly forgot," Lady Catriona said. "I'd promised Madam Curdred a Sparring. Johns, some more torches for the Sparring ring. Come now, Madam Carlyle, Miss Rya. My nephews are some of the finest swordsmen in the country," she said. "It'll be a sight you won't soon forget."

A flight of steps connected the upper lawn to a sunken Sparring ring surrounded by stone benches. My mind numb, I sat next to Gwyn as Daired and the captain engaged each other. I watched the Sparring, but what I saw was Anjey's face, tearstained and hopeless, trying to hide how deeply Brysney's silence hurt her. Back and forth I reeled between disbelief, shock, and anger, even as the men locked swords in a clash of bright steel and bloodred pommel stone.

Anger won.

The more I thought of it, the more convinced I became. I didn't know exactly how he'd interfered, and I no longer cared; he'd done it *somehow*, and that was all that mattered. Daired bore the responsibility for the anguish Anjey had felt with every stroke of her unanswered pen, for months of quiet heartbreak and disappointment, and for that I could never forgive him.

The Sparring came to a dissatisfying end minutes later, with Daired's blade across the captain's throat. Curdred cheered, Gwyn and her mother clapped politely, and Lady Catriona pointed out three or four things both her nephews had done wrong. Daired ignored them all. He sheathed his sword and met my poison-arrow gaze, a satisfied smirk on his lips.

Never before had I hated anyone as much as I hated him in that moment.

I laid a hand on Gwyn's shoulder. "If you don't mind, I think I'd like to go home."

"Is everything all right?"

"I'm not feeling well."

At Gwyn's request Lady Catriona was happy to release us for the evening. We left Edan Rose followed by Captain Edmund's fond farewell and Lady Catriona's promise to invite us over again soon. Daired alone did not see us to the gate.

MY DREAMS THAT NIGHT WERE SHAPELESS AND TROU-bled. I woke twice, heart pounding, head aching, palms sweating, nursing an anger too big for my sleeping mind to hold. Dawn couldn't dispel it, but the morning light brought back the calm I'd lost, and as I dressed, I came to a decision. The damage was done; Daired had made sure of that, but until I could figure out how to reverse it, I'd not waste my energy hating him. He didn't deserve even that.

At breakfast I apologized to Madam Carlyle and Curdred for cutting their evening at Edan Rose short. Distracted by her task of convincing Rya that the Curdreds' porridge was as good as any she'd had at the Manor, Madam Carlyle said not to mention it.

Curdred blinked for a full three seconds before answering me, in shock that I'd broken our agreed-upon silence. "I *do* hope you're not still, er, unwell, Miss Aliza?"

"Much better, thank you. Lady Catriona serves stronger wine

than I'm used to. Speaking of which, do you think you'll be able to get that stain out from your sleeve?"

Curdred beamed, and Gwyn gave me a curious look as he lamented how challenging it would be to restore his suit to its usual state of perfection, but how kind I was to inquire after his efforts. I smiled into my teacup. Curdred had made a home for my friend, and she wasn't unhappy. After all, I told myself, there were worse things in the world than well-dressed men with a habit of overemphasizing.

Halfway through breakfast the maid slipped in and handed Gwyn a letter. "Just come from the Rose, ma'am. Messenger says 'e'll wait for your answer."

Gwyn broke the dragon crest in gold sealing wax. "Ah. It looks as if we have plans for the afternoon," she said when she finished reading the note. "Aliza, Mother, Rya, Lady Catriona has invited us to tea with her at Edan Rose."

"How *splendid*," Curdred said as Gwyn ordered notepaper and ink from the maid to pen our acceptance. "Didn't I tell you, Madam Carlyle? Her Ladyship is a woman of her word. Now, you must tell me what you think of the interior when you return. I'm quite sure you've never seen the like!"

CURDRED WAS RIGHT. INSIDE AND OUT, EDAN ROSE WAS a house without equal. We took tea in a room twice the size of the Great Hall at Merybourne Manor, our circle of sofas and tea tables clustered in the corner closest to the fireplace. Close, but not too close. Without the chain mail fire screen in place, we wouldn't have needed much effort to toast our scones. Nor, for that matter, our faces. Twin dragons curled over the mantelpiece, mouths open in stony snarl, as if encouraging the flames to greater and entirely unnecessary ferocity.

Lady Catriona made and served the tea herself. Madam Kiery hovered in the background, her expression fixed in the peeved resignation of a servant watching her master do her job. We were the only guests. I wouldn't have minded if Captain Edmund joined us, but my resolution not to waste energy hating Daired was much easier kept when he wasn't actually in the room.

"I hope you're feeling better, Miss Aliza," Lady Catriona said as she handed me a cup.

"I am, thank you."

"Edmund was sad to see you go. Thought you might've been disappointed with his Sparring performance. Truth be told, I wouldn't blame you if you were. The boy spars like a berserker on a bad day. He has no *discipline*."

"I thought they both fought remarkably well," Gwyn said.

Lady Catriona shrugged. "Alastair did all right, but there's always room for improvement. Miss Rya, would you like some tea?"

Rya looked at her mother. Madam Carlyle patted her head. "Go ahead. Tell Her Ladyship what you'd like."

"Sweet apple tart and honeycomb cake, please!"

Lady Catriona laughed as her mother turned red. "Not before lunch," Madam Carlyle said, but Lady Catriona didn't listen. She cut a sliver of tart and honeycomb cake and handed them to Rya with a beneficent smile.

"What's the harm? There you are, my dear."

"You're so kind to invite us here, Lady Catriona," I said before Gwyn's mother worked up her courage to scold Rya and Her Ladyship in the same breath. "Edan Rose is stunning."

"Yes, it is rather lovely, isn't it?" she said, looking around the room with an air of abstracted fondness. "Lots of room for one old lady."

"Do you have any children?"

There was a long silence, broken only by the gentle *clink* of her teacup settling in its saucer. "Not anymore," Lady Catriona said at last, staring into the fire.

"I'm—"

"Oh!" Gwyn gasped. "Mother, quick, come feel! The baby's moving."

Lady Catriona beamed as Gwyn placed her mother's hand on her stomach, my question and the memories it'd stirred forgotten, or at least buried far enough to hide from strangers. Talk of Gwyn's child and childbirth filled the next half hour, during which I sipped my tea, nibbled on a slice of honeycomb cake, and prayed I'd be able to unhear some of the things Lady Catriona, Madam Carlyle, and even Gwyn discussed with astonishing frankness. In that little circle, the lines between Riders and *nakla* dissolved; motherhood made all women equal.

Once we were out of tea and cake, my gaze wandered to the rest of the room. Dragons ran rampant everywhere: bracing themselves against the wall as sconces, or embroidered in the cushions, or carved as a motif along the wainscoting. I followed the panels to the far side of the room, where the dragons stopped their wooden march at a door large enough to admit a young dragon, a full-grown wyvern, or three Lord Merybournes. It stood ajar. Beyond I could just make out the rich reds and deep forest-greens of a magnificent tapestry, shimmering in sunlight streaming from unseen windows.

"Miss Aliza, Alastair tells me you're an artist."

The name jolted me back to the conversation, his as much as mine. "Oh, aye. I mean, I draw a little," I said, wondering what else he'd said about me. He wouldn't have wasted his breath in compliments.

"You must have good taste. I see you've already spotted the gallery."

"Do you have many paintings?"

"More than I know what to do with, and tapestries and statues and Thell knows what else. My father fancied himself a connoisseur and had no concept of the rubbish heap."

I snuck another glance.

Lady Catriona chuckled. "Good gods, girl, go look! You needn't feel like a hostage here. Madam Curdred, have you seen the gallery yet?"

Gwyn shook her head but declined any desire to go exploring, one hand still resting on her belly. Madam Carlyle also said she was happy to stay put, although with a stuffed and sticky-fingered Rya fast asleep on her shoulder, she didn't have much choice. I thanked Lady Catriona and headed for the gallery.

It suffered from no lack of paintings. From watercolor studies of a dragon's eye to a sweeping pastoral of Edan Rose and grounds, frames large and small covered the walls, but I could only manage a cursory glance, for the tapestry on the eastern wall bore no competition. The shining figures of Edan Daired and his dragon, Aur'eth, charged across the cloth, leading a band of Arlean settlers into battle against the Oldkind. Each drop of sweat stood out on Edan's forehead, and I felt the tension in his muscles as he drew his sword. His battle cry filled my ears, strong and proud and terrible, even in the silence of imagination. Aur'eth bared his teeth at the foe, his neck arched, ready to flame. I could feel waves of heat rolling from his open mouth. The woven sun gilded the spikes along his back with threads of silver silk, fine as a spider's web. I had to lean close to make sure it was truly a tapestry and not a painting.

Somewhere behind me, a door shut with a soft *thud*. Boots clicked against the floor.

And stopped dead. "What are *you* doing here?"

I closed my eyes and took a deep breath, flirting with the idea that Daired might go away if I pretended not to hear him.

"Miss Bentaine?"

I opened my eyes and turned around. "Good afternoon, Master Daired."

"What . . . why are you here?"

"Your aunt invited us over for tea."

"In the gallery?"

"She said I could look around."

"You didn't—I thought . . ." His voice wavered and he fell silent.

Curiosity buried any anger lingering from the night before. An impressive feat, as there was a lot to bury, but seeing Daired flustered came with a certain degree of satisfaction. No doubt a *nakla* intrusion within the hallowed halls of Edan Rose had caught him off guard. I couldn't let the opportunity go to waste. "Tell me, do you know who made this?" I asked, running my fingers through the fringe at the bottom of the tapestry.

"No."

"Shame. It's beautiful."

"Why are you really here?"

For the same reason I gave thirty seconds ago, halfwit. "This morning Lady Catriona sent a note to Gwyn, asking if we wanted to join her for—"

"You know that's not what I meant."

"I'm not sure I ever know what you mean, Master Daired."

"You . . ." he began, then seemed to change his mind. "Do you like Edan Rose?"

"It's magnificent."

"Then you do like it?"

"There's not much to dislike."

He came closer. "But there is some?"

"Well, I haven't seen a single hobgoblin."

A smile flashed on his lips, brief, bright, and entirely unexpected. "My aunt's gardener knows his business. How long are you staying with your friend?"

"A few more days; maybe longer, if Gwyn wants. And speaking of Gwyn, I should go. They'll be wondering what happened to me. Good afternoon."

"Miss Bentaine." He reached for my arm, his grip gentle but unyielding as steel. "Wait."

"Sir?"

"Listen to me. As long as you're here, don't say anything to my aunt about the Witherwood. Please. She can't know you rode Akarra."

"I wasn't planning on telling her," I said, scowling at his hand on my wrist.

He released me. "Make sure you don't."

For a moment we stood staring at each other—me waiting for an explanation, him waiting for gods only knew what. "Master Daired, you can't say something like that and then expect me *not* to ask why."

"My aunt would tell Herreki."

"And what would she do?"

"For both our sakes, Miss Bentaine, pray we never find out."

CHAPTER 15

STEEL, STONE, AND SMITHCRAFT

A tinkle of china and the murmur of voices from the adjoining room broke the spell of his ominous words, and without so much as a "good afternoon," Daired retreated through the opposite door.

We didn't stay long after I rejoined the others, as Gwyn was struck by a sudden bout of nausea. With murmurs of sympathy and a prescription of hot ginger tea, Lady Catriona saw us to the front hall, where she wished Madam Carlyle, Rya, and me safe travels back to Hart's Run.

Curdred was gone when we returned to the house. The maid said he'd been called away on magisterial business and expected to miss dinner—with, as she said, his *profoundest* regrets. We didn't see him again until the next morning, where he did his best to make up for his absence.

"It really is *such* a pleasure to have you ladies visit. It's a shame you can't stay longer," he said over his breakfast of orange marmalade, the slice of toast beneath it small enough to be an afterthought. "I was just saying to Gwyn last night, 'Darling, I can't remember the last time our home played host to someone without a beard down to—'"

Gwyn touched his hand. "You're rabbit-trailing, dear."

"Oh, goodness, you're quite right. Well, Gwyn and I were wondering if you would like to accompany us on a tour of the village today. It's unfortunate you'll see it *after* visiting Edan Rose, of course, since the comparison isn't worth mentioning, but Forgemaster Orordrin agreed to give us a special demonstration this afternoon. It's one we'll not want to miss!"

Madam Carlyle, no doubt relieved at the idea of a full day's entertainment for her youngest daughter, leapt at the offer, and I, eager to see the famous Forgemaster, had no objections. After breakfast we started out.

Hunter's Forge spread along the bottom of a valley, the east side divided from the west by a narrow river. Houses rose almost three stories over the banks, some tilting this way, some that way, and some built so far out over the river they met their counterparts on the opposite side, making odd-looking bridges every few blocks. Curdred led us down the street on the west bank, bowing and smiling at all the townspeople who greeted him. Gwyn walked at his side, her arm through his.

"Miss Aliza, look down this street here," he said, pointing with his cane as we approached an alley near the smithies. "Do you see that gray building? You'll never believe it, but Edan Daired *himself* laid the cornerstone for that house. In good light you can still see the dragon crest etched in the mortar. In fact, we just might be—Master Hamden, whatever's the matter?"

A red-faced man with a bull neck and the burns of a baker stormed out of the shop next to us, holding a boy by the scruff of the neck. The man flushed even redder when he saw Curdred. "Beggin' your pardon, Magistrate. Ladies," he said, touching four fingers to his forehead. "Don't mean to cause a fuss, but Jeoffy's been snitching. I won't hold with that kind a behavior in my shop." He shoved the boy off the stoop. "Go find other work, if you can. You're not welcome back here."

Curdred caught the lad by the arm before he fell. "Jeoffy, I'm appalled! After all Master Hamden has done for you?"

"Picked you up out o' the gutter, boy!" Hamden said. "And this is the thanks I get?"

Jeoffy stared at the ground and said nothing. Tears left streaks in the fine layer of flour that covered his face.

"Magistrate, I want him locked up and made an example of. Don't want my other apprentices ratting out my secret ingredients to those *sludge slingers* on Savory Row."

Curdred released Jeoffy. "Sorry, Master Hamden. What?"

"The boy went off and blabbed the recipe for my banshee brown bread all up and down the market this morning."

"You must forgive me; I'm afraid I misunderstood you. The lad hasn't *stolen* anything?"

"Well, no," Hamden growled. "But he has been snitching on my secrets!"

"I din't know it was secret, Magistrate, I swear!" Jeoffy sniffed. "Bill and me just got talking and he asked about the bread, so I told him. I weren't gonna lie." He clasped his hands. "Please, sir, don't send me to prison! I got five little brothers that need taking care of."

Curdred patted Jeoffy's head. "Don't worry, my lad. Master Hamden, you can't sack the boy for talking to his friends."

"I can when he talks about *my business!*"

"No, sir, I'm afraid you can't," Curdred said. "He hasn't broken any laws. In fact, I'd say you suffer only from having an honest young man working for you, which is a *great* deal more than I can say for some shopkeepers in this town."

Hamden looked away, his face now nearly crimson.

Out of the corner of my eye I saw Gwyn smile.

Curdred pulled a handkerchief from his pocket and brushed some flour from his sleeve. "And if you wish to keep your recipes secret, might I take the liberty of suggesting you *mention* this fact to your apprentices? It'll save you ever so much trouble in the future."

"Fine," Hamden grunted. "Come along, boy. There's work here needs doing."

Curdred took Gwyn's arm again. "Oh, and, Master Hamden? *Do* consider investing in a good apron." He eyed the oil splatters and crusts of dried flour that covered the baker's shirtfront. "Madam Hamden will thank you on laundry day."

He and Gwyn strolled on ahead, followed by Madam Carlyle and Rya. I stumbled along after them. We might've passed all four wonders of the world, a harbinger of rabid valkyries, and King Harrold himself dressed in motley; I wouldn't have noticed. For all its charms, the town couldn't compare to this new Curdred. *Who is this man, and what has he done with the joke that was Wynce Curdred?*

Little things between him and Gwyn now leapt to my attention, things I'd failed to notice for the simple reason that I'd never thought to look for them. The way she leaned into him to hear his comments on the perfectly *dreadful* flower arrangements in the milliner's window, nodding when he suggested they send her some lilacs from their garden to remedy the catastrophe. Her smile when he paused at the sweetmeat vendor to buy her a bit of marzipan. His occasional glances at her growing belly, his expression wavering among wonder, terror, and excitement.

I misjudged him. The realization struck me like a troll's fist to the gut. Gwyn had called herself content, and for her sake I'd been willing to give Curdred the benefit of the doubt. I'd never imagined he'd be capable of erasing those doubts altogether.

"Mama, look at that!" Rya cried as we set foot on the opposite bank. She pointed to the cavern yawning at the end of the street. Smoke spilled from its stony mouth. "Master Wynce, is the hill on fire?"

"Good gracious, my dear, of course not! That's the smithy of Forgemaster Orordrin."

"Can we take a closer look?"

"Why, you're in luck today, Miss Rya. That is *precisely* where we're headed."

Carved out of the hillside on the edge of town, the great smithies of the forge-wights formed the burning heart of Hunter's Forge. The gate to Orordrin's smithy was a masterwork of wrought-iron artistry, depicting the diamond sigil of the Fourfold God. At the topmost point, Odei's lightning bolt pierced a circle of iron. To the left and right were the leaf and shield of Janna and Mikla. The empty circle of Thell sat at the bottom of the diamond, and crossed in the center were the hammers of the forge-wights.

A muscular young man stood guarding the gate, his arms bare beneath a leather apron, every inch of exposed skin glistening with sweat. "Morning, Magistrate," he said, pulling open the gate. "Forgemaster's expecting you. Morning, Madam Curdred. Ma'am, miss, and . . . little miss." He grinned as Rya looked up at him in awe.

Heat washed over us as we passed from sunlight to firelight, accompanied by the clank of iron tools and a curious smell. Curious, and curiously familiar. I wrinkled my nose, trying to identify it. Like metal, but not quite metallic, it smelled spicy and dangerous and exciting, like the first wind of an approaching thunderstorm.

Minutes later, I remembered. It was the scent of dragonfire.

Mixed with the cacophony of hammers and the roar of the forge fires was a bubbling sound from deep in the cavern. I asked the gate-keeper, who'd appointed himself our guide, what it was. He tapped the grate on the floor in front of us with his boot. Beneath I could see the dark glint of rushing water.

"There's a spring coming up from the heart of the hill, miss. We've got channels running beneath the forge to keep water close at hand. You'll want to mind your step," he said as we crossed the grate.

Deeper in the smithy, dozens of young men and women bustled around worktables, dressed in heavy aprons like the gatekeeper. Many wore leather hoods pulled down over their eyes. Some polished weapons, from swords and daggers to battle-axes and silver spear-tips. Some labored with hammer and pincers over the scroll-work on wrought-iron lamps, laughing and swearing in turn as their neighbors bumped their elbows. Others weighed out copper ingots, noting the impurities and passing off suitable ones to a foreman. Absorbed in their work, not one of the smith-hands acknowledged our group as we passed them.

"Goodness, how big is this place?" Madam Carlyle asked. "They must've hollowed out the whole hill!"

I craned my neck to make out the roof high above. Firelight danced along the rocky surface, reflected from the deepest part of the forge, where furnace mouths gaped like glowing eyes. A trickle of sweat rolled down the back of my neck. "Aye, I think they did."

The gatekeeper paused near the largest of the furnace doors, taking care to stand well to the side. "Forgemaster?" he called into the flames. "Magistrate Curdred and his guests have arrived."

Curdred patted Gwyn's hand. "Isn't this exciting, darling? I've never met a forge-wight while he's *working!*"

Forge-wight. My mind flashed back to the gallery at the Manor House, and the blue flames dancing on the palm of the Faceless Minister, the forge-wight who was no longer a *Shani*. Despite the heat, an icy hand gripped my insides.

The doorkeeper frowned at our group. "Er, you all might want to stand back."

We took a few steps away from the forge.

"Maybe a bit more."

We were nearly against the far wall before the man was satisfied. "Ready, Forgemaster!"

"Thank you, Jerremy." The unseen Orordrin's voice shook the forge. "You may return to your post. I'm expecting another guest shortly."

Jerremy bowed. "Been a pleasure, ladies. Magistrate. Enjoy your visit," he said, and left us to face the mysterious Forgemaster.

"Now then, let me have a look at you."

With a crackle and a roar, the furnace strode out to meet us.

Rya shrieked. Madam Carlyle went pale and squeezed her daughter's hand. I shielded my eyes from the brightness and the stinging heat. The forge-wight Orordrin wasn't merely the master of the forge; he *was* the forge. Standing twice as tall as the tallest human, he filled the mouth of the furnace, a statue of living fire. Without its master, the forge flames inside died down to coals.

"You must pardon my attire, Magistrate Curdred. It is difficult to keep track of time in the fire, and I didn't have a chance to change. If you will give me a minute, I can remedy that."

"Yes, of course!" Curdred said. "Orordrin is the oldest of our forge-wights," he explained as the Forgemaster moved to the spring at the far end of the cavern, leaving glowing footprints in the stone. "My clerk thinks he's been alive for *hundreds* of years. They say he forged the sword that Saint Marten used to slay the sphinx of the Silent Citadel," he said, raising his voice to be heard over the explosion of steam from the spring. "Can you *imagine?*"

White clouds billowed from the surface of the water as the

Forgemaster emerged, the armor enclosing his fiery flesh now dull and cool. Seams of light glowed between the chinks of the metal plates. He spoke from beneath a mask of steel, smooth and unmarked save for two eye slits, each burning with a hot blue flame. "There," he said. "Easier on human eyes, I think. Will you introduce your guests, Magistrate Curdred?"

"Ah, indeed. I don't believe you've met my wife. Gwyndolyn Curdred, Forgemaster Orordrin." Gwyn curtsied. "This is Gwyn's mother, Madam Carlyle, her sister, Rya, and her dear friend Aliza Bentaine, all of Merybourne Manor, Hart's Run."

"An honor, ladies Carlyle. You are welcome in my forge."

"P-pleasure, sir," Madam Carlyle stammered.

"Hello!" Rya said, standing on her tiptoes to see as much of the forge-wight's face as she could. "Aren't you hot under there?"

"Rya!" Gwyn and Madam Carlyle said together.

Orordrin laughed, his mirth rolling over us like liquid sunlight, hot and bright and heartening. The coldness I'd felt at the memory of the Faceless Minister vanished. "Yes indeed, dear one. If I weren't, all my fires would go out and I would be of little value to the world."

"Really?"

"For instance, I wouldn't be able to do this."

From the nearest worktable he picked up half a copper ingot. The metal grew bright as he poured his heat into it, and with deft movements the Forgemaster pulled and pinched the softened copper, shaping it into the form of a phoenix in flight, trailing copper feathers as fine and delicate as real ones. Rya clapped as he held out the statuette, but he pulled it away before she could reach for it.

"I'm afraid it needs time to cool. Kepharous!" he bellowed, and as if by magic a smaller forge-wight appeared at his side, also masked and armor-clad. Orordrin handed him the copper phoenix. "Have the apprentices take care of this. It will go home with the little girl."

The forge-wight Kepharous ducked his head and disappeared again.

Orordrin turned to me. "Miss Bentaine. I'm pleased to meet you too."

"As am I, sir. Your forge is incredible."

"I'm glad you think so. You and I have something in common, I believe," he said, the glowing slits of his mask fixed on my face. More sweat gathered on my brow. "Odei's spark also burns in your spirit. You create too, do you not?"

"Oh, Miss Aliza, he's found you out!" Curdred said. "Gwyn always did say you were quite the artist."

I blushed. "It's nothing compared to your work, Forgemaster."

"Small or large, no honest art is unimportant." A man coughed behind us and Orordrin looked over my shoulder. "Yes, Jerremy?"

I turned to see the gatekeeper, clasping his hands in front of him and looking apologetic. Daired stood next to him, his sword in hand. Daired's eyes darted from Curdred to Gwyn to Madam Carlyle, settling at last on me with something akin to panic.

"Sorry, Forgemaster," Jerremy said. "He's a bit early."

"I didn't realize you had guests, Forgemaster," Daired said. "I'll come back later."

"No, young man, I'd like you to stay. You had a most intriguing request, and I thought it might serve as an illuminating demonstration for—"

"No!"

"I'm sorry?"

Sweat dotted Daired's forehead. "I mean, no thank you. I'll wait."

"It's no trouble," Orordrin said. "It's been so long since I've held the heartstone blade. I should like to get reacquainted."

Daired answered him in Eth.

The steel mask gave no hint as to Orordrin's expression, but I felt the shiver of heat as he turned to look at me, his gaze as blistering as it was puzzling. After a moment he replied in the same language.

Madam Carlyle leaned over to me. "What are they saying?"

"I have no idea," I whispered, though I wished I did.

"Very well, Master Daired. I understand," Orordrin said in Arlean. "My apologies, friends. It seems Master Daired must postpone his errand, which means I cannot show you what I wished today. For that and for the brevity of our visit, I am truly sorry, but the fire calls me back. I must return to my forge. Jeremy will show you what other small wonders my smithy has to offer." The Forgemaster bowed. "Family Curdred, Family Carlyle, and Miss Bentaine, may you always burn brightly. Farewell," he said.

As his foot crossed the threshold of the furnace the embers roared into flame, and like a soul returning to its body, his entrance breathed life into the forge again.

"Small wonders, eh?" Jeremy said, scratching his head. "I suppose he means the Mirror Room. It's this way." He glanced at Daired. "Will we see you another time, sir?"

"No, I'll stay," Daired said. "I've never been up to the Mirror Room."

Keeping my thoughts about that to myself took a real effort of will. Twice he'd tested my resolve now; another encounter like this and I'd not be able to maintain the façade that courtesy demanded. Still, if avoidance wasn't an option, perhaps I could do something better. Perhaps I could get the truth out of him.

Putting on my brightest, falsest smile, I fell into step with Daired as Jeremy took us on a meandering circuit of the forge, pointing out interesting features to a rapt Curdred and a slightly less rapt Madam Carlyle and her daughters. "I confess I'm surprised to see you in Hunter's Forge, Master Daired. I didn't think the muster would end for at least another fortnight."

"The king let most of us go last week."

"Master Brysney too?"

The corner of his mouth turned up in the hint of a smile. "In a manner of speaking."

"What does that mean?"

"The king decided it's time to honor Cedric and Charis for their slaying of the Lesser Lindworm. He's holding a banquet for them on the first day of summer."

My heart sank. Summer was almost two months away. "If that's the case, do you know when he's coming back to Hart's Run?" *Or if he is?* I thought, but dared not say aloud.

Like a flame starved for air, Daired's smile flickered and vanished. "Why so interested in Cedric, Miss Bentaine?"

"Just curious." Ahead of us Jerremy and the others disappeared up the curve of a winding stone staircase near the apprentices' worktables. I started after them, Daired hard on my heels. "The Manorfolk miss having a Rider at North Fields. We're all anxious to know when we'll see him again."

"You should ease their minds. The king's asked them both to stay on at Edonarle, or at least until after the banquet."

"Why?"

"There's a lot to plan."

I frowned. "I'd think that's what the royal stewards were for."

"Clearly you've never met the king."

The darkly self-satisfied way he said it brought me to a standstill. If Brysney stayed in Edonarle, it meant even more time away from Anjey. *But without Daired to interfere, their letters might still make it through*, I told myself, clinging to what hope I could, *if Brysney hasn't given up.* I knew Anjey hadn't.

Daired noticed I'd stopped. "Don't you think we should join the others, Miss Bentaine? Or are you not interested in the Mirror Room?"

I kept climbing.

A moment later he caught up. "What does your friend think of Hunter's Forge?"

"She likes it." *Blast, how long is this staircase?* "Lady Catriona's been very welcoming."

"She thinks Curdred made a good choice."

"He did."

"Your friend should be proud. It's not easy to impress a Daired."

Yes, I know. Over the past few months you've made that abundantly clear. "Perhaps your aunt has better judgment than most."

"Aliza—Miss Bentaine. Wait. When I asked you in Hart's Run if you wanted to take up the blade, that was poor judgment on my part, I admit. You're no warrior. You're not made for that life." He paused on the steps as his eyes sought mine. "But you can't want to stay at Merybourne Manor forever."

"Excuse me?"

"I—never mind. There's something I need to see to. Good afternoon." Turning on his heel, he disappeared around the curve of the stairs.

Odd.

At the top, I found Jerremy showing my friends around a small room, the walls covered with the retired blades and armor of famous Arlean warriors, each piece polished to a mirror sheen. Seeing the war-scythes, greatswords, and maces glittering on every surface, I wondered why Daired hadn't climbed the last few steps.

Of any of us, he would've appreciated these deadly furnishings the most.

After admiring it all we returned to the forge floor, and as Jerremy couldn't think of anything else noteworthy to show us, he led us to the gate. Kepharous waited there with the cooled phoenix statuette. He presented it to Rya with a bow, and though he didn't speak, the flames hidden by his steel mask danced with the merry twinkle of a smile. Over her daughter's delighted squeals, Madam Carlyle thanked him, and both Jerremy and the forge-wight bid us farewell.

CHAPTER 16

A FINE PROSPECT

The next day I had to myself. A messenger at break-fast called Curdred away on urgent magisterial business, and Rya woke up with a headache and sore throat, which bound Madam Carlyle to her bedside for the better part of the morning. At first I planned to pick through Curdred's library and settle down with a book, but with Gwyn's encouragement I packed up my drawing supplies and headed outdoors instead.

"Not that I wouldn't love to have you around," she said after breakfast, "but Mother told me we need to *talk*." Her eyebrow shot up at the last word, and I understood. In their father and husband's absence, the Carlyle women had much to discuss. "There's a lovely view of Edan Rose from the hill at the end of the lane," she said. "You should see it."

By the time I reached the clearing at the top of the hill, I was panting and sweaty. Bark sloughed from the trunk as I sank down against an obliging sycamore to catch my breath. Gwyn was right; before me spread an incomparable vista of Edan Rose, its brown-stone towers glowing golden in the late-morning sun. I unpacked my parchment and charcoals and set to work capturing its splendor.

A few hours passed before I sat back to ease my cramping fingers. Sketches littered the ground around me. I set my charcoals aside, leaned back against the trunk, and closed my eyes, stretching my hand and taking pleasure in the play of shadows and sunlight that danced across my face. A robin chirped. The breeze rustled the boughs over my head. From somewhere nearby came a soft metallic *clink*.

My eyes flew open. Daired stood at the edge of the clearing. "Miss Bentaine?"

"Master Daired! Wh-what are you doing here?"

"Your friend told me you'd come up this way."

I scrambled to my feet. "Is something wrong at the house? Is Gwyn all right?"

"What?" he said, as if he'd forgotten who Gwyn was. "Yes, of course. Everyone's fine."

"Oh. Um, good."

He came forward and stopped in front of me, resting one hand on the hilt of his sword. Awkward silence stretched between us, giving me time to notice that he'd shaved, and the surcoat he wore over his armor was more richly embroidered than any I'd ever seen. In the dappled light, the silk shimmered crimson and copper. A golden dragon clasp secured his high collar at the throat, and draped across his shoulders was a magnificent direwolf pelt, blacker than a starless night.

He looked profoundly uncomfortable in it.

"Is there, ah, anything I can do for you?" I said at last.

"You—" His eyes fell to the parchments scattered on the grass. "What are you drawing?"

"Edan Rose."

"Ah." He made a motion as if to look over his shoulder and compare the likeness, but abandoned it halfway through, staring instead at the tree trunk behind me. "It's a good view."

"It's lovely. Master Daired, is something the matter? Or did you really climb up here just to talk about art?"

"No, I didn't." He paced to the nearest tree, leaned against it, changed his mind, and returned to the first place he'd stood. At last he clasped his hands behind his back, fixing me with the most peculiar look. "I can't do this anymore."

"Do what?"

"I've been in many battles in my lifetime. I've slain monsters by the hundreds and won more victories than I can count, but against this there's no defense. From the moment we met I tried fighting it—gods, I've tried. Nothing works. I thought I'd be safe at the other end of the country, but the minute I heard you were coming to Edan Rose I flew here as fast as Akarra would take me."

Words drifted through my mind, sound and reasonable questions as to what he meant, why he was telling me, and, most importantly, whether or not he was intoxicated, but my tongue refused to cooperate.

"I'm a Rider and you're a *nakla*," Daired said. "There's nothing we have in common. There's nothing we *should* have in common. Your birth, your bloodline, all of it—it's beneath me. I know all of that, and it hasn't changed a thing. I've lost, Aliza. You've defeated me."

He reached for the pouch at his hip, and it was then I noticed his sword hilt. The pommel gem was missing.

"If this is a battle, then I surrender." From the pouch he withdrew a bloodred stone in a golden brooch. "This is the heartstone I cut from the Broodmother Crone of Cloven Cairn on the darkest day in my memory, and nothing save Akarra means more to me than what this stone represents."

I opened my mouth, closed it, frowned, and gave up. "I don't understand."

"I love you."

The wind tossed the branches above the three of us: me, Daired, and the words that hung like a living thing between us, too enormous for me to begin making sense of them.

He knelt. "Aliza Bentaine, say you'll bear my heartstone. Say you'll be my wife."

The final word roused me out of my stupor, and gathering my scattered wits, I replied the only way I could. "I . . . can't."

For a few seconds he stared at me, his expression wavering between shock and disbelief. After a small eternity he stood. "Is that it? That's all you're going to say?"

"There's nothing else to say."

"If you're going to toss me aside so casually, I'm at least entitled to know why."

"I don't *want* to marry you."

"Why not? You'll marry someday, and there's no one remotely worthy of you in that little Manor of yours." His fist tightened around the brooch. "The Daired name isn't something you turn down lightly."

"It's not your name I'm refusing to marry, sir. Just you."

"I don't understand."

"What's not to understand? I never liked you, Master Daired, and as far as I can tell, you've never liked me much either."

"I just told you I love you!"

"You don't even know me!"

"I know enough—"

"*Enough?* Aye, my birth and bloodline being 'beneath you' summed it up pretty well."

He reddened. "I didn't mean it like that."

"Oh, you meant to insult me in a kind and considerate way?"

"What did you want me to say, Aliza? Pretend I'm not a Daired and you're not a *nakla*? Even for you I can't deny who and what I am."

"I never asked you to. I never sought your affections, and frankly, you haven't given me a single good reason to return them. From the moment we met you've been nothing but rude and unpleasant to me and the people I care about, and Rider or not, if that's how you show love, then forgive me for saying I want nothing to do with it."

"Tell me how I've treated you with any less respect than you deserve."

"We can start with the fact that you introduced yourself by kicking one of my friends across the garden."

Daired grunted and turned away. "It was a *hobgoblin*, and I didn't see it! Are you really rejecting me because I tripped over some garden vermin a few months ago?"

"*His* name is Tobble, and that's exactly what I'm talking about! You have no regard for anything smaller or weaker than yourself, *nakla* included. I could never be your wife."

"This is what you really think of me?"

"You haven't given me any other choice."

"And nothing I can say will change your mind?"

Anger and frustration burst like a dam inside me, and words spilled out, harsher words than I might've intended if I'd been able to think straight. "How could it? Even if I did like you, after what you did to Anjey and Brysney, what makes you think *anything* you say would make me want to be your wife?"

"I don't know what you're talking about."

"Anjey wrote to Brysney every week since he left Hart's Run, but she never heard a word from him. *You* made sure of that."

"What?"

"You intercepted their letters during the muster in Edonarle, didn't you?"

"For Thell's sake, Aliza, I already told you I don't know anything about their letters!"

The blood rose in my cheeks. "Then look me in the eye and tell me what kept him from writing to her, because I know it wasn't indifference."

"I didn't touch their letters . . . but yes, if you must know, I did warn Cedric to keep away from your sister. I told him he'd be better off without her." He paced the grass in front of me, his step jerky and agitated, ignoring my open mouthed outrage. "Cedric has fallen in love more times than I can count, and it's never ended well. Your sister was nothing new: a poor, pretty girl who understands Cedric's weakness and uses it to her advantage." He stopped. "Oh, even you must admit it. She practically threw herself at him!"

Only the distance between us kept me from slapping him. "How *dare* you talk about Anjey that way? She loves Brysney, and every day they've been apart has been a dagger in her heart. She never cared about his fortune, or his fame." A new thought struck me. "And you're such a hypocrite! You'd turn Brysney away from my sister because she's a poor *nakla*, but you'd marry me without a second thought?"

"You think I *didn't* put any thought into this, Aliza?" he said. "You think I didn't struggle for months trying to forget you? Trying not to fall in love with you?" He passed a hand over his forehead. "I did. It didn't work, and in any case, I knew you didn't care about money. I made sure of it."

"I don't remember you asking me."

"I didn't need to. You turned down the extra dragonbacks for Lord Merybourne's horse."

The scene in my father's study came to mind and I remembered Daired's smile as I handed back the purse. It only made me angrier. "I turned them down because it was the right thing to do, not because I wanted to impress you!"

"I didn't—"

"And what you did to Anjey isn't the only thing I have against you. You were cruel to *nakla* long before we met, and nothing you've shown me suggests that's about to change."

He went still. Eerily, frighteningly still.

"What do you mean, *before we met*? Who've you been talking to?"

"Someone who knows you better than you'd like to admit. I've heard one side of the story, Master Daired. Now it's your turn. Why did Wydrick leave House Pendragon?"

Like a lit match dropped into a keg of black powder, Daired exploded. Roaring something in Eth, he flung the heartstone brooch away and closed the distance between us, eyes burning hot and furious not inches from mine. I held my ground.

"How did he take you in, Aliza?" he said, his voice hoarse. "Tell me! I need to know he's a man and not a ghost sent to torture me, because that's what it feels like. Do you know what I did to keep him away from you? Do you have *any* idea? I arranged the muster to get that man out of Hart's Run. A thousand Riders and countless Rangers from all over the country—all that, and for what? I find out that he's already filled your head and your heart with his lies. What more do I have to do?"

"*You* were responsible for the muster?"

"I—yes."

"How?"

Breathing hard, he retreated a few steps. "You mentioned once that it'd be a mistake to make an enemy of House Daired. The king's of the same opinion. He'll not deny me a favor. Aliza, he isn't . . ."

He spat a curse through clenched teeth. "I should've cut off that Ranger's head when I had the chance."

I drew myself up to my full height. "Thank you, Master Daired. You've convinced me. You are, without a doubt, the last man on earth I'd ever marry. Good afternoon, *sir*."

Without waiting for an answer I turned on my heel and headed down the hill.

Only when I passed the Curdreds' garden gate did I realize I was crying.

BY THE TIME I REACHED THE HOUSE, I HAD A POUNDING headache. Between the tears, the anger, and the outright shock, it was all I could do to take Gwyn aside and tell her I was unwell. She didn't ask me to explain. I latched the door behind me and collapsed on the bed in a sniffling, undignified heap.

After a few minutes I roused myself. As the shock wore off, so did the tears, leaving me with burning eyes, a damp coverlet, and a head that, while not clear, was at least a little less muddled.

"If this is a battle, then I surrender . . . I love you."

He loved me? Alastair Daired loved *me*? I couldn't believe it. *He doesn't even know me! How could he love me and say those kinds of things about me and my family?*

Doubt and outrage swirled inside me, a tempest I didn't have the least hope of calming on my own. I sat up, then slumped down again, imagining a letter to Anjey. *Hello, dearest, hope you're well. Remember that Rider no one liked much, the one I danced with at the banquet—Alastair Daired? Wouldn't you know he's been infatuated with me all these months? I know! He wants me to be his wife. Fancy that. I said no. Gwyn is doing well. Growing like an enchanted pumpkin; she'll be showing in earnest soon. Love always, Aliza.*

I shook my head. A story like that should be told face-to-face, if told at all, and to tell it to others I'd first have to believe it myself. Again and again I turned his words over in my mind.

"*I surrender . . . I love you.*"

The more I thought of it, the more confused I became, and not feeling up to the task of facing the Curdreds and the Carlyles, I did the only sensible thing left to me. Not bothering to change out of my day dress, I curled up under my coverlet and fell into an exhausted, dreamless sleep.

THE SUN WAS LOW IN THE SKY WHEN I WOKE. GUILT AND weariness warred within me as I lay there, wondering if Gwyn would forgive me if I decided to stay in bed for the rest of the evening. Guilt won. Pretending everything was normal was the only way to cope until I figured out what I felt, so I showed up to dinner and did my best to act interested in Curdred's tale of the town clerk's lost spectacles.

It didn't take long for Gwyn to see through the act. Later that night she walked with me back to my room. "Is everything all right, Aliza?"

I considered telling her what had happened, but Madam Carlyle's voice drifted up the stairs and I changed my mind. "I'm fine. My time of month," I said, hating myself for lying.

"Oh, bad luck. Do let me know if you need anything."

I didn't sleep well. For hours I drifted in and out of a restless haze, both mind and body unable to settle. The chirrup of birdsong outside my window finally urged me out of bed, and in the predawn dark I dressed and slipped outside. I needed to walk, to move, to do *something*, and the sketches and charcoals I'd left on the hilltop yesterday gave me an excuse to leave the house. The dew would've ruined the parchments, but those sticks of charcoal were some of the best I owned and I wanted them back.

The morning breeze was crisp and the air misty as I started down the lane. A farmer driving his goats to pasture on the outskirts of town waved hello as he passed; otherwise I reached the foot of the hill unobserved. I hoped my luck would hold until I returned.

It didn't.

Akarra sat on the ridge overlooking Edan Rose.

CHAPTER 17

AKARRA'S TALE

She sat motionless, a dark silhouette against the dawn-streaked sky, wings folded along her back and her tail wrapped around the sycamore trunk. My sketching materials were nowhere to be seen.

"Good morning, Aliza."

"What are you doing here?"

"I thought you might come back for your drawing things." She turned and looked at me. "Alastair told me what happened yesterday."

My survival instincts screamed at me to run, to get as far away from her as possible and contemplate the wisdom of angering a Daired dragon from a safe distance. Some other instinct—stubbornness, or perhaps suicidal curiosity—rooted me to the spot. So I faced her and did the bravest thing I could think of. I told her the truth. "You can't change my mind, Akarra. I won't marry him."

"I didn't come to change your mind, Aliza. Your heart is your own business. I only came to set the record straight. You accused Alastair of some serious things yesterday, and I'll not have him slandered unjustly."

"Oh." Wearier than I had any right to be, I sank onto a nearby stump. "Did you know?"

"That he'd fallen in love with you? I'd suspected partiality on his side for a while now, but I didn't realize what he intended until I saw his heartstone missing. He had Orordrin make the brooch the night before last. I *wish* Alastair had told me, and not just for his sake. It might have spared you both pain." She heaved a bellows' sigh. "Then again, maybe not. He can be rather pigheaded."

"Did you know he arranged the muster?"

"Yes."

A breeze ruffled the leaves, damp and chilly. "Why did he do it?"

"He told you. He wanted to protect you."

Protect me, aye. At what cost? "What about the people I love? Did he think what it might do to them?" The words came out with more bitterness than I intended. "Do you know what my sister went through because of the muster?"

"Ah. That." Akarra hung her head. "While regrettable in retrospect, I promise that his interference between Cedric and your sister was motivated by the best intentions. As fond as I am of Cedric, he is a man of rather . . . easy affections."

"Maybe, but my sister's not. She loved him. She *still* loves him."

"That was poor judgment on Alastair's part, and I'm sorry I condoned it. We'd seen Cedric hurt too deeply to risk it again, and your sister does resemble the last woman he loved," she said. "You look surprised."

Surprised was too weak a word. Thinking of Brysney with anyone but Anjey felt awful, like seeing someone's head on the wrong body.

"Who was she?"

"A *nakla* from Hallowsdean. Rosamund was beautiful, charming, witty, and she had no heart. A month before their wedding, Cedric found her in bed with a stable lad. He broke off their engagement and fled to Edonarle, and gods know why, that woman followed him. I think she just liked to watch men suffer. Cedric took Lord Merybourne's contract to get out of Edonarle, to someplace Rosamund wouldn't follow. Of course, then he met Anjey, and—well, you know the rest. When Alastair warned Cedric off, I promise he only wanted to protect him from further heartbreak."

The knowledge that Brysney had not only loved but also been engaged to another woman shook me, but in some small corner of my heart, I began to understand Daired's motivation. With roles reversed I'd have done the same to protect Anjey, and done it without a second thought. "That still doesn't explain the missing letters."

"Alastair told me what you said. Aliza, he never touched Cedric's letters, or your sister's. I'm prepared to swear it."

Though it left a whole new mystery to solve, I believed her. "Then what about—?"

"Yes?"

I eyed her talons. I'd misjudged Daired's feelings regarding Wydrick; to do the same with Akarra might have more serious consequences.

"I think I know what you're going to ask," Akarra said. "I promise you have nothing to fear from me, and you never will. So ask."

"What about Master Wydrick?"

Her wings drooped. "*Wydrick*. Oh, Aliza, I wish I could convey to you just how devastated Alastair was when he realized that man had gotten to you. What did he tell you?"

"Wydrick said Daired killed Wydrick's mother's horse as a warning not to compete in the Rider trials."

She snorted, a short, fiery blast that singed the grass beneath her. "A barefaced lie."

And I'd believed it. I'd been happy *to believe it.* "What did happen?"

"Wydrick was the bastard son of a Ranger friend of Lord Erran Daired's. When the boy's mother died, Lord Erran took Wydrick in as his ward. I watched him grow up with Alastair." She lowered her head so that she looked me in the eye. "Do you know how we choose our Riders?"

"I thought only Riders knew."

Her lip curled in a smile. "I'm sure they like to think so, but it's no great secret. When we're young, all dragons memorize tales of the Flamespoken Sire, who first bound dragons and humans through his *khela* Edan Daired. Carrying on Aur'eth's legacy and finding a *khela* of our own is our greatest honor. When the children of House Daired reach the age of binding, they make the journey to the Standing Stones at the foot of the Dragonsmoor Mountains and call a dragon. Our kind watch Family Daired from the egg," she explained. "If we like what we see, when that boy or girl reaches the Standing Stones and calls for a dragon to face them, we'll answer their challenge."

"Is that where you fight?"

"No, Aliza. That is where we *dance*. You've seen Alastair in the Sparring ring, haven't you? The principle is the same. No man or woman can hide their true character in the heat of battle. If they are cruel or needlessly violent, we see it. If they are reckless, we see it. If they are brave or merciful, we see that too. If the Sparring ends with each impressed with the other, the bond is struck, the oath is sworn, and we are companions for life. If not, we go our separate ways. Alastair tells me it's a dreadful shame for a Daired to be rejected by a dragon."

"I take it that's what happened to Wydrick."

The growl reverberated in her throat, and the leaves on the lowest bough trembled. "Young Wydrick was the most insolent, spoiled, lazy brute ever to disgrace the halls of House Pendragon.

He could, however, be quite charming when he put his mind to it, and from the way he insinuated himself into your acquaintance my guess is that's not changed."

I decided not to answer that.

"For some reason only the gods know, Lord Erran loved him. Wydrick and Alastair trained together as children, and Alastair even used to speak of the times when they were something like friends. When the time came for their first solitary venture, Lord Erran allowed them to go together against a pack of direwolves. A dangerous and unusual assignment, but Wydrick begged Lord Erran for the chance, and Alastair—whom I'm afraid has never been one to pass up a challenge—had no objections."

"I heard about that. I didn't know Wydrick was involved."

"Because he wasn't." Akarra's horned eyebrows drew together into the dragonish equivalent of a frown. "Together they might have had a chance, but the coward abandoned Alastair just as the wolves attacked. Nearly got him killed. That was the day Alastair met Charis and Cedric, and Family Daired owes the Brysneys greatly for their valor. Wydrick, on the other hand, returned to House Pendragon in disgrace. Lord Erran stripped him of his weapons and armor and sent him back to start his training afresh. Alastair and I were bound soon after that, and we didn't hear much of Wydrick until after Lord Erran died." She gave me a sidelong look. "Has Alastair ever spoken of his sister, Aliza?"

"He mentioned her once at North Fields." *Gianna? Julia?*

"Julienna is several years younger than Alastair, and Lord Erran allowed Wydrick to train alongside her after his demotion. The summer following Lord Erran's death, Alastair and I returned early from our rounds of Arle to be with Julienna when she called a dragon. On our way to the house, we saw Wydrick battling a dragonet among the Standing Stones."

"I thought the dragons didn't like him."

"Most didn't, but Mar'esh has the kindest heart of any *kes-ah* I've ever known, and I think he pitied Wydrick, standing there with no one to answer his call. Alastair and I hid and watched the fight. Kind he might've been, but a fool he was not, and Mar'esh soon saw what kind of man Wydrick was. He wanted nothing more to do with him, so he disarmed him and flew back to the eyries. Alastair and I returned to the house and I didn't think much of it, except to rejoice that Wydrick had been put in his place. The next day was Julienna's trial. Any ideas who answered her call?"

"Mar'esh?"

"Yes. And he liked her very much. Alastair told me he'd never seen a pair so evenly matched."

"Weren't you there?"

She closed her eyes. "No, and not a day has passed that I don't regret my absence. The Nestmothers had called me on important business to the eyries that morning. I didn't want to leave Alastair and Julienna alone with Wydrick, but the Drakaina was visiting and I couldn't refuse. After his defeat, Wydrick put on a contrite air and begged until Alastair was too embarrassed to deny him. I think Alastair planned to send him away from Dragonsmoor afterward." A second growl rumbled in her chest as she opened her eyes. "He never got the chance. Wydrick struck the moment Mar'esh declared Julienna his *khela*." She extended one wing above my head, and I stared at the parchment-thin hide spanning the slender wingbones. Veins pulsed just under the skin. "He maimed Mar'esh from shoulder to wingtip for choosing Julienna over him.

"If I'd been there he wouldn't have lived past the sheathing of his sword. Alastair wanted to kill him too, but Mar'esh was losing blood too quickly and Julienna couldn't stanch the wound by herself. Alastair chose to save his sister's dragon instead of avenging him," she said, her voice quiet. "He told me what you said about him being cruel to *nakla*, Aliza. I won't deny it; Alastair does take pride in his position as a Daired and a Rider, and he doesn't apologize for it, but that doesn't make him a monster. The standard of House Daired—do you know what it is?"

"No."

"*Tey iskaros.* 'We serve.' His life is sworn in the protection of the weak and defenseless. Despite what you think, he honors Mikla before Thell, like all true Riders."

A weight settled on my shoulders with each new facet of Daired Akarra's story unveiled. It took me a moment to name it. *Guilt.* "What happened to Mar'esh?"

This time when she spoke I could feel the dry lick of dragonfire in her words. "He lived, but he'll never fly. In those first few weeks he wanted to die. Julienna was the one who kept him alive. He told her to leave him, to find another dragon to claim her as *khela*, but she wouldn't." Akarra scanned the distant spires of Edan Rose, where Whiteheart danced above the battlements. "I don't think I need to describe to you Alastair's reaction to this."

The curses, the burning black eyes, the whisper that cut like a knife—they all made sense now. "No, you don't."

"Now that you know the truth, I trust you'll not judge Alastair too harshly."

"I feel as if I can't judge him at all."

Akarra straightened and stretched both wings, sending me to my feet to get out of the way. "Well, you have my permission to judge him a *little*. I may not be human, Aliza, but I am female. If he told me what he told you, even I'll admit he was far from charming."

"Honestly, I don't know what to think about yesterday."

"You're an intelligent woman. I trust you can come to your own conclusions." She stepped up to the rocky outcrop that ran along the ridge of the hill. "But whatever you decide, know this: for all his faults, my Alastair does care for you." With that she dove off the ridge, leaving me alone with the ponderous weight of my thoughts.

AS SOON AS I KNEW MY LEGS WOULD CARRY ME WITH-out trembling, I returned to the Curdreds' house. Akarra's story had taken the teeth out of my anger, and without them I felt naked, defenseless. My prejudices had been shattered to the core, and I hadn't the slightest idea where to start picking up the pieces, or even if I should try.

For days I put on a convincing show of normalcy for the Curdreds and the Carlyles, but inside I turned over Akarra's words in a fruitless attempt to discover how I felt. On the night before we were to leave Hunter's Forge, I at last confessed the whole thing to Gwyn.

She took it better than I expected. "If it's any consolation, I know how you feel. You and I both misjudged the men in our lives." Seeing my look, she smiled. "Aye, I know what you're going to say. Wynce can be a bit flamboyant, but his heart is in the right place, and I've never doubted he cares for us. No child could have a more doting father, and I . . ." She rested a hand on her belly and looked away. "Well, one of us should."

"I'm glad for you, Gwyn. For all three of you," I said, and it was the truth.

THE NEXT MORNING, GWYN KNOCKED AT MY DOOR AS I finished packing my trunk. She entered with a flushed face and a gleam in her eyes. "Aliza, Wynce found this in our letterbox."

She handed me a thick envelope, and my insides turned to water as I traced the dragon crest stamped in gold sealing wax. I sank onto the edge of the bed and broke the seal. Several loose scraps of parchment and a few sticks of charcoal fell onto my lap. In a daze I swept them aside.

"Do you need a moment?"

"If you wouldn't mind," I said. She slipped out after making me promise I'd share anything important with her. I read.

Aliza,

You'll forgive me for neglecting to deliver this letter in person, but in accordance with the sentiments you made so clear at our last encounter, I would not presume to trespass on your time any more than absolutely necessary. I ask only that you would do me the honor of reading this letter and know that I have now done all in my power to resolve the conflicts that stand between us.

Akarra told me that she visited you and explained my family's connection to that accursed Ranger. I trust she did the story justice. If I frightened you with my reaction the other day then I apologize, but now at least you may understand the reasons behind it. A dragon is the heart and soul of a Daired, and the sky is our birthright. He took all that away from my sister. Even Mar'esh begged her to leave him when he learned he would never fly again, but she refused. Julienna may be the noblest Daired of our family, for even when she knew what it meant, she would not break her oath to her dragon. Nevertheless, she's suffered for her choice in a thousand small ways that only a brother could see, and it is that which sustains what I hope you will acknowledge is my just rage toward that man.

He was a deceiver and a trickster from my earliest memory of our childhood together, and I can say without hesitation that he would think no more of harming you than he did of maiming Mar'esh if he realized you knew of his infamous past. Aliza, if you

will not have me, then at least take my advice: if the Rangers ever
return to Hart's Run, stay far away from him.

In the matter of your sister, however, I fear I can only reiterate
what I told you earlier: I did not touch Cedric or Miss Bentaine's
letters, nor do I know who did. If my advice to Cedric caused your
sister pain then I apologize, but know that in the protection of a
friend I could do no less.

I do not expect a reply to any of this, nor do I imagine we will
ever see each other again. Consider this only my warning, my
apology, and my farewell.

I wish you every happiness the gods can bestow.

Alastair

I folded the letter and collected the fallen scraps of parchment
and charcoal, then tossed them aside, smoothed out the letter, and
read it again. And again as I hurried down to catch breakfast. And
once more after we'd bundled ourselves into the carriage and said
our goodbyes to the Curdreds. At the fourth reading, Madam Carlyle ventured to ask about the letter's contents, and with that I came
back to myself. Brushing it off as news from home, I tucked it into
my pocket and stared out the window as the countryside rolled by.
There would be time enough to pore over it when we returned to
Hart's Run.

We stayed the night at the little inn we'd visited on our way to
Hunter's Forge. The innkeeper gave us a lively rendition of the local
gossip as he served us dinner in the common room. According to
him there'd been a troop of Rangers visiting just days before, bringing news from the wider world. My ears pricked up in alarm at the
word *Ranger,* only to relax as he named the Selkie's Keep Regiment.

"Tremors in the ground all through them northern hills, the

capt'n tells me," the innkeeper said as he ladled out our stew. "'No good'll come of that,' I tells the capt'n. ''Tis a sign o' trouble, you mark my words!'"

Whether or not the captain of the Rangers had marked the innkeeper's words remained a mystery, for before he could continue the next table over called him away. We finished our meal and went to bed soon afterward.

I was relieved no one brought up the letter again.

THE THIRD DAY FROM HUNTER'S FORGE DAWNED DARK and overcast as we set out from another wayside inn, which in everything but name was indistinguishable from the first. Thunder in the east grumbled the promise of rain. By noon it kept its promise. A light drizzle blurred the outlines of the surrounding hills into watercolor streaks of gray, white, and green. With a whimper, Rya buried her face in her mother's shoulder each time it thundered, clutching the phoenix statuette close to her heart.

"There's nothing to be afraid of, love," Madam Carlyle said, stroking Rya's hair.

There was only one other passenger in the carriage, an older woman called Freya Trenowyth, who we'd picked up at the second inn. She had the booming voice, gray robes, and authoritative air of a cantor of the Fourfold Faith, and told us she was returning to her abbey in Lesser Eastwich.

She leaned closer to Rya. "Do you know what causes thunder, young lady?"

"Papa says it happens when the air gets angry."

"Tush. Would you be surprised to know we're listening to the saints feasting in heaven?"

A rare smile softened Madam Carlyle's features as her daughter pondered this with all the gravity of a child. "Do they drop lots of things?" Rya asked.

"Good gracious, no!" Trenowyth said. "You see, the food is simply so delicious, they can't help but give a great big belch every once in a while. Here, I'll show you. Listen carefully."

Rya waited with bated breath for the next roll of thunder.

"Ah!" The cantor threw up her hands. "There. That was Edan the Fireborn."

Another peal of thunder sounded overhead, louder than the first, and even I jumped a little. Rya clapped her hands in delight. "Who was that? Was that Saint Ellia?"

"Heavens, no, child. Saint Ellia is much too well-mannered to belch. By the tenor, I'd say that was Saint Marten."

"Meanwhile, the Fourfold God starts to wonder if they should raise the standards for sainthood," Madam Carlyle said, and winked at Trenowyth. "They'd—"

A third *crack* shook the carriage.

"Was that Saint Marten again?" Rya asked. "He must be eating an awful lot."

I wiped the condensation from my window. A sea of green-tinged mist met my gaze. "I don't think that's thunder."

The carriage lurched and skidded to a halt.

"What's going on?" Madam Carlyle asked, clutching Rya closer to her.

Trenowyth opened her door and peered out. "What's wrong, coachma—oh, good gods, will you look at that?" She sat back in her seat. "Hope none of you were in a hurry."

I looked out. The road ahead of us had disappeared beneath a small mountain of boulders. The carriage swayed, and with a rumble like distant thunder, a stone the size of a cow tumbled from the hilltop to our left. One of the horses screamed and reared as the boulder crashed into the road a bowshot from our front wheels.

"Steady, old girl! Steady! No getting through this way, ladies." The coachman's voice drifted down to us, pinched with worry. "Soon as I get these horses turned about we'll start for the southern road into Hart's Run."

"Blast it all if I sit here while he does that," Trenowyth said. "Young lady, you look like you could keep your calm around jittery animals," she said. "Aliza, isn't it? What say you and I go help the man?"

Even with all three of us, it took a quarter hour to maneuver the frightened horses to a place in the road wide enough to turn the carriage around. By the time we'd finished, I was wet through and muddy as a newborn hobgoblin. Trenowyth clapped me on the back as we bundled inside.

"You've a steady hand with the beasts, Miss Aliza. It's a good thing they weren't any faster though, or we—" She broke off at a look from Madam Carlyle. "We wouldn't get to enjoy each other's company for quite so long."

"Did you see what caused it?" Madam Carlyle asked. "Was it a mudslide?"

"Must've been." Trenowyth smiled at Rya, who looked close to tears. "Now, Miss Carlyle, tell me more about these forge-wights you met. I want to know everything."

The coachman whipped the horses away from the blocked road as fast as he dared. I watched the trees rush by as Trenowyth endeavored to take Rya's mind off our close encounter. My fingers traced the folded letter in my pocket. I tried not to think of the innkeeper's comments, and of the sleeping dread they stirred inside me.

"'Tis a sign o' trouble, you mark my words!"

THE COACHMAN DROPPED THE CARLYLES AND ME OFF AT the Manor House just before sunset, or what would have been sunset on the other side of the clouds. Trenowyth waved goodbye, telling us to visit her sometime in Lesser Eastwich.

Anjey met us at the front door. "What on earth happened to you?" she asked, seeing the state of my dress. "We were expecting you hours ago."

"What *didn't* happen to us? Help me with this trunk and I'll tell you all about it."

Together we carried my luggage back to our rooms. As I changed, I told Anjey about our adventure on the road.

"How odd," she said. "Henry said the same thing's happening up near Harborough Hatch and Eastwich."

"Have you felt anything on the Manor?"

"No, nothing at all. It's been awfully quiet in general, with you and Gwyn gone." Her expression clouded. "Too much time to think."

"Anjey," I said, tremors and mudslides forgotten, "I saw Daired at Edan Rose."

"Really?"

"He—"

"Was Cedric with him?"

"No."

Anjey pulled out a pile of crumpled laundry from my trunk and threw it on the bed. "Too bad. I'm sure he missed a lovely time."

The careless way she said it broke my heart. "The king's holding a feast for him and Charis on the first day of summer. He has to stay until then. After that, I'm sure he'll be back."

"He can go or stay wherever he likes," she said, folding my clothes as though her sanity depended on it. "Obviously there's nothing here worth coming back to."

"Anjey, he didn't get your letters."

The dress in her hands fell onto the bed. "What?"

"Your letters. Daired said they never got through to him; I don't know how. But I promise Brysney hasn't forgotten you."

"Are you sure?"

"I've never been surer. He loves you, Anjey. Don't give up."

Hope and confusion warred in her eyes as she stared at me. After a minute she picked up the fallen dress and shook it out. "How . . . how's Gwyn doing?"

"She's well. She's changed."

"In a good way?"

"Better than I expected."

"I'm sure Master Curdred's made it his business to see her done up in the most fashionable maternity gowns he can procure," she said, and smiled.

I returned the smile, but couldn't maintain it for long. *Sooner or later I'll have to tell her.* I took a deep breath. "Anjey, something else happened at Hunter's Forge." And quietly, hesitantly, I told her everything, from Daired's proposal to the letter left in Curdred's letterbox.

When I finished she let out a low whistle. "He *loved* you? Right from the start?"

"So he says."

"He was so unpleasant!"

"True. He also wasn't the complete cad we—the cad *I*—painted him as," I said. "As for Wydrick, he's worse than I could've ever imagined."

"Shouldn't we tell Papa? Or His Lordship? Or *someone*? What if the Rangers come back?"

"No! No, you mustn't say a word. Wydrick will want to keep his history with the Daireds a secret, and if we know nothing we're no threat to him. We're safest if we keep quiet. Please, Anjey. Promise you won't say anything."

"Fine, but he shouldn't be running around Arle a free man. He deserves the gallows."

"I think so too, but there's nothing we can do now."

"No, I suppose not." She reached for my hand. "Now tell me, Aliza. How do *you* feel?"

"About Daired? I don't know."

She raised an eyebrow.

"Honest! I don't. He may be a better man than I first thought, but that doesn't change the fact that he's a Rider and I'm—not." I took the stack of folded undershifts from her arms. "And it doesn't matter. Odds are I'll never see him again."

I didn't admit—not to Anjey, not even to myself—what that made me feel. Alastair Daired was gone from my life.

It was time to move on.

CHAPTER 18

THE DANGERS OF LISTENING TO ONE'S AUNT

Summer arrived in all its sweaty, sticky glory. The children of the Manor spent most days paddling around the River Meryle, shouting and splashing each other with all their might. Lord Merybourne said they had to make up for the fun they had sacrificed when the gryphons ruled, and even encouraged the adults to join them in their play. Many did. In fact, of all the Manor-folk, only one avoided the general merriment. Leyda, who would've once leapt at any opportunity for mischief and excitement, stayed indoors.

At first it didn't worry me. After all, I could imagine worse pastimes than her sudden attachment to the Manor library. Mama and Papa didn't think anything of it, and even Anjey didn't seem bothered by the change.

"So? She's reading. I'd rather that than have her running around flinging mud balls at the stableboys," Anjey had said. "Don't worry about her, Aliza."

So I tried. One week after Midsummer Quarters, I lost my patience.

It began at breakfast. Papa brought a letter to the table. "Any guess who sent this, girls?"

Anjey looked up, the name *Cedric* forming on her lips. Papa shook his head. After what I'd told her about their letters, she'd continued writing with renewed hope of hearing from him, or even better, of seeing him again, but as yet there'd been no word.

"Gwyn?" I ventured.

"Guess again."

Mama sighed. "Oh, for heaven's sake, Robart! Just tell them."

"Uncle Gregory and Aunt Lissabeth. They're coming to visit." All of us brightened at the news, even Anjey. We'd not seen our aunt and uncle from Edonarle in years. "Only for a night, unfortunately," Papa said. "They have urgent business in Lambsley."

"Is everything all right?" Anjey asked.

"Depends on who you ask. They're going to see Great-aunt Essie."

"*Ugh.* Why on earth would they do that?" Leyda asked, pushing her eggs around her plate. Aunt Lissa's hometown of Lambsley was four days' ride northwest of Hart's Run, right on the borders of Dragonsmoor, and our aunt made no secret that she and her mother weren't on the best of terms. As Aunt Lissa said, Essie had never forgiven her daughter for running away with the family gardener. "The old hag hasn't apologized, has she?"

"As close as she's ever going to get to it, I'm afraid. Gregory says she's ill. She asked for his help."

"She must be *very* ill," I said.

"Fellfever. They left Edonarle just after posting this letter, so they should be here tomorrow or the next day. Gregory said they'll stay the night and head for Lambsley in the morning. He thinks he might need help with his herbal draughts, Aliza. They'd like you to go with them."

I thought about it. The idea of another journey over rough country roads didn't thrill me, but I longed for a change. As Anjey had said, the quiet life of the Manor left far too much time to think. "Aye, Papa, I'd love to go."

A fork clattered to the floor and Leyda bent to pick it up. "Of course you would."

"What's that, dear?" Mama asked.

"Of course Aliza gets to go. Why should the rest of us have any fun?"

"She'll be boiling sick rags and scrounging for feverfew on the moors," Papa said. "I'd hardly call that fun."

"It's more fun than anything that'll ever happen *here*." Leyda shoved her chair back. "Sorry, Papa, I'm not hungry anymore."

"Leyda?" Papa said, but she'd already rushed out of the room.

I excused myself and followed her.

It didn't take long to find her hideaway. The Manor library filled a long gallery above the Great Hall and rarely received visitors. Beams of sunlight slanted down on the sagging shelves, illuminating books filled with fading ink and silverfish. Leyda sat hunched on the window seat overlooking the front courtyard, surrounded by journals, scraps of letter paper, a half-filled inkwell, and two or three tea saucers, each covered in crumbs.

She wiped her nose on her sleeve and looked out the window as the door creaked open. "Go away."

"No." I sat next to her. "Something's wrong, and I'm not leaving until you tell me what it is. Come on, Leyda, talk to me. I'm worried about you."

"Don't be."

My eyes fell to the scraps of paper scattered on the cushion in front of her. Several looked like the beginnings of letters, and I caught the name *Tristan* on one of them before Leyda swept them out of sight. Her cheeks flamed crimson. "Is this about a boy?"

"No."

"Leyda."

"Not like *that*. He's a friend. From, um, Trollhedge. It's just . . . he has such an exciting life. He tells me about all his adventures, and all I can think of is how I'm stuck here on the Manor." She nudged the book with her toe, *Tales of the Seven Saints* printed across its spine. "All I can do is read about the great things everyone *else* does. Even you and Anjey have adventures. A handsome Rider saves Anjey from a gryphon attack. You run off to Hunter's Forge and have who knows what kind of fun, and now you're going north with Aunt and Uncle. You're always doing something interesting, Aliza." She wiped her nose again. "I'm always the Bentaine girl who gets left behind."

"What about Mari?"

"Mari doesn't *want* an adventure! She's the one who wants to read the stories everybody else writes. If she stays at the Manor for the rest of her life, she'll be happy. Not me."

"Dearest, you're only sixteen. You have plenty of time for all sorts of adventures." I tucked a stray strand of hair behind her ear, tilting her chin up so she met my eyes. "And if an adventure doesn't come to you, you should go and make one for yourself."

"You think so?"

"Absolutely. You don't need anyone else's permission to go do something worthwhile. Just don't mope around in the meantime."

She brushed a few crumbs off the windowsill and managed a smile. "Thanks, Aliza."

I kissed the top of her head. "Now come on, you've got a plate of eggs to finish."

UNCLE GREGORY AND AUNT LISSA ARRIVED AT THE MANOR two days later. "Glory be, Lissa, do my eyes tell me the truth?" Uncle Gregory said as he climbed out from their carriage, all sharp elbows and grass-stained trousers and beaming smiles. "I thought we had little sprouts for nieces, not these lovely flowers."

Aunt Lissa embraced Mama. "Gregory, please. They're girls, not gardens."

"They take about the same effort," Papa said as he shook his brother-in-law's hand. "Good to see you."

"And you, Robart, and you. It's been far too long. Now, who do we have here? Gracious me, is this my Sweet Alyssum?" Uncle Gregory said, using the nickname he'd given me during the summers I'd stayed with them in Edonarle. He wrapped me in a big bear hug, his graying beard tickling my nose. A warm, earthy smell hung around him, as comforting and familiar as childhood.

"Hello, Uncle," I said.

"Still as lovely as her name. Ready to brave the moors with us, my girl?"

"I wouldn't miss it for anything."

THAT NIGHT, UNCLE KEPT US AWAKE LONG PAST MID-night with news from Edonarle. When he finished, Papa contributed with a few much less thrilling tales of life on the Manor, though his account of the Riders did pique Aunt Lissa's interest.

"Daired?" she said as Papa named them. "*Alastair* Daired? Fancy that!"

"Know him?" Mama asked. "Hold still, for goodness' sake!" she told Leyda, who'd asked Mama to braid her hair before bed.

"Oh, he's lord at House Pendragon. You can see the house and grounds from Lambsley."

The needle I was mending with slipped through a hole in my thimble and pricked my thumb. Hard.

"Quite right," Uncle Gregory said. "And a fine view it is too."

I could feel Anjey's gaze, trying to gauge how this news affected me. In the months since Daired's proposal, I'd done my best to forget the whole incident, which naturally meant that I relived every word at least once a day. Still, it was easier to pretend in a place like Hart's Run. In Lambsley, under the shadow of his family's ancient estate, it wouldn't be so easy.

I fell asleep that night clinging to the hope that our paths wouldn't cross.

In the rush of packing the next morning, however, my uneasiness faded, replaced by excitement over our journey. By the time we'd stuffed ourselves into the carriage and waved goodbye to my family, I'd almost forgotten about Daired and House Pendragon altogether.

Almost.

DUSK HAD LEACHED THE LAST OF THE COLORS FROM THE sky when our carriage stopped in front of Essie's house at the northern end of Lambsley. Not a moment too soon either. The roads to Dragonsmoor were hard and rocky, and four days bouncing around a cramped carriage had given us all an unlooked-for empathy with churned butter.

"Looks like the whole place's gone to seed," my uncle said.

In the fading light, the windows in the stone façade of Aunt Essie's house left me with an impression of staring eyes. Moss crept across the front walk and weeds grew up from the cobbles, and only one of the lanterns hanging by the door had been lit.

Uncle Gregory leaned close as we walked to the door. "Ready, my dear? The old girl may have the fever, but I'd bet she'll still be pricklier than a briar patch."

"Oh, hush," Aunt Lissa said. "She'll be thrilled to see Aliza."

Thrilled wasn't the best word. After the servants settled us in our guest rooms, Aunt Essie's head maid showed us into the sick chamber. The old woman lay propped up on an overstuffed divan, a miserable-looking cat sprawled on her lap. Essie's eyes fluttered open, bloodshot from the fever but sharp as ever. Though I hadn't seen her in years, I remembered those eyes: gray as steel and just as cold.

"Who's this?" she croaked. "Marta, who are these people?"

Aunt Lissa held up a hand before the maid could answer. Without gloves or a veil over her mouth she couldn't touch her mother, but she came as close as she dared. "Mother, it's Lissa. Lissabeth and Gregory and your great-niece Aliza."

"*Hmph.* Didn't ask for the whole bloody kingdom," Essie mumbled. "Just want the gardener to mix me one of his potions and leave me alone."

Uncle put a hand on my shoulder. "Maybe you should get some sleep, Aliza," he said as Aunt Essie's mumblings faded into a wordless whine. "Lissa and I'll make her comfortable for the night. You and I can start on the draught tomorrow."

I gladly took his suggestion.

THE NEXT FEW DAYS REDEFINED MY UNDERSTANDING OF patience. Most of my time I spent helping Aunt Lissa in the kitchen, boiling water, chopping feverfew, and mixing the colorless broth that was the only thing Essie would eat. From dawn to dusk her complaints echoed through the house, stretching my poor uncle's nerves thinner than a spider's web. One morning he came into the kitchen after a struggle to feed Essie and crumpled onto a stool, rubbing his temples and asking where Marta kept her store of belladonna.

Aunt Lissa gave her husband a light swat on the shoulder. "Oh, hush."

"Not that it would do any good. I don't think you could kill the old woman if you tried. The fever's not had much luck yet."

"But she's not getting better," Aunt said.

"Aye, I know. I've done what I can with what we have here in the house, and despite what she says, I don't think she'll get any worse. Aliza, have you scouted the local flora yet?"

"Not yet." From what I'd seen of the windswept crags of the moors, it didn't look promising.

"Best start this afternoon. We'll need a good deal of hush, some yarrow, angelica, and mint. Lissa darling, you know the area best. Would you go with her?"

Aunt Lissa didn't have to be asked twice. That afternoon we bound back our hair, armed ourselves with baskets and pruning knives, and set out. The main road sloped up through Lambsley between rows of tall brick houses to the heights of the open moors beyond. We only had a little ways to walk before the wall bordering the road gave way to hedgerow.

"Thank the gods we're out of there!" Aunt Lissa cried. "Now, you mustn't think I don't love my mother, Aliza. I just find it easier to love her from a distance. Up close it's so . . . so . . ."

"Maddening?"

"I was going to be a little less blunt, but yes, maddening." She bent to inspect the shrubbery for any promising leaves. "She's a changed woman, my mother. When my father was alive, she was full of laughter, full of mischief. Full of *life*. When he died, part of her died too. And she still hasn't forgiven me for marrying Gregory and moving to Edonarle."

"Still? It's been twelve years."

"She doesn't like the fact he's got wood-wight blood." She snorted. "Well, she liked it plenty when he was the gardener, just not when he was going to be her son-in-law. Called him the bastard whelp of an *Idar* when I showed her the heartstone he gave me. Said it right to his face too."

I tucked a strand of hair back into my braid. This speech sounded as though it'd been weighing on my aunt's heart for a long time, and I was glad to hear her out.

"I just wish that she would see what Gregory *is* to me. He's everything my father was to her, but she just can't accept it. Sometimes I think she never will, and—I say, is that yarrow growing there?" She peered at a clump of white flowers near the roots of the hedgerow.

"No, it's snow-in-summer."

"Blast. Well, we're doing a masterful job." Aunt Lissa eyed the few sad stalks of mint at the bottom of her basket.

"There aren't any town gardens in Lambsley?"

"Hardly. This is it." Somber brick houses clustered below us, their cobblestone lanes bereft of growing things. "We could try the moors, but I doubt we'll find much more than heather and sedge. Although . . ."

"What?"

"We're awfully close to House Pendragon."

Whatever expression crossed my face must have been extraordinary, because Aunt Lissa burst out laughing.

"Goodness me, did Lord Alastair make *that* bad of an impression?"

I had a wry response to that, but my voice turned traitor and I settled on a shrug.

"Then what are we waiting for? We can be up and back here before lunch. I know the kitchen gardens at Pendragon have more than enough of what we need."

"Aunt Lissa, I'm not going to steal."

"Janna preserve us, I wasn't thinking of *stealing!* I know any number of staff up at the house. Half the chambermaids grew up with me. I'm sure someone won't mind allowing us in."

"Are you sure? I mean, won't Master Daired be home?"

"Certainly not. We would've seen that dragon of his flying around the grounds. See?" She pointed north through a break in the hedge. "No dragon in sight."

A crescent of iron-gray mountains jutted from the edge of the moorlands, their summits dusted with snow. Out of the shadow of the nearest mountain rose the slender pillars and shining roofs of House Pendragon.

"*Oh.*"

"I take that as a yes? Good. Off we go." Aunt Lissa hiked up her skirts and started up the incline. At the end of the lane she ducked left through a hole in the hedge, revealing a path that twisted into the mountains.

I followed as she began climbing the steep stone steps, my mind in a tumult. *Of course his house is splendid.* Had I really expected anything else? *Blast it all, why can't I just forget about him?*

After twenty minutes, the slope of the hill blocked the sight of the house, but Aunt Lissa showed no signs of slowing. I trudged after her, sweat stinging my eyes and my breath coming ragged between parched lips.

Then we were there. The stair ended at a high wall and a narrow archway, barred by a gate of wrought iron with the dragon crest of the Daired family worked into the center. Aunt Lissa tugged on the bell chain. A few minutes later a stooped man with a nose like a hawk's hurried out into the courtyard.

"May I help you, madam?" he asked.

"*Tom? Old Tom?*" Aunt Lissa clasped her hands in delight. "Great gods, look at you! You haven't aged a day, ironically enough."

The man's rheumy eyes widened. "Lissabeth Martens? Toby Martens's little Lissa?"

"The very same."

"Great gods indeed! What are you doing here? I thought you and the gardener—"

"Yes, Gregory and I live in Edonarle now. We're just in town visiting my mother."

"Bless you, my poor child. But what are you doing *here*? And who is this young lady?"

I curtsied. "Aliza Bentaine, sir."

"My niece. While we're here she's an apprentice of sorts to my husband. We're looking for herbs to help my mother through the fever, and I thought you might be able to spare a few from the gardens. We've searched all through town and can't find anything useful."

Old Tom glanced into the courtyard, looking doubtful.

"We won't be long, and we won't take much. On my word."

"Oh, all right. I suppose there's no harm," he said at last, unlocking the gate. "But don't for one second think this is for your mother, Lissabeth."

Aunt Lissa didn't argue.

"Right this way, if you please."

House Pendragon had a different kind of beauty than that of Edan Rose. Lady Catriona's estate was all warm stone and grassy rolling lawns; the ancestral home of the Daireds had a spare, stark splendor to it, reflecting the harshness and the majesty of the mountains. Pillared colonnades and archways of white marble led into shadows of blue and violet. The courtyard bustled with life, from stableboys in golden livery leading bloodred mares and bright chestnut stallions, to the climbing wisteria that covered the outer walls, to the mosaics sparkling in shades of sapphire and emerald at the bottom of the central fountain. Only a few servants bothered to give my aunt and me curious looks as we hurried after Old Tom. I guessed House Pendragon often played host to visitors on business with Family Daired, though probably none as disheveled as us.

"Just through here." Old Tom ushered us toward an arch at the far end of the courtyard, beyond which I could see and smell evidence of a first-rate herb garden. We followed him inside. "Now the herbs you'll be—oh, goodness me! Begging your pardon, Your Lordship."

A thrill of horror ran through me, keener and more piercing than any blade. The terror I'd felt during the gryphon attack, my escape from the troll troop, even the dread I'd felt confronting the Faceless Minister—nothing compared to this.

A shirtless Daired sat on a bench next to the herb beds.

CHAPTER 19

HOUSE PENDRAGON

My face burned so hot, I thought it a miracle my eye-brows weren't singed. Daired's leather hauberk, tunic, and scabbard lay in a heap on the ground, and he had a rag soaked in something green and pungent pressed against a gash just under his ribs. Head bent, he winced as the poultice seeped into the wound.

"Everything all right, sir?" Old Tom asked.

Daired looked up. "Oh, good. Tom, I—"

Our eyes met.

Daired flushed a brilliant, violent crimson. I wanted to look away, to look down, to look at the sky, at the house, at the mountain, anywhere. Impossible. Shock robbed me of speech and turned my legs to stone.

It did not, however, stop me from observing. And, from a purely aesthetic point of view, there was a great deal to observe.

Unruffled by both the presence of the master of the house and his half-naked state, Aunt Lissa swept forward and dropped into a curtsy. "We're so sorry to intrude, Your Lordship. My name is Lissa Greene, formerly Martens of Lambsley. This is my niece Aliza Ben—"

"Aliza Bentaine of Merybourne Manor, Hart's Run," he said, sounding dazed. "Yes, I know Aliza. What are you doing here?"

"I'm so sorry, Lord Alastair," Old Tom said. "That would be my fault. Madam Greene is an old friend. Her mother is sick, and they needed herbs for the fellfever draught."

Daired rose and came toward us, still pressing the cloth to his side. I tried not to stare at many things, none the least of which were the purplish-yellow marks of an old bruise on the left side of his face. Just days before it would've made a fine black eye. He stopped in front of me. "But what are *you* doing here?"

Wishing with all my heart I wasn't. I prayed the earth would split open and swallow me alive. It had been obliging less-eager Arleans all over the kingdom with tremors and mudslides for the past few months; I thought it bad manners it couldn't do me this one favor. "My uncle is an herbmaster," I said when I felt sure my voice wouldn't shake. "I'm here to help him."

"Are . . . ?" he began, then glanced down and broke off. "Pardon my attire. Help yourself with whatever you need from the garden, and, Tom, if they can't find something, ask Madam Gretna to bring up the stores from the larder."

"Certainly, sir."

"You're very kind, Lord Alastair," Aunt Lissa said. "We're in your debt."

"I'm glad to help. Excuse me, Madam Greene. Aliza," he said, and sweeping his armor off the ground, he fairly ran out of the garden.

I watched him go. I hadn't moved an inch.

"My, what a coincidence," my aunt said. "Extraordinary fellow, that one. And *rather* good-looking. You failed to mention you knew him so well, my dear." She brandished her pruning knife. "But we'll get to that later. Right now there's a great mass of mint over there just begging to be thinned."

COUNTLESS PLANTS SUFFERED UNDER MY KNIFE OVER the course of the next half hour. I considered them fortunate; they narrowly escaped being torn up by the roots. *How could I have such bad luck?* I asked myself for the third time as I beheaded a hapless yarrow plant. *After everything we said to each other . . .*

As the shock faded, the bitter aftertaste of shame took its place. Months spent trying to erase the memory of Hunter's Forge hadn't done any good; one glimpse of Daired and everything came flooding back, forcing me to face what I'd tried so long to ignore. His words might've been cruel, but he'd at least spoken the truth. A callous truth arrogantly told, perhaps, but truth nonetheless: about Wydrick, about Brysney and Anjey's letters, about all of it. And what had I wielded in reply? Wild speculation and the regurgitated lies of a man I hardly knew. I'd defended Wydrick and rejected Daired; he had every reason to never want to see me again.

So why did he let us stay?

"Aliza, love, have you seen any angelica?" Aunt Lissa called from the other end of the garden. "I've got mint and yarrow and a bit of hush, but I can't for the life of me remember what angelica looks like."

"It's got—"

"Yellow flowers?"

My basket tumbled from my hands. Daired stood behind me—dressed, thank the gods, but that was little comfort. "Master Daired! I . . . you . . . I'm sorry, what?"

He bent down and helped replace the fallen herbs. "Your aunt asked about angelica. It does have yellow flowers, doesn't it?"

"Oh. Um, aye. Whitish-yellow. Do you have any?"

"By the fountain."

"Splendid!" Aunt Lissa called. "Thank you, Lord Alastair!"

I straightened as he did, desperate to say something, to say *any-*

thing, but as before words deserted me. Daired adjusted his leather armbands, fiddled with the dagger at his hip, studied the ground, studied the garden, studied me. At last he cleared his throat. "So how long do you plan to stay in Lambsley?"

"It depends. My uncle's tending my great-aunt, and we're staying with her until she recovers. Or until she, ah, doesn't."

"Didn't your aunt say she has fellfever?"

"She does, and we have more than enough herbs to treat her now. Thank you for your generosity. I'm so sorry I—I mean, I'm so sorry for having intruded. We didn't think . . . we should go." I started down the path, craning my neck to find my aunt. "Aunt Lissa?"

"Aliza? Aliza, wait!"

Boots thudded on the flagstones behind me. Part of me wanted to keep walking, to pretend I hadn't heard him, but for some reason I couldn't. Like the solidness of earth after a flight through stormy skies, his voice drew me to him. "Sir?"

"Would you and your aunt like to stay for lunch?" he asked in a rush. "Akarra will want to see you before you leave."

"She's here?"

"She's visiting her Nestmother, but she'll be back."

As if Daired's invitation had conjured her out of the air, Aunt Lissa appeared at my side. "What's this? I heard something about food."

"I'd be honored if you'd join me for lunch, Madam Greene. My dragon is a friend of your niece's. She'd never forgive me if I let her go now."

"Oh, how lovely!" Aunt Lissa said, then caught my expression. "Unfortunately, we need to get back to my husband with these herbs."

"Dinner then. Tonight."

"Uncle Gregory couldn't possibly leave Essie for so long. Right, Aunt Lissa?" I said through clenched teeth.

"Nonsense! Get Gregory's draught in her and Mother will do perfectly well on her own. It's the only company she likes. Lord Alastair, it'd be our pleasure."

"Excellent! If you're finished, may I see you back to the village?"

"No!" I said. "No, Master Daired, we'll be all right. Good afternoon." Without waiting for an answer from either of them, I hurried out the garden gate.

Aunt Lissa caught up a minute later. "My dear, dear girl, it seems you left *quite* a lot out in your account of your acquaintance with Lord Alastair. You'd better start explaining."

As we made our way down the path I told her the whole story, from my first encounter with Daired to the last words of his letter. "I wish we'd never come," I said when I'd finished. "I feel like such a fool!"

"Why is that?"

"How would you feel if the person who rejected your marriage proposal turned up uninvited in your garden?"

"I'd thank Janna for the second chance and pick them a bouquet."

"Be serious, Aunt Lissa."

"Oh, darling, I couldn't be more serious. If I found our paths had crossed again, I wouldn't waste the opportunity. It's a foolish woman who spits in the face of fate."

I kicked a pebble down the steps. "I'd hardly call crossing paths today *fate*."

"No?"

"No. Just really bad luck. You wouldn't be angry to see me again?"

"Not at all. Not if I truly cared for you."

"Even after I called him cruel and a hypocrite and just about slapped him in the face?"

"You *slapped* him in the face?"

"Verbally."

She laughed. "No wonder he likes you! Courage is a trait they admire, your dragonriders."

"They're not *my* anything."

"Aliza, stop." When I didn't, she set her basket on the ground and blocked the path. "Listen to me, love, because this is important. Look me in the eye, tell me that man is angry with you, and I'll drop this right here. We'll make excuses for tonight and you'll never have to see him again. But"—she held up a finger before I could speak—"you have to make me believe it."

"He's . . ." My argument died on my lips. No matter what I said, I couldn't deny the fact that he'd invited us to dinner. "All right. Maybe not *angry*."

"You said in his letter he wished you every happiness. Lord Alastair doesn't strike me as someone with frequent experience with sarcasm, so my guess is he meant it. And the man we just met was pleased to see you. Shocked, yes, and frightfully embarrassed, but pleased too, and if you think otherwise, you're deluding yourself."

"Aunt Lissa, I don't know *what* to think anymore!" I cried, loud enough to startle a rabbit nibbling the grass at the side of the path. "Maybe he did care for me once, but any feelings he might've had are long dead by now. He's a Daired, a dragonrider, and a warrior; I'm a poor *nakla* who hates flying and doesn't like the sight of blood. Whatever else he is, and whatever else I am, that hasn't changed."

"If I recall what you told me correctly, wasn't that his initial objection?"

"Aye, but—"

"And you were quite keen to point out that such things shouldn't matter?"

"Sort of. Aunt Lissa, I didn't—"

"Then why the sudden change of heart? So you weren't born with a dragon-claw rattle in your mouth. What of it? My dear girl, don't tell me now that you think you aren't deserving."

"That's not the *point*," I said, struggling to find a way through her logic. It was a little too insightful for comfort. "Even if he did still like me, and even if I liked him, Master Daired—Lord Alastair—and I have nothing in common."

"Don't you?" Her eyes twinkled. "Seems to me you're both loyal, passionate, spirited young people with enough stubbornness between the two of you to tame the wildest *Tekari*. Trust me, Aliza. Lambsley-folk raise their children on tales of the dragonriders living on our doorstep, and I know them all by heart. It's true; they may be Riders, and they may be proud of it, but that doesn't make them bad, or even unpleasant," she said. "Just for tonight, give Lord Alastair a chance. If he's truly the pretentious ass you've described, then you'll have the pleasure of proving me wrong. And if he's not . . ."

Then gods help me, you'll never let me live it down. "Fine. I'll go to dinner, but don't expect anything beyond that."

"I'll take what I can get."

"I'm not promising anything, Aunt Lissa."

"No, but I am." She patted my shoulder and picked up her basket. "Consider yourself warned, my girl. I'm looking forward to causing you all kinds of trouble."

UNCLE GREGORY RECEIVED NEWS OF OUR EVENING plans with no less wonder than his wife. He waved away my concerns about Essie. "The old lady will be fine. If the fever hasn't killed her yet, it's not going to do it tonight, and Marta will keep an eye out after I get this draught into her. I say, it was really Lord Alastair?"

"In the flesh," Aunt Lissa said. "Quite a lot of it, in fact."

"And he invited all of us?"

"Unless you'd like me to bring my other husband, yes. All of us."

Uncle sprang to his feet. "Then there's no time to waste! Aliza, make sure the angelica steeps for three minutes, no more. Don't let the leaves burn. Lissa, my love, this hush needs a little more honey. I'm glad I brought my good coat," he said, bustling toward the door. "I'd better tell Marta." His ruminations on the *finest gardens north of Edonarle* continued until he was out of sight.

As afternoon stretched into evening, my dread dissipated. Slowly, and not altogether, but enough to keep me from feeling sick with apprehension as the sun sank in the west. I couldn't imagine facing Daired again without embarrassment, but Aunt Lissa's promise that he *didn't* hate me worked wonders for my agitated mind. *It's just dinner,* I told myself for the tenth time as I donned the nicest dress I'd brought. No matter what had happened between us, we could be cordial to each other for one evening.

Uncle stilled Aunt Essie's protests at our going with the first cool sip of his fellfever draught. After muttering something about the "fickleness of young people," she fell asleep. It spoke to my uncle's skill as a herbmaster that the booming knock at the front door an hour later didn't wake her. Marta answered it, gasping at the sight of the coachman's dragon-crested livery.

The coachman wouldn't hear of us walking. "My master's explicit orders, ma'am," he said as he handed me into the carriage.

"Well now, we mustn't disobey Lord Alastair," Aunt Lissa said. "Isn't that right, Aliza?"

She was already having a splendid time.

The main road to House Pendragon curved around the south side of the mountain. Out the left window spread the wilted patchwork of the southern lowlands, disappearing in a line of bluish-purple haze at the horizon. On the other side of the carriage rose the slopes of the Dragonsmoor Mountains, the peaks above us the color of bleached bone. And there, shining atop the nearest ridge, was the house itself.

If the back courtyard had impressed me, the rest left me breathless. Marble pillars glowed in the long evening light. Flashes of color broke the monotony of stone, spilling over balconies in masses of roses and spiky, star-like clematis. Uncle Gregory was giddy with delight by the time the coachman halted the carriage.

"Lissa, pinch me," he whispered, staring at the rhododendrons lining the terraces. "I think I—ow!"

Aunt Lissa smiled. "Don't ask if you don't mean it. Collect yourself, my dear. Our host is coming."

One look out the carriage window and all my nervousness came flooding back. Daired had traded his armor for a surcoat the color of the sky after a thunderstorm, and for the first time since I'd met him, he wore no weapons. I smoothed the front of my dress as the coachman opened the door.

"Madam Greene, welcome," Daired said, helping her down. "And you must be Master Greene."

"D-delighted to make your acquaintance, Lord Alastair," Uncle Gregory said. "So kind of you to invite us here."

"My pleasure," he said, but he was no longer looking at my uncle. "Miss Aliza."

Polite. Courteous. Cordial. I sucked in a deep breath and took his hand.

It was a good thing he held on to me, for just then a roar from the house sent me nearly jumping out of my skin.

"Great gods, what's *that?*" Aunt Lissa cried.

Daired smiled. "Ah. If you don't mind delaying dinner for a few minutes, there's someone I'd like you to meet."

THE INTERIOR OF HOUSE PENDRAGON MATCHED ITS EX-terior grandeur for grandeur, from the corridors paved in marble to the lace-like stone latticework that divided the rooms. Evidence of the family's winged counterparts could be seen all around, from the height of the ceilings to the notable lack of carpets and other flammable materials. I felt smaller than a gnat and just as important as I trailed after Daired, lost afresh in wonder at every new room.

"You're welcome to visit the gardens as long as you're in town, Master Greene," Daired said, holding back one of the silvery curtains hanging between the pillars of the gallery. I looked closer as I stepped through. The curtains weren't cloth at all, but finely wrought chain mail.

I bumped into Aunt Lissa, who'd stopped dead. "Oh. Oh my goodness," she said.

In the center of the courtyard, a dark-haired girl and the most beautiful dragon I'd ever seen were fighting tooth-and-talon, the dragon's sapphire scales and the girl's twin blades gleaming in the last rays of the sun. Having witnessed a Sparring before, I understood what was happening, but by the way my aunt and uncle winced at each blow from the dragon's tail, I could tell they feared for the girl's life. Daired must've realized it at the same moment. "She's not in danger. Here," he said, and whistled.

The combatants fell apart, the dragon with a rumbling grunt of annoyance. It seemed he'd been winning. The girl sheathed her swords and came forward.

"This is my sister, Julienna," Daired said.

Julienna Daired didn't look at all as I'd imagined. She was

younger than I expected, perhaps fifteen or sixteen, and though no one who saw her could doubt she was a warrior, her face had an open, honest expression that I liked at once.

"This is Master and Madam Greene of Edonarle," Daired said, "and this is their niece, Miss Aliza of Merybourne Manor. I've asked them to dine with us."

"Welcome to House Pendragon. I would've met you out front, but *somebody* forgot to mention we were having guests," Julienna said, glaring at her brother.

"You were busy."

She turned to me. "You wouldn't happen to be Aliza *Bentaine* of Merybourne Manor, would you?"

I dropped into a curtsy, uneasy at the idea that Daired might've relayed some of our less pleasant interactions to his sister. For some reason I couldn't explain, I wanted Julienna Daired to think well of me. "Lady Julienna. It's an honor."

"No, no, Miss Aliza, the honor is mine. I can't tell you how much I've heard about—"

"Julienna, aren't you going to introduce Mar'esh?" Daired asked.

"Oh! Of course." Julienna spun on her heel and threw her arms out as if to embrace her dragon. "This my friend and brother-in-arms, He-Whose-Eye-Holds-the-Dawn-Spark. *Ah-Na-al Hon-she'an-Mar'esh,*" she said in Eth. "Mar'esh, Miss Aliza and the Greenes."

Mar'esh extended his wing in greeting. Like a raindrop to a bitter sea, the ragged hole gaping between his third and fourth wingbones drew my eye, but if he saw me staring, he gave no sign of it. "Pleased to make your acquaintance," he rumbled. "Now, not to be rude, Alastair, but didn't you mention something about dinner?"

WE ATE IN A PILLARED ROOM WITH A CEILING SO HIGH IT was lost in shadows, though with two dragons in attendance it didn't feel the least bit cavernous. Akarra joined us just after the servants laid out the first course. She filled the room in a flurry of opalescent scales and wings and booming laughter.

"Aliza, what a lovely surprise! I didn't know you were visiting."

"We're staying in Lambsley with my great-aunt," I said. "My aunt and I only met Master Daired by chance." I emphasized the last word.

"Well, what a fortunate chance. It's been a long time since we've seen each other," Akarra said as she settled down next to the table, moving so as not to disturb the tureens of turtle-and-lemongrass soup. "Too long."

"Aye, it has."

I wondered if she remembered the last time we'd spoken the same way I did. *How much has changed since then?* My gaze drifted toward Daired. Again our eyes met, and the intensity of his look struck me like a physical weight. He didn't appear upset, or contemptuous, or even uncomfortable, merely puzzled, as if trying to read my thoughts by sheer force of will. I wondered if it'd be worth telling him what a pointless endeavor that was. I could hardly make sense of them myself.

"Ah!" Akarra said in a much louder, much happier voice as a servant led in a pair of bulls. "Good. I'd started to wonder if they'd run off."

Mar'esh leapt up, his talons extending with a disconcerting *snick*. I set my spoon down and swallowed, then swallowed again. When Mar'esh had said *dinner*, I hadn't imagined they'd be eating with us.

Before he could spring for the frightened creatures, Akarra smacked him over the head with her wingtip. "Honestly, *kes-ah!* Where are your manners? We have guests." Crestfallen, Mar'esh retracted his claws. "Some humans find this a little unpleasant," Akarra told us. "Mar'esh and I can take our meal outside if you like."

"You . . . er . . ." Uncle Gregory said. "No, by all means. We wouldn't want to trouble you. Please, ah, carry on."

A moment later the animal nearest Mar'esh made the fascinating albeit short-lived discovery that dragons could dispatch a full-grown bull with a single blow from their tail.

I turned away before I could see anything else, but that didn't keep me from hearing the crack and slump of Akarra's bull as she snapped its neck, or from feeling the singeing smart of dragonfire as they cooked their dinners. Sweat started at my temples as the temperature rose, but they finished roasting the carcasses in seconds.

Mercifully, they went about the eating part without gratuitous noise.

With hardly a second glance at the slaughter-and-roast happening behind us, Julienna turned to me and begged to hear my account of her brother's time in Hart's Run. "Alastair's talked more of that gryphon horde in the past year than of every other battle he's fought since. Did you really *kill* a gryphon, Miss Aliza?"

Aunt Lissa and Uncle Gregory looked at me in surprise.

"I didn't mean to. It just sort of . . . happened."

"Really? Alastair made it sound like you tracked the beast for miles."

"Julienna, I never said that," Daired said, refilling my uncle's wine glass. "You misunderstood."

"No, I didn't. Either way, I'm glad you killed the beast, Miss Aliza. And speaking of gryphons, Alastair, weren't you supposed to look into the sighting on the south slope today? The shepherds near Ramshead said one of them had been picking off their flock."

Daired smiled. "Not anymore it won't."

"Only because my Alastair is a *fortunate* idiot," Akarra said, returning to the table. Years of living side by side with humans must've made Daired dragons tidy eaters. I couldn't find a spot of blood on her. "You were supposed to wait until I got back to go after it."

"You'll notice I did very well on my own."

Aunt Lissa perked up. "A gryphon attack? Is that what happened to your chest? Forgive me, Lord Alastair, but I'd been wondering about that gash. It looked so . . . painful."

Dragonfire had nothing on the blush that burned in my cheeks. With her wide, placid eyes, plump face, and tone of innocent curiosity, it was almost impossible for Aunt Lissa to give offense, but I also knew my aunt, and innocence was the last thing on her mind.

At least she hadn't asked about the black eye.

Daired and Julienna didn't seem bothered by the physical intimacy posed by Aunt Lissa's question. Like death, battle wounds were their stock-in-trade, as was the flesh that bore them. "Just a scratch," Daired said. "You're kind to be concerned."

"I'd be glad to mix an herbal dressing for you, sir," Uncle Gregory said. "If you like."

"It's all right; I've seen to it. But that reminds me. How is your mother-in-law?"

"Still holding on, poor thing."

Aunt Lissa murmured something about *poor thing indeed.*

"Fellfever's contagious, isn't it?"

"Aye, sir, but we've been careful."

"Is there any reason you couldn't tend to her while staying somewhere else?" Daired asked. "Here, perhaps? My coachman could take you into Lambsley whenever you're needed."

I quelled the rising panic as Aunt Lissa nudged Uncle Gregory. Whatever trouble she'd planned on causing for me tonight was succeeding beyond her wildest dreams. I cursed the fact that she sat too far away to kick under the table.

"You'd be free to take anything you needed from our gardens," Daired said.

Uncle Gregory brightened. "In that case, we'd be delighted."

"Gregory and I will need to return to the house tonight, of course," Aunt Lissa said before Daired could summon his steward. "Mother will want to know what's become of us. But I don't see why you shouldn't stay, Aliza dear. We can send your trunk up with the coachman. Fellfever does have *such* a terrible effect on young people." Aunt Lissa smiled at the fearsome look I gave her. "We'd never want to risk your health."

"Miss Aliza?" Daired asked. "Would you like to stay?"

Once I might've been angry with him for asking my permission after everyone else's, but not anymore. There was no hint of presumption in his request, no expectation of obligation. I wondered if he asked me last because he feared my answer most.

"Oh, do stay," Julienna said. "There's so much I wanted to ask you about Hart's Run."

I opened my mouth to answer the only way I thought I knew how. *I'm sorry to disappoint you, Lady Julienna, but I can't. I have a duty to my aunt and uncle, to Essie, to myself . . . it's not proper . . . it's too sudden . . . I can't stay in Alastair Daired's house, not after what I said to him . . . not when he's looking at me like that . . . I need time . . . I need space . . . I can't . . .*

"Thank you, yes. I'd love to stay."

A whole second passed before I realized what I'd said. Another passed before I realized I didn't regret a word.

CHAPTER 20

JULIENNA

Soon after we finished dinner, the two dragons retired for the night, Akarra to the crags above House Pendragon, Mar'esh to the stony valley below it. Uncle Gregory and Aunt Lissa left not long afterward, promising to send my trunk back with the coachman. The triumphant gleam in Aunt Lissa's eyes said what she couldn't as they climbed into the carriage and waved goodbye.

"Have you ever had *kaf* before, Miss Aliza?" Julienna asked as the carriage lanterns swung out of sight.

"Not that I know of."

"Julienna, it's a little late for that," Daired said.

"It's never too late for *kaf*." She took my arm. "Come on, I think you'll like it. We'll ask Barton to bring some to the courtyard."

I certainly liked the smell of *kaf*. Rich and spicy, it wafted ahead of the steward, who arrived balancing filigree cups and a silver pitcher on a tray the size of a hassock. The three of us sat at the edge of the Sparring courtyard, the gardens lit by torches and the sliver of a waxing moon. Julienna took the tray before the steward could pour.

"Thank you, Barton, that'll do."

"Very good, my lady. Will you need anything else?"

She shook her head and Barton returned to the house. I watched as she poured the foaming black *kaf* into the cups, my interest born in part from the need to avoid meeting Daired's eyes again. He sat too near for comfort. He could've been on the other side of Arle and it would've been too near for comfort. The questions he asked with his silence stirred strange feelings in me, and moved me to even stranger answers.

And I realized, with a little shiver of alarm, that I quite liked being looked at that way.

"There." Julienna handed me a cup. "If this is the first time you've tried it, you may want to start slow."

"Thank—ow!"

I sprang from my seat as a paw snaked out from the shrubbery and buried needle-sharp claws into my calf. Steaming *kaf* splashed over the flagstones.

"Pan!" Julienna cried.

Daired darted forward, pulling from beneath the bench what looked like an armful of shadow. It hissed and tried to wriggle free, but he held on until it gave up and flopped over his arm. Yellow eyes stared out of a furry, pointed face of absolute black. One long canine shone milk-white against its lip.

"I'm sorry," Daired said. "We forgot he was out here."

I set what remained of my *kaf* on the bench. The strange creature had the shape of a cat, if a cat was the size of a sheepdog, but the ears were too pointed for a cat's, and those luminous eyes far, far too big. "What is it?"

"Stoorcat." Daired grunted as one paw whipped up and batted him across the face. A sound like small thunder reverberated in the creature's throat. "We think."

"I've never heard of them."

"They're not from around here," Julienna said. "Pan snuck into a barrel of *makaf* beans from the Garhad Islands when he was a kit. Got himself shipped off to Arle and dropped on our doorstep. He's a nasty piece of work on a good day."

"Only because he knows you don't like him," Daired said. As if he'd understood his master's words, Pan hissed at Julienna.

She made a face. "Quite right too."

"Are stoorcats Oldkind?" I asked.

"If they are, he's forgotten to mention it." Daired released Pan, who landed lightly on his feet. The cat twined around his master's legs, the top of his head grazing Daired's knee. Daired bent down and scratched behind those saucer-sized ears, which seemed to restore him to the stoorcat's good graces. Pan leaned into his hand and purred loudly enough to agitate the *kaf* in my cup.

"He's beautiful."

The purr fell silent. Pan fixed me with a look of deep suspicion before sauntering off into the shadow of a nearby rhododendron.

Daired straightened. "And not very friendly. He didn't hurt you, did he?"

"Surprised me, that's all." That wasn't entirely true; my calf still stung, but I ignored it. I settled back on the bench, pondering the incongruity of what I'd just witnessed. There was something pleasantly jarring about the image of Alastair Daired wrestling a housecat. Absently, I picked up my cup and tasted the *kaf*.

Julienna laughed at my expression. "Don't like it?"

"I'll tell you in a minute." *Kaf* tasted nothing like it smelled. It was bitter, earthy, and, after a second, more cautious sip, oddly invigorating. "It's interesting."

"How long will you'll be here again, Miss Aliza?" she asked.

"As long as my aunt and uncle think is necessary."

"Then we'll have it every morning."

"We'll have whatever Aliza and her aunt and uncle want, Julienna," Daired said. "They're our guests, not your converts."

I finished the cup. Once past the first shock of bitterness, it wasn't bad. I didn't, however, ask for a second. "My uncle Gregory would like it."

"This is the same uncle who taught you herblore, isn't it?" Daired asked.

"Aye," I said, surprised he'd remembered.

"He—" There was a discreet cough from somewhere in the rhododendrons, and Barton stepped into the torchlight. Daired closed his eyes. "What is it, Barton?"

"Begging your pardon, my lord. A message's just come for you."

"Can't it wait until morning?"

"I'm sorry, sir; it's from the lord general."

Daired swore under his breath and opened his eyes. "I'm sorry, I'll have to see to that." He stood and bowed. "Goodnight, Aliza."

I noticed he'd again dropped the *Miss*, and wondered that I hadn't the least inclination to correct him. "Goodnight, Master Daired."

"What, don't I get anything?" Julienna asked as her brother started after their steward. "No goodnight?"

"Don't stay up too late."

She rolled her eyes at his retreating back but did as he said. Half an hour later, after Julienna's second cup of *kaf*, the sullen reappearance and subsequent disappearance of Pan, and a few traitorous yawns from me, she led me to the guest chamber. The room was spacious and comfortable, but as the night had grown cool, I was glad to see a brazier burning in the corner. My trunk sat next to the door, a small square of parchment tucked under the latch.

Julienna stopped me before I could read the note. "Akarra told me you're a wonderful artist, Miss Aliza. I couldn't try and persuade you to sketch Mar'esh and me while you're here, could I?"

"You wouldn't have to try hard, Lady Julienna. I'd love to."

"Oh, thank you! And none of this 'Lady Julienna' business. We've drunk *kaf* together, so as far as I'm concerned, it's Julienna or nothing."

"Only if I can be Aliza."

"Perfect." She started to close the door, then paused. "I'm glad you decided to stay. Truly. I haven't see Alastair smile like that in a long time. Goodnight." She shut the door softly behind her before I could string my thoughts into a sensible answer.

I picked up the card. Written on it in a firm, familiar hand, were two words.

Sleep well.

It might have been the *kaf*, or the note, or the simple fact that I was a guest at House Pendragon, but I hardly slept at all.

For hours after Julienna left I lay awake, tracing the bas-relief figures that decorated the ceiling. Moonlight filtering in through the curtains gilded the characters of Arlean myth, from Saint Ellia of the Shattered Bow to Aur'eth the Flamespoken, but even as my gaze wandered over the depiction of Saint Ellia's doomed stand against the sea-serpent, my mind strayed back to Daired. I relived each word, each motion, each look from our meeting in the garden to his farewell in the courtyard. The more I considered it, the more I realized Aunt Lissa was right: the pompous Daired I'd known in Hart's Run had yet to make an appearance in House Pendragon. Another man had taken his place, one who teased his sister and remembered details about my extended family. Who kept a cat and brought my trunk up himself and opened his home to *nakla* strangers.

In short, one I wouldn't mind getting to know better.

That left me only one coherent thought as I at last drifted off to sleep. *So what on earth am I going to do about it?*

DAWN BROKE OVER A RARE SIGHT: ME, OUT OF BED BE-fore the sun, and of my own free will. Cold water from the ewer basin chased away the cobwebs of sleep but did nothing to calm my nerves. I paced the room, fiddling with my braid and rehearsing conversations in my head. *Morning, Master Daired. Lovely weather, isn't it? Yes, I'd like some breakfast. While you're at it, would you please describe your feelings for me? You've changed since we last met, and I'd like to know exactly who I'm dealing with now, because gods know I'll never sort out what I'm feeling until I do.*

A tap sounded at the door, and a plump, middle-aged woman in an apron bustled in with a breakfast tray.

"Morning, Miss Bentaine! Didn't think you'd be up quite so early, or I'd have fetched you for breakfast with the master. Madam Gretna, Pendragon housekeeper." She set the tray down and curt-sied. "His Lordship said to bring you whatever you needed."

Perhaps it was her confidence, or the remarkable speed at which she laid out tea, toast, and scones, or perhaps it was just her air of being everyone's mother, but I liked the housekeeper at once. I thanked her and set into the scones as she made the bed.

"Is Master Daired already up?" I ventured after a minute.

"Goodness, yes! He and his sister are early risers. Up before the sun, they were, and looking forward to seeing you. Lady Julienna's all excited to have her portrait drawn. As soon as you're done I'll take you to them."

I finished quickly.

Madam Gretna took me through the house, pointing out interesting features as we passed. I glimpsed hallways lined with books, corridors covered in murals, alcoves lit by glass skylights, and a number of rooms with no discernible purpose save to bewilder guests. When we at last paused in the pillared gallery Daired had shown us the day before, I was relieved to see something familiar.

"Right through there, miss," Madam Gretna said.

The clap of wood striking wood echoed through the courtyard. I pushed aside the chain mail curtain and watched, half hidden by flowering shrubs, as Daired and Julienna crossed quarterstaves in the middle of the pavement. Neither noticed me.

"Pivot! Don't turn your back," Daired said.

Julienna bent backward to avoid the sweep of her brother's staff. "That'll be so useful when all my enemies come at me politely, one at a time."

"Which is why you never take a contract alone. Only show your back to another Rider."

"The same way you did on your little excursion to Ramshead the other day?"

"That wasn't a contract. That was exercise."

"Of course it was." They circled each other, muscles tensed, testing each other's defenses. Julienna twirled her staff without breaking eye contact, first with one hand, then the other. "But what does it matter? I'll never be alone. Mar'esh will be with me."

Daired lunged and knocked the staff out of her hand. She caught it just before it clattered to the ground. "Like Mar'esh is here now? The battlefield is chaos, Julienna. Never bet your life on what someone else will or won't do." Their staves met again in midair with a crack like a breaking bone. "Even your dragon."

"Be glad Akarra didn't hear you say that."

"She'd say the same thing. Our work is life or death." A light tap sent Julienna stumbling back, rubbing her shoulder. "And you'd better start treating it that way, or I'll make sure you're stuck here chasing stray gryphons away from Ramshead for the rest of your life."

"You could try."

"My privilege as your older brother, Julienna. I won't let you die before me."

"Mikla save us, is Alastair Daired actually getting *sentimental?* She is a good influence, isn't she?"

"Mind on the fight, Julienna!"

She deflected his next attack. "Whatever happened to *mind your surroundings?* I'll start paying attention to all that advice you're so fond of doling out as soon as you do. Don't you think that's fair, Aliza?" she called over her shoulder.

Daired straightened as I stepped out from behind the greenery.

Julienna delivered a stunning blow to his stomach with the butt of her staff. "Mind on the fight, brother dear. Good morning, Aliza!"

"Morning, Julienna," I said, torn between asking if Daired was all right and laughing at his comical expression. "I hope I'm not intruding."

"Not at all," Julienna said.

"Did you—sleep well?" Daired said. Or rather, wheezed. "Would you like breakfast?"

"Madam Gretna brought me a tray, but thank you."

Julienna tossed her staff to her brother and took my arm. "Would you still mind taking our portrait? I promise Mar'esh and I will be good models."

"I've been looking forward to it."

Leaving Daired in the courtyard to put away their weapons, Julienna showed me to the gardens adjacent to the herb beds. A little wooden chest sat on the edge of the fountain, next to a stool and a makeshift easel. Inside the chest I found a wondrous assortment of parchments, paint pots, charcoals, whittled pencils, quills, and even a few jars of Noordish ink.

"Is that all right?" she asked. "We weren't sure what you'd need."

"It's more than all right." I unrolled a square of parchment. The skin ran smooth and seamless beneath my fingers, nothing like the rough stuff I used at home. "It's *perfect*. Where did you get all this?"

"We found it in one of our mother's old rooms. If you don't need anything else, I'll be back in a minute." She disappeared behind a clump of whitethorn.

I closed the chest and touched the crest carved into the lid. A feathered creature spread its wings across a waxing moon, its surface embedded with mother-of-pearl. Beautiful, and strange. It was the first article I'd seen to come out of House Pendragon that lacked the Daired dragon.

Something rustled in the bushes. I looked up just in time to see a greenish lump sail toward me, trailing floppy sleeves. It landed in my lap and uncurled with a flourish, revealing the chubby, smiling face of a baby hobgoblin.

"*Wheee!* Ma's not lemme do that in *forever!*" she said in broken Arlean. "You new here. I like your face."

"Er, thank you! I like your face too. What's your name?" I asked in Gnomic.

The hobgoblin child's eyes brightened and she bounced onto my outstretched palm. "Hilly! Ma'll like you too. You're a friend. I can tell," she said in Gnomic. She put her hands on her hips and sniffed. "You smell like flowers after they got rained on. What do the Big Folk call you?"

"Aliza." I stood and curtsied. "Pleased to meet you. Is your mother around here?"

"Ma's digging up breakfast with the gnomes. I told her I'm gonna see a dragon!" Footsteps on stone drew our attention at the same time, and Hilly pointed down the path as Daired strode toward us. "It's the dragon man! Miss 'Liza, I know him."

I held her closer to my chest; against the green of my dress she was almost invisible. She gripped my finger and rested her chin on her hands, watching him approach with wide, lilac-colored eyes. "Thank you for the drawing materials, Master Daired," I said.

"You got them? Good. I'm—"

"Dragon man!" Hilly cried in Arlean.

He started, looking first at the hobgoblin, then at me, as if unsure of what to say, or which of us to say it to.

"This is Hilly, Master Daired." I watched his face. "She lives in your garden."

"Good morning, ah, miss," he said at last, and then did something I didn't expect. He bowed to the little hobgoblin child in my arms. "I'm Alastair."

Hilly looked up at me, cupped her hands around her mouth, and said in Arlean in a voice that wasn't at all a whisper, "He smell like smoke and sunshine. Good, but yours better."

"It's a pleasure to meet you, Miss Hilly," Daired said in fumbling Low Gnomic.

I almost dropped Hilly. "You speak Gnomic?"

"Akarra taught me a few words."

"*She* speaks Gnomic?"

He smiled. "Of course."

"Who'd Akarra?" Hilly asked, looking up at the two of us.

A rumble from the far end of the garden announced an addition to our party as Mar'esh's sapphire head popped up over the garden wall.

"Morning, all. Sorry I'm late. Lost track of time." He moved with a sinuous grace, clawing over the balustrade and using his ruined wings for balance. Julienna followed him through the gate.

"Oh. That's a *big* dragon." Hilly tugged my sleeve, and switched back to Arlean. "Miss 'Liza, I gonna go find Ma now."

Daired held out his hand. "Allow me."

"Thank you, dragon man! 'Bye, Miss 'Liza." With a grin big enough to make her eyes disappear in rolls of baby fat, Hilly leapt into Daired's arms and gave him directions to their Underburrow.

"Where would you like us, Aliza?"

Julienna's voice brought me back to the moment. There'd be time enough to contemplate Daired's transformation later. "In front of the fountain is fine. I should warn you though, this'll take a while. You'll have to stay still."

Mar'esh ruffled Julienna's hair with the tip of his wing. "I can sit like a stone. She's the one you'll have to worry about."

Julienna patted her hair back into place with a scowl and said something in Eth that made Mar'esh laugh even harder.

I set to work.

CHAPTER 21

FIRE ON THE MOUNTAIN

Mar'esh was right. After twenty minutes he'd not so much as twitched his tail, but Julienna fidgeted as she leaned against his foreleg, and after capturing their outlines I let them relax. It gave me time to solve a conundrum. Whether on purpose or by chance, Mar'esh had posed with his torn wing draped over Julienna's shoulder, presenting me with a perfect view of Wydrick's work. It would've been easy enough to disguise it, to hide the broken flesh with a few strokes of my charcoal, or to position Julienna in front of the wound and avoid drawing it altogether, but that didn't feel right.

Then again, I didn't want to emphasize it. I saw the longing in Mar'esh's eyes as he followed the swallows diving above our heads, and the way Julienna pressed her lips together as she watched the silhouettes of dragons flying to and from the distant eyries. What I didn't see, I could imagine. From their flatware to furnaces, every facet of House Pendragon served as a reminder of the birthright that Wydrick had stolen from Julienna and Mar'esh. I'd known them for less than a day and I felt their pain; any longer and I'd begin to empathize with Daired's desire for vengeance.

So I compromised. I drew what I saw, wound for wound and

scar for scar, but on the second pass I took some liberties, sharpening one line here, smudging another there, until what wrapped around Julienna wasn't so much a wing as a column of blue fire, licking through her hair like a halo.

Daired joined us after he'd seen Hilly back to her mother. He sat on the edge of the fountain and watched me draw and, when charcoal couldn't capture the details anymore, watched me paint. Once his scrutiny might've bothered me, but the play of sunlight over Mar'esh's scales and the complexity of Julienna's expression of ferocious serenity had me captivated, and in my determination to do them justice, I hardly noticed him.

It took Madam Gretna's arrival with the announcement of lunch to convince me at last to set down my paintbrush. "Afraid your aunt and uncle can't make it up here today, Miss Bentaine," the housekeeper said as she and her maids set out the meal on a nearby terrace. "Carson just came from collecting their extra things. He says your uncle told him Essie'd taken a turn for the better, and she's not letting him out of her sight until she's on her feet." She smiled as she said it, half amused, half sympathetic. I wondered if she knew Essie.

While I felt for my aunt and uncle, news of their delay came as a bit of a relief. It gave me a little more time to sort through my feelings before Aunt Lissa stepped in to make a delightful mess of things. I was doing that well enough on my own.

Over lunch I painted a second portrait. It was a mental portrait of Daired, awash with colors and details I'd never noticed before. The gentle way he teased his sister for her preference of raw potatoes over cooked ones. The deep, rolling sound of his laughter as something his housekeeper said amused him. The muddy handprints on his leather jerkin, left in love and carelessness by a hobgoblin child.

He hadn't wiped them away.

WE RETURNED TO THE GARDEN AFTER LUNCH. MAR'ESH and Julienna took turns posing as I painted, and after I'd finished with her, Julienna surprised me by bringing out a set of silver panpipes. She sat cross-legged next to her brother and polished the pipes on her sleeve.

"I didn't know you played," I said.

"Alastair forgot to mention it?"

"It never came up." Daired leaned back on his elbows. "Aliza, you'll be happy to know that my sister is the best piper in Dragonsmoor."

Julienna wrinkled her nose. "Coming from you that hardly counts as praise. You can't tell panpipes from a pipe organ. Don't ever, *ever* let him sing for you, Aliza."

Whatever musical deficiencies he suffered, Julienna more than made up for them. The notes she drew from the panpipes took on a life of their own, warbling with the warmth and strangeness of a phoenix's song and tingeing the long afternoon light with an almost magical quality. The next few hours passed quickly.

"There." Adding the last flecks of emerald in Mar'esh's eyes, I set down my brush.

Julienna stopped playing to inspect my work, and I held my breath as her gaze swept over Mar'esh's wing. *Don't hate it. Please, please don't hate it.* She smiled and said something in Eth to Mar'esh, who gave a rumbling grunt of approval. I released my breath.

"That's remarkable, Aliza," Daired said, leaning over my shoulder. "I almost . . ."

I looked up as he trailed off. Mar'esh had bent his head close to Julienna's, deep in debate as to where the painting should be hung. "Is it his wing?" I asked Daired quietly.

"No, it's not what you did; it's what I can't do. I can't see it properly."

It took a moment for the memory to surface that gave his words meaning. In all that had passed between us since the banquet at Hall-under-Hill, I'd almost forgotten Daired was color-blind. "What do you see?"

"The lines, the shapes, the light and dark. It's the colors I don't understand." His eyes swept over the dark emerald of Mar'esh's underbelly and the lighter turquoise of his wingtip. "What I can see is that you have a gift. I hope it's enough."

I blamed the heat rising to my cheeks on the sun, now balanced like a golden ball on the westernmost peak of the Dragonsmoor Mountains, and fixed a nonexistent smudge along Mar'esh's painted foreleg. He and Julienna had switched to Eth to continue their debate in more heated, albeit still playful, tones. Daired stood.

"They'll go all evening if we let them." He offered me his hand. "Dinner should be ready soon. Are you hungry?"

"I am, thank you." I took his hand, realizing as I did that, in many ways, this was the closest we'd been to each other since that disastrous day on the hilltop at Hunter's Forge. Again I traced the shape of his eyes, remembering a time when I'd refused to let myself think of them as anything but nicely symmetrical. Now I knew better. I knew him better, and I knew myself better too.

And they were, without a doubt, beautiful eyes.

THROUGHOUT DINNER I FOUGHT AN ODD FEELING IN my chest, as if something inside me had shed a great weight, or as if I'd woken up expecting a dreary day of lessons, only to realize the holidays had already begun. The meal must've been splendid; I didn't notice a bite of it. We finished as the deep blue of evening crept across the sky, swallowing the remnants of a magnificent sunset.

Neither of the dragons ate with us. Julienna explained that

Akarra often spent evenings training Mar'esh near the Standing Stones. "He's going to beat her one of these days," Julienna told her brother as we took our wine onto the adjoining porch. "Wings or no wings."

"When that happens, neither of you will ever let us live it down, I know," Daired said. "Speaking of which, shouldn't you be practicing with your longsword?"

"Now? Really?"

"I let you off last night, so tonight you're going to make up for it. I promised Aunt."

"I don't see why I need to know how to decapitate something with one sword when I can already do it well enough with two. Better than you, in fact."

"Best me in a longsword Sparring and I won't make you practice anymore."

"You're going to regret saying that one day," she said, but accepted defeat and bid us goodnight.

"Thank you for what you did today, Aliza," he said when she'd gone.

"It was my pleasure."

"Not just the painting. *How* you painted them. It meant the world to—them."

"Then it was worth every second."

The wind rustled the leaves in the garden below us, and only then did I realize how quiet it was. No servants bustled nearby; no dragons flew overhead. We were very much alone.

He set his wine glass on the balustrade. "If you're not too tired, there's something I'd like to show you."

At that moment, I cared for sleep about as much as I did pickled cabbage or which lords planned to join the Great Stag Hunt in the autumn. That is to say, not at all.

"No, I'm not tired."

I followed him back through the dining room and out into the hall. For the length of a corridor we walked in silence: him with hands clasped behind his back, me torn between a dozen feelings so strong and strange I couldn't begin to make sense of them. Our shadows flickered together in the light of the torches as we climbed the staircase at the end of the hall. I smelled sweet oil and the hot, smoky scent of dragons that permeated the house like perfume.

The stair opened onto a small balcony overlooking the mountains. Above us, summits like knifepoints serrated the sky; beneath us was only blackness. No crickets sang. Besides the torch on the wall, the only light in a hundred leagues came from the young crescent moon and the stars, each one burning colder and bluer than I'd ever seen in Hart's Run. Before we'd been alone; now it felt like we were the only two living things on earth.

"What did you want to show me, Master Daired?"

"You know, you can call me Alastair," he said, and pointed toward the peak.

Only moon-softened darkness and the brilliance of the stars met my eyes, and for several minutes I said nothing, wondering if he'd only meant to show me the sky. Beautiful, but not quite what I expected.

As if I had any idea what to expect.

"I spoke to Cedric," he said at last. "About your sister. I told him I was wrong, that Anjey wasn't like the others. I told him I'd misjudged her, and that he was a fool if he didn't go back and tell her what he felt. And . . . I told him that his letters to her hadn't made it to Hart's Run."

"What did he say?"

His lip curled in a rueful smile. "Say? Nothing. He punched me."

"He *what?*"

"He thought I meant I'd kept his letters from her."

Judging by the state of his black eye, their conversation couldn't have taken place much more than a week ago. "How did you explain it?"

"I told him the truth, that I didn't know what happened to his letters. When I left Edonarle he was making plans to return to Merybourne Manor."

My heart swelled. *That meant all would be well again! Anjey and Brysney will marry, Mama will be thrilled, and . . .*

"There! It's starting." He put one hand on my shoulder, and I felt the warmth of his touch through the fabric. "Look."

Night stretched unbroken above us. "What am I looking—?"

From the highest peak of the Dragonsmoor Mountains, a fiery flower exploded in the darkness. I gasped. Flames roared in blue and crimson and white, lighting up the mountain in a wild rhythm of light and shadow, each burst a note in the song the dragons were spinning out of fire and silence. Every drop of blood tingled in my veins.

"What's happening?"

"The Nestmothers are christening their dragonets. Akarra calls it their baptism into fire."

"It's *beautiful*."

We watched without speaking until the blasts grew intermittent, then faded altogether. The stars beyond the peak looked more brilliant than ever, as if the dragonfire had burned away the last grimy veil between earth and sky.

"Did you get my letter?" Daired asked when the last flicker of flame winked out.

"Yes."

"You can think of me however you want, Aliza, but I hope you'll at least absolve me of injustice toward—that man."

"On the contrary, I think you treated Wydrick most unjustly."

Anger and confusion warred in his eyes as he turned on me. "How can you say that? You know what he did to my family."

"Yes, I knew. Now I *understand*. I've seen what he took from Julienna and Mar'esh, Alastair, and I think it was injustice when you didn't run him through on the spot."

A moment of satisfying silence passed before he found his voice. "Thank you." He smiled. "We can go inside. The christening's over."

"If you don't mind, I'd like to stay out here," I said, and touched his wrist.

He stiffened, staring at my hand on his as if he thought I'd made a mistake. When I didn't move, he brushed his fingers along my arm, hesitant at first, then bolder as he reached for my waist. Half my mind shrieked at the contact, screaming impropriety, and danger, and *oh gods, what am I doing?* The other half saw only the awe and the terror in those beautiful eyes, and felt the wild gallop of his heartbeat, and wondered how I'd ever managed to hate this man.

"Aliza, I know what you think of me," he said quietly. "When you look at me, I know you see a brute, and a cad, and a selfish man. And yes, maybe that's what I was once, but I need you to know I can be more than that. *Different* than that."

He raised my hand to his lips, and I forgot I was chilly. I forgot cold existed at all. Like his dragon, Daired had fire all his own.

"I can learn how to heal things, like you do. How to be kind. How to forgive, even if it means—" His face twisted as he fought some inner battle. "Even Tristan."

Tristan. Uneasiness nibbled at the edges of my memory, but the sensation of his hand on my cheek swept it from my mind.

"Tell me I have a chance. If it's a seed that'll take a thousand years to grow, I don't care, but don't ask me to wake up another morning without hope." He tilted my chin upward. "Please, Aliza. Give me at least that."

"Alastair, I . . ."

Then I remembered.

"Wait. *Tristan?*"

He backed away, looking at me as if I'd buried a spear in his chest. "Yes, Tristan. Thell knows I hate that man, but if it meant you'd—"

"Tristan *Wydrick?*"

"That's his name. I thought you knew . . . Aliza?"

I covered my mouth. My legs felt watery, and this time it had nothing to do with Daired's touch. *Tristan—Wydrick—Leyda's mysterious friend.* It couldn't be a coincidence. *What does he want with her?* "Oh gods."

He took me by the shoulders. "Aliza, tell me what's wrong. What has he done?"

In the quietness of the house below us, something shrieked.

Daired's fingers dug into my arm. No dragon made that noise, and no human either. It was the cry of a wyvern in distress. Again the shriek sounded, and this time a man's voice accompanied it, faint but frantic. "Alastair! For gods' sakes, *Alastair!*"

It was Cedric Brysney.

We sprinted downstairs. Brysney, Silverwing, Barton, and Julienna milled about on the front portico in varying states of confusion. Julienna still held her longsword.

"Cedric, what's going on?" Daired said. "What on earth are you doing here?"

"Haven't you heard?" Brysney panted. "Scouts from the north passed through Little Dembley yesterday morning. They told me the news."

"What news?"

"Alastair, they—" Brysney caught sight of me. The color drained from his face. "Aliza! What are you doing here?"

"She's visiting Dragonsmoor with her aunt and uncle. Cedric, *what news?*"

"Those tremors we've been feeling," he said. "They weren't earthquakes. Alastair, the Greater Lindworm is awake."

CHAPTER 22

OLD, DEEP THINGS

"What?"

"The Riders I spoke to saw it themselves," Brysney said. "Two days ago it broke ground north of Harborough Hatch. They say it's five times the size of the Lesser Lindworm. It's already leveled any number of towns."

"How many dead?" Julienna asked.

"Dozens. Hundreds. Nobody knows. And it's not alone. Creatures are joining it from all over Arle. *Tekari*, even some *Idar* are flocking to the Worm—gryphons, direwolves, valkyries, trolls, all of them. It's an army, and it's coming."

Julienna sheathed her sword. "But why now? What woke it?"

"Revenge." Brysney's shoulders sagged. "What else? Charis and I killed its spawn. The Worm must've felt it."

Silence fell as that sank in. With startling clarity the page dedicated to lindworms in Mari's bestiary leapt to mind.

Ten times the length of a full-grown dragon, with scales as hard as stone, the legendary lindworm may sleep for hundreds of years buried deep in the earth, spawning but once a generation, not stirring until disturbed—but woe to those who disturb the Great Worm. Its poison is vicious, its sting incurable, its appetite insatiable, its progress unstoppable. The foes of humankind will follow it, for in its wake it leaves naught but death and destruction.

The drawing accompanying her description showed a snake-like creature dragging itself through the ruins of a town on two legs the size of tree trunks, its mouth yawning open to swallow a yoke of oxen whole. Brysney and his sister had done the unimaginable by slaying the Lesser Lindworm of Harborough Hatch. Terror washed over me as I realized what Brysney's look meant. *They won't be able to do it again.*

The steward murmured a prayer. Julienna tightened her sword-belt.

"Where was it heading?" Daired asked.

"South. All the Riders and the Rangers in the country are mustering at the borders of Harborough Hatch to stop it before it reaches Hatch Ford."

"Then there isn't much time. Barton, bring my armor. Julienna, wake Mar'esh and Akarra. Aliza—" His grim look softened. "I'm sorry. Julienna and I have to leave."

"If your coachman can make the trip in the dark, I'll go back to Lambsley tonight," I said, hoping I sounded brave. I didn't feel it.

"Aliza, wait," Brysney said. "That's not everything. Alastair, stay a moment. You need to hear this too. I've just come from visiting Anjey at Merybourne Manor." He took my hand. "I'm sorry, but your sister Leyda has done something terribly foolish."

It felt as if Brysney had reached inside my chest and wrapped his hand around my heart. Each word squeezed it a little tighter. "What did she do?"

"She ran off to join the muster."

Part of me wanted to sink to the ground, to curl up in a ball and cry. Another wanted to run, to curse, to hurt something. Or better yet, hurt someone. Blood sang in my ears, hot and fierce and loud—and *angry*. *Wydrick*. Tristan Wydrick, with all his grand tales of adventure, all his lies. *Did he put you up to this, Leyda?*

Dimly I heard Brysney confirming what I feared. "She left with a regiment of Rangers out of Trollhedge. Anjey didn't find her note until they'd left."

"Where are they now?"

"I don't know. Somewhere between Hart's Run and Hatch Ford, but that's just a guess. Aliza, I'm so sorry."

I turned to Daired, willing my tears to mind their own business. Now I had to be strong; my family needed me, and if I started crying I might never stop. "I need to go home. Tonight."

"Agreed," he said. "Cedric, tell my sister that Akarra and I will join you at Hatch Ford as soon as I've taken Aliza back to Hart's Run."

Brysney nodded and hurried inside, Silverwing with him.

"Alastair, no," I said. "I just need a carriage. You can't come to Hart's Run. They need you and Akarra on the front lines."

"I'll be no good to them if you're not safe. You heard what Cedric said; *Tekari* are crawling out from all over Arle. The roads from Dragonsmoor won't be secure until the Worm is dead." His hand brushed my cheek. "Aliza, if I can't do anything else before the battle starts, let me do this. Let me take you home."

The words he hadn't said hung between us. *Before I go to what may be my last battle. What may be the last battle for any of us.*

Hands numb, heart cold, head on fire, I nodded.

Barton appeared at the door bearing his master's armor, and Daired pulled away from me, his expression hardening as he dressed for war. "My people will make sure your aunt and uncle are well looked after. Write them a note and I'll have it sent it to Lambsley before we leave. And, Aliza?" he said before I went inside. "Wear something warm. We'll have to fly fast."

When I returned to the porch a few minutes later, the Daired of the past few hours had disappeared. Again I saw Daired as I first knew him, battle-scarred and forbidding, his heartstone blade secure in its scabbard at his back. Akarra paced at his side, growling in Eth, each word accented in flames. She wore a war-saddle strapped between her spikes.

Daired handed my letter to Barton and helped me climb into the saddle. "It's not the flight she's worried about. They say lindworm scales are impervious to dragonfire."

"You can stop it though, can't you?"

He swung up behind me. "Barton, be sure that letter gets to Master and Madam Greene at the Martens' house in Lambsley."

"Of course, Lord Alastair. And, sir? Good luck."

"Thank you. Julienna, wait with Cedric and Charis at Hatch Ford. Cedric, she doesn't fight without me. Understand?"

Before either Julienna or Mar'esh could protest, Akarra leapt into the air with a roar that shook the mountainside, spread her wings, and started southeast, toward home.

AN UNMOTIVATED DRAGON MIGHT'VE FLOWN FROM House Pendragon to Merybourne Manor in a little less than a day.

Akarra was not unmotivated.

The speed with which we rushed first over wild countryside, then over a patchwork of fields and towns as the moon rose, nearly took my breath away. Clouds swallowed the stars soon after we set out, leaving us in darkness, broken once in a while by the twinkling lights of a town or village far below. It was cold. Bitter wind snatched at my shawl and tore at my hair. I tightened my grip and tried not to think of the flight ahead.

Daired leaned forward, putting his mouth close to my ear. "I'm sorry about your sister. Would I could . . ." The wind blew away his final words, but I guessed they had something to do with *help*.

Words weighed on my heart, an answer I dared not speak aloud for fear of making it that much more real. *I think it's too late for that.*

"We'll stop in another hour or two so Akarra can rest her wings," he said.

I leaned into him, but my mind was far from the warmth of his arms around me. I was too angry to be miserable, too anxious to feel sad, and, as the dark hours stretched toward the sunrise, too tired to think of anything much at all. Daired didn't speak again. Save for the wind and the sound of Akarra's wings laboring beneath us, the night slipped by in silence.

I didn't notice we'd started our descent until Daired tightened his grip around my waist. Akarra landed with a thud that rattled my bones, and I slipped out of the saddle onto soft, springy turf. The moon cast a little light behind the clouds, enough to see Daired dismount but not enough to see where we'd landed.

"Where are we?" I asked.

"A meadow on the borders of Middlemoor, I think. We can't stay long, but you'd best get some rest," Akarra said, settling down and spreading her wing. "Come, I'll keep you warm."

We huddled next to her and she lowered her wing, covering us in a living, leathery tent. Daired unbuckled his sword-belt and sank next to me with his scabbard across his knees, the hilt of his sword within easy reach.

I settled my head against Akarra's foreleg and prayed for dreamless sleep.

THE CRACKLE OF FLAMES WOKE ME. FOR ONE PANICKED second I forgot where I was, but sore muscles gave me a hasty reminder. I sat up, stretching the crick in my neck, and peered out from under Akarra's wing. Above the rim of trees, a line of gray spread across the horizon, coloring the world in shades of ash. Around us, wildflowers twisted in the morning breeze and the first birds of dawn chirped under the eaves of the forest. Mist pooled in the hollows of the meadow, a pearly blanket under the lightening sky, and in the midst of such serenity, everything about the Worm felt faint and far away, like a half-forgotten nightmare.

Everything except Leyda.

"We'll have to wake him soon," Akarra said as I stood. She folded her wing back over Daired, who still snored softly, his chin on his chest. "I need to hunt, and you two need to eat before we can fly again."

A circle of scorched earth smoked in front of her, the square of peat she'd laid in the center burning with a fitful flame. I crouched next to the fire. "Akarra, will you tell me something?"

"Of course."

"Will you tell me the truth?"

She lowered her head, opal eyes staring into mine. "Always."

"My sister Leyda. Do you think . . . is there any chance she's still alive?"

"Oh, Aliza. Don't ask me to answer that."

"Please. I need to know."

"There's always a chance."

Tears spilled down my cheeks. "But not much."

"No." Reaching out with her wingtip, she brushed away the tears. "Not much."

I stood, drying my face with my sleeve. I needed to do something, or I'd go mad. "I'm going to find us something to eat."

"Don't go far," Akarra called.

The meadow was fertile, and I didn't have to search long before finding a clump of blackberry bushes. The fruit was small and sparse, but with our meal at House Pendragon only a distant memory, I'd have settled for less. Daired was awake and Akarra was gone by the time I returned to our makeshift camp. The blackened body of a grouse lay next to the fire, its feathers charred and smoking. He knelt beside it, cleaning a second one with his knife. I deposited the berries on the ground. "Where'd those come from?"

"Akarra brought them down for us," he said without looking up. "Here."

Together we worked in silence. I took the cleaned birds from him, skewered them on sharpened sticks, and set them to cook more evenly over the coals. The meat was tough and tasteless, but I scarcely noticed. Daired said nothing as we ate, not about the food, or the battle, or my sister, or even what had passed between us on the balcony. Worry lines creased his face, lines that hadn't been there yesterday. He looked tired, and older, and defeated, as if he'd already fought the battle and lost. He avoided looking at me if he could. When we finished, he stood and moved away from the fire as a tremor ran through him, like wind over calm water. His shoulders heaved once and were still.

"Alastair?"

"No. Don't. I need to say this."

I waited.

"You know what's on the other side of this journey, don't you? You know what you're going to hear at Merybourne Manor."

The broken pieces of my heart splintered again as I forced the word past my lips. "Yes."

"If we can't hold the Worm beyond the river, it'll come south. All of Hart's Run will be in danger." He spoke faster. "I can take you to safety. Akarra and I can get your family out of there, to Edonarle or somewhere on the coast. Say the word, Aliza, and I'll do it, Greater Lindworm and all the *Tekari* be damned. I can't let—"

"No."

He turned and looked at me.

"Your place is with the Riders, Alastair, not with me."

"I need to protect you."

"You have. You *are*. But Arle needs you too, and I won't take you from them." *No matter how much I want to.* My eyes fell to his lips, and for one wild instant I wanted to press mine against them, to let him know how much my feelings had changed, but it wasn't the time. Daired needed to be strong, to be hard. He had a war to win, and I couldn't—I wouldn't—distract him. I stood as Akarra landed at the end of the field. "If you can't save us from this thing, no one can."

"Aliza, you know we can't save everyone."

"Maybe not." With the toe of my boot I turned over a loose clump of sod onto the fire. It flickered, smoldered, and went out. "But you can still save thousands." *Thousands who still have a chance.*

He nodded once and said nothing.

We set off a few minutes later.

NOT LONG AFTERWARD I SAW THE FIRST SIGN OF HOME. The River Meryle twinkled beneath the eaves of the forest surrounding North Fields, shimmering in the summer heat that did nothing to thaw my cold heart. Akarra followed the river to the Manor, scattering a handful of stableboys as she landed in the courtyard.

"You there!" Daired called to one of them. "Find Sir Robart and tell him Aliza is back."

The lad stared at him with wide eyes.

"*Now!*"

With a yelp, the stableboy ran for his life.

"Thank you," I said as Daired helped me down. "For everything."

He leaned close, his forehead almost touching mine. "I wrote it once, and I mean it still. Whatever happens in the next few days, I want you to know that I wish you every happiness the gods can bestow. If I don't—"

"No." I brushed four fingers against his temple. "May Odei give you strength, Janna give you courage, Mikla keep you safe, and Thell take your enemies. You're coming back."

He raised my hand to his lips. I'd scarcely felt the heat of the kiss before he released me and swung onto Akarra's back.

She extended one wingtip and rested her claw on my shoulder. "This is it, I suppose. *Hysehkah, shan'ei.* Goodbye, my friend."

"Goodbye, Akarra. I'll—I'll see you soon."

"Pray so."

And then they were gone, dark specks against the gray sky.

"Aliza!"

Anjey's voice rang through the courtyard. She ran out and threw her arms around me, and I clung to her like a rock in a raging river.

"How did you get here?" she asked when I let go. "Where are Aunt and Uncle?"

"Daired brought me home." I led her inside, telling her of Brysney's appearance at Dragonsmoor on the way. "Anjey, what happened?"

She slumped into a chair, her eyes red and swollen. "A band of wyvern Riders flew through here on their way to warn Edonarle. They told us the news."

"When did Leyda leave?"

"Right after the Riders had gone, but I didn't find her note until just before Cedric left. Aliza, we were all so *blind!* I should've seen it. Wydrick came back to Trollhedge after the muster with some of the other Lower Westhull Rangers. Leyda had been writing to him for weeks."

It made sense; Leyda wouldn't have been able to send letters to Wydrick from much farther away without someone noticing. My blood boiled to think that snake had been under our noses for months. I wanted to scream, to throw something. *Why didn't I ask her who Tristan was? Why did I tell her to make her own adventure? It wasn't supposed to be this!*

"The rest of the regiment cleared out of Trollhedge the next morning and so had Leyda." Anjey rose and left the room, returning a moment later with a sheet of notepaper. "She left this on her bed."

> *I'll be gone by the time you get this. Don't bother coming after me.*
> *I know I'm only sixteen and nobody thinks I'm good for anything,*
> *but I want my share of adventure. Tristan's promised me that*
> *and so much more. I can't disappoint him. I'm going north with*
> *Tristan's regiment to help defeat this lindworm creature. When*
> *I come back to the Manor, I'll finally be the Bentaine girl worth*
> *noticing.*
>
> *Leyda*
Lower Westhull Regiment

Going by the crumple marks, I guessed both Papa and Mama had read her note and balled it up in despair, only to smooth it out again to hunt for some sign that this was all an elaborate joke, that Leyda would come skipping around the corner and admit how pleased she was to have taken everyone in. I read it twice before handing it back to Anjey. "She doesn't think Captain Forstall will allow her to fight, does she? It's murder!"

"Papa's sent letters after the regiment, but it doesn't look good. Everyone's leaving Harborough Hatch."

"There *must* be something we can do."

"There's nothing we can do, my girl."

Papa stood in the doorway of the drawing room, his eyes puffy and his face pale. Seeing him like that broke down the last of my self-control, and I found myself sobbing into his shoulder. He held me tight, smoothed the hair from my forehead, and let me cry.

"I know, I know," he said. "We've all been in a state since reading her letter."

With a sniff I pulled away. "What are we supposed to do?"

"Wait. Pray. Hope that she'll come to her senses and run as far away from that creature as she can." He spoke in the flat, dull tone of someone who talked of hope when he had none left. "Besides that? All we can do is comfort each other."

HOW DO WE DO THAT? HOW CAN WE COMFORT EACH other?

I wondered that more than once over the next few days. Before I'd arrived, Mama had locked herself in her room, and when at last she allowed us inside, I saw someone I almost didn't recognize. Stooped and shaking, her red-rimmed eyes stared at some point beyond us, too full for tears. Here was our mother without schemes, without intrigues, without theatrics, without even her enthusiasm to hold her up. Grief had stripped her raw.

Mari alone bore the news without weeping. When I found her, she had her head buried in her book. "Mari? Are you all right?"

"I'm fine."

"Because you don't have to—"

"Look," she said, pushing her bestiary into my hands. It was open to her chapter on sphinxes. "Read that. I found it ages ago in Uncle's library in Edonarle."

I read where she indicated. She'd copied the line in her spidery handwriting beneath a sketch of a roaring sphinx.

While the sphinx and their close cousins the lamia and the ladon are creatures most deadly, they are also the most word-wise and cunning of the *Tekari*. Their kinds possess the secrets of all the Oldkind, from the resting place of the fearsome sea-serpent to the waking hour of the mighty Worm.

"Mari, I don't see what this has to do with Leyda."

She snatched the book from me. "Don't you *see*? *The waking hour of the mighty Worm!* Other *Tekari* are already flocking to it. Maybe they knew it was coming. Maybe they can tell us how to defeat it!"

Then I understood. Mari didn't mourn for her sister, because she alone hadn't given up hope. In the one small way she knew how, she was trying to save Leyda.

And she might even be right. What had the Elsian minister said? "*All* Tekari *whisper it to each other . . . It is coming.*" Perhaps they had known. I decided not to tell her we had a better chance of slaying the Worm ourselves than we did of cornering a sphinx and forcing it to tell us the secrets of the Greater Lindworm. It was hope, no matter how slim. "That *is* good news," I said. "Keep looking. And, Mari?"

"Hmm?"

I hadn't said it to Rina nearly enough, and I hadn't said it to Leyda when she needed it. I wouldn't make the same mistake with another sister. "I love you. You know that, don't you?"

She looked up. "Of course. I love you too, Aliza."

Again she bent over her book, and I smiled. It was the first time in a while.

NEWS FROM THE NORTH CAME IN FRAGMENTS AND RU-mors over the next few days. Madam Carlyle swore that the Riders and Rangers had held their ground outside of Hatch Ford, turning the Worm and its army away at the Ford with only minimal casualties, the Daireds and their dragons cutting a fiery swath through the enemy. Lord Merybourne assured us that their lines were holding, though many warriors had lost their lives in the battle. Henry Brandon told me in a grave voice that only a few Riders and Rangers were left, many were injured, and the Worm would soon be crossing the river and descending on the south.

I didn't believe Madam Carlyle's optimism, but I wouldn't let myself believe Henry either. *They can defeat it,* I told myself over and over. *All of them together. They have to.*

That did little to comfort my family. Four days of bloody rumors had crushed our hope that Leyda had survived the first attack. As I watched the fifth day dawn from my window, a cold, detached thought sprang to mind: sooner or later, one of us would have to clean out her things. *Might as well be sooner. And it might as well be me.*

As I reached for the rope to lower the curtain, a winged shadow fell over the courtyard.

I flew down the steps to the front hall three at a time and elbowed my way through the Manor-folk gathered in the courtyard, staring at the unexpected arrival and whispering among themselves. Akarra stood in the center of the pavement, her wings outstretched. Daired had just dismounted. When he saw me he started forward.

He held a sobbing Leyda in his arms.

CHAPTER 23

THE ROAD SOUTH

I collapsed with a cry. Perhaps I tried to say thank you, to tell him what it meant to see them again, but I could only manage a few pathetic gasps before bursting into tears. Someone reached down and helped me to my feet, and I blinked back the tears to see Papa and Anjey on either side of me. They were both weeping.

"Her leg's broken," Daired said. "I didn't have time to see to it properly. Sir Robart, do you have someone here who can set a bone?"

"Anjey, run to the kitchens and fetch Madam Moore. Bless you, sir, bless you, bless you!" Papa said, following Daired into the house.

Daired set Leyda down on the first available divan. Sobs racked her body as I inspected her leg. Her leggings were torn at the knee and I could see the break midway up her shin, but it looked clean and the bone hadn't pierced the skin. She clutched my skirt as I stood.

"Aliza, I'm sorry . . . so sorry . . . I didn't know . . ."

"Shh, dearest, it's all right. You're safe now."

Anjey arrived a minute later, bringing Mama and Madam Moore. Mama shouldered her way past Daired and threw her arms around her daughter, her wails drowning out Leyda's tearful apologies.

Daired drew me aside, and for the first time since he'd landed I got a good look at him. A long gash gaped above his eyebrow, clean but otherwise untended. Scuffs, gouges, and spatters of dried blood covered his once shiny armor. He walked with a slight limp. "I need you to take me to Lord Merybourne," he said.

"What's wrong?"

"The battle's not going well."

Daired didn't bother to knock when we reached the study. Lord Merybourne stood at the window, peering into the courtyard, and at our entrance he dropped the curtains he'd been holding back. "Master Daired, what are you doing here?"

"We couldn't hold the Ford," Daired said. "The Worm is coming south. If it doesn't change direction, it'll be at the borders of Hart's Run in a few days' time."

"*What?*"

"Get your people out. Head for the coast; Edonarle if you can, but whatever you do, you have to leave now."

A world of emotions passed over Lord Merybourne's face, from incredulity to terror to despair. "Very well," he said at last. "Excuse me."

"How did you find my sister?" I asked Daired as the door swung shut.

"I was looking for her."

"And Wydrick?"

Shadows gathered behind his eyes. "Blood for blood. I gave him what he deserved."

"Was he with Leyda?"

"He's the one who broke her leg. He . . . was going to use her as bait."

I swallowed the rage that rose like bile in my throat. *He's gone. He's gone, and Leyda's safe. Let it go.* I traced the gouges across Daired's breastplate. "I don't know how we'll ever be able to thank you."

"Only promise me you and your family will leave tonight. I can't fight this creature unless I know you're safe."

"We will. Of course we will. You can kill it, can't you?" *Don't ask me to watch you fly away again without knowing that.*

His sigh sounded like the last breath of a dying man. It was the only answer he gave.

"We'll leave as soon as we can," I said.

"Thank you." He raised his hand as if to stroke my cheek, but checked himself at the last moment. "Goodbye, Aliza. I didn't say it before. I—goodbye."

"Alastair. Alastair, wait!" I cried, but he was already gone.

LORD MERYBOURNE'S VOICE CARRIED ALMOST AS FAR AS the bells he ordered to ring in the south tower, calling all Manor-folk to the Great Hall. Children shrieked as he announced the Worm's approach. Most of the men and some of the women began talking all at once, debating how to best arm themselves for the road. At least one of the stable lads fainted. No one, however, disagreed with Lord Merybourne's decision. It didn't matter how many things we had to leave behind; Merybourne Manor would be empty by dawn.

Our family apartments were eerily still. Mama tended Leyda in silence as Papa collected supplies for the road. Anjey, Mari, and I packed carpetbags with the little that we couldn't live without. I took my charcoals, adding Brysney's dagger at the last minute. "*Tekari are crawling out all over Arle,*" Daired had warned. The road to Edonarle wasn't as wild as the one from Dragonsmoor, but I felt better having the dagger close, even if I prayed I never had to use it.

The first caravan left Merybourne Manor at sundown. Papa made sure we were in the second, promising he'd follow as soon as he could. Neither Lord Merybourne nor anyone else on the Manor's staff would leave until they were sure everyone else was safe.

Leyda lay on one side of the carriage with her leg propped up and Mama's arms around her, protecting her from the jolts and jostles as our coachman whipped the horses away from the Manor. Madam Farris sat on the other side of Mama, her twin boys in her lap. Anjey, Mari, and I crammed together opposite them, clutching our carpetbags and staring out the windows as the only home we'd ever known went rushing past. I couldn't bring myself to feel sorrow, or fear, or grief. What I held most dear couldn't fit in a carpetbag, and I hadn't left it at the Manor.

In any case, I'd already cried myself dry.

We spent the night at a crowded inn in Trollhedge, all five of us squeezed into a tiny room next to the stables. When morning came I expected Mama to bundle us into the carriage and continue south, but over our meager breakfast, she told us otherwise.

"No. We're staying here."

"Mama, you heard Lord Merybourne," Anjey said. "We need to get to Edonarle."

Mama clutched Papa's brown heartstone, which hung on a chain around her neck. "We're not going any farther without your father, Angelina."

After that none of us tried to change her mind.

The sun rose on a steady procession leaving Trollhedge. By noon the next day the road south was clogged with carriages, carts, wagons, and even a few men and women on foot. Anjey and I watched from the inn windows as Henry helped Rya Carlyle and her mother onto a cart. He'd volunteered to stay with our family until Papa joined us.

"We'll be safe here, won't we?" Mari asked as the last carriage pulled away, taking with it the innkeeper and the rest of the inn's occupants. "Papa won't be much longer."

I thought of Betsy and Henshaw and the other servants at the

North Fields lodge. They wouldn't have known about the evacuation unless someone from the Manor rode out to tell them. "We'll be fine."

Henry pushed open the inn door, a cloud of dust trailing after him. "That's the last of them. With everyone heading south, they won't get far today."

"It might be far enough," I said. "The Riders will stop the Worm before it gets here."

"Aye, I'm sure they will," Henry said in a tone that suggested he didn't believe a word of it. "In the meantime, what say we find some food? I hope that whey-brain of an innkeeper left the larder unlocked."

With what stores we could find in the abandoned kitchen, Henry, Anjey, and I managed to cook a passable supper. We served the meal in the common room, where, at Leyda's request, Henry sang for us "The Lay of Saint Ellia of the Shattered Bow."

Just as he reached the part where Ellia loosed her last arrow against the sea-serpent, the door creaked open and Papa stepped inside. "Robart!" Mama cried, and rushed to him. "Oh gods, we were so worried! What took you so long?"

"Henshaw wouldn't leave the lodge. Moira, why didn't you go south with the others?"

"We weren't leaving without you."

Papa dropped his carpetbag and wrapped his arms around his wife. They held each other long and tight, firelight glistening on the tear-tracks that stained Papa's cheeks. He wiped them away with the heel of his hand. "Bless you, Henry, for staying with them."

"You couldn't have sent me away if you tried, Sir Robart."

"We'll set out in the morning," Papa said, settling on the bench with one arm around Mama and the other around Leyda. "But for now, how about you finish that song? You were just at the best part."

SLEEP DIDN'T COME EASILY THAT NIGHT. I LAY BACK-TO-
back with Anjey in the narrow bed, trying to keep warm. It'd been
almost three days since Leyda's return. Doubt and desperation
warred inside me as I tried to guess how the battle was going, tried
to calculate the Riders' chance of success against the crushing odds
of defeat. They could win. They *had* to win. *But when will we know?*

"Aliza," Anjey whispered. "Do you hear that?"

I strained my ears—

And heard the glorious sound of wingbeats.

Anjey and I bolted out of bed and ran to the window. Horsetail
clouds swept the night sky, glowing with a mother-of-pearl sheen
in the moonlight, and my heart leapt at the dark shape descending from the north. "Akarra!" I cried, and rushed out of the room. I
burst onto the deserted street, waving my arms like a madwoman.
"Akarra! Alastair!"

Akarra checked her flight and dropped onto the road in front of
me. She was alone. "Thank the gods, I thought you'd gone farther
south. We have to hurry. There isn't much time!"

"What do you mean? Where is he?"

"We were charging the Worm . . . a gryphon came at me from
below," she panted. "I banked too soon. He missed his stroke and . . .
I didn't mean—"

Dread opened like a pit in the bottom of my heart. "Akarra,
where is Alastair?"

"He's been stung."

No. Please gods, no. Not him.

Alastair Daired couldn't die. If I knew nothing else, I knew that.
I won't let him. I spoke before I knew what I was saying. "What can
I do?"

"Come with me. You're an herbmaster; you might be able to
do him some good, but whatever we do, we have to hurry! They've

taken him to the lodge at North Fields, but the Riders won't be able to keep the *Tekari* back for long."

"Akarra, there's no cure for lindworm venom."

She lashed her tail. "You think I don't *know* that? I can't just watch him die! I have to try *something*, and you're the only one I could think of who might help. Come with me," she said again, dropping her head so she could look me in the eye. "Please. I left the battle for this. I'll . . . I'll do anything."

For the space of a heartbeat, I weighed her words. Going with her meant flying into danger without the guarantee I'd return, and for all that, Daired might still die. But she was right. We had to try something.

"Give me a minute."

I pushed past both my parents on my way to our room. "Aliza? What's going on?" Papa asked. "Aliza!"

I ignored him, taking the stairs two at a time. Even as the blood pounded in my ears, an irrational calm drifted over me. I'd made my decision; what happened next was out of my hands. I caught a glimpse of Brysney's dagger at the bottom of my carpetbag as I pulled out a pair of trousers, and once again the words of the Elsian minister came rushing back, his deadly smile glinting like the edge of that knife.

"All Tekari whisper it to each other . . . It is coming."

Hope bloomed inside me, then wilted just as fast. Even if the minister had told the truth about the *Tekari*, and even if Mari's book was accurate about what sphinxes knew, they were desert creatures, and Arle had no deserts. The closest was in Els, and that was hundreds of leagues from Arle's shores. Daired had a day, maybe two at the most. Akarra couldn't cover a quarter the distance in that time.

But she could get to Cloven Cairn.

I slipped the sheathed dagger into my boot. Maybe we couldn't get to a sphinx, but I'd bet anything that Akarra knew where to find a coven of lamias.

"Aliza?" Anjey said from the threshold. "What's going on?"

"The Riders are holding the Worm at North Fields. Daired's been stung," I said, and she gasped. "I'm going with Akarra. I have to help him."

"You know Papa won't let you."

"I don't care. I'm going."

"Aliza, *no!*" She blocked my exit. "Please! Listen, I'm sorry for Daired, but I'm not going to lose another sister. You can't do this."

Tears filled my eyes as I put a hand on her shoulder. "If it was Brysney lying in that lodge with the Worm's poison in his veins, what would you do?"

She backed away as if I'd slapped her.

"Please don't try to stop me."

"Then I'm coming with you," she said.

"No."

"I can't let you go alone!"

I slipped past her into the hall. "Akarra's coming with me. Anjey, I'm sorry, but there's no time to argue. You all need to leave tonight. Go farther south, as far as you can make it. If you love Cedric, stay safe. It's the only thing you can do for him now."

She looked away, and closed her eyes, and nodded.

"Thank you," I said. "Now come on; we need to wake the girls."

Leyda stirred as Anjey lit the lamp on the table in their room. I knelt at Mari's side of the bed and shook her awake. She blinked and sat up. "Aliza? Anjey? What's wrong?"

"Mari, I need you to answer something for me," I said. "It's a matter of life and death. Would the lamias of Cloven Cairn know a cure for the sting of a lindworm?"

"What? I don't know . . . I think . . ."

"Mari, *please!*"

"If it existed, aye, I think they would. Aliza, what's happened?"

With a kiss to the forehead I bid my sisters goodbye, hurrying away before they could see me cry. *I might never see them again,* I thought as I raced down the stairs. In some small corner of my heart I felt the awful pain of that, but the rest of me had gone too numb to do anything except keep moving.

Papa met me downstairs. "Aliza Bentaine, what is going on?"

"I'm going back to the Manor with Akarra."

He seized my arm. "You'll do no such thing!"

"I'm sorry, Papa," I said, and wrenched out of his grasp.

"Aliza!"

I ran from the inn before he could stop me. Akarra paced in the street. "How far is it from here to Cloven Cairn?" I asked, breathless.

"Are you out of your *mind?* What could you possibly want at the Cairn?"

"There are still lamias there, aren't there? Or did Alastair kill them all?"

"No, he and Lord Erran never made it to the breeding pits. But they—"

"My sister thinks the lamias might know a cure for the Worm's poison."

"That's insane."

"Do you know for certain that they *don't?*"

She growled. "I meant you have no idea how dangerous that is! The coven lives in a cave beneath the Cairn. If you go in there, I can't come with you. I can't protect you."

Despair settled hard and icy in the pit of my stomach. *A coven of lamias at my throat, swinging their war-scythes to take off my head, and they might not know anything about the Worm.* I could die in vain without ever seeing Alastair or my family again.

Then again, if I didn't take this chance he'd die anyway, and if there was even a fool's hope of saving him, I could do no less. I climbed onto her back.

"We have to try."

"Very well." Akarra spread her wings. "Hold on tight."

FIELDS AND FORESTS SPED BY BENEATH US, PALE AND ghostly in the moonlight. Without Daired's arms around me I felt doubly exposed, buffeted on all sides by the cold night wind and by my own growing fear. I flattened myself against Akarra's back and held on, both for my life and for his.

Hours later the sky ahead of us began to lighten, first gray, then warming in shades of orange and gold as the sun rose, revealing the landscape below. An ugly gash lay across the countryside where the Worm and its army had crawled south, leaving trees torn up by their roots, streams poisoned and muddied, and towns in ruins. Akarra swooped low over one of the smaller villages, and I saw the broken bodies of a horse and its rider crushed into the mud in what had once been the main street of the town. The figure's red cloak made its shroud. I closed my eyes and turned away.

Akarra started her descent as the crags grew higher around us, rising out of the earth like broken bones. The sun still shone high in the sky, but mist hung between the towering columns of stone, twining around them with greedy, insubstantial fingers. She landed on a scree-covered slope just below the highest crag. At its summit stood a pillar of white stone, its point sundered and blackened by lightning. Below the cloven stone, a slit of darkness opened like a knife wound in the hillside. I swung off Akarra's back.

"This is Cloven Cairn," she said. "Be careful. They'll know we're here. You're a woman, so they won't kill you on sight, and if they don't think you're a threat, they just might let you speak. Good luck, Aliza."

My legs shook as I started for the entrance, not daring to think either of the chaos behind me or the deadly danger before me. A foul stench rose from the mouth of the cave. Pressing my sleeve to my nose, I took a deep breath through my mouth and stepped into the darkness.

CHAPTER 24

THE BATTLE OF NORTH FIELDS

The cold blade of a scythe scraped my throat.

"*Hsssst!*"

"I'm not armed!" I cried, raising my hands and hoping my terror made the lie believable.

"Yesss, and that isn't a *dragon* pacing outside." A voice spoke from the darkness, soft, hissing, and just human enough to make my skin crawl. "No dragonrider would enter our domain without their preciouss weaponss."

"I'm not a Rider."

The scythe twitched beneath my chin. "Sso what are you, sstranger? Jusst a *fool?*"

Whatever ground I'd won with my audacity I felt slipping away. "*You're a woman, so they won't kill you on sight.*" *Why wouldn't they kill a woman?* I wished I had Mari's bestiary, or better yet, Mari herself. She'd know what to do. I could only guess. "I heard the Broodmother Crone could answer a question that's been plaguing me. My . . . brother told me I was wrong, that the lamias know nothing and would kill me anyway." I knelt and bent my head. "I can see he was right. You may as well kill me now," I said, and held my breath, and waited to see if I'd pay for my gamble with my life.

A minute of silence passed, each second sharper than the blade that grazed my skin. At last the sentry scoffed. "What answsers do you sseek?"

"Take me to the Broodmother and you'll see."

She spat and lowered her scythe. "Yess indeed, we shall ssee. On your feet." Her blade settled between my shoulders as she pushed me deeper into the cave. I stretched my hands in front of me, feeling each step with my toe. "Fassster, human!"

"I can't se—"

The ground gave way. I screamed and plunged down a flight of stone steps, landing hard on my knee. The instant I opened my mouth, a chorus of hissing rose around me.

"Ssssst! That wasss a human voice!"

"I ssmell blood. Human *indeed*."

"Iss it a Rider?"

"Lightsss! Let there be lightsss!"

The last voice rang with authority. No sooner had it spoken than the entire cavern blazed with torchlight, and at last I could see the creatures I'd been foolish enough to seek out. Writhing, hissing lamias filled the pit into which I'd fallen. From the waist down they were snakes; from the waist up they looked like gaunt, spectral women, clothed in the flayed hides of creatures I didn't wish to name. A hundred mouths opened as I scrabbled to my feet, giving a glimpse of fangs and forked tongues.

"What have you brought uss?" the voice that had called for lights demanded.

Again I felt the scythe between my shoulder blades. "A human child sseeking answswerss from the Broodmother Crone," the sentry said, pushing me toward the center of the pit. Lamias on either side parted to let us through. "Kneel here, human, and assk your quesstion. Ssee if we cannot prove thiss man wrong."

I sank to my knees in the stone ring at the middle of the nest and risked a glance over my shoulder. A patch of daylight shone just beyond the lip of the pit, so close, yet so impossibly far.

"Well?" the authoritative lamia asked. She couldn't be anything but the Broodmother Crone. Black wings stretched from her shoulders, webbed and bloodless as a bat's, and she wore a crown fashioned from a split skull. A *human* skull.

"Honorable Crone, my brother told me that you kill anyone who enters your Cairn, even if they come seeking your wisdom. If he's right, I'd only ask that you give me an answer before taking my head."

The Crone hissed. "Your *brother?* Your brother iss a fool. I will answwer your quesstion, but in return for your ssafe passage from my Cairn, you musst promise to answer one of mine."

"Agreed."

"Assk your question."

"What will cure the poison of a lindworm?"

The Crone flapped her wings and crowed. "Oh-ho! The human world has felt our cousin's ssting! My sisstters and I rejoiced at the waking of the Worm, little girl. It has sslept far too long. It will lead the *Tekari* to victory againsst you human ussurperss and your traitor allies, and we shall sspread across this land once again, to kill and blight and sspawn as we will."

"Is that your answer?"

"You are impatient as well as foolish. Yet I admire your courage, and sso I will tell you how to ssurvive its ssting. You may not be glad when you know." Her tail twitched as she fixed me with a ghastly smile. "To be sstung by the Worm and yet live, someone musst do to it what it tried to do to you. It musst be slain, and to cure its poison you musst eat its heart."

"Thank you," I said, and backed toward the stairs. "That's all I wanted to know."

"One moment, human. You have yet to answer my quesstion. And beware! I will know if you lie to me, jusst as I know you have no brother."

I froze.

The Broodmother laughed. "Yess, I sspoke truly when I ssaid I respected your courage. I do not resspect your clumsy attempts at a deception. So sspeak honestly, or you will never again see the light of the sssun."

"What's your question?"

"What iss the name of the poisoned one?"

In an instant I saw the trap they'd laid for me. The Brood-mother Crone was right; knowing the secret of the Greater Lind-worm hadn't made me glad. It'd only added false hope to the death sentence I'd signed by arriving at Cloven Cairn on the wings of a Daired dragon. Of course they'd recognized Akarra. No one, least of all the Broodmother, could forget the slayer of her predeces-sor. Even if Daired hadn't managed to kill all of them, I could only imagine the mountain of lamia corpses he'd left behind. The lamias around me didn't have to imagine it.

"Sspeak. What iss the name?"

So be it. I straightened and met the Crone's soulless stare. "His name is Alastair Daired."

And I turned and ran for my life.

Hisses and shrieks erupted behind me as I caught the stone lip and swung out of the pit. A long-nailed hand clawed at my boot and I kicked free, my heel crunching against scales and bone. The lamia screamed and fell back, giving me a half second head start as the snakish creatures swarmed over their fallen sister and up the steps, blades swinging. I dared not look back as I plunged toward the sliver of daylight. "Akarra!"

A scythe caught my shoulder and I twisted away.

"AKARRA!"

"Aliza, run!" Akarra cried.

I burst into open air. With a roar that sent showers of scree cascading down the mountain, Akarra arched her back and exhaled a column of dragonfire into the mouth of the Cairn—

Too soon.

My second scream was stillborn as smoke clogged my lungs, accompanied by a crisping sound and an awful smell. Gasping, I rolled down the slope. Gravel scraped my palms and tore at my cheek. The roar of the flames stopped and I looked up the slope to see Akarra half running, half flying toward me. No lamias followed.

"Your shoulder!" she said.

My sleeve was split open at the seam. Blood flowered crimson along my arm and trickled down my back from a long cut above my shoulder blade. "It's fine," I said, pushing the pain away as I climbed into the saddle. My head felt light. I reached up. The dragonfire had seared my braid clean off.

"Did they know?" Akarra asked. "Did they tell you?"

I bent over the saddlebow and rested my forehead against her scales, the singed ends of my hair sticking to my sweaty brow. "He has to eat the heart of the lindworm."

Akarra leapt into the air and wheeled west, toward Hart's Run and the impossible cure.

MORE THAN ONCE I DRIFTED OUT OF CONSCIOUSNESS, only to jolt awake, clinging to the saddle with strength borne of sheer desperation. She flew as fast as she dared. *What good is any of this if the Worm can't be killed?* I thought as we flew over the Worm's destruction. The sun was dropping close to the horizon when the landscape grew familiar. Hills dark with evergreens rose beneath us, and I could make out the crags of the Witherwood below.

Akarra banked to the left, and over the crest of the last hill the grassy slopes of North Fields came into view.

It was a scene of slaughter. The Worm lay sprawled at the east end of the fields, more terrible than I'd pictured even in my nightmares. The sketch in Mari's bestiary didn't do justice to the grotesque, maggot-white hide, the red, rimless eyes or the mouth that split its enormous head like an ill-healed wound. A ripple ran down the length of its body until it reached its tail, and with a reflexive jerk, it tore trees up by their roots. The carcasses of dozens of Riders, Rangers, wyverns, beoryns, and horses lay beneath its claws, some of them half eaten. I retched to see the mangled remains of a red cloak hanging wedged between the Worm's teeth.

Around it, the battle raged. Armor-clad centaurs galloped against beoryn Riders and horse-mounted Rangers, their spears and crossbow bolts clashing against swords and shields. I picked out Mar'esh at once, his sapphire scales standing out in the midst of the blood-drenched ground. He and Julienna fought alongside Nerissa Ruthven and the Rangers, Mar'esh with tail and teeth and talons, Julienna with buckler and longsword. Smoke roiled up from the Arleans' left flank, where half a dozen forge-wights held the line with Ruthven and Burrumburrem. Their swords glowed with a blue-hot heat, burning through the enemy's lines, but there were too few of them, and too many *Tekari*. At least one forge-wight had already fallen beneath a centaur's spear, his body smoldering on the broken earth.

In the air, the remaining Daireds and a handful of wyvern

Riders battled a horde of gryphons, a knot of wings and flames and feathered shrieks writhing just out of reach of the Worm's mouth. Valkyries circled the Worm's head like an unholy halo, watching the battle and laughing at each blow struck against the Arlean defenders. Hanging back from the hottest part of the fight, a pack of direwolves howled and bayed, savaging the bodies of the dead. Trolls lumbered here and there, sometimes lunging at a Ranger, sometimes at a Rider, sometimes even at the *Tekari*. Over it all echoed the screams of the banshees hidden beneath the eaves of the forest, guarding the rear flanks.

The Worm's mouth broke open in a gruesome grin, its tongue snaking out as it relished the destruction it had inspired. Poison dripped from the barbed tip, black as old blood.

"Akarra, where's Brysney? I don't see him!"

"There!"

She glided to land on the hill overlooking the battle, where a few Riders and Rangers tended to their wounds beyond the reach of the advancing *Tekari*. Charis leaned against her mare as her brother wrapped her arm, her face tight with pain. She gasped when she saw us. "Akarra? Where in Thell's name have you been?"

Brysney swore as I lurched off Akarra's back. "And Aliza? What are you doing here? Is Anjey all right?"

"She's fine," I panted. "She's safe. Is Daired still alive?

"Yes. Barely. Henshaw's with him in the lodge."

"We know what will cure him."

Every Rider in earshot turned to us, and I told them what I'd learned. Charis and Brysney listened without speaking. Charis hardly breathed, her eyes fixed on my face. When I finished, she looked away.

"But what good does that do us?" asked one of the wyvern Riders I didn't know. He had a bandage wrapped around his left eye, which, judging by the blood dripping from his chin, was no longer there. "Take a look, miss. We're doing all we can to stay alive against the *Tekari*. We can't risk going against the Worm on the word of some *nakla*, not even for Lord Daired."

Akarra hissed. "You'd say that, Sadler? After what Alastair did for you? That gryphon was about to *gut* you."

Sadler shifted under her searing gaze. "I'm not ungrateful. I thank Mikla for each and every *Tekari* head Lord Daired's taken, but he's long past saving, and we have another battle to fight right now."

"He's right, Akarra. We need every warrior we have left. We can't throw our lives away against something that can't be killed," Brysney said. "Aliza, you need to get out of here. There should be a horse at the lodge. If you can't ride, find someone there who can. We need to get word to Edonarle. The king needs to be ready."

I looked from Brysney to Akarra to Sadler, and back to Brysney. "No."

"What?"

Words came to mind, stupid, impossible, foolish words, and the truest I'd ever spoken. "If I have to, I'll cut the Worm's heart out myself. I will not let him die."

Charis turned and looked at me.

Sadler scoffed and returned to bandaging his wyvern's leg. Brysney said something sharp to Akarra in Eth, to which she responded even more sharply. Their argument grew heated, angry voices cresting like waves, mixing with the roar of battle that rolled over us in an endless song of fury and death. My temples throbbed.

Charis came toward me. "How do you know the lamias were telling the truth?" she asked, so softly only I could hear.

"They meant to kill me. They wouldn't lie to a dead woman."

"You have no idea how foolish that was. Foolish and reckless and mad and—*why* did you do it, Aliza?" She seized my arm, a wild look in her eye. "Tell me!"

"*Because I love him!*"

The wild look melted into something else, something that made me forget the pain of my injuries and the hopelessness weighing on my heart. Charis Brysney was crying. "Will you do what you said?" she whispered. "Will you save him?"

"I'll do whatever I have to do."

She closed her eyes. When she opened them, her tears were gone. "Then so will I."

"Charis, we need—what are you doing?" Brysney said, finally noticing us.

She released me and swung up onto her mare. "You're wrong, Cedric. The battle's not over yet. The Worm can be killed."

"Don't be a fool. You know we've tried everything. People have *died* trying everything."

"Not us. Not me."

"What are you talking about?"

"Goodbye, brother."

And she wheeled to face the Worm.

"You want revenge, slug-spawn?" she screamed. "Come and take it!"

"Charis, NO!"

A roar rose from the enemy lines as they caught sight of the tiny figure on horseback streaking across the fields, dodging ally and adversary alike. The Riders and Rangers who saw her cried for her to stop. None of the *Tekari* tried to attack her. She had challenged the Greater Lindworm, and the Greater Lindworm alone would answer. Its tongue lolled from its mouth as if to welcome the latest course of its despicable meal. She rode on, heedless of the head that lowered at her approach, her battle cry echoing shrill and terrible across the hills as the Worm's mouth opened wider, wider . . .

Just before it closed, Charis stood up in the saddle, drew her sword, and thrust it deep into the creature's upper palate.

A thunderous growl shook the ground as its jaws shut over horse and Rider.

Brysney screamed and fell to his knees.

The Worm inched forward, then stopped, its throat heaving and convulsing as it swallowed. It swayed once, bellowed, and advanced.

The sound shattered the spell Charis's death had laid on us. Roaring like a madman, Brysney sprang onto Silverwing's back as the *Tekari* surged across the fields, following their monstrous general.

"Aliza, get on my back!" Akarra cried. "*Now!*"

Fear gave me strength I never knew I had. I swung into the saddle, clinging for life and all it was worth as she dodged a lunging valkyrie. Over her wing I saw Brysney and Silverwing dive toward the lindworm, wheeling out of reach above its head. The Worm roared again, rising on its segmented belly to follow their flight. Silverwing sped upward, taking Brysney away from the glistening teeth and barbed tongue and slim silver glint of a blade still wedged in the upper half of the Worm's jaw, deeply, but not deeply enough . . .

The Worm threw itself after them, Silverwing's tail just yards from the tip of its poisoned tongue, then only feet.

In midair, Brysney drew his sword and flipped backward off his wyvern.

"Brysney, *no!*" I cried.

His blade came down in a singing arc as he tumbled past its open mouth, severing the barbed tongue. It snaked through the air, trailing black blood as it fell. Brysney fell with it.

With a sound like slabs of rotten meat colliding, the Worm's mouth snapped shut, driving home Charis's blade.

A shudder ran through the Worm as blood bubbled out from between its teeth. Trees came up in clumps, torn from the ground by the Worm's frenzied death throes as the creature collapsed on itself, its massive body crumpling with the force of an earthquake.

Silverwing dove, catching Brysney moments before he hit the ground.

"Aliza, hold on!" Akarra cried.

A gryphon barreled into her from her left. She twisted out of reach and leapt a few feet into the air, jaws snapping, but the motion caught me off guard. My grip broke and I slipped from her back.

The ground came sooner than I expected, slamming the breath from my lungs. For an instant I lay still, gasping, too stunned to move, too afraid to look where I'd fallen. *Get up get up get up!* I sucked in an agonizing breath and rolled to my feet. Not far away, the Worm lay shuddering in its last throes. Silverwing landed next to it. It didn't react as Brysney climbed onto its snout, the maggot-white flesh half buried in the earth. One red eye stared up at him, glazed with the creeping stupor of death.

Brysney drew his sword and drove it into that eye with all his might. He withdrew and stabbed again, and again, and again, until his blade was black with blood and the Greater Lindworm moved no more.

Something *twanged* behind me.

I sprawled flat as a bolt from a centaur's crossbow whistled past my ear. The bolt buried itself in the ground, but the centaur didn't try shooting again. A direwolf crouched between the two of us, its graying snout dyed red with the blood of the horse it'd just mauled. Seeing me alone, unarmed, and unprotected, its mouth fell open in a wolfish grin.

No, not unarmed.

It pounced in the same instant I drew Brysney's dagger. My own scream sounded faint and far away as I fell to my knees, its jaws missing my head by inches. With every last ounce of strength I possessed, I thrust my knife upward into its exposed throat.

I felt blood, and heat, and crushing weight, and pain, and then . . . nothing.

CHAPTER 25

HEART'S BLOOD

A steady rocking motion stirred me back to full con-sciousness. Bleary-eyed, I blinked away the cobwebs. It took a second for the face above me to swim into focus, with its dark skin, glowering brow, and the three scars that marked that grizzled jawline.

"Ruthven?"

I sat up, or tried to. I didn't get far, though in trying I realized why the world was moving. Ruthven was carrying me toward the lodge. His wife walked at his side, her face grave and flecked with *Tekari* blood. Burrumburrem paced a little behind us. I didn't see Bluescale.

"Better not, miss," Ruthven said gruffly.

"What's going on? What about the battle?" Panic seized me. "The heart! Daired needs the heart!"

"They're cutting it out now," Nerissa said. "Cedric and Julienna and Akarra. The battle is over and the *Tekari* are retreating. You'd best not move. You're hurt."

Even as she spoke, the worst of the pain came flooding back. Both wrists ached, and judging by the awkward way my knee hung over Ruthven's arm, I'd done something nasty to it as well. The scythe cut along my shoulder throbbed. Each time it brushed Ruthven's gardbrace, I felt the dried blood crusting beneath the sleeve of my ruined dress.

My fragmented memories of the last few minutes began to pull together. "The direwolf. Did I kill it?"

A ghost of a smile creased Ruthven's eyes without making its way to his lips. "No."

"Julienna finished it off," Nerissa said as we reached the lodge. "But you did make its last moments rather unpleasant."

Ruthven maneuvered the two of us through the door and deposited me on the nearest sofa. I stood, took one step, stumbled, and caught myself. "Where's Daired?"

"You need to rest, Miss Aliza," Nerissa said. "You're not strong enough."

"I am for this. Please. I need to see him."

She sighed. "He's in the parlor with the others."

Henshaw had turned the North Field lodge into an infirmary, with wounded Riders and Rangers draped on every available surface. I limped past men and women with broken limbs and bloody gashes. Midway through the room I had to stop, shocked to see Ranger Ned Dennys's face fixed in the surprised expression of the newly dead. A centaur's arrow protruded from his gut. Laid out on a pillow next to him was the tiny body of Lieutenant Punch.

I covered my mouth as tears ran down my cheeks.

Over the edge of the sofa a small green head swung into view, homely and comforting and utterly unexpected.

"Tobble?"

Tobble jumped. "Aliza! Good earth, what are you doing here?" His wilted dandelion eyes darted to the door. "What's happening out there? Is everything all right?"

"Aye." I wiped away the tears with the heel of my hand. "The Worm is dead and the rest of the *Tekari* are fleeing. What are you doing here?"

"We can't do much, us garden-folk, but this is our home too." He reached down and closed Ned Dennys's eyes. "We do what we can." He put his hand on mine. "Your shoulder!"

"It's fine."

"Let me get a bandage."

"In a minute. I need to see Daired."

Tobble nodded to the cot spread out in the far corner of the parlor. "He's over there."

Daired tossed and turned in a feverish doze, shaking despite the blankets Henshaw had piled on top of him. I knelt next to the mattress, ignoring the protests of my sore knee. *Oh gods.* The three fingers that remained on his left hand stuck out from beneath a bandage, which reeked of some sour poultice. He had a new cut along his brow, and along with part of his eyebrow, his enemy's blade had nicked off the top of his left ear, but awful as they were, those injuries didn't worry me. Heart in my throat, I pulled back the makeshift dressing on his right shoulder.

A hole gaped where the Worm's barbed tongue had pierced his armor. The wound oozed black blood. Black too were the veins that ran along his arm, pulsing sluggishly beneath my touch. His hand was cold.

Tobble climbed up onto the mattress. "We cleaned them all, but I don't think it did that one much good."

"Don't worry. He's going to live," I said, more to myself than to Tobble. The front door banged open as I smoothed the hair from Daired's sweat-slicked brow. *He has to live.*

"We have it!" Julienna cried, rushing into the parlor, her face blood-spattered but triumphant. She held the Worm's heart above her head. It was smaller than I'd expected, pale and wrinkled like some dreadful, unclean raisin. Brysney followed her.

I touched Daired's shoulder. "Alastair? Alastair, wake up!" For one horrible moment he didn't move. I shook him again. Slowly, painfully, he stirred, but seeing him conscious didn't bring the comfort I thought it would. The whites of his eyes were shot through with black.

"You have to eat this, Alastair," Julienna said, setting the heart in front of him. "The Broodmother Crone told Aliza that it would save you."

Daired looked at his sister, then at me, and tried to speak, but Brysney wouldn't let him. "Cut it up, Julienna. He's too weak to eat it on his own."

Julienna drew her dagger and began slicing the heart into pieces. I turned away and studied the floor, unwilling to leave but unable to watch. A trail of blood had followed Julienna, the thick drops soaking into the wood floor and spreading a horrible black stain. *After all I've been through, I am not going to be sick now. Blast it all if I . . .*

Something glinted at Julienna's feet. I bent to look closer. That was no bloodstain.

Could it be?

As soon as I touched it, I knew. No larger than a peach pit, the stone reflected emerald lights deep within its faceted surface. I picked it up, my disgust forgotten.

I held the heartstone of the Greater Lindworm.

"Brysney?"

He turned and I offered him the heartstone. Surprise and anguish filled his face, and he closed my hand around the gem. "No. You keep it."

"I can't."

"Yes, you can. Please. I don't want it. It belongs to Charis, not me, and if anyone had to bear her heartstone, she would've wanted it to be Alastair." He lowered his voice as Julienna carved the last bit of the heart. "You know as well as I do that yours is the only one he'll ever accept, and he—Aliza?"

I never knew if Brysney's confession or my own injuries overcame me at that moment. My name was the last thing I heard before falling down in a dead faint.

THE SWEET SCENT OF HONEY AND HUSH WORKED BETTER than smelling salts, or at least a good deal more pleasantly. I woke in a goose-down bed to the blissful sensation of someone laying something cool over my torn shoulder.

"I think Akarra owes you an apology," Daired said.

I stared at him, thanking every facet of the Fourfold God at once. The color had come back into his face and the whites of his eyes were no longer shot through with black. His left arm, and the mass of bandages that enclosed his ruined left hand, hung from a sling. He moved slowly, but he moved, and that was more than enough for me.

"How long have I been asleep?"

"Since yesterday evening," he said. "It's dusk now."

"And you're all right?"

"I'll live," he said, undisguised wonder in his voice. "Which is more than I might've said for you if you'd been a few feet closer to Akarra when she ignited," he said, adjusting the honey-and-hush-soaked square of cloth that covered my shoulder.

Only then did I notice that I wore nothing beneath the covers but the ragged remains of my trousers and a chemise, though calling that scrap of cloth a chemise was nothing short of generous. Someone had cut off the sleeve, leaving my arm free for the poultice. *Mama would have a fit*, I thought vaguely before realizing, with a pleasant jolt of surprise, that I no longer cared what she—or any-one else—thought about my current wardrobe. Close encounters with death put things like propriety into perspective.

And in any case, I wasn't about to ask Daired to stop.

"I'm sorry about your hair," he said. "What in *Thell's* name was Akarra thinking?"

"She saved my life."

He set the bowl of honey and hush down hard on the night-stand. "I mean what was she thinking taking you to the Cairn?"

"We needed to find the cure for the Worm's sting."

"Yes, Cedric told me. Why did you go to the lamias?"

"My sister Mari thought they might know the cure."

He sighed. "Aliza, it's not that I'm not grateful. I am, truly. But that's not what I meant."

"What do you mean?"

"Why did *you* have to go?"

I smiled. "I couldn't let you die. Neither could Akarra. She loves you, you know."

He didn't answer for a long time, clenching and unclenching his right fist. "What did you say to the lamias?" he asked at last.

"I told them I'd made a bet with my brother that they couldn't answer my question."

"Clever."

"It only worked because they let it. The Broodmother Crone knew I was lying. She recognized Akarra, and she remembered you."

"Good." He stood and moved to the window, resting his good hand on the sill. "How is your sister?"

"Leyda? She's all right, I think. Her leg will heal."

"And the rest?"

"I'm not sure. Ever since Rina died she's talked of becoming a warrior, but now . . . now I don't know."

"She's about Julienna's age, isn't she?"

"Sixteen." There was a clatter and a thump from the direction of the stairs. "Nearly seventeen now."

"Old, but maybe not too old," he said quietly. "Not if she wants to learn."

Footsteps pounded in the hall outside.

"Learn what?"

"Riders start their training at four, but I've heard of some—" He broke off, peering through the glass. "Oh no."

"What's going—?"

Julienna burst into the room. "Alastair, Aliza," she said. "I'm sorry; I heard voices."

Daired pointed out the window. "What is *she* doing here?"

"She said to tell her the minute Aliza woke up."

I struggled to sit upright. "Who?"

"The Drakaina's outside. She wants to speak to you. Alone."

"Now?" Daired said. "Julienna, she's hurt. She needs to rest. Even the Drakaina could—"

"Now."

There was a weighty pause. "I'm sorry, Aliza," Daired said. "You should go."

What on earth does the Drakaina want with me? It was all I could think as Julienna flung a dressing gown over my shoulders. I pushed the loose strands of hair away from my face. The ends still smelled smoky, and I fought the urge to reach for the braid that no longer existed as I followed Julienna outside.

The sun had dipped below the rim of the hills, plunging the whole valley into rich blue shadow. In the distance I could just make out the carcass of the Worm. Around it milled dozens of Riders and Rangers, still working to collect the bodies of their fallen comrades. The Drakaina paced the flagstone courtyard in front of the lodge, flexing her wings and hissing under her breath.

Somehow I managed to curtsy. "You wanted to see me, Drakaina?"

Herreki stopped pacing. "Aliza Bentaine, you have done House Daired a grievous wrong."

"I'm sorry?"

"You have defiled the sacred bond of *khela* and dragon, and you have publicly disgraced my own fire and blood. Don't pretend you don't understand," she said. "You rode *Ahla-Na-al Kanah-sha'an-Akarra* into grave danger without training, without armor, and without consent of Lord Alastair."

"Akarra asked me to come with her."

"Foolish girl! Akarra is blinded by sentiment. She knew as well as you did what dishonor it would bring to bear a *nakla*, but she couldn't look beyond her precious *khela*. Still, I might forgive her for her faults of fondness sooner than I can forgive yours."

"What faults are those?"

"Your arrogance! Your thirst for glory! You'd risk Akarra's reputation and your own sorry life for the praise only due a Rider." She growled, and this time I could feel the dry lick of dragonfire in the air. "I'll not allow our noble name to bear the stain of your insufferable presumption. None of your deeds will ever be sung when they tell of the slaying of the Great Worm, and you will leave Arle by next fortnight. You—"

"No."

"What?"

"I'll do no such thing, Drakaina. I don't care whether or not the bards sing about me, but I won't leave Arle."

"You selfish, insolent—"

"Because you're wrong. I didn't risk the journey to Cloven Cairn for glory."

A laugh like unforgiving thunder rumbled deep in her throat. "Don't think you can play games with me. I was told what you said on the battlefield. You *cannot* love Lord Alastair. You may think yourself infatuated, but you hardly know him. Pretending you do will not help your case. You wanted glory, nothing more." A victorious gleam glittered in her eyes when I didn't answer. "Yes, *nakla*. You should've realized long ago that a girl like you could never be worthy of a Daired."

"Maybe I'm not," I said, my voice sounding thin through the pulse humming in my ears. "And maybe I don't know him as well as you, but I know enough."

Warrior and killer, defender and guardian of Arle; whatever else he was, or whatever else he could be, Alastair Daired was a good man. I'd seen it firsthand, even when I didn't want to. He'd helped mend Anjey's relationship with Brysney. He'd saved Leyda. He'd risked the wrath of his fellow Riders to warn the Manor of the Worm's approach. He'd fought and bled and nearly died to protect the people of Hart's Run. To protect *my* people.

I met Herreki's fiery gaze. "Maybe I don't love him the way you think he deserves, but at least I'm willing to learn. If it takes the rest of my life, well, so be it. I'm not going anywhere."

The moment the words left my lips, I realized they'd be my last in the land of the living.

With a roar that shook the lodge, Herreki lunged.

"*NO!*"

Like a stone Akarra fell from the sky. The pavement cracked as she landed between us, spreading her wings to shield me from the Drakaina.

Herreki reared. "Stand aside! Isn't your disgrace enough?"

"There's no disgrace in what we've done, Drakaina."

"You broke our sacred tradition!"

"We saved the lord of House Pendragon and Lady Catriona's heir," Akarra said, a growl accenting each word. "No tradition means more than that!"

"I said stand aside, you rebellious little *fewmet!*"

"No."

"What's this girl to you that you'd dare defy me?"

"She's my sister-in-arms, and I do defy you."

"I owe that ill-bred country wench no respect, and neither do you! She's no Rider."

"No, she's not." Daired's voice rang out across the courtyard, small compared to Herreki's but full of power. "But I am." He strode from the lodge and placed himself in front of Akarra, heartstone blade drawn. He held it clumsily in his stiff right hand, but he held it, and I'd no doubt he'd strike if needed. "By your oath to my family you *do* owe me respect, and I say Lady Aliza has proven herself worthy of any Rider ten times over. You will not touch her."

The Drakaina roared a second time and lashed her tail, but even as the air crackled with dragonfire, she raised her wings and sprang into the air, flying toward the ruins of the Worm and leaving Daired unchallenged, Akarra unhurt, and me—incredibly—alive.

Weak with relief, hunger, and two of the most terrifying days of my life, my knee at last gave way and I slumped forward. *Oh, blast dignity.*

Akarra's wing darted out, catching me before I hit the ground. "Aliza! Are you all right?"

"Aye, I'm fine. Just . . . just tell me one thing, will you?"

"Yes?" she and Daired said together.

"If there are any more angry dragons or rampaging *Tekari* we need to face today, could they at least wait until after dinner?"

THE NEXT DAY I SET ABOUT THE SERIOUS TASK OF REGAIN-
ing my strength, a process which involved a lot of rest, a lot of Tobble's fussing with various poultices, and many, many cups of tea.
Daired saw me in the morning and evening, but duty kept him and
the other Riders and Rangers away, occupied with the solemn business of recovering the remains of their fallen comrades. He didn't
say how many friends of his had died. I cut moorflowers from the
garden and laid them at the stone feet of Thell, and didn't ask.

When I told him what Charis had done to bring down the
Worm, he turned away from me, buried his head in his hands, and
wept.

I saw even less of Brysney. He and Silverwing left the lodge
before dawn and returned long after dark, haggard and silent. That
night I woke to the sound of his cries from across the lodge, pleading with his sister, even in his sleep, to stop before she reached the
Worm.

The following morning, the creak of a wagon outside the lodge
alerted me to the arrival of a few familiar faces. Lord Merybourne
climbed out first, his hair and beard threaded with streaks of silver
that hadn't been there the last time I'd seen him. Papa and Anjey
were with him.

"Aliza!" Anjey cried, and rushed forward to embrace me.

"*Ow.*"

"Oh! I'm sorry." She backed away, taking in the sight of my bandaged shoulder and short hair. "What happened?"

Papa gently but firmly moved her aside before I could answer.
His face looked crumpled and worn as old parchment, and I had
the horrible feeling he hadn't slept since the night I'd left Trollhedge. "Yes, what *did* happen here?"

"A wyvern Rider found us last night and delivered the news. He didn't give us any details," Anjey said. "All he could tell us was that the Worm was dead, and that you weren't. We set off as soon as—"

"Anjey?" Brysney stood in the doorway of the lodge, his haunted eyes drinking in the sight of my sister like a desert traveler at a freshwater spring. "Is it really you?"

Anjey ran to him, threw her arms around his neck, and, in front of our father, Lord Merybourne, Daired, and Julienna, she kissed Brysney full on the mouth.

For a moment, a minute, an eternity, they held each other and said nothing.

They didn't need to.

CHAPTER 26

THE FINAL PYRE

Lord Merybourne and Papa spent the day with Lady Catriona and the chief Riders. Together they surveyed the ruin of North Fields, assessing the damage and its cost to the Manor. I didn't envy their task. In the summer heat the Worm's corpse had already begun to smell, and by late afternoon even a breeze from the north had become almost unbearable. Papa told us the Riders and the forge-wights planned to burn everything that evening, and sunset couldn't come soon enough.

Anjey and I stayed in our room at the lodge while we waited for dusk. To pass the time she explained what had happened after I left with Akarra.

"Were Mama and Papa angry at me for leaving?" I asked.

With a *snip* a few strands of hair fell to the floor. Anjey was busy evening out the singed ends of my hair. "Angry? Not really. Scared, yes. We were all scared for you."

"I was scared for me too."

She set the shears down on the table. "I know why you did it, Aliza, and I don't blame you. You were right: I'd have done the same for Cedric without thinking twice. Whatever anyone else says when we get home, I need you to know that. You did the right thing."

What she didn't say, I heard. *I forgive you.*

I took her hand. *Thank you.*

"Henry's already working on a ballad," she said with a smile. "I heard him practicing before we left. It sounded as though your exploits might feature in several verses."

"Oh dear. He'll make me sound *dreadfully* romantic. He does know I didn't actually kill the Worm, doesn't he?"

"That doesn't make what you did any less heroic. I can't imagine facing a lamia coven by myself. You were very brave."

I stiffened. I was kneeling once again in the Cairn, face-to-face with the Broodmother Crone. A thrill of horror shook me to my core, and I wrapped my arms around my knees, willing the memory away. It didn't fade easily. *And it never will,* I realized. Some part of me would never leave the Cairn, would never be able to forget the blank stare of the Broodmother's skull crown, or her hissing laughter. My shoulder throbbed. "I was *terrified.*"

"The two aren't mutually exclusive, you know."

Footsteps sounded in the hall and Papa appeared in the doorway, pale and shaken. "Aliza, my girl, be glad I'd never seen that creature before. I'd have locked you in the root cellar before letting you go within a hundred leagues of it."

"What did Lord Merybourne say about the fields?" Anjey asked, and I silently thanked her for changing the subject, unwilling to dwell on what would've happened if he'd stopped me from going with Akarra.

"They'll be a ruin for years yet. We're only thankful the Worm didn't make it farther. The Riders are almost ready to burn it," Papa said. "And, er, Aliza, there's someone here who'd like to speak with you." He moved out of the doorway.

"Charming place, this lodge," Lady Catriona said as she stepped into the room. "You must be Angelina Bentaine," she said as Anjey dropped into a startled curtsy. "No need, no need. Miss Aliza, I'd like a word."

I followed her across the hall into a room scattered with sleeping rolls, mind racing to think what she'd have to say to me, and what on earth I could possibly say in return. She shut the door behind her.

"How can I help you, Lady Catriona?"

The scar across her cheek pulled taut as she raised an eyebrow. "Oh, come now, young lady. Neither of us have time for small talk. Herreki visited you yesterday, didn't she?"

I nodded. My heart began to pound.

"She accused you of a serious thing."

"She said I'd dishonored your family by riding Akarra to Cloven Cairn."

"And you are aware that, by the traditions of our house, this is forbidden to a *nakla?*"

"Aye."

"Then I only have one question for you, Miss Bentaine, and I'd suggest you think over your answer carefully."

I held my breath.

"Would you do it again?"

"I'm sorry?"

"If Alastair ever found himself in danger, would you do something like that again? A simple yes or no will suffice."

The answer came without hesitation, a single word spoken from my heart. "Yes."

Lady Catriona smiled. "Well then, I suppose that's that. Good evening." She turned to go.

"Your Ladyship, wait. You're not going to send me away?"

"Send you away? Mikla save us, girl, of course not!" She placed a hand on my good shoulder. "I suppose it'd be difficult for you to understand, not knowing me like Alastair does. As a Rider it's my duty to protect Arle; as a Daired it's my duty to protect my family. Herreki has sworn herself to House Daired, but I'm afraid the two of us have differing views on what that means," she said. "Herreki sees herself as defender of our name, our honor, and our traditions."

"And you?"

"I let her do as she sees fit. Respect is never a bad thing. My concern is with people. So when I say you've broken tradition by riding Akarra to Cloven Cairn to save Alastair's life, you must understand I only care about one of those things. No matter how foolish or insubordinate your actions might've been, my nephew owes you his life, and that means more to me than all the honor in the world."

I opened my mouth to reply before realizing I hadn't the faintest idea what to say.

She chuckled. "He did tell me you were one for stunned silences."

"Thank you, Lady Catriona."

"Yes, well, in any case, I have the feeling Herreki's scruples may be answered soon. After all, it's no crime for a Daired to ride a Daired dragon." She patted my shoulder, eyes twinkling. "The funeral ceremonies will be starting soon, and I expect you'll want to be there. You'd best get ready."

WHAT SHE MEANT, I REALIZED LATER, WAS THAT I should've avoided dinner.

The setting sun cast long shadows as Anjey and I trudged up the last slope between the lodge and the battlefield. Anjey gasped as we crested the hill. I fought a wave of nausea. Seeing the scene spread out before us, I realized why it'd taken so long to prepare the Worm's body for burning. Its scales may've been impervious to dragonfire, but its insides were not, and the Riders and Rangers had spent the whole day hewing away the outer hide from its inner flesh, which now glowed white and revolting in the dusky light. Mounds of brush lay heaped against its sides.

To the left of the Worm, rows upon rows of makeshift pyres lined the fields, holding the wrapped remains of the one hundred and thirty-three Arlean warriors who'd fallen in the Battle of North Fields. With solemn steps, the forge-wights moved between the pyres, their gauntleted hands resting for a moment on the head of each warrior. Flames pooled around their fingers, igniting the pyres and entombing the fallen in a shroud of fire.

They've only missed one. My eyes traveled down the length of the lindworm's carcass. *This is her pyre.*

At the foot of the hill we stopped. A line of Riders, Rangers, and their mounts stood in front of us, stretching to the edge of the forest. Brysney stood in the center, holding an unlit torch. One of the forge-wights separated from the others to speak with him, his voice rumbling warm and familiar in my chest even though I couldn't understand the words. It was Forgemaster Orordrin. Brysney nodded and Orordrin closed his hand around the end of the torch, then stepped away as it burst into flames.

Brysney buried the blazing brand deep in the brush piled around the body of the Worm. As the fire roared upward, he drew his sword, threw it on the ground in front of him, and fell to his knees with a cry, screaming his sorrow to the stars.

Together the rest of the Riders unsheathed their weapons and followed his example, adding their voices to the wild, discordant lament. I closed my eyes. *May the Fourfold God grant you peace*, I prayed, pressing four fingers to my forehead, my lips, and my heart.

Minutes later the lament faded, then fell silent. The line of warriors splintered as some returned to their makeshift camp, some to the woods to take up guard duty, and some to continue their mourning in private. Several stayed by the burning carcass, watching with hollow eyes as the flames consumed the creature. Anjey left my side and made her way to Brysney. She knelt next to him, wrapped her arms around his heaving shoulders, and cried with him.

"Miss Aliza, may I have a word?"

The flickering light disguised my surprise at being addressed by Captain Edmund Daired. "Yes, Captain?"

He waited to answer until we were out of earshot of the other Riders. "I have a favor to ask of you." He untied a satchel from his belt and handed it to me. "When the time is right, will you return these?"

"What's—?" An envelope fell out. My blood ran cold, then hot as I realized what I held. "*You* took their letters?"

"No. Charis did."

I stared at him.

"She never meant to hurt Cedric, I swear," he said. "She only wanted to protect him."

"Why didn't you tell me at Edan Rose?"

"I didn't know. Charis only gave them to me when we were called to Hatch Ford, before she saw her brother again. She—she asked me to burn them, but I couldn't do it." He looked away, drinking the sight of Charis's pyre down to its bitter dregs. "For whatever happiness this has taken from Cedric and your sister, know that I'm truly sorry."

"Thank you for telling me, Captain."

"Thank you for taking them. I hope the gods grant both you and your sister every happiness. Good evening." He bowed and backed away, melting into the shadows.

It was her all along? I clutched the bundle of letters to my chest and closed my eyes. Charis had lied to her brother. She'd forced my sister through months of doubt and heartache. For almost a year she'd stolen and cheated and done everything in her power to take away their chance of a life together.

And in one day, she'd given it all back.

I looked toward the burning Worm. Anjey and Brysney still knelt by the fire, heads bent, their bodies racked with sobs. I wouldn't have far to go to return their letters, to explain who was responsible for keeping them apart. A few words exchanged, the satchel handed over, and they'd know the truth about Charis Brysney.

I crossed the field, skirted the Riders, and threw the bundle of letters into the fire.

"Aliza?" Daired spoke from behind me. "What are you doing?"

Repaying a debt, I thought with a pang of sorrow, but the gentleness in his voice pulled me away from the cold ledger of the dead, back into the vibrant, painful, beautiful world of the living. I turned from the pyre. "Nothing."

"Walk with me, will you?"

The rising moon peeped out from the veil of clouds hanging low over the hills, bathing North Fields in silver light as we moved away from the fires. "How are you feeling?" I asked.

"Well enough. You?"

"Aye, I'm well," I said, and as I spoke, every emotion I'd felt in the past day rushed over me at once. "I didn't lose my head to the lamias, the Worm is dead, my family is safe, my sister is with the man she loves, and you . . ."

"And I what?"

"You're still alive."

"You know as well as I do who's responsible for that." Daired stopped and faced me. "Aliza, you're not a cruel woman, so don't trifle with me. I love you," he said, "more now than ever before. You're peace and beauty and kindness and courage, and I want you with every fiber of my being, body and soul. After all you've done, I want to think you love me too, but you've never said it. Not to me."

"Alastair—"

"If you don't feel the same, then for gods' sakes, tell me so right now," he said in a rush. "Akarra and I will leave Hart's Run tonight and you'll never see us again." He hesitated, and when I said nothing, he moved closer. "But if you do . . ."

I took his good hand. He was trembling, or perhaps I was. Maybe we both were.

"I do," I said. "I love you, Alastair."

And then, because I'd fought through dragonfire and death and knew at last what courage looked like, I kissed him.

I thought I knew everything there was to know about fire. I'd smelled it, touched it, almost tasted it, but for all that, I had no idea. *This* was the fire that bound the Daired bloodline to dragonkind. Love, and passion, and wildness—all burned in that single touch, searing my lips even as it seared my soul.

When we separated we were both breathless.

Daired smiled—a true smile, open and honest. "I'm sorry I don't have a brooch this time. I had Orordrin put my heartstone back." With difficulty he drew his sword and held it hilt upward between us. "The next time we're in Hunter's Forge I'll ask him to make another."

Only then did I remember what Brysney had given me. I reached into my pocket and withdrew the heartstone of the Greater Lindworm. Its emerald facets glinted in the moonlight. "You'll have to ask him for two."

He lowered his sword. "Where did you get that?"

"Brysney said Charis would've wanted you to have it, and he's right. She did, and I do. It's yours, Alastair, if you want it."

Daired sheathed his sword and took the heartstone. Sadness

flickered in his eyes as his hand closed over the gem, but it passed in a moment, and his smile returned. "I take it this means you'll be my wife?"

"If you'll have me."

"I'll have no other," he said, and kissed me again.

DAIRED AND I RETURNED TO THE LODGE SOON AFTER-ward. Brysney and Anjey met us there with news of their own: Brysney had asked Anjey to marry him, and she had said yes.

Neither Anjey nor I slept much that night. We stayed up long past midnight, talking, planning, crying, laughing, and wondering how our family would take our announcements. "Papa won't know what to think," Anjey said. "We'll have to tell him first thing in the morning."

We should've timed it better.

Red-eyed and yawning, Papa met with us in the parlor just after dawn. "What's all this about, girls? You just about raised the dead with your knocking."

Between the two of us, we told him everything that had happened the previous evening. When we finished he sat back and ran a hand through his hair.

"*Engaged? To Brysney? And you, Aliza, to Daired? But they're Riders!*"

"You do approve, don't you?" Anjey asked.

"I don't see how I couldn't. We owe them both too much for that. But, girls, it *can't* be true." He reached a hand to each of us. "I simply won't believe that I'm going to lose *two* daughters on the same day."

"Tell you what, Papa," I said. "I have every intention of marrying Alastair, but if it'll ease your mind, I promise not to do it on the day Anjey marries Cedric."

"In that case, I give you both my blessing, and give it gladly. We'll have a lot to celebrate in the midst of this—" His face fell. "Oh gods. I just realized something."

"What?" Anjey and I asked together.

"Who's going to tell your mother?"

MY SISTER AND I KEPT OUR PROMISE. SHE AND BRYSNEY wed in Edonarle, to the delight of Aunt Lissa and Uncle Gregory, who'd returned from Dragonsmoor after the death of the Worm, and to the unspeakable rapture of our mother. Our entire journey to Brysney's rented seaside villa consisted of nothing but Mama's praise for his accomplishments. I was glad Brysney had elected to fly rather than ride with us. Since the death of his twin, he'd grown graver and quieter, and though his feelings for Anjey never wavered, we could all see that the Battle of North Fields had left him a changed man. Both Anjey and I cringed whenever Mama brought up the slaying of the Worm, and we even went so far as to ask her never to mention it in Brysney's presence.

Three days after we arrived in Edonarle, Anjey and Brysney were married.

Mari, Leyda, and I stood at Anjey's side during the wedding, Leyda balancing on crutches. Anjey had offered to provide a chair at the front of the abbey, but Leyda refused, wanting to stand with the rest of us. If the encounter with the Worm had changed Brysney, it had transformed our little sister. The day before the wedding I found her sobbing in her room, her splinted leg stretched out in front of her on the window seat. I sat next to her, took her head on my shoulder, and rocked her as she cried.

After a few minutes she gave me a sniffly smile. "I'm sorry, Aliza. I didn't mean to break down like that. It just hit me all of a sudden."

I smoothed the hair back from her forehead. "Do you want to talk about it?"

"No, I don't. But I think I need to."

In a quiet voice, she told me how she'd smuggled her first letter to Wydrick through one of Madam Moore's apprentices, and of how she'd been so delighted with the attention when he replied that she hadn't thought twice about doing as he asked and hiding their correspondence. She'd told him of her admiration for the Rangers, and how she hoped someday to be like them. Wydrick had in turn described his adventures and encouraged her to join the Free Regiments, promising that with him as her tutor, she would take to the fighting arts like a phoenix to fire.

"I believed him," Leyda said. "When news came about the muster, I knew it was my chance. I thought, if I don't go now, I never will. I didn't plan on doing any actual fighting." Another tear fell, splashing onto the hands clasped in her lap. "I just wanted to help. To do something important."

"Did Forstall know?" I asked.

"No. Wydrick hid me, and by the time we reached Hatch Ford, nobody cared anymore. Even when we got there, it was all excitement and adventure for a little while. I hardly saw the first battle. Then the *Tekari* broke through, and everyone got scared and pulled back. That's when Wydrick . . . when he turned into something else. He'd always been so charming. I had no idea what kind of monster he was. After the Worm crossed the Ford, the Rangers retreated to a town on the borders of Eastwich and tried to regroup. He—" She closed her eyes.

"You don't have to, Leyda."

"Yes, I do. When the Worm stopped advancing, he came back from the front lines for me. I didn't want to go. He said someone needed to make the sacrifice, or all of Arle would be destroyed. That's when he broke my leg."

"Oh, dearest. I'm so sorry."

"Believe me, so was I. I would've been sorrier if Daired and his dragon hadn't found us. Akarra got me off the battlefield. Daired stayed behind. I didn't see what happened to Wydrick."

"Alastair said Wydrick is dead." I took her hand. "He won't hurt anyone ever again."

Leyda looked up at me. Pain and betrayal had hollowed out her gaze, and there was no pity in her voice. "Good." She squeezed my hand. "Will you tell Daired thank you for me?"

I wrapped my arms around her and hugged her tight.

"Of course."

DAIRED ACCOMPANIED OUR PARTY TO EDONARLE, AS did Akarra, Julienna, and Mar'esh. I felt confident the residents of the other villas had never witnessed a finer gathering than the Brysney-Bentaine wedding party, with a number of high-ranking Riders, two dragons, and dozens of wyverns and beoryns in attendance. Even Lady Catriona came.

The Drakaina did not.

Saying goodbye to Anjey after the wedding was hard, but not as hard as I'd feared. It made it easier knowing I'd see her again at my own wedding in a few weeks. Daired asked that we be married at House Pendragon, and with the alternative being the Great Hall at Merybourne Manor, I had no objections. That meant, however, that my family had another four-day journey ahead of them only a week after they'd returned from Edonarle, and if my husband-to-be hadn't been lord of such a grand estate, I think even Mama would've voiced a complaint or two. As it was, she contented herself with the fact that, with a Daired and a Brysney in the family, she'd be able to introduce her youngest girls in any circle of Arlean society with justifiable pride.

Gwyn came to Dragonsmoor as well, her rosy-cheeked, curly-haired infant son and impeccably cravated husband in tow. For a while she seemed surprised at our engagement, thinking both Alastair and I had laid our relationship to rest after my stay in Hunter's Forge, but when I described our encounter at House Pendragon and the events of the following weeks, she heartily gave her blessing.

As for Aunt Lissa and Uncle Gregory, Alastair wrote their invitations himself, and when they arrived, he greeted them with nearly as much affection as I did. Uncle Gregory remarked on it as the four of us wandered the Pendragon gardens the night before the wedding, savoring the last moment of calm before the celebratory storm.

"We're indebted to you, Lor—I mean, er, Alastair," Uncle Gregory said after he'd spent many minutes working up the courage to speak to him, not as lord of House Pendragon, but as his future nephew-in-law. "You've been so extraordinarily kind."

Alastair smiled. "I think, Gregory, that I'm the one indebted to you."

"Really?" Aunt Lissa asked, brightening. She'd had far less trouble accepting Alastair as family. "How so?"

"If you hadn't invited Aliza to Dragonsmoor, none of this would've happened."

"We both owe you for that," I said.

"Well, in that case . . ." Aunt Lissa said, a solemn twinkle in her eye. "Aliza, Alastair, promise us something, will you? You've already passed through peace and war, fire and blood, and gods know you'll pass through more of it before the end. This life you're trying to make together won't be easy." She smiled. "But then, nothing worthwhile ever is. Promise you'll never stop fighting for each other."

Small as it was, I felt the weight of the bloodred brooch pinned to my shoulder, heavy with memories new and old, bitter and sweet and sacred. My gaze rested on the green heartstone Alastair wore on a chain around his neck before meeting his eye.

"Aye." *That we will.*

THE END

ACKNOWLEDGMENTS

There isn't a thank-you big enough for the team who made this book happen: Thao Le (agent extraordinaire, dispeller of authorial panic, and champion of all things awesome), Rebecca Lucash (first-class editor, dragon airspeed velocity expert, and general font of knowledge), Paula Szafranski (layout wizard and designer of beautiful pages), David Pomerico (master of the proverbial baton transfer), and everyone else at Voyager who helped craft this story into everything it could be.

To Kelsey, the Original Swan: for the beta reads, the midnight brainstorming conversations, the tough love, and the endless encouragement, thank you. And to Stephanie, Bailey, Abi, Rachelle, Aleena, Britain, and all the rest of the Ragged Blue Monkeys: you showed me how to embrace the blue life. This book wouldn't exist without you.

To Colleen, Arleen, Ron, and the entire Jennings family: thank you for your constant support. Same for the countless friends, colleagues, and coworkers who stood next to me from day one, even when you weren't sure what you were getting yourselves into. You're the best cheerleaders any author could ever ask for.

To my on-call experts: Lauren, for the equestrian know-how, and Melanie and Alex, for the medical advice. Thanks for keeping me grounded.

To Nicole, Arista, Tina, and the entire fan fiction community who saw *Heartstone* in its infancy—I don't know all your names, but I'm glad you stuck with me to the end. I hope it was worth the wait.

And finally, to my family, who first introduced me to the beauty of the Word: thank you doesn't begin to cover it. Here's to living with no regrets.

ABOUT THE AUTHOR

A textbook introvert who likes to throw out the (meta-phorical) textbook every once in a while just to see what happens, Elle grew up in Buffalo, New York, where she learned valuable life skills like how to clear a snowy driveway in under twenty minutes and how to cheer for the perennial underdog. When she's not writing, she spends her time drinking tea, loitering in libraries and secondhand bookshops, and dreaming of world travel. *Heartstone* is her first novel.